**RED ROWAN BERRY**

Staindrop pushed Janet through the arch and kept his hand on her arm. They could hardly see one another.
"Lie down," he said.
"Are you out of your mind?"
She jerked her arm away but he caught hold of her cloak.
"I said, lie down," he said between his teeth and began to force her down to the grass. Janet bewildered, resentful and more than a little frightened tried to resist him. The episode became brutal.
They struggled in the dark and Staindrop cursed ceaselessly at her, calling her by the foulest names he could think up as she tried to break away from him. He hit her on the face with his fist, after which she staggered back dazed and sick, her head singing and fell over a fallen roof-slab in the grass.
"You'll do it," he grunted, "you'll do it if I have to break your damned neck!"

**Also by the same author, and available in Coronet Books:**

The Heroine's Sister

# Red Rowan Berry

# Frances Murray

CORONET BOOKS
Hodder and Stoughton

First published in Great Britain 1976
by Hodder and Stoughton Limited

*Coronet edition 1978*

---

*The characters and situations in this book are entirely imaginary and bear no relation to any real person or actual happening*



Printed and bound in Great Britain for Hodder and Stoughton Paperbacks, a division of Hodder and Stoughton Ltd., Mill Road, Dunton Green, Sevenoaks, Kent (Editorial Office: 47 Bedford Square, London, WC1 3DP) by C. Nicholls & Company Ltd The Philips Park Press, Manchester

ISBN 0 340 22004 X

For Margaret

Secretary-companion designate

in memory of various islands

wet feet

the Eighth Fleet

and marauding cows

A peat water burn,
In stark brown heather;
And a wavering birch,
In windy weather:
A grey Northern land,
From Wall to Sule Skerry;
Heather moor, dark hill
And red rowan berry.

# I

THE FUNERAL WAS over. John Laidlaw had stood grimly by while his daughter Janet supervised the food and drink distributed to the members of the ceremony; not many, for his wife had had a sharp tongue and had taken little part in the affairs of the district, and when they took their departure he endured the wordless handshaking in the little-used front porch of the farmhouse. Then, with Janet and Jock, her brother, on either side of him, he watched the guests bumping down the rough track to the lochside road in a variety of traps and governess-carts held to a walking pace behind the Minister who stalked in front with his wife holding up her skirts and breaking into a trot every so often to keep up with him. Mr McMurdoe considered the prevalence of personal transport in his parish as a symptom of the degeneracy of the generation among which it had fallen unto him to minister.

"Aye," John Laidlaw had said, "so that's it by with."

Janet, white-faced with grief and lack of sleep, had felt this was hardly adequate comment on his wife's death and burial but he did not give her time to dwell on this reflection. He pulled the huge silver watch out of his waistcoat pocket.

"Make another cup of tea, Janet lass," he instructed. "I've just an hour and a bittie before the steamer and there's her will to read yet."

"I've a bed made up for you," Janet said.

"I'll not be staying. I've business at the yard the morn's morn and there I must be."

Janet brought a tray into the parlour which was still chilly despite the fire lit early that morning in the shining black grate and handed round the tea to the family seated on the much-polished, little-used chairs in the half light which filtered through the draw blinds.

"That's the best cheeny!" exclaimed Jock's wife, Kirsty, swathed in crape and wearing a close black bonnet which made her look more than ever like a fat ferret. "The rose-patterned tea service my mother gave her at her wedding. Time it was put past now the guests are away."

Janet said nothing but handed round the milk and sugar. Kirsty sniffed and handled her cup with exaggerated care.

"There's some folk not fit to have good stuff," she observed, "using the best cheeny for every day."

Janet sat down on the stool which was the only seat left.

"Thirty years my mother had that service," she said quietly, "it was washed twice a year but it was only used three times. Once for Jock's baptism, once for mine and then for your wedding. Three times in thirty years. Surely death is an occasion great enough to use the rose-patterned tea service?"

Kirsty sniffed and drank without more words. Betsy, the grieve's wife, gulped noisily and her husband, Dick, stood behind her clutching his best black bowler as if it, too, was to be the subject of dispute. John Laidlaw drank his cup quickly and then rose to pull up the lace-edged blinds, ignoring Kirsty's flounce of outrage.

"Best to get on with the business," he said. "I'll read the bit that concerns you and Betsy first, Dick, and then you can go yoke the mare to take me down to Luss pier for the steamer. I'm for Glasgow the night."

What he read was not strictly speaking a will. No lawyer had been concerned with its drawing up. Elspeth Laidlaw, knowing her death near and with her husband in Glasgow, had written him a letter in which she asked him, among other things, to dispose of her possessions. There were not a great many of these.

". . . Dick is to have the wag-at-the-wa' clock," she had written, "for he has kept it going with his feather and neat's foot oil these twenty years. Betsy is to have the rose-patterned tea service because she admired it so much . . ."

Kirsty flounced again and Betsy sobbed aloud into her best black sateen apron.

"And for the long years of faithful service they have given me and mine they are to have the croft and cottage in Inverbeg which my grandfather left me. It is not much of a place and old Angus has let it go back these past few years but it will be a roof over their heads when they need one."

Kirsty's face slackened with shock and Betsy ceased her sobbing to stare for an incredulous moment and then resumed more grievously than ever. Dick put a huge gnarled hand on her shoulder and Laidlaw raised his eyes from the letter.

"Did she not mention this?"

Dick shook his head.

"The more credit to you both, then," said Laidlaw. "I will have the deeds sent. I am glad she has done this, for you have kept my mind easy, the two of you, all these years I have been away. You are to have the furniture in the cottage as well and she asks me to see that you have a good pair of horses and two good cows and ten sheep and a ram which you are to choose for yourself for stock. This will give you a start."

He looked at the tearful old woman and jerked his head at Dick.

"Take her outby and give her a dram from the corner cupboard," he said. "And then yoke the mare."

When the door was closed behind them he glanced round the room, at Janet staring out of the window at Ben Lomond, lowering over the grey waters of the loch, at Kirsty, her lips pressed tightly together to contain her spleen, and Jock sitting uncomfortably on the very edge of the parlour chair.

"There's little more," he told them. "Her bitties of jewelry are for Janet, all but the ring which the old laird gave her father, and Jock's to have that."

He raised the letter again.

"Janet can have my furniture or what she wants of it except for the parlour cabinet . . ."

They all looked at the rosewood cabinet with its gleaming glass panes and carved panels where the rose-patterned tea service had dwelt for thirty years.

". . . I want that to go to Mistress McMurdoe for she has always admired it and I know she will care for it and it is but seldom she can have what she likes, poor wifie, with yon sour-faced stick of a man she's married on . . ."

Jock looked shocked and mumbled a protest about respect being due a man of God and Janet withdrew her gaze from the ben and chuckled aloud. Kirsty clucked offendedly at the sound.

"It was her very voice I heard saying that," Janet explained, "she was aye sorry for Mistress McMurdoe."

"Evidently," agreed her father drily, "this is how she goes on, 'Give the poor body my best grey silk with the braided bodice that I wore for Jock's wedding and tell her to burn yon weary old Sunday gown she's worn these twelve years and more. Janet'll not need it and it'll never look at Kirsty the way she's put on flesh since she married our Jock.' "

He paused to turn the sheet.

"The very idea!" Kirsty exploded. "A solemn testyment is no place to pass personal remarks."

Her father-in-law ignored her.

"Give Jock the big Bible with the brass clasps that was my great uncle's who was a Minister. He's fair set on quoting the Good Book to serve his ends. This will maybe help him get the words right once in a while."

It was John Laidlaw's turn to chuckle and Jock glowered at his knees and tried vainly to find a quotation which would fit the situation. After this Laidlaw read out her instructions to give some of her friends round about 'some wee mindings' as she called them which varied from a book to a long coveted china ornament. The widower read these briskly and then stopped abruptly, frowning at what he read.

"The rest is for me," he told them and folded up the paper. "And this is for Janet."

He held out a sealed paper.

"Read it later," he advised and then rose to his feet. "I must be on my ways if I'm to catch yon steamer."

Jock and Kirsty gaped at him. Jock half rose to his feet but Kirsty was on hers before him.

"That's never all there is to it?"

Laidlaw raised his bushy brows.

"What's that?"

"The place, man!" Kirsty said impatiently. "What about the place? Glenfoot was hers was it no?"

"No," said Laidlaw. "Glenfoot is mine. It came to me when her father died."

"But she aye spoke of the place as her own."

"And who had a better right?" demanded Laidlaw. "She was born in the room above this, lived here all her days and when her father died she worked the land . . . aye and worked it better than he did, or I would have done. She's made Glenfoot the best farm on Loch Lomondside . . . as well you know."

"But father . . ." Jock began heavily.

"My Jock's her son, it's due he should have the place!" Kirsty shrilled.

"Glenfoot is mine," Laidlaw reiterated. "Content yourselves with Braeside."

"But father," Jock persisted, "my lease at Braeside is near up and the factor said he thought the laird had another man in mind and I thought with mother ill and . . ."

"Did you so?" said his father harshly, "well, you'd best see the laird and change his mind for him."

"What in the Name do you want with a farm?" demanded Kirsty, "and you biding upby in Glasgow from one year's end to the next. You've no wish to plaister with cattle beasts and dung and the like. You've your ships and engines and that."

"If you're wanting Glenfoot," said John Laidlaw and opened the parlour door, "I doubt you'll have to buy it in."

"Buy!"

Kirsty's face was red with anger and disappointment.

"Buy in his mother's place which should be his by rights!"

"I've a use for the money," said Laidlaw. "Dick, is the mare yoked?"

"And who's to take it on till it's sold?" asked Jock.

"Janet. She's been working it this six month past with Elspeth laid away, have you no, Janet lass?"

"Me! But I just did what mother said," said Janet anxiously. "And Dick was aye there to set me right . . ."

"A lassie! Janet to take on Glenfoot!" Jock protested.

"Best find a buyer fast, John Laidlaw," advised Kirsty scornfully, "or damn the farm you'll have to sell in a sixmonth."

"I'm in no hurry," said her father-in-law. "You'll do fine, Janet, I've no doubt. Your mother thought well of you and Dick's aye there yet. And maybe Jock'll lend a hand where i's needed for all the good that'll be."

He gave a scornful glance at his son who had sat down again and was gnawing the rim of his hat.

"Goodbye, Janet lass. I'll write. And you'll see to it yon wee mindings go where your mother wished."

"Aye, father."

He nodded at them from the door, a tall, grey-haired figure with a bony unsmiling face in which his vivid blue eyes seemed inappropriate. Then he was gone and they heard the trap rattle away down the stony track.

"It's no decent, that's what it's no," said Kirsty indignantly. "No even to bide the night and his wife new coffined."

"Father's a busy man," protested Jock and held out his cup, his rose-patterned cup. "Have you another cup in the pot, Janet?"

Janet refilled it from the rose-patterned teapot and looked enquiringly at Kirsty, who was simmering like a saucepan.

"It would choke me," she declared, "it would choke me. Fancy asking me to drink from this service which should be mine by rights. It was my mother gave it her. To give it away to yon Betsy! The very idea . . . what use has a coorse old wife the like of her for a good cheeny tea service?"

"I daresay she has a cup of tea whiles," returned Janet, "and maybe a friend to share it."

This last remark appeared to infuriate Kirsty.

"Do you mean to say that *I've* no friends?" she demanded angrily. "You just keep a civil tongue in your head to your betters you impident wee besom. I've plenty friends."

"I meant nothing of the kind, Kirsty."

"Did you not, then."

Jock waded in with both feet.

"Och, Kirsty, you've no need for tea services . . . you've the wedding cheeny put past and never used. The only folk who come about the doors at Braeside are the Minister and Mrs McMurdoe and they aye get the old blue crocks . . ."

Kirsty snorted with temper.

"They are *not* the only folk . . . and I can see myself getting out the good stuff for that one. A nursery governess she was for all her airs and never a penny-piece to her name."

"Mistress McMurdoe put on no airs," contradicted Janet, "my mother said she'd to ask the Minister's leave to breathe."

"He'll be spry enough to give her leave to take yon good cabinet I don't doubt, aye . . . and to wear yon good grey silk. They'll not let that go past them, oh, no!"

Kirsty's voice rose.

"What I'd like to ken is what your mother thought she was at!

To leave stuff to folk not even in the family and nothing for her own son but an old-fashioned ring no one would be seen dead in. A ring! When in the Name would Jock wear a ring? And nothing whatsoever to me . . . her own son's wife . . . or her grandchildren. No even a mention."

"She did so mention you, Kirsty," protested Jock.

"Aye," agreed Kirsty, "so she did. To say I was over stout to wear her grey silk! Just like her. If I had my rights and Jock had his we should have fair half of everything . . . furniture, cheeny, jewelry . . . everything. And the very idea of leaving yon wee croft at Inverbeg away from her own flesh and blood when Jock's been at her for years to have it to put his young stuff on . . . it's no natural, that's what it's no . . . aye, and it's no fair! Yon's no a right testyment, Jock. We should get a lawyer to it."

Jock, unsuccessful in placating her, tried blunderingly to turn the subject.

"Are you finished the sowing yet, Janet?"

Janet nodded.

"We've the Wee Field to roll, that's all. If the rain holds off we'll get at it the morn's morn."

"What have you in?"

"Barley."

"Aye . . ."

Jock searched for further comment but his hesitation gave Kirsty time to start again.

"A lassie working a farm . . . whoever heard of such a thing. Forbye it's no decent-like you living your lone. You'll be a speak for the whole parish."

"I'll not be alone. There'll be Betsy and Dairy Jean."

"You'd best leave the place to Dick and Jock and come to Braeside. It'll be handy, for Donald's about the doors most days . . ."

Donald was her brother.

"You can keep an eye to the bairns for me too," she added.

"No thank you," said Janet firmly. "I'm fine where I am."

Kirsty sniffed.

"Time and high time you were married," she declared, "you're near twenty."

"Och, our Janet needn't be in any hurry," interrupted Jock,

"she's half the lads in the district after her. She's the bonniest lass in the land of Lennox."

This was true. Janet had taken all the best features from the family for her own: her mother's cloud of dark brown hair, the fine-boned face and clear skin which had been her Skye grandmother's, her father's brilliant blue eyes with a fringe of long dark lashes. She was tall like her father but had her mother's slimness so that she walked gracefully and well. However, this observation did not please Kirsty, tightly corseted to squeeze into last year's dress and all too conscious of the contrast between them.

"Huh!" she ejaculated, "Handsome is as handsome does."

"Our Janet does fine," Jock protested, "she's a grand cook and a . . ."

"Man, hold your wheesht! Fine I ken the sun rises and sets on the limmer. If you'd half the notion of your own family that you have of your sister we'd be the better off. I'm deaved with Janet this and Janet that . . ."

"Och, haivers . . ." said Jock.

"It is *not* haivers! And I'll tell you this to your head, Janet Laidlaw . . . looks don't last for ever. If you play fast and loose with the chances you get you'll end on the shelf for sure and certain. You think yourself too good for the lads about here with all your books and reading and sic-like dirt!"

"I do not," protested Janet, flushing with anger.

"Yes, you do, and so did that mother of yours for she chased the lads from your door without a by-your-leave. And why else would you give our Donald the go-by at the Luss games and dance with the Minister's son and him not twelve years old."

"I'd promised him," said Janet. "You'd not have me break a promise to a bairn."

"You'd have done better to break that one . . . a fine larruping he got from his father when the Minister found he'd been to the dancing and after all he'd said about it in the Kirk."

Janet looked dismayed at this news but Jock reassured her solemnly.

"He's young yet . . . it'll maybe save his soul," he said and added, "forby he told me the dance with you was worth a touch of the tawse."

Janet laughed at this. Kirsty gave her a look of dislike.

"It's no decent, so it's no, to be laughing and daffing in a house of death."

"Mother'd not heed . . . she dearly liked a laugh," said Janet and rose to collect the teacups.

"Especially at the expense of her neighbours," snapped Kirsty. "Now you just sit down, Janet Laidlaw, and hear me out."

Janet took no notice.

"I'll tell you that your mother would have done better to laugh less and mess with this place less and pay more heed to her proper business."

Janet looked at her incredulously.

"And what was that, pray?"

"To get you properly married. When I was your age I was married and had two bairns already . . ."

"Aye," said Janet drily, "we all ken you wasted no time."

This hint that Kirsty's wedding to Jock had been a trifle hurried she regretted as soon as it was out. Kirsty went a deep plum colour and began to shout.

"You're at that, are you! Well, let me tell you this . . . we sinned, maybe, Jock and me, but it was no more of a sin than your mother living away from your father these seventeen year. If she'd been a right wife to him she'd have gone to the town. I'd be shamed to let my Jock live himself that way."

Janet had borne a great deal and she could never stand to hear her mother criticised. She put down the tray of china on the dresser and turned to Kirsty.

"My mother," she said evenly, "was worth six of you or any other tattling jaud in this parish or any other. She was the best housewife and the best farmer in the district. What would a woman like her have done in the town?"

"She'd have done her duty! She was a bad wife to John Laidlaw and I don't care who hears me say so."

"Don't you speak so of my mother!"

"I'll speak as I find . . . never in six year was she civil to me . . . never! She was an ill-tongued bitch and aye thought herself too good for her company."

"I don't blame her . . ." said Janet, "she'd no patience with fools . . . and she'd no *law* for women who'd drag a man to the Kirk the way you did."

Jock, alarmed and distressed at the turn of events, tried to come between the two women but was pushed aside by his wife with a shove from her elbow which sent him reeling back against the cabinet destined to grace the manse.

"And let *me* tell you a thing or two, mistress," Janet went on, "as long as you're so free with my mother's name. It's a better thing, to my mind, to live apart from your man than make him a speak and a joke over the whole parish for the way you mistreat him. A real grey mare he took to his stable, my poor Jock, and a sore penance he's had to pay for a few minutes' pleasure at the harvest . . . if pleasure it was . . ."

Kirsty gobbled incoherently at her.

"You've made a dog's breakfast of his farm for him with your interference and while I won't come and have an eye to my wee nephews it's time and high time somebody did, for they're dressed like tinks and let run wild!"

For a few seconds Janet thought her sister-in-law would have a fit. Her face was purple with anger and her throat swollen above the tight, high-boned collar of her dress. However, the moment passed.

"Come, Jock," she got out at last, "damn the help you'll give this throughither bitch. I'll see to it, mistress, for he'll not come his footlength near Glenfoot if you get down on your knees and beg. I'll see him burn in Hell rather."

She marched out into the lobby, where Betsy just managed to dodge back into the kitchen from her station at the keyhole, and climbed into the waiting trap where she sat and bawled for Jock like a calf bellowing for its mother. Jock, dithering on the door-step, shook his head mournfully at his sister.

"You shouldn't have spoken that way," he observed mournfully, "she's awful easy riled."

Janet looked at her brother's woebegone face and knew a pang of remorse. If she knew anything about her sister-in-law it would be Jock who would suffer most for what she had just said.

"I'm sorry," she said. "truly sorry. But I'm as short in the temper as cat's hair just now and there was no bearing what she said about mother."

"Aye," he said and shook his head, "but for all she should never have said what she did, she was right enough. A wife's place is at her man's side. 'Every good woman buildeth her house: but the foolish putteth it down with her own hands.'"

"And if you misquote Proverbs at me," returned Janet sharply, "you mind that there are other texts in the same book: 'It is better to dwell in the corner of the housetop than with a brawling woman and in a wide house.' You take my advice, Jock, and make Kirsty bridle her tongue. The laird cannot abide a troublemaker. Leave your prayer-meetings and tract-carrying for a while and pay some heed to your family. Good night to you."

Jock turned on his heel and stalked out muttering some incoherent remark about the godless and joined Kirsty, who was still bawling for him. Janet shut the front door, not with a slam for it was far too stiff for that, but with sufficient force to close it without the need to apply her shoulder. She turned to find Betsy at her back shaking her grey head.

"Lassie, but you made a right piece of work there. They'll not be back in a hurry."

"Good riddance," said Janet between her teeth.

"You'll be sorry for it. Blood's thicker than water."

"To speak of mother that way and on the very day she was buried . . ."

Janet overwrought with anger and grief began to cry at last. Betsy hustled her into the warm kitchen and put her into Dick's elbowchair with the patchwork cushions.

"There, lambie, there . . . greet away. You've sore need to. There . . . there!"

In an hour's time Janet was tucked up in her bed with a 'het-piggie' wrapped in flannel at her feet and a glass of hot milk well-laced with whisky inside her. She was still catching her breath occasionally from her long fit of crying: the storm subsided slowly and Janet, worn out with nursing and a turbulent mixture of grief, anger and the guilt that survivors feel that they are yet alive and glad of it, was about to blow out her candle and sleep when she remembered the letter from her mother which her father had given to her lying still unread in the pocket of her black silk apron. The letter was easily found but Janet stood by the window for a minute holding the curtain back and staring out at the scene. A pale half moon was scurrying through scattered clouds and the loch waters glinted silver between the dark hills. It was a peaceful scene, as comforting in its serenity as all Betsy's ministrations.

The letter was rambling and long and the writing wavered

from time to time, eloquent of the weakness of the woman who had penned it.

Jennie-lass, [she had written] when you read this I shall be dead. Don't grieve too much for I'm a burden to you and a weariness to myself and better it's all by with. But I've a few words to say to you before I go. Don't be coarse on your father, lass. He'd his way to make and it was no fault of his that it was never mine. We should not have married. Ours was a made match. John's father did not wish to divide his farm and John was the younger son. My father needed a man for Glenfoot. I was the only bairn he had and he had no notion of a lassie farming the place so the Parlanes and the Laidlaws made it up between them. It was a good downsitting for John for my father promised he should have Glenfoot after him, and his father would not let him give the arrangement the go-by. I was happy enough for all I wanted to do was to stay on Glenfoot and John was a fine lad and all the other lasses jealous; but John had a lass already and never let on to me. When the kind folk hereabout told me all about it I was wild angry and hurt and somehow things never did go right for us though we warstled along well enough when you and Jock were bairns. If his lass had lived and married another body it might have been fine but she died young and single still and I aye fancied she was in his eye when he looked my way and it was hard to be civil whiles. And he never had a real notion of the place the way I did and when you were up and my father dead he left the work of the farm more and more to me while he plaistered in his workshop, for he was more interested in the machines and the like of that.

I never got at the rights of it but he invented some contraption for a steam engine and selled it to folk making engines for the steamboats. After that he was aye in Glasgow and working for these folk and he came home less and less and I got so that I told myself I didn't care. He wrote a while back would I come to the town where he'd bought a grand house and I thought I would go but the hay was cutting and when it was all in I'd had time to think again and I knew fine I'd never thole living in a town. He wrote again but after a while he stopped writing.

So, you'll understand there's faults on both sides, Jennie-lass. Your father's a good man for all he's so dour. He's borne with me and my bitter tongue and never cast it up to me that I wasn't the one he'd wanted to wed. Whiles I've wished he would, for all it's a bitter thing to be taken for your land and gear and no for yourself.

There's another thing that's in my mind. He's a partner with these ship-building folk now. They're real taken up with him and his contraptions from what he says. He borrowed on Glenfoot to buy in with them till my heart was in my mouth over the risk but that's all by with now and the money paid back: but I doubt he'll be rid of the place when I'm dead. He's a clever man and not one to hang on the breeching and be content with what he has. If the money will help him I don't begrudge it: it's all I ever had to give him, it seems to me now, for you were my bairn from the start, bonnie wee thing that you were, and Jock was a poor soul, a sapsie bairn, aye scared of his father and no very clever at the school.

Jennie-lass, whiles I fret for you. You're that bonnie and I cannot see how you will go on without me to see after you. There's never a lad hereabout fit to tie your shoe, and you'll not meet anyone while you're tied to Glenfoot. You cannot bide with Jock for yon wife of his will drive you gyte in a week. I've seen to it Dick and Betsy will have a roof to offer you if you need it but what would you do there at the back of beyond? Don't hang back from going to your father in the town because of anything you might fancy between him and me. And don't marry the first lad that offers for the sake of a hearth and home of your own. An ill marriage is a weariness all your days.

Goodbye, my own dear lass,

Your Mother.

Janet folded up the sheets of paper and put them under her pillow. After a minute or two she blew out the candle and lay awake looking out at the moonlit waters of the loch and considering her situation. In the distress and confusion of her mother's sickness and death it had not occurred to Janet to wonder what would become of herself. It was characteristic of her mother that she should have foreseen what would happen. The letter spoke so clearly with Elspeth's voice and stressed so much what Janet had lost with her death that she wept again for the grim humour and commonsense and the astringency of her tongue and grieved for the unhappiness revealed in the letter. However, she was too weary to cry long and fell asleep on a wet pillow with her hand below it holding the letter as if it were her mother's hand, as in a sense it was.

# 2

Kirsty was as good as her word: as the hard, cold spring gave way to a wet summer neither she nor Jock came near Glenfoot. Jock waylaid his sister occasionally, when Kirsty was occupied elsewhere, and enquired tentatively if all was well, but even had it not been there was little he could have done. Janet struggled with the lambing and the potato planting and the flood which came in April-month without more help than Dick and the men could give. She took the stirks to market herself because Dick had to mend fences on the boundary where her cows had trampled Kirsty's father's hay, and a poor price she would have got for them after the business of getting them on and off the steamer except that the auctioneer remembered Elspeth.

"Aye, gentlemen!" he had bawled, "Don't ask me to take yon price for these beasts off Glenfoot. I'm over near my latter end and Elspeth Laidlaw will be waiting for me wherever she's gone, the soul, if I don't get her lass a decent price!"

The buyers had laughed at this apprehension and bid and Janet had gone back to the laid hay and the grey weeping sky above it with a lighter heart. However, she was not wholly without help, of a kind. Donald Patterson came about the doors, twice and three time in a week. Kirsty, whose eye to the main chance was unaffected by anything so commonplace as a quarrel, did not fail to remember that her young brother still lacked a bride; Donald in his turn was willing enough to court a girl who had insulted his sister (the story had grown in the telling) on the offchance that John Laidlaw might see sense and there would be a good farm to go with her. As Kirsty said, it would be all in the family. Donald's mother said with a sniff that yon Janet could count herself lucky and his father, while less sanguine about Donald's merits, was not displeased at the prospect, for Glenfoot marched with his farm on its upper boundary.

Donald's wooing was not exactly subtle: a conviction of his own excellence and worth was strongly rooted in him and fostered by his mother and sister, both blinded by affection to his defects. Such defects included a notion that to wash was unmanly and he did so with reluctance only on Saturday nights before donning the Sabbath's clean semmit and shirt . . . not to mention socks. From Tuesday on, unless the weather was very cold, it was advisable to hold converse with Donald out of doors and keep to windward of him at that. Indoors, conversation with him was made even more trying by his inability to talk below a bellow, a trait induced by a natural indolence which led him to prefer shouting across a gap to walking across it . . . an indolence which made his offers of aid limited in actual application. He preferred shouting advice from the field gate or barn door to taking off his jacket and getting down to work. He left Janet in no doubt of his intentions because he could be in no doubt of her welcoming them. He was at no pains to propose she should marry him but merely took it for granted that she would: a tactic difficult to counter.

Janet found these continual visits at first an inconvenience, then a joke and then after three months when he evidently considered that his wooing need no longer confine itself to shouts, a persecution. Elspeth would have wasted no time in sending him to the rightabout, as she had done with a number of previous suitors, but for Janet it was a persecution hard to avoid situated as she was. Jock was in too much fear of Kirsty to help her, for when Janet on one of their rare meetings applied to him to rid her of this affliction he pressed her to accept Donald, giving as his reason for this wish that Donald would be a useful neighbour and was his good friend. He expatiated on the advantages of the match at some length and with great earnestness. Janet heard him out and realised she would find no help in that quarter.

"Friends! Neighbours!" she returned bitterly, "you live three miles away . . . and upwind!"

Jock pretended not to know what she meant.

Nor would the men on Glenfoot help her. They all knew that yon Donald would have to be thrown off the place, neck and crop, for he was not a man to heed hints even if he had understood them and as none of them were certain what Laidlaw intended for Glenfoot they did not wish to offend old Patterson who might some day offer them a job. Good places were hard to come by.

In the first week of June the clouds lifted, the sun came out and the hay dried. Janet and Dick laboured all the hours of daylight to cut, dry and stack it, like every other farm in the district. With the hay all in and better than anybody would have believed possible in May, Janet drew breath for a while and considered a visit to Glasgow to discover what plans her father might have. The time was near when she and Dick would have to consider the work for the coming year. Her father's letters had been unusually few and far from informative. She had got no further than considering this when she had a brief note from him to say that he had despatched a box of books for her by the steamer and that it should arrive on the following day. She harnessed the mare into the trap and went to Luss pier to meet the midday boat. The steamer fussed into the pier with her paddles churning and a cloud of gulls round her like the cloud of flies round a cow in the pasture. The *Prince Consort* edged in carefully and a group of passengers gathered on the paddlebox where two crewmen were ready to put out the gangway and hand over the pile of parcels and bundles to the piermaster with whom they exchanged cheerful insults in a mixture of Gaelic and English as the gap closed between them. Janet looked idly at the passengers to see whether there was anyone she knew, but they were strangers for the most part, barring the herd from Glen Douglas and his wife who had been to their son's wedding in Balmaha. Among them was a tall, fair-haired young man with a close-cut beard wearing an Inverness cape and carrying a selection of rod-cases. Janet guessed that he would be the lodger expected by the widow Maxwell at Camstradden. Mary Ann had been up for eggs and some prints of Betsy's butter the previous evening. She eked out a tiny pension for her man killed long since at Balaclava in the Crimea, by taking in visitors who came for the fishing and for whom she had kept her husband's boat, by now elderly and leaky. She had worked as a cook at Camstradden House and her visitors considered her cooking worth the risks they ran in her boat, for they came again and again and sent their friends. Janet had not seen the tall young man before but no doubt he would have been recommended in this way. The fishers were a close fraternity.

Alec, the *Consort's* purser, waved at her and indicated the box at his feet. Evidently the books had arrived. She waved back and waited for the passengers to come off before she went to collect it. There was the usual scatter of small boys trying to earn a halfpenny for carrying baggage and she saw the tall angler confide his valise and rods to one of these while he lifted the heavy box and strode down the pier with it. Janet climbed down hastily and opened the tailgate of the trap so that he could put it in, which he did with a smile of relief.

"Whew!" he exclaimed and smiled at her, "is it bricks you're having sent you?"

Alec watching the little group from his post on the paddlebox as he sorted out the rest of the parcels, gave a little chuckle and thought pleasurably of the dram he would have tonight in the inn at Balloch from the half sovereign he had been given. The fisher had been much struck with the sight of Janet. Alec, who had known her since she was a wee lass in a pinafore, allowed that she had become a real bonnie woman and accepted the coin offered for the privilege of taking the box to her. He and the fisher had found a common passion in the taking of trout, though Alec's fishing, as he freely admitted, was mostly nocturnal. He considered he had done Janet no disservice; had he been asked he would have described his acquaintance as a 'decent lad for a Perth man'.

Janet latched the tailgate and held out her hand in thanks to her new friend, an offer which he accepted enthusiastically.

"Alec is a real rogue," she told him, "he has no call to make use of folk in that way. He could have carried down the boxie himself. That was very kind of you."

"It was a pleasure," he assured her as if he meant it.

"It's heavy because it's books," she explained. "My father sends me some from Glasgow from time to time. I like to be at the reading. You'll be for Mary Ann Maxwell's?"

"I think so."

He produced an old envelope with an address sprawled across it.

"Camstradden Cottage."

"It's about a mile down the shore," said Janet. "It's on my road home. Put your rods and bitties in the back there and I'll take you up."

The angler agreed with evident pleasure. The small boy ran

off with a whole silver sixpence, unheard-of riches, and gave his mother a vivid description of the 'great rich mannie who was going in Janet Glenfoot's trap'. His mother went out to feel the clothes hanging in the garden and saw for herself, and later discussed the matter with some cronies, who agreed that it was a forward thing for a lassie to do and shook their heads over it.

The young man introduced himself as they clopped sedately up the road from the pier between the neat grey stone cottages.

"My name is Simon Lamington," he said.

Janet told him her name and pointed out the steading of Glenfoot on the hill above the loch road and promised to wave if she saw him out in the Widow Maxwell's boat. By that time they had reached the gate of the cottage, where Lamington jumped down and retrieved his belongings. Mary Ann had been on the watch for him and tried to persuade Janet to join them in the 'wee cuppie' she had prepared and which could be seen through her front door, overflowing the kitchen table with scones and pancakes and other delicacies. Janet refused, mindful of the similar spread which Betsy would have ready by the time she returned, and Simon Lamington watched the slim upright figure disappear round the corner before he turned back into the cottage kitchen determined to find out all he could about Janet from his hostess.

This presented no difficulty at all. Mary Ann was only too delighted to be encouraged to talk about the one subject on which she was an expert, the district and the people of that district. Before long Simon had had the whole history of the Laidlaw family back to the third and fourth generation. He heard how James Laidlaw, Janet's great-grandfather, had walked from the Border country with a flock of sheep back in 1793 when the old laird's father was putting the wee crofts together to make farms. He listened to how Laidlaw had been ostracised by the crofters who were left and how summarily he had dealt with sheep-stealers;

"Into the loch they went," said she, "and Devil the bit did he care could they swim or not and one lad was near drowned afore they pulled him out."

Janet's grandfather had brought in machinery to work the land, and met with further opposition.

"Not that they gave a docken," declared Mary Ann, "they Laidlaws, they don't give a snap of their fingers for the Devil himself. He brought in a winnowing-fan, so my father told me, and the Minister of the time, he was wild-angry, it was a contrivance of the Evil One, he said, and preached against it one Sabbath in the Kirk, saying it was flying in the face of Providence."

Simon, well-accustomed to the inability of the better part of mankind to keep to the point, for he was a lawyer, accepted another scone and honey and wondered when Mary Ann would come to Janet herself. However, he knew better than to hurry her. He had plenty of time and it was just as well, for Mary Ann knew even more about the Parlanes, Elspeth's family, for, like Mary Ann's own people, they had lived thereabout for generations. Simon heard stories of ancient clan battles, of cattle-lifting raids across Glen Douglas by the MacGregors and how they had been beaten off; he heard scandal too, about a Parlane daughter and the son she had borne to an unknown, but not unguessed-at, father and the good farm of Glenfoot which had subsequently come into the hands of the Parlane family.

"She was the bonnie one," said Mary Ann reminiscently, "she was a good age when I knew her but there wasn't a lass in the whole lochside to hold a candle to her. Janet's her image, they say. The Parlanes never have that many bairns . . . the farm came to her son in time and Janet's his granddaughter."

At length Simon, replete with tea and scones and family history, left Mary Ann to prepare an equally vast evening meal and went out to look at the boat drawn up on the pebbly beach below the cottage. He considered it doubtfully and decided to make one or two much-needed repairs before he made use of it. His gaze wandered towards the low grey steading of Glenfoot and with a confused memory of Mary Ann's tales tried to picture Janet in that setting. After a few minutes he told himself he was a fond fool to become thus obsessed with a pretty face within a few seconds and then strolled along the loch too preoccupied even to see the multitude of concentric ripples as the evening rise began. He pulled himself up at a clump of alders and said aloud, "Such things do not happen . . . this is just not feasible," and then walked back with his eyes upon the grey steading so that he stumbled more than once on the stones of the shore.

He might have been gratified had he known that Janet had

been distracted from the new novel by Mr Trollope which her father had included among a bundle of more improving material (such as a reprint of the Reverend Chamlers' sermons) which she had taken to the kitchen window to read while Betsy prepared the men's supper. She had watched the tall figure strolling along the waterside and wondered where he came from and what he did and whether he was thinking about her as she was about him. She had just told herself firmly that she was behaving like one of those daft creatures in a novel and returned her attention to the book when a letter fell out of it.

"I imagine you'll be at this first," her father had written, "so I'll tuck this note into the first chapter . . ."

Janet was forced to laugh at this masterly summing up of her taste and her readiness to have the best first.

"Just a note to say that I've had an offer or two for the place but that there's nothing settled yet. You and Dick go ahead and settle what's to be done in the back end. I doubt you'll not hear from me until October month and by then, from what I hear, you'll not be caring, one way or the other."

Janet puzzled over this last sentence for a second or two but her eyes wandered to Simon bending over the old boat and she forgot it in wondering whether Mary Ann had had Farquharson the Carpenter to look at it or whether it was still as unsafe as ever. Dick who was mending harness on the other side of the kitchen asked if she had had a letter, and she was forced to take her attention from Simon and explain to him what her father had said. Dick seemed a little put out and was going to say something when there was a demanding knock on the door. Betsy's mouth tightened and she went to remove her patchwork cushions from the elbowchair. Dick gave a grunt of evident disapproval and went out into the dairy, filling his pipe as he went. Donald had arrived for an evening visit.

Janet did not rise from her perch on the window seat (which was wide enough only for one) and kept her eyes on the book, firmly, and latterly rather tartly, refusing to go for a walk, go into the parlour or even to pay attention to her visitor's stentorian comments on the weather and the prices at Balloch and other matters of general interest. Betsy darned industriously and ignored broad hints to take herself off. Janet ignored even broader hints that some refreshment would be in order after a long walk from the Patterson place, merely replying that her tea was past and then concentrating on her book. Donald, unheeded and unwelcome, eventually decided to seek livelier company at Luss and left. It was fairly typical of him that as he went down the path he should feel complacently that he had done his duty by his intended. Betsy swept the floor and wiped his chair before she replaced her cushions with a muttered:

"Faugh! the clarty, nasty creature!"

Janet dropped her book on the table and stared out of the window at the waters of Loch Lomond which lay patterned by the erratic winds and seemed to be draining the light out of the evening sky. Down by the bay she could see the chimney of Mary Ann's cottage trailing a veil of blue smoke against the dark green of the trees on Inchtavannoch and outlined against that bright water a tall figure still hammering away at the boat. She remembered the newcomer's pleasant face and easy manner and contrasted it with the stocky figure now stumping down towards his cronies at the Inn, his hands thrust into the pockets of his unspeakable breeches and his greasy cap on the back of his head. Donald saw the figure at the window and knew a swelling of certainty:

"She's her eye on me, surely," he assured himself and swaggered on his way.

At that moment Simon straightened his back and considered the tingle he had tacked over the worst of the rotten boards and privately returned thanks that he could swim. Almost without his volition his eyes turned towards the steading: just then Betsy lit the big reading lamp and put it at Janet's elbow so that he saw her plainly for a moment before the curtains were drawn.

"Feasible or not," he muttered, "it's happened."

In Mary Ann's over-crowded little parlour he wrote a letter to his mother and another to his partner and arranged to extend his holiday by a week or so.

His 'week or so' extended into the first days of the harvest which was hastened that year by a spell of glorious July weather. Janet was delivered from Donald's visitations, for Patterson, short-handed, kept his son at home. The long sunny days were not ideal for Simon who spent much of his time in Camstradden Bay trailing an idle line and watching Janet at work in the fields by the lochside. He had met her again twice; once when she had brought

Soldier, one of the great Clydesdale pair which were the pride of Glenfoot, down to the smiddy to have a cast shoe replaced and once on Inchtavannoch. This was an island just across from the bay where Janet rented pasture for her young beasts and from time to time she rowed across to see that all was well with them. He had seen her rowing over and had landed immediately round the point and met her 'accidentally'. Mary Ann, as always, had been generous in the matter of sandwiches and they had shared them, fighting off the onslaught of determined wasps, and talked during the long hot afternoon of books and travel and life in towns. Simon described his work as a lawyer in Perth and the vagaries of his clients. Janet told him about her mother and the farm and about her father's work in Glasgow and was startled and proud to learn that Simon knew of him.

"A clever man, they say," Simon told her, "he's expected to do great things."

They both had to explain themselves that night: Janet to Betsy who had endured a bellowed interrogation from Donald across the burn about her absence from the harvest field, and relayed his promise to visit again as soon as the back of the work was broken.

"I telled him no to hurry himself," said Betsy drily, "and said you were away on the island. You were long enough there in all conscience."

Janet bent her head over Mr Trollope.

"The beasts were all over the place," she said truthfully enough. She said nothing of the companion she had had in looking for them.

Betsy, whose eyesight was good and who liked to keep an eye on Janet's comings and goings on the water, remembered the smaller boat towed behind Janet's coble and the figure rowing and smiled to herself. Mary Ann had already made it her business to reassure Betsy about her lodger.

"For he's fair taken up with your Janet, mistress," she had remarked during the negotiations for eggs, milk and a boiling of late peas.

"Do you tell me that, now?"

"Aye. Mind, she could do worse, the lassie. He's a decent creature and an awful bonnie lad. They'd make a grand pair so they would. And there's money, forby, he's a lawyer and in a good way of business, so my Mr Douglas tells me, and they're partners in the business in Perth."

So, Betsy had made no comment and drew her own conclusions from Janet's reticence.

Earlier, Simon's rather conscious, "I met with Miss Laidlaw" had called forth no more from Mary Ann than a smile and an offer of a scone and honey to tide him over till his tea should be ready.

Nor were theirs the only eyes to have noted the meeting. Kirsty in Luss to collect some grainbags from the steamer heard the rumours flying about and went hot foot to her brother urging him not to miss his chance.

"They're cunning brutes, lawyers," she told him, "and fine they know a good property when they see it. He'll be after her like a cock at a grosset."

Donald smiled at the very idea that his intended should prefer someone other than himself, and his father, eating a belated dinner, his hair and clothes dusty from the barley, looked anxiously at the sky.

"Donald can wait till we've the hill field carried and stacked," he said. "He's no time to waste courting with a thunder-plump on the way."

Janet, down in the lochside field, was looking at the same high-piled black thunderclouds. She and Dick and the men had eaten their dinner of bread and mutton and cold tea as and when they could and there was no more than one load left to carry. There was a flash of lightning and a grumble far in the distance beyond the Ben. Janet between the horses' heads looked across the loch which lay leadenly under the yellow livid light. Soldier tossed his head and nickered his alarm and Janet stroked the hairy pink nose comfortingly.

"Easy lad," she reassured him, "not much longer now."

As she waited for Dick's wordless cry which would tell her that it was time to move on she looked at the boat far out on the loch. A tall figure flicked a fishing line. Janet smiled.

"Simon's in for a right drooking," she confided to the horses.

As the first warm drops splashed on to Janet's sunbonnet so that the starched brim flapped down over her eyes, they were leading that last load. The barn door was open and they took the cart with its huge top-heavy burden right inside at once. The horses were unyoked and led away to their stable and the men prepared to stop work.

"It'll do in here till the morn, mistress," said Dick.

Janet agreed and he went away to get his tea from Betsy. No doubt, thought Janet, he would give thanks in his grace before meat for the goodness of Providence in delaying the storm long enough to let them lead the loch field. Janet remembered her mother standing where she was standing in the barn door and looking out at the bare fields of stubble. She savoured the freshness and coolness after the heat of the day. The hens murmured contentedly and from the byre came the champing sound of cows milked and fed. They need not go out till the storm was past, less chance then of their poaching the grass in the top field; there was hay enough to spare for one feed. In spite of everything it had not been too bad a year.

She wondered in an undefined fashion whether her mother was in a position to appreciate the number of stacks and the full hayloft. She knew of heaven from Mr MacMurdoe in Luss Kirk but found it hard to picture her mother, harp in hand, praising God in white linen in company with the angels. She remembered Elspeth as she had been at the harvest last year, gaunt, grim and busy, her old grey woollen gown kilted up over the striped petticoats and her big man's boots all muddied. Last year they had not been so lucky with the weather.

"Providence," Elspeth had said with her eye on the weeping sky, "has an unco way with it. I doubt it'll be a week before the loch field's dry enough to cut."

Janet had had the feeling that if her mother could have got her hands on Providence things would have been very different . . . the irreverent thought struck her that maybe she had. She could see the beloved shabby figure daring Providence to let the storm begin before the loch field was all led. She found such a picture comic and comforting and laughed.

By evening the rain was past and the air smelt fresh and earthy and there was a good breeze of wind.

"I think I'll just row over to the island again," Janet told Betsy. "That was a fair storm we had. I'll just see that the beasts haven't done themselves a mischief."

Betsy was about to protest that Dick had better go, for if there was a beast in trouble there was little that Janet could do to help it, when she saw Dick wink at her from the fireside where he was plaiting straw ropes for the thatching of the ricks. Betsy closed her mouth and Janet took the oars from the shed and walked down the farm-road to bail out the boat at the jetty, nearly half filled with rainwater.

Out on the water beyond the point Simon heard the regular splashing sound as she bailed and looked round. He was soaked but happy because he had two sizeable trout in the boat already and was well into a third which promised to be even bigger. He played it carefully hoping to land it before Janet could disappear into the thick woods of the island. A picture grew in his mind of Janet and himself sitting beside a driftwood fire on the beach and maybe a fish grilling at it. He braked his reel and took away his hand to pat his pocket, making sure he had brought matches. The trout chose that moment to set off for Ardlui at the other end of the loch, jerking the rod out of Simon's hand. He grabbed for it, rising as he did so, and placed his foot on the fish he had already caught. He slipped and his foot went right through the rotten boards. The boat rocked crazily, water cascaded through the great hole and Simon decided, rather hastily, that it was time to abandon ship. The boat filled and sank as he struggled to get his boots off in order to swim the hundred yards or so to the shore of the island.

By that time Janet had stopped bailing, cast off and was rowing strongly towards him. She arrived just as he was beginning to wonder whether he would, after all, be able to reach the shore, for the water was bone-chillingly cold and the struggle to remove his boots and his heavy tweed jacket already soaked in the thunderstorm had left him breathless and exhausted. She reached an oar to him and hauled at it till he came alongside and could hold on to the gunwale.

For a short while all he could do was hold on while he struggled to get his breath back. After a minute or so he tossed the wet fair hair out of his eyes and grinned gratefully at her.

"Thank you," he panted, "what a daft thing to do."

"That boat of Mary Ann's was a death-trap," Janet declared, venting the anger which had followed her relief, "a good riddance to it. It should have been burned long since. How will you get in?"

He took stock of the little coble.

"You get right up into the bow," he told her, "and throw me the painter. I'll haul myself in over the stern with it. Not so dangerous."

Dick called to the kitchen window by Betsy's cry of alarm considered this move with approval.

"Knows what he's about in a boat," he declared, as the dripping figure emerged from the water and tumbled into the coble in an undignified flurry of legs and arms. Even at that distance they could see Janet laughing at the sight. Simon shook his fist at her in mock reproof, took the oars and began to row strongly for the shore.

"I'll liven up the fire," said Betsy leaving her post of observation, "and I'll fetch those old duds himself keeps in the press and air them. Away you and yoke the trap to bring them up before he gets his death."

"Goodsakes, woman! Mary Ann's is just on the water there."

"Mary Ann's off on the ferry to Rowardennan to her niece with the new baby and left him a cold supper and gave him the key and I'll lay you the key was in the pocket of his jacket. She told me when she was upby for her eggs."

Dick didn't argue further but ran in the direction of the stable. However, quick as he was, he met Janet and Simon halfway along the farm-road. Simon was limping badly and leaving a trail of blood from a cut foot. Janet looked up thankfully when Dick appeared.

"You saw what happened, then?"

"Aye," said Dick and turned the mare, "herself said it would be a cold hearth at Mary Ann's. She's some dry duds of Mr Laidlaw's airing for you at the fire."

He gave Simon a hand to climb into the trap and shook his head.

"You're a fortunate man, Mr Lamington."

Simon, his teeth chattering, nodded his agreement.

"I've Jan . . . Miss Laidlaw to thank."

"Aye, have you," said Dick and gave the mare the office to go.

At Glenfoot Betsy was bustling about.

"Draw the blinds, mistress," she instructed, "and away ben the room till I get him stripped and into dry clothes. You'll catch your death man!"

Janet did as she was bid and was joined in the chilly stiff parlour by Betsy, who was chuckling.

"He put me out and all. Said it was years since he'd had a nurse and he was quite able to do his buttons up himself."

John Laidlaw's clothes fitted Simon well enough, for the two men were much of a size, and after a meal and a hot drink he was anxious to set out for Mary Ann's, but neither Betsy nor Dick would hear of this.

"Haivers!" said Dick. "You've had a sore shake and your feets is all cut. You'll bide here the night and I'll send downby to Mary Ann and let her ken."

He put on his old-fashioned bonnet and went out to find a messenger in the bothy.

"I'll away up and make up a bed in the attic room," said Betsy, "and I'll put in a 'het-piggie'. Janet'll sort your feets. She's the doctor about this house."

Simon's feet were bruised and cut from walking barefoot up the rough farm-road. Janet got out her basket of scraped lint and soft rags and took down the jar of arnica ointment.

"I doubt you were never a barefoot laddie," she observed as she surveyed the damage.

"Only in summer," said Simon, "and that was a while ago. We used to go to my aunt in the country at Moulin and I'd run wild. But I was not allowed to go barefoot in the town."

He told Janet something about his boyhood in Perth as she dressed the cuts and wrapped bandages smeared with arnica over the worst of the bruises.

"I was the only son of my mother and she a widow," he explained, smiling, "so many of my pleasures were illicit."

"And in a town too," she reproved.

"As to that, Perth is a country town," he told her. "There's nowhere in Perth where you can't look up and see the hills round about. And the River Tay runs right through the town. I used to go fishing in it with a stick and a bent pin on a length of linen thread from my mother's workbasket."

"So this won't be the first time you've had a drooking?"

Simon laughed.

"Oh, not by a very long chalk," he agreed. "My stepfather, bless him, was a fisher himself and he used to smuggle me into the house by the back door and Mamie the cook would scold like a Newhaven fishwife and then go and bring down my dry clothes under her apron right past my mother's door."

"I like the sound of your stepfather. Did you have some little stepbrothers to lead astray?"

"No," he said regretfully. "No, they were both too old by the time they were married. I'd have liked that. I was the only one. But my stepfather treated me like his own son. He was good to me. He put me to the University in Edinburgh and then took me into his business. When he died he left me a share of it, my mother has another and I have a partner."

Janet tied the bandage and began to ease the foot into a grey woollen sock of her own knitting.

She began bathing the cuts on his other foot and Simon began to elicit details of her earlier life. She told him about being a child on the farm among the animals and how she had enjoyed going to the village school.

"The dominie said he'd a job to get me to go home when I was wee," she said, "and I worked away at my letters with my father till he was deaved."

She described how her father had eked out the instruction she was given at the school when she and Jock were older.

"Home he'd come from Glasgow, maybe twice in a sixmonth, with a boxful of books. I didn't mind, I like the reading well enough, but Jock could never abide being indoors with his nose in a book. But he kenned fine my father would be at us to tell him what was in the books the next time he came so I'd tell Jock what was in them and woe betide me if I got it wrong."

"What happened when you left the school?"

"I helped my mother. She'd need of help then for my father was never home and Jock was married and away before he was eighteen. She'd let me read all I wanted but I had to have my jobbies finished before I could open a book. And she was good at figures . . . she showed me how to keep the accounts and the like."

"And your father still sends you books, as I know. Do you get much time for reading now?"

She smiled up at him.

"You can aye find time to do what you like doing," she said. "But Betsy doesn't approve. She says I'll waste my eyes with all that reading and be blind before I'm thirty."

Simon considered the vivid blue eyes in front of him and saw no sign of approaching blindness. He was conscious of a certain breathlessness; it was evidently shared by Janet who looked down hurriedly and put on the second sock upside down so that the heel bulged from the top of the instep. She was correcting this, her face pink, when the back door opened violently, crashing back on to the dresser, and admitted Donald Patterson. He stamped his boots on the flagged floor.

"Have you missed me, lass?" he bellowed.

# 3

Janet, already put about, had jumped at this sudden din and upset the bowl of water over the rag hearth-rug.

"Not particularly," she said with marked restraint and went to the scullery to find the floor-cloth.

Donald, grinning at the effect his arrival had had, planted himself in front of the fire and took in the occupant of the armchair. His complacent smile faded. Simon's appearance did not please him. The newcomer was tall and well-proportioned and might have put readers of Mr Kingsley in mind of Viking heroes. His hair was fair and worn rather long and he had grown a neat beard in an attempt, not entirely unsuccessful, to look mature, reliable and dignified. Simon had inherited his stepfather's law practice at a sadly early age and had found that clients mostly considered wisdom a concomitant of age. While he was young enough to dispute this opinion he was also wise enough to admit its weight in affecting his (and his mother's) income.

If Simon's appearance did not please Donald, there were certain aspects of Donald's presence which could please no one. It was Friday after a hard, hot working week and he was standing before the fire. He glared down at the newcomer.

"And who might you be?" he demanded belligerently.

Simon was a trifle startled at such a tone. He had taken Donald for a farm-servant. Before he could answer Janet returned.

"Move yourself," she instructed her swain curtly, "you're in my road. And don't sit there on Betsy's clean cushions."

Donald ignored this trifling embargo and sat down on the other armchair, his cap tipped over his unshaven face and one boot, which declared unequivocally his various preoccupations that day, from cows to pigs with a horsy interlude, dangling over the wooden arm.

"What kind of a welcome's that?" he shouted.

"What kind do you expect?"

Janet mopped the last of the spilled water and stood up. Donald became sentimental in an attempt to demonstrate his prior claims before the interloper. He caught hold of her skirt and pulled her down on his knee.

"A wee kiss wouldn't come amiss."

Simon did not miss the expression of revulsion on his hostess' face as she pulled herself free. Donald's face darkened with annoyance.

"Is that a way to go on after I've been a week away? I couldn't help it. I'd to help at home. I came right after the work was done."

From a safe distance Janet eyed the filthy boots, the stained breeches and the unsavoury shirt.

"You've no need to tell me that," said she.

"And what do I find?"

No one answered this rhetorical question.

"Him!" he shouted, pointing at Simon. "What the devil's he doing here with Dick away down to the loch and Betsy nowheres to be seen. And you plaistering away with his clarty feet!"

Janet caught Simon's eye and detected amusement among the embarrassment. Donald who, like his sister, was quick enough to detect slights, real or imagined, did not miss this exchange and his bluster turned to spiteful bad temper.

"You're enough of a speak living your lone here," he shouted, "without entertaining all the goingabout bodies you pick up out the dykes and dubs. You mind your reputation, my lass, for I'll no bed with spoiled goods, so I'll no."

The faint smile vanished from Simon's face and Janet went white.

"Indeed?" she remarked.

"Aye," her suitor bellowed on, "I'll not have folk sniggering at me ahint my back, no if you brought me all the farms in the parish."

"You," said Janet dispassionately, her hands on her hips, "would wed a midden for its dung, and though it's no for me to say it, you'd be well-matched."

"Ye limmer!" yelled Donald at this masterly reading of his character, "ye footy jaud!"

"And this is my house," Janet continued, "and I'll invite whom I please into it, without asking leave of you or any other body."

Donald scrambled to his feet.

"You are my intended and you'll heed me!"

Simon moved forward on his seat, his hands on the arms, ready to rise and intervene.

"I've got a right . . ." Donald insisted.

"You've got no rights in this house," Janet told him, "but what I allow you and those don't include incivility to my guests. As for intentions . . . I'll not speak for you . . . but mine don't include wedding a man who stinks like a brock and bawls at me like a rutting stag."

This statement, which for force and directness would have been hard to better, left both men staring at her. Simon was ready to applaud but Donald was aghast: he saw the bright bubble of a prosperous, uxorious existence vanish utterly.

"We're promised," he protested.

"We are *not*," said she. "You never bothered yourself to ask me. If you had I'd have said no. I might not have been so plain with you but I'd have said no. Now, go your ways home. I'd liefer your room than your company."

She opened the door. Donald hesitated, his swarthy face flushed with anger, his head lowered like a bull and his fists clenched. At that Simon rose to his stockinged feet, his head on a level with the polished brass lamp above the table. Donald moved to the door. He stopped under the lintel and glowered at Janet.

"Just you wait till I tell folks what you're at!" he threatened and stumbled outside into the gathering dusk. "You're a bad woman . . . a wicked limmer . . ."

The last part of the observation came from the middle of the farm-yard. His parting shot was delivered from the barn corner thirty yards away, safe, as he must have thought, from an angry stocking-soled Viking . . .

"And don't you prig at me to father your chance-come bairn!"

Simon had moved to Janet's side on the doorstep, beside which was a basket of early potatoes from the kailyard which Dick had left there earlier in deference to Betsy's forcibly expressed views on 'clarty boots'. Simon stooped and picked up a healthy specimen weighing close on half a pound and hurled it at the retreating suitor. It missed, but Donald, feeling the wind of it, turned abruptly and lumbered down the farm-road, without dignity and without delay.

Janet turned to her guest and held out her hand.

"It was *just* what I wanted to do more than anything," she told him fervently, "how I wish I could throw like that."

"Perth is a great town for cricket," explained Simon, and held the door for her to go inside again. "We used to play the officers from the Queen's Barracks on the North Inch."

Janet bent to clear up the scraps of lint which were still lying on the rug.

"I'm sorry to have had such a tirrivee in front of you," she apologised.

"I would bring it in as marked provocation," said Simon smiling at her embarrassment. "And you should be proud, not apologetic. That was a masterly set down."

"Things are a bit difficult . . ." she said awkwardly, "his sister's married to my brother and he's been . . . well . . . you saw what he thought. I've been waiting for a chance to . . ."

"Well, it looks as if you've sent him away for good."

Janet looked doubtful.

"He's got a hide like an elephant. And an awful temper. I must learn to mind my tongue. The times it's got me in trouble when I lost my temper."

"Aye, lass," said Betsy, bustling in, "you're as sharp as your mother before you when you're provoked. Oh but . . ."

She gave a chuckle of reminiscent laughter.

"You gave him his kail through the reek, right enough. It was a pleasure to hear, was it no, Mr Lamington?"

"It was all that," agreed Simon and they both laughed till Janet had to join them.

Betsy considered Donald's visible traces and the smile left her face. She stripped the cushion of its cover.

"Glad I'll be to be shot of the nasty, clarty creature," said she. "I doubt he'll not be back."

But she was wrong. He came back that same night just before midnight, well-fortified by whisky, and prowled about the house making coarse and raucous enquiries about the whereabouts of the guest. He hammered on the back door and bawled pot-house insults at Janet. Janet flung on a dressing gown and pattered barefoot down the staircase, closely followed by a drowsy Simon somewhat affected by the hot milk and whisky which was Betsy's panacea for everything from grief to a cut foot and negotiating the steep attic ladder with care. Just as he joined Janet in the darkened kitchen Donald began to hurl stones as well as insults. One of them came through the kitchen window and covered Janet with splinters of glass, which wakened Simon thoroughly. The din awoke Betsy and Dick, who slept in the big box-bed in the kitchen, and they unsealed themselves and turned out. Betsy took the spill which Simon was kindling at the range and lit the lamp. Both of them hovered round Janet, removing the slivers of glass from her hair and gown. Dick pulled his breeches over his nightshirt without a word and climbed the ladder to the kitchen attic with a speed surprising in so large and deliberate a man. He reached into the darkness and produced a gun which might have seen the light of day at Drummossie Muir. He came down with this and an ancient powder bottle, and while Betsy swept the floor with care, Janet holding the lamp to see where the glass might be, he went to the dresser and began to load it. Simon watched with horrified fascination. He poured in more than an ounce of coarse black powder, loaded the veteran with a selection of bent nails and metal scraps which he had stored in a drawer; these he topped off with a measure of bird-shot and a wad cut last winter from Betsy's outworn flannel petticoat. He cocked this formidable piece and went out into the dark in a purposeful way. Betsy blew out the lamp and the three in the kitchen waited. Simon suddenly made a move to join him but Betsy grabbed him by the arm.

"He'll do him no harm, Mr Lamington," she assured him, "it's just to give him a big fright."

Outside Dick waited with his eyes shut to accustom them to the dark. A rattle of stones on the wall at the front of the house indicated that Donald had hit the window only by accident. A familiar voice bellowed an obscenity. Dick raised the bell-mouth of the gun in the direction of the voice, pointed it at the black outline of the hills above Glen Fruin and pulled the trigger. It was a noble explosion which rattled the windows. The insults ceased. There came the sound of feet stumbling over assorted obstacles to the garden gate. They found their uncertain way into the distance. Dick smiled, lowered his smoking weapon and returned to the kitchen. There he found Betsy relighting the lamp.

"We'll just have a wee cuppie," she declared and put her hand on the front of her elaborately embroidered nightgown. "I'm real put about. The drunken brock . . . we should have the police to him."

"I expect he's had a lesson," said Dick. "I didn't hit him but the old gun fair spreads the shot about. He'll have heard the bitties landing all about him."

"There'll be trouble about this," prophesied Betsy, "as sure as I stand here there'll be a stushie. Old Patterson'll no stand for it."

"I'll need to write to father," said Janet. However, she knew a certain sinking as she said it; John Laidlaw had little time for situations such as this . . . or for the people who provoked them. He would not be pleased.

Trouble came sooner than any of them had expected. Dick, the milking done, took the cows up to the field by the burn and came striding back to the farmhouse, seething with rage. Betsy, Janet and Simon were just sitting down to breakfast.

"Do you ken what he's done, the bastard?" he burst out.

Betsy made a face and tut-tutted at the language. Janet rose and looked anxious.

"What mischief has he done?"

"I'll tell you what he's done! He's put a fence our side of the burn and the beasts cannot get their water. It's just a rickle of sticks and hurdles but they'll not get by it till I pull it down. And when I went to do it he . . ."

"Who?" enquired Simon. "The noisy lad who was here last night?"

"Not him!" said Dick scornfully, "he'll be stinking in his bed yet, the drunken brock. It's his father, old Patterson, and yon futtrick-faced grieve of his. The both of them, laughing at me fit to give themselves their kill and when I went to pull down yon contraption he pointed a gun at me and said no to lay a finger on his fence . . . his fence, if you please . . . if I didn't want an arseful of shot. I'm back for my gun."

He reached for the ancient weapon which lay on the dresser. "I'll give him an arseful!"

"No!" said Simon, coming painfully to his feet and limping

across to the angry grieve. "No, leave that. It would just play into his hands."

Dick glared at him.

"You pay heed," said Betsy. "Mr Lamington kens what he's about. He's a lawyer-body."

"But the beasts upby is bawling for water," said Dick.

"Don't put yourself in the wrong," said Simon. "It'll do no good. Can't you put them on the stubble by the loch, just a wee while till we get things sorted out?"

He jerked his head at the gun in Dick's hand.

"That's no way to deal with a bit of spite."

"Mebbe I could," said Dick reluctantly. "There's some feed down by the water . . . and the gleanings forby . . ."

He put the gun back on the dresser.

"But I take my orders from the mistress."

They all looked at Janet, who was standing behind her chair. She was trying to think what her mother would have done in the circumstances and thinking miserably that her mother would never have been foolish enough to get herself into such a pickle. Simon, considering her anxious face and the hands clenched round the chairback, knew an impulse to run out and deal with this Patterson, and his son, whatever the consequences might be. Then he would take her home on the steamer and she would never need to bother her head about such things . . .

"Best shift them," said Janet in a small voice, "I'll go down to Luss and telegraph to my father this morning."

"Aye, he'll sort them," agreed Betsy, but there was little conviction in her voice. Glasgow was a long way off and John Laidlaw was a busy man.

Dick whistled up his dogs and set off for the hill field without another word, but his face was as black as the sky had been the day before. Janet sat down wearily.

"The spiteful brute," she said. "Fine he kens the field's no use to me without water. We can't cart water that far and it's by far too poor to plough."

"It'll be the milk, likely," suggested Betsy.

Janet supplied milk to the Inn and to a number of houses round about. Old Patterson, who prided himself on his milking herd, had coveted this outlet for some time.

"Likely enough," said Janet.

"It'll mebbe be a lesson to you to mind your tongue, lassie," remarked Betsy, not without sympathy, and added more hot water to the teapot from the huge black kettle on the range, "you've aye been too free with it."

Simon accepted another cup and considered Janet thoughtfully. She refused Betsy's offer and went to stare out of the window at the loch, wondering how long it would take for her father to reply to her telegram about this problem. Meanwhile there were the beasts to consider: she began to think of ways and means.

"Come and sit down, lass," coaxed Betsy. "Don't let old Patterson spoil your breakfast."

Janet obeyed listlessly and Betsy went away to fetch another print of butter. Simon had done her oatcakes full justice. When she was in the dairy he reached for Janet's hand and squeezed it.

"Don't worry," he said, "it isn't the end of the world. There could be a very easy answer."

She let her hand lie in his and knew a sense of great comfort.

"I know. It's just that it seems to have been one thing after another since my mother died. There were floods in the spring and we lost any number of lambs and the ploughing was late and the hay-making was late and with father away I don't . . ."

She pulled herself up abruptly; she must not whine. Her mother had a scornful word for those who whined about their misfortunes and Simon . . . Mr Lamington . . . was a comparative stranger for all he . . . The comparative stranger squeezed her hand again and let it go as Betsy came back. He spread another oatcake and remarked thoughtfully, "Mary Ann said this farm was your father's own. Is that right?"

Janet nodded and then she smiled and looked mischievously at him.

"Right enough. And no doubt you'll have heard about my great grandmother's wee mistake too?"

Simon shrugged and grinned at the two women.

"As I understood it, that was your grandfather," he said.

"Mary Ann's another one with her tongue hung in the middle," disapproved Betsy.

"Is Patterson's farm his own too?"

"No, no . . ." said Betsy, "he pays rent to the laird like everybody round here. But his father had the tack before him and like enough Donald'll get it after him. The Pattersons is far ben with the laird."

Simon looked at Janet.

"Have you got the deeds of the farm in the house?"

Janet looked blankly.

"The deeds?"

"The title-deeds. The papers which give you possession. They ought to describe the boundaries and the water rights and so forth. If the boundary's on Patterson's side of the burn he must remove the fence. If it's on yours you may find you have the right to water beasts at the burn. Either way we can make him take down the fence without using Dick's gun. I could draft you a letter and put it in the post today . . ."

Betsy gave a great snort of laughter.

"That'll sort him. Old Patterson's real frightened of lawyers since Mathieson took him to court over they beasts in his garden and he'd to pay for all the plants."

"The deeds might be in yon box of my mother's."

"It's put past there in the kitchen attic," said Betsy, "away up there the pair of you while I get at the dishes. I'm all behind today, like the cow's tail."

The attic above the kitchen was crammed with the junk of more than a century. Simon, bent double under the thick adze-cut roof beams, looked with interest at the litter of worn-out straw baskets, broken harness, furniture and clothes.

"Lord," he said in awe," have your people never thown out anything at all?"

"I doubt it," agreed Janet. "Every time I wanted to burn anything or throw it on the midden my mother would say that I'd be sure to want it the very day after I'd done it. And she was usually in the right of it. This is the box."

It was lying under a drift of old clothes; there was a homespun coat with huge worked silver buttons and a riding cloak with capes and several long old-fashioned waistcoats with flapped pockets.

"These must have been your great grandfather's," said Simon.

"His father's more like . . . oh, dear!"

The box was crammed full of letters and papers and scraps of newspaper. The idea of finding a single item in that tightly packed mass was daunting. However, they cleared a space on the floor of the attic and began to sort it into piles. Janet found innumerable letters from various cousins in all parts of Scotland and in Canada, cuttings which described weddings, funerals and baptisms, and odds and ends like yellow kid gloves and two tiny battered objects which she recognised as baby shoes which must have belonged either to Jock or to herself. A lock of soft dark hair tied in a faded blue ribbon she knew for her own and wondered that she had not seen this streak of sentimentality in her mother.

"There's more here than your mother's collection," said Simon, "this must date from the French wars."

He held up a yellowed scrap of paper torn from a notebook with a scrawl of writing on it which described the death of one James Parlane at Fuentes D'Onor.

"My great-uncle," said Janet rather absently, "he was with Sir John Moore . . ."

She had come upon a packet of more recent letters tightly bound with a leather thong. They were in her father's writing and addressed to her mother. With a sense of guilt she slipped off the binding and opened one.

'. . . a fine house and not long built,' he had written, 'from the front door you look across the park to the river. It would be hard to realize that you were in the town but for the smoke over the river at night. I look forward to your coming. At this present Jimmie Gillies and I are camped in a corner . . .'

It was, for John Laidlaw, a cheerful, enthusiastic letter, but the ones which followed were less so. He had begged and pleaded with his wife to sell the farm and come to the fine house he had bought for her. Two paragraphs stood out: '. . . surely you don't still hold my friendship with Libbie McPhail against me? She is long dead and you are my wife. I work and think and plan for you and our children . . .' and from the last letter in the bundle a sour note: 'I must have the money which Glenfoot will bring. My affairs will not wait. If I cannot sell I must borrow. If things go wrong you may find yourself here at Woodside in any event.'

Janet leafed through the little bundle and wondered why her mother had kept them. John Laidlaw was not a good letter writer but there was a note of sincerity in those first letters. He had genuinely wanted to have his family with him and had been wounded deeply by his wife's refusal to come. Nor was it all the need for money which had prompted him. Various phrases jumped out at her: '... Janet is a clever little thing, she would benefit from the seminaries here. Even Jock would improve if I could win him a place at the High School.'

She smiled at that, remembering Jock's hatred of school. Did her mother think of poor Jock among the sharp-witted town boys, she wondered.

'... it is by far the best part of the town. You will not suffer from the bad air ...'

'... why will you not even come to see the house. I am sure you would be pleased with it ...'

But her mother had not gone. Janet had never before questioned her decision. The idea of her mother away from the fields and steadings and beasts of Glenfoot had been unthinkable, her father unreasonable to suggest it. With these letters before her she began to wonder. John Laidlaw was no farmer, why should he not follow his bent: and having done well should he not expect his wife to join him. It was no more than any man could expect. And yet ... and yet ... Janet tried to picture her busy mother in a town house with little or no garden and no cares but the household. It was a picture so incongruous that she almost smiled. Simon looking up from a crackling wad of thick parchment, saw tears on her cheeks and forgot what he had been going to say.

"What is the matter?" he demanded.

Janet shook her head and bundled the letters into their thong again.

"Nothing which can find a remedy now," she replied and impulsively went on to explain the situation. Simon listened sympathetically, the deeds in his hand. When Janet had finished he offered the clean handkerchief which Betsy had supplied and watched her dry her cheeks.

"It has always seemed a little unjust to me," he reflected, "that a man must follow his star but that a woman must follow a man and his star. Normally this doesn't matter too much, but it's plain enough that your mother had a star of her own. Mary Ann said she was the best farmer in the district and I've heard that from other people who might be better judges. What would she have done in the town? She would have died of boredom."

Janet looked at the little bundle of letters.

"She died young anyway. She wasn't fifty. I think she was eaten up with knowing she should go with father and wanting to in a way and yet knowing she couldn't leave the place."

Simon nodded.

"It's true. People must be at peace with themselves. Guilt and hatred and jealousy: they can hollow a person out and leave just a shell . . ."

Janet said nothing to that but remembered her mother as she had been during those later years, gaunt, ill-tempered and never still as if she wished no time to think and none to lie in her bed awake. Simon sat still watching her.

"Your father never did sell the farm, did he?" he reminded her. "He must have had some notion what it meant to her. This means he must have understood why she could not come."

For some reason Janet found this a discomforting idea.

"But how must he have felt when his wife preferred a puckle of earth and grass and rocks to himself?" she asked.

"He had his work," said Simon.

"All that unhappiness," Janet burst out impatiently.

"It's by," he insisted, "it's over. You can do nothing. Don't make yourself unhappy as well. Look . . ."

He tried to distract her.

"I've found the deed. But I'll need to read it carefully. We'll put these away and go down."

But Janet carried down that bundle of letters and burned them one by one as Simon studied the cramped eighteenth-century handwriting. After a while he gave an exclamation of triumph.

"Here we are," he told her, "the boundary is held to be on the far side of the burn. Old Patterson hasn't a leg to stand on."

Janet looked where he pointed.

"Fine," said she, "but what do we do now?"

Simon looked at the wag-at-the-wa' clock which had been left to Dick. He folded the parchment and handed it back to Janet.

"My holiday should have been over this past two weeks," he told her. "I'll go now and pack my traps and catch the midday steamer. I'll be back at my desk tomorrow morning and the first thing I'll do is have my clerk write two letters. One to old Patterson telling him to remove the fence or be brought to court and the other to the laird enclosing a copy and explaining the situation."

Janet smiled.

"Tomorrow's Sunday," she reminded him.

"They'll have those letters by Tuesday evening," he promised, "and the cows will be back in the field by Wednesday."

He hesitated.

"Unless your father would prefer his own doer, of course."

Janet thought of the business of explaining to her father and waiting for him to act and the town lawyers he would be sure to employ who would not understand how cows need water and made up her mind.

"No," she said, "it would be most kind of you."

"It will be a great pleasure," he assured her.

They stood for a long moment looking at one another, and Betsy, peeling potatoes for the men's dinner in the scullery, held her breath. Janet, conscious of sensations she had never known before, broke the silence almost brusquely.

"I'll yoke the mare," she said.

In the stable, her fingers wrestling with the straps and buckles, she managed to regain her poise. The idea of Simon's departure had given her a jolt. She realised that she did not want him to go and hoped more than she had ever hoped for anything that he would return quickly. The thought crossed her mind, 'this is the man for me . . .' and she blushed again so that she could scarcely look at him when they sat together jolting down the farm-road. Simon, for his part, held his tongue, wondering whether he had gone too fast for her.

On the way down they passed an old rowan tree. At one time there had been a croft-house built on the corner and the rowan tree had been planted as a protection against witches and warlocks. The old cottage was now no more than a rickle of stones with a riot of nettles hiding the place where it stood, but the rowan had become a noble tree and already it was laden with glowing scarlet berries. Janet pulled up the mare and handed the reins to Simon: she pulled down a branch and broke off a spray of berries.

"They're for good fortune so the old people say," she told

him and tucked the spray into the buttonhole of John Laidlaw's old coat. "They'll bring you luck and keep you safe from the Good People."

He caught her hand and held it against him.

"You wish me well, then?" he enquired.

"Oh, yes . . ." she said, rather breathlessly.

The mare jerked her head and stamped. Simon handed her back the reins and reached up for a cluster of the berries which he placed carefully in her dark hair.

"You'll make me look like Jessie McPhee the tinker-wifie," she protested.

"But I must insist that you are as well protected as I am," he said.

Janet blushed and flapped the reins so that the mare trotted on with a contemptuous flick of her tail.

"I'm not the one who keeps tumbling in the water," said she.

This exchange led Simon to the conclusion that he was not going too fast and he cursed at the necessity which was taking him back to Perth.

At Mary Ann's there was a letter waiting for him. He excused himself and read it while Ann exclaimed and lamented over the accident of the previous day. Janet tried to soothe her and help her pack Simon's few garments into the valise, but she was conscious that the letter had contained bad news. Simon said nothing of it while they were in the cottage and put the envelope in his pocket, while he promised Mary Ann that he would pay for another boat and asked her to get Farquharson to make one. She was unwilling to take it but he persuaded her at length and commissioned Janet to see Farquharson herself, which she promised to do. Mary Ann waved him off from the door tearfully.

Once in the trap he wasted no time in telling Janet what was the matter.

"That was from my clerk," he explained. "My partner, Mr Douglas, is ill and not expected to recover. And he hints that my mother is none too well either. It's as well that I'm going home."

They turned into the village and trotted briskly down the street, for the *Prince Consort* could be seen manoeuvring to approach the pier.

"The devil's in it," he said as Janet drew up at the gate, "but I won't be able to come back as soon as I hoped. May I write . . . and will you write to me?"

Janet nodded. Simon jumped down and reached for his baggage.

"I must go," he said and caught her hand. He kissed it and then put her palm briefly against his cheek and smiled.

"Till our next meeting," he told her and she blushed again.

Janet waved at the rapidly diminishing figure on the paddle-box of the *Consort* and found herself wishing that she could have found more to say when they parted. Janet had been tongue-tied by the revelation of how she felt about this kindly stranger. She waved again, telling herself fiercely that she was foolish and worse to imagine he was . . . interested in her. People like him, she reminded herself, did not marry farm-women. She drove the mare slowly back and made herself unhappy picturing the elegant, gently-bred woman he would marry. Betsy, seeing her mood, kept her busy for the rest of the day. Dick, when he was told what Simon proposed to do, became gloomy.

"You'll get no help from the laird," he said. "Glenfoot's aye been a thorn in his side, right in the middle of his land. He's offered a good price to your father more than once, as I hear, and it's my belief that John Laidlaw would have sold to him long since but for your mother, God rest her."

On Wednesday the postie brought a letter from Simon to say that he had posted the letter to Patterson and the one to the laird and that they should have them by the time she received his.

". . . I was monolithically legal,' he wrote, 'and if he can decipher what it is I said he should take some action. In case it's not what you expect you had better ask Dick to stand by with the gun. I enclose a copy."

Janet read this to Dick and gave him the copy and watched him scratch his head over it. He smiled and gave it back.

"I doubt he'll draw in his horns," he said. "He's no fool is old Patterson and fine he kens that there's nobody profits from going to law but the lawyers."

He went away up the hill to see what Patterson was about and

Janet was left in peace to read the rest of the letter. It was not as long as she could have wished but this was readily understood.

> . . . My partner is in a bad way [he went on]. I have taken on his work but as long as he is alive I cannot take in another partner for this would finish him. I expect to be very occupied. To make matters worse my mother is none too well and she wishes me to go north to Strathpeffer with her to drink the waters. I think I must do this for she is old, though reluctant to admit it, and at this present has no one able to go with her. I could wish that all this had happened at another time for I would like very much to return to Luss and discover what result my interference has had. I also want to see you again, more than anything. My regards to all at Glenfoot and believe me when I call myself,
>
> yours,
> very sincerely,
> Simon Lamington.

Janet had not finished reading this for the tenth time when Dick came triumphantly into the kitchen.

"You never did a better day's work than pulling yon billie out the loch," he told Janet. "There was Donald pulling down the fence and as sulky as a bear. We can use the field again, mistress. I'll put the beasts up there after the evening milking."

Janet wrote a note in the graceful handwriting which she had learned at Luss school to tell Simon this good news, to thank him and send good wishes from all at Glenfoot and she was his grateful friend, Janet Laidlaw. This she sent to the address in George Street which was on the letter and found an excuse to take it to the post before the evening boat.

It seemed that the summer ended the day she took that note to the post office. The weather turned cold and wet and the wind blew constantly out of the south-west, churning the loch into a pattern of white wavecrests. The fields were a sea of mud and the work was held up. Janet watched for the postie but he rarely came up the Glenfoot road. Her father wrote to say that she would be glad to hear that the arrangements were well in hand and enclosed this mysterious information in a box of books. Janet puzzled over this for about half an hour and then decided that a letter must have gone astray and wrote to ask what arrangements these might be. The following day there came another note from Simon, dated from Strathpeffer, and very brief. He thanked her for her note, regretted that it was impossible for him to come to Luss in the near future because he was due to go to Edinburgh to the courts there. He promised that he would come as soon as was possible and was, again, hers very sincerely.

Janet was slightly chilled by this note. It sounded hurried and perfunctory. This was hardly surprising, for Simon was doing his best to carry on his business by letter and spent most of his days at a very inadequate desk in a hired house, but he did not explain this. Janet replied equally briefly with a few comments on the weather and the work of the farm and the fishing on the loch. It effectively concealed her depression and uncertainty . . . and her longing to see him again. Simon, opening it eagerly, was conscious of a vast disappointment. The truth was that neither of them was blessed with a bent for literary expression and Janet, schooled by her mother, to a stoic attitude to life, found it hard to express any kind of emotion at any time. It was more than a week before Simon, back at his desk in Perth, found time to write again at more length.

Some three days after she had written this letter the weather cleared and Dick set about the ploughing. Janet, conscious of the race there would have to be between the plough and the coming of the frost, still knew a lifting of the heart as the faded stubble was turned in and the rich brown earth began to pattern the low fields. She and Dick were at the barn door after midday dinner on the third day of the good weather discussing the work which would have to be done before the onset of winter, while Janet kept her now daily watch for the postie when a procession of farm-carts turned in at the road-end and began to bump and sway up the farm-road. Dick stiffened and peered at them under his hand.

"What in the Name . . . ?" he exclaimed. "They're Braeside beasts . . . and yon's your brother Jock sitting on the shaft, idle brute."

Neither Jock nor Kirsty had been near Glenfoot since the day of Elspeth's funeral. Janet looked again and saw that Dick was right. Not only was Jock on the shaft of the leading cart but Kirsty was sitting beside the driver of the second, her son in her arms and her Sunday hat on. The carts were loaded with farm implements and furniture. Behind them plodded a string of bony cattle.

"What in Hell do they think they're at?" demanded Dick, but Janet realised at once what had happened and she felt sick.

"Either Jock's bought in Glenfoot . . ."

Dick snorted his incredulity.

"Him! Never, mistress. What his wife doesn't spend on her back he gives to the Kirk. He's never bought it in."

"Then it's sold to the laird and Jock's got the lease of it."

Dick nodded slowly and Janet could see the dismay on his weatherbeaten face.

"Aye, that'll be the way of it, likely."

In the silence they watched the procession wind its way up to the steading.

"What will you do?" Dick asked at last.

"Pack," said Janet.

# 4

KIRSTY WASTED NO time in letting her wishes be known.

"You'll just move out of yon wee roomie at the front," said she. "The bairns is to go in there and Jock and me'll take the big room."

She considered the furniture which had stood in its place for a century.

"I'll get the men to put your bits of sticks in the shed outby and you can get Jimmie the carrier to lift them up to Braeside. And mind you don't leave them cluttering the place too long."

She surveyed her new domain complacently.

"That Betsy and her Dick can take themselves off to Inverbeg, the morn," she went on, "and you can move into the wee boxie bed ben here. It'll be handy. If you're to bide here with us you'll do your share. None of your gallivanting about the place with the fishers and dirt the like of that, giving the family a bad name."

She shook a pudgy finger at Janet.

"I've told your father I'll give you houseroom till you and Donald are wed but you'll not come the fine lady over me and you needn't think it."

"Donald and me are wed?" exclaimed Janet, startled out of the enduring silence which she had adopted as the best defence "what haivers is this?"

Kirsty's eyes narrowed.

"So that's the way of it," she snapped. "You're to play the jilt are you?"

"Haivers," said Janet again.

"Let me tell you, my fine madam, you'll not upset things at this stage. Everything's ready. Donald's got your father's permission and a bit of a tocher with you . . ."

"He has what?"

"No much, but it's fetched him a beast or two. He's to take on Braeside. The laird was down about it last Tuesday and they shook hands on it. Donald's upby now at the ploughing with his new pair."

Janet got her breath back and tried to remain calm.

"He may have got my father's permission," she said quietly, "but he certainly hasn't got mine. And what is more, Kirsty, he won't get it."

"But your father's arranged it all," shrilled Kirsty, "sent me the money for the bridal . . . it's to be from here. Donald's to come the night to take you down to the Manse to set the day with the Minister and get you cried in the Kirk."

"Donald can turn about and go again," Janet retorted, "I'll not have him in the house after . . ."

"This," Kirsty reminded her maliciously, "is *my* house now and my own brother's aye welcome to it."

"Welcome or not," said Janet, still keeping a rigid control, "I'll not marry him."

"So you're still hankering for your fancy-man," enquired Kirsty spitefully. "Well, you can put him out of your head. He'll not show his face here after what he's done to my father, the coarse brute. The laird was wild-angry, so he was, and his doer's wrote a letter'll settle his hash. Interfering like that in what was none of his affair!"

"It's nothing to do with him," said Janet angrily, "for I'd not marry Donald if he was the only man alive."

"Oh, he's not good enough for you, is that it? Well, let me tell you you'd best be shot of your fancy notions and airs and graces my lass! If your brother's good enough for me, mine is good enough for you . . . and better than you deserve after the way you've been carrying on."

She sniffed.

"What in the Name of the Kingdom gave my father the notion I'd marry Donald," Janet persisted, "not me, I promise you."

"He's been courting you all summer," said Kirsty.

"Courting? Is that what he was at?"

"What else?"

"Folk who come courting don't get as drunk as a fiddler's hinny and come around the doors shouting filth and putting stones through my window," remarked Janet.

"Fine I ken what happened that night," shouted Kirsty, "and a damned disgrace it was. Donald to come down here and find his intended plaistering away with a stranger. You're the speak of the parish, so you are . . ."

Janet's temper snapped at last.

"If I'm the speak of the parish it's because you've made me so, you long-tongued bitch! "

Kirsty put her hands on her hips.

"You watch your tongue when you speak to your betters! " she shouted. "Just you mind on this. This is my house. I'll house you till you're wed. But if you're coarse with me or you'll not have our Donald you can get out and stay out."

Her face was flushed with triumph.

"And then what can you do?" she went on spitefully. "You've not got a halfpenny of your own. You can't do nothing genteel for all your reading and books and dirt. And you'll not take a job as a farm-girl, no you. You're too much of a fine lady for that. You'll bide here and do as you're telled and it's me will do the telling."

She flounced out, a ridiculous figure in her over-trimmed Sunday hat, to bawl directions at the men in the yard. Janet took a tight hold on her temper, walked out to the field gate and stood there for nearly an hour staring out over the ploughlands and thinking of her mother standing in the same place watching the horses at work. The rain began at last and she turned away and went back to the farmhouse. Betsy appeared in the kitchen with a bulging valise and wearing her second best cloak and bonnet.

"Dick and me's taken our due," she announced. "Yon Jock wasn't best pleased but Dick had the lawyer's letter and he's had to thole it. We're for Inverbeg this very day. I've packed your duds in this baggie, mistress, and Dick's put your bitties of furniture in the shed . . ."

"Aye," said Dick, coming in and lifting the straw baskets on the box bed, "and I've the key of the shed in my pooch and there it'll stay, mistress, till you're needing what's inside."

He jerked his head at the window.

"I've Soldier yoked in the old cart and Bella tied on behind."

Bella was the best of the young cows and Soldier had been bred on the place and broken by Dick himself.

"Tam the herd says he'll bring up the sheep in a week or two," he went on. "I'll not bide here with yon woman and nor will Betsy."

"And you'll just come with us, lambie," said Betsy. "Marry yon drunken dirt of a Donald! The old mistress would turn in her grave."

Janet looked at the cheerful old couple and she calmed down. Here were they, turned out of their home and, what was more to both, their life's work, at a moment's notice and she had been thinking of nothing but her own petty affairs. The tears came to her eyes: she felt angry for them and helpless.

"I'm sorry . . ." she choked, "I'm sorry . . ."

Betsy engulfed her in grey camphor-smelling folds.

"Never heed her, the wicked limmer," she comforted, "never heed her."

Janet disengaged herself gently and blew her nose.

"I'll fetch my cloak and bonnet."

During their slow progress down to the loch road in the pouring rain Janet had time to recover herself. The shock of the morning's events wore off and her sense of humour stirred again at the sight of Kirsty, her Sunday hat forgotten in her fury, shouting objurations from the doorstep as the flowers and feathers drooped under the weather. She began to think more clearly. As they negotiated the rutted muddy track which led to Luss she made a decision.

"Leave me at the pier," she told them. "I'm for Glasgow."

The old couple stared in consternation.

"Look," Janet begged, "I can't be a charge on you . . . I'll not do it. You're going to have enough of a struggle; Inverbeg hasn't been worked right in ten years and for the last year it hasn't been worked at all. You're going to have a real hard winter. I can't help you much but I'll not make matters worse with an extra mouth."

She overrode their protests and after a deal of argument they left her at Luss pier to wait for the steamer.

"I'll be fine with my father," she told them, "he can't turn me out of doors and maybe I can be useful to him, keep the house or the like of that."

They agreed rather doubtfully. John Laidlaw had always been a grim and distant figure to them.

"Besides," Janet added meaningly, "I'm sorely needing a word with him over the head of this Donald business."

Betsy laughed under the sack which Dick had put over her head for shelter.

"Aye," said she, "maybe he'll think twice before he hands you over without asking you a second time. But mind, you've aye a place with us, lass, if you're needing one. I promised your mother I'd see after you and so we will as long as we've a sup and a bite."

"Which we'd not have but for her," Dick added.

They drove off at last reluctantly but anxious to reach Inverbeg before dark. As they turned the cart and coaxed Bella to follow, Janet remembered something.

"Betsy," she called after them, "Betsy . . . did you mind and pack the rose-patterned tea service."

Betsy smiled and patted the wickerwork trunk under her feet.

"Allow me, lass . . ." she called back, "allow me!"

Before the boat arrived Janet remembered something important and called in at the post office. Lachie, the Postie, was out on his round but his old mother was there in the dim cottage, peering at Janet with her faded eyes.

"It's Janet Glenfoot, mistress," Janet said clearly. Lachie's mother was more than a little deaf; not that she was ever prevented by this disability from keeping abreast of events, as her reply proved.

"Aye, aye, it's yourself, Janet. Your brother's to have Glenfoot I hear."

"Aye," said Janet.

"Are you to bide there with Kirsty, then?"

The old woman grinned over the polished counter, well aware, as all the village was, of the state of affairs between Janet and her sister-in-law.

"No," said Janet uncompromisingly and the Lachie's mother cackled with amusement.

"I'm for my father's," Janet continued. "That's how I'm here. Would you ask Lachie to send on my letters to Woodside?"

"I'll do that, lassie," agreed the old woman and cackled again. "Certie, but you've wasted no time."

Janet, unwilling to talk about her hasty removal wished her good day, picked up her valise and walked down to the pier. It was, perhaps, a pity that she had not made sure of what Lachie's mother had written down. Like a number of deaf people she was reluctant to admit her difficulty; in her case she could often fill in unheard or half heard remarks from her intensive knowledge of local affairs. Aware of Donald's 'intentions', as who in Luss was not, and aware of his being about to take on Braeside, the half-heard 'Woodside' became Braeside. When, the following morning, Lachie found Simon's letter among the morning packet from the steamer he duly delivered it at Braeside where, as Donald was still living with his parents, it was to lie unheeded for a month.

It was long after dark when Janet reached Glasgow and engaged a cab to take her to Woodside Terrace where her father's house was. She peered out of the dingy windows at the shining wet cobbles which gleamed in the gas-light and caught glimpses of town scenes; gaudily dressed women parading the pavement, skinny barefoot children and smallish men with grimy caps pulled down over their eyes and mufflers about their throats talking in small groups under the gas lamps with their clay pipes in their mouths. Other cabs trotted busily past and carts and drays with every kind of load. Her driver drew up once for a pathetic procession of four weeping women and a man behind a small coffin on a handbarrow. To someone used to the quiet of the country the din was bewildering. Gradually the lights became fewer and farther apart, the shop-windows gave way to trees and bushes and forbidding iron railings and the noise died away. The cab-horse slowed to a walk and toiled uphill with the driver cracking the whip and hurling abuse at it. At length it came to a halt at a house in a long curving terrace and the driver, helping Janet down on to the mounting block, looked doubtfully at the darkened windows.

"Nobody home, but?" he suggested.

Janet, however, had seen a light in the area, down under the imposing flight of steps which led up to the front door. The cabfare and trip took nearly all the money she had left; when the driver clattered off she went up the stone steps and pulled at the brass bell-pull, determined she was not going to creep into her father's house by the area door. After a long wait she saw a light moving behind the transome above the door and she heard the bolts being undone. A frowsy, unkempt head peered round the door.

"You'll be Jimmie Gillies, likely?" said Janet, remembering her father's letter to her mother.

"Aye, that's me," agreed the frowsy grey head, "and who might you be when you're at home, as a lassie should be this time of the night?"

This was scarcely welcoming.

"Janet," she said. "Janet Laidlaw . . . John Laidlaw's daughter."

The grey head emerged still farther to reveal a collarless and grimy shirt and a long unbuttoned waistcoat which had belonged to a larger man. The lamp was held up, smoking distressfully in the chill wind from the river, to illuminate Janet's face.

"Aye," said Jimmie Gillies after a moment's contemplation, "you're his daughter right enough. Aye. Have you come to bide?"

He eyed her baggage with dislike.

"I have," said Janet, picking up her valise and marching inexorably into the hall. Jimmie picked up what was left on the step and followed her in, muttering in no very complimentary style.

"We're all at sixes and sevens," he grumbled, "it's no place for females."

Janet ignored him, stripped off her gloves and her bonnet.

"I haven't eaten since breakfast," she announced, "can you find me something?"

He jerked his head at the gloomy kitchen staircase at the back of the wide hall.

"There's meat downby."

Later that night Janet lay uncomfortably on a horsehair sofa, from which the horsehair seemed determined to attack any occupant, in the stuffy, tobacco-scented back room which was her father's study. To lie down she had had to remove a drift of papers, blueprints, news-sheets and letters. From Jimmie she had learned by a process, not unlike pulling teeth, that her father was out to his dinner and would be late back; that there were just the two beds in the house, her father's which Jimmie would not permit her to use and Jimmie's, which Janet was as unwilling to use as he was to let her. The 'meat' had proved to be stale baker's bread which tasted suspiciously of chalk, and a slice of cold boiled mutton, tasteless as leather and just as tough. Exploration showed her that only the huge kitchen, Jimmie's frowsty den beside it, the study in which she lay and the bed chamber above were furnished at all and that Jimmie's notions of cleaning were distinctly sketchy. The rest of the house echoed empty, bare and magnificent: superbly proportioned rooms with elaborate plaster mouldings, a wide stone staircase with broad shallow steps and elegant cast-iron banisters. The huge windows were blank and uncurtained, mirroring Janet and the lamp she bore against the black night outside.

Jimmie had volunteered nothing more but a half-inch of tallow candle in an encrusted holder and a couple of musty blankets. However Janet noticed that painters had begun work. The drawing room was hung with a figured flock wall-paper (very fashionable had Janet known it) and the intricate carvings and mouldings around the huge mirror over the chimney-piece had been regilded. In the hall below were ladders and pots and rolls of carpet. On the landing were huge bundles wrapped in sacking which might have been curtains. Janet wondered drowsily why he should be decorating the house after so long and supposed that he might be about to sell it. It was by far too big in any event. As she speculated on the kind of house he might be about to buy she fell asleep and did not hear her father come in: if she had she might have heard an exclamation at Jimmie's informing him of her arrival which suggested that it was neither expected nor welcome. Nor did she waken when he peered round the door of the study and lifted his candle to have a look at her. The musty blanket had slipped to the floor and he stooped and pulled it over the sleeping girl very gently. For a second he stood looking down.

"Aye, aye," he said to himself, "a bonnie lass, a real bonnie lass."

This softening, however, was not in evidence when, the following morning, he demanded to know the reason for her unheralded arrival on his doorstep.

"In the Name of the Kingdom of Heaven, father," said Janet indignantly, "did you not sell Glenfoot over my head without a word of warning to me?"

Her father stared at this accusation.

"Haivers," he returned, "and were you not provided for?"

"Provided for! Do you mean Donald Patterson?"

Her father began on the bowl of porridge which Jimmie set before him.

"It seemed to me an excellent arrangement."

"Excellent for whom?" asked Janet. "Not for me. I wouldn't touch the man with a ten-foot pole."

Her father looked up at that and frowned.

"Jock said you were pleased with the idea."

"Jock!" said Janet bitterly, "Jock has said no more than a dozen words to me since mother's burial. How would he know what I thought? And when I did see him I asked him to be rid of the man Donald for I was deaved with him and his dirt and his bawling. Jock said to you what Kirsty told him to say. And why, I would like to know. Kirsty has no law for me why does she want me to marry her brother?"

"Kirsty would like her brother to marry any lass with a thousand pounds," returned her father.

"Ah," said Janet, "now I see."

"There's more to it than money," said her father and chuckled drily. "You've fairly put the cat among the pigeons coming away like this. But I thought you'd know all about it. I thought Jock would be about the doors at Glenfoot all the time."

"Not he," said Janet, "I'd words with Kirsty on the day of the burial."

"I might have known," said Laidlaw, and sighed. "Why did you not say so in your letters?"

"I didn't want to worry you. I was managing."

"Do I take it then you never knew about any of this?" asked her father.

"Nothing. Unless you count Donald's coming about the place as if it belonged to him. Why on earth didn't you write to me and tell me what was afoot. All I had from you was yon note with the books you sent . . . and that was no more than a half a dozen lines. You might have told me how you were . . . disposing of me."

Her tone was acid.

"Now, then, lass," said her father, "just you watch your tongue. I'd no notion you were managing on your own."

"Dick was there. I'd have been nowhere without him and Betsy."

"You did well, Dick or no. Confound it, girl, I made sure that

Jock would be about the doors whenever and wherever if only to get out from under the cat's foot."

Angry as she was, Janet had to smile.

"You see, lass, I wrote letters to the both of you. I'm a busy man and it saved me writing the same thing twice over. It saved the stamp forby. When Jock wrote back I just took it that you knew what was afoot and agreed."

"I saw none of your letters . . . not one," said Janet. "Did you never wonder why I didn't answer?"

"I'd messages from you in Jock's letters."

"Messages from Kirsty, more like."

Her father sighed.

"Aye . . . well, I should have known."

He chuckled again.

"They'll be in a fair old stushie upby the morn. It's all arranged, you see. I sold Glenfoot to the laird on two conditions. The first was that Donald should have Braeside."

"The laird wouldn't be too pleased about that. Donald's no worker."

"He wasn't," agreed her father, "he wasn't unco happy about the second either."

"What was that?"

"That Jock should have Glenfoot."

Janet put back her head and laughed aloud.

"And I'll tell you another thing," she said, "Donald's spent some of the tocher on stocking Braeside."

"Has he so," said Laidlaw, "well, he'll need to get his father to lend him the money to pay for he'll get no tocher from me if you're not to wed him. I'll write the laird and withdraw the conditions today."

He rose and pulled on his heavy tweed ulster which Jimmie Gillies was holding ready.

"I'm sure I don't know what's to be done about you, lass. You can't stay in this house. It's not fit. And I'm to be married before the New Year. A widow-woman with two young daughters of her own. She told me flat she'd not be willing to take on another. That's why I was pleased to hear you were promised to young Patterson."

At the door he turned back.

"We'll talk about it, the night."

He went away to his work in the shipyard and left Janet to digest this unexpected information under Jimmie's sardonic eye. For the second time in two days she felt the ground cut away from under her feet. She told herself fiercely that she ought to have expected something of the kind. There seemed to be nowhere she could go and nothing she could do. She wondered rather forlornly when she would hear from Simon again.

As a gentleman's gentleman Jimmie Gillies left a good deal to be desired in every way. After breakfast was over he took himself off with a market basket and an indescribably greasy 'book' to buy food. Janet left to her own devices and her own uncomfortable thoughts decided that she would not mope about but try to make the big basement kitchen rather less like a troll's den. She had discovered scrubbing-brushes, soap and pails in a deep, dark and unfrequented cupboard when the painters arrived and set to their work whistling and singing in the echoing empty rooms. By midday Jimmie had not returned and Janet had cleaned both kitchen and larder from end to end. The foreman painter came down to ask for hot water for tea and looked about him admiringly.

"My, but you've made a differ here," he said, "the old yin'll think he's come back to the wrong house."

Janet agreed feelingly and made eight large mugs of peat-brown sweet tea which she carried up to the workmen. They stopped work at her appearance and produced their 'pieces'. Janet, accustomed to the generous 'mid-yoking' provided by Betsy, noted the small size and unappetising nature of most of them and then considered the men themselves, pale and underfed compared with the farm-servants. She smiled at them and went back to the kitchen to build up the fire and make a vast baking of scones. One of Elspeth's dictums had been, 'aye do the work which lies to your hand'.

Jimmie returned as they came fragrantly out of the oven and sniffed appreciatively. For a fleeting moment he looked almost pleasant and then he saw the gleaming walls and the scrubbed flags and the white wood of the table revealed after years of concealment below grease and stains, and his habitual scowl returned.

"Damned women!" he grumbled, "never happy with anything.

Here, since you're that busy with my affairs . . . there's beefsteaks for the dinner. You can cook them. It'll be a week afore I'll be able for to find anything in this place."

He vanished into his den, leaving a powerful whiff of whisky and pipe-tobacco behind him. Janet considered his basket and the tough and elderly beefsteaks which lay in it and sighed. She had begun the process of converting these into a stew and was busy preparing a supplementary dinner of tea and scones for the painters when the first and largest of the series of brass bells which hung above the dresser quivered and rang. It rang the more loudly for being cleared of cobwebs.

"Jimmie!" called Janet. "The front door."

"It's yon damned woman," Jimmie called back from the murky gloom of his room, "Just let her wait. The painter lads'll let her in fast enough."

From which Janet gathered that the caller was her prospective stepmother.

Mrs Hannah Lampeter was a tall, well-corseted woman in her early forties. She had a strong-boned face and quantities of greying brown hair and she made the most of these assets. Her figure was good, her walk elegant and her hair elaborately coiffed. She came of a very well-connected Leicestershire family: her mother's preoccupation had been the 'keeping-up' of these well-bred connections while her father's interest in breeding had been rather more direct. Hannah was the seventh child and fifth daughter in a family which attained the total of fifteen before her father broke his neck one Boxing Day, trying to fly a five-barred gate without previously ensuring the co-operation of his mount. Her mother's grief at this sudden bereavement had been tempered with a certain satisfaction that she could hereafter concentrate her energies on marrying off her daughters suitably without having to provide an annual addition to her problems.

Mr Lampeter had been the second son of a Scottish peer of a very minor and recent creation and when that was said there was little else left to say about him. Hannah was, one must remember, the fifth daughter. Mr Lampeter had died young, quietly and unobtrusively, of pneumonia brought on by shooting over his father's Caithness estate during an autumn sleet storm and had left his widow to the uncongenial business of keeping up appearances on a very inadequate jointure. Fortunately the family connections on both sides were sufficiently well maintained for her to be able to depend upon frequent invitations to wealthy houses, which helped to eke out her income and provided her with a venue in which to parade her two daughters. Phoebe and Aramintha favoured their father and like him tended to be swamped in their mother's wake, though they were usually discovered to be a pretty enough pair whenever anyone looked at them for long enough to see them.

During the previous year invitations of a suitable nature had become scarcer and Hannah, anxious not to be cast too much upon her own resources at a time when Phoebe and Aramintha were about to 'come out', brought them to stay with her mother-in-law, Lady Angela. Lady Angela Lampeter, on her husband's death, had thankfully relinquished the draughty castle in Caithness to her elder son and bought what she described as a 'neat town house' in Glasgow's Woodside Terrace. In this town her title gave her a certain cachet which she might not have enjoyed in Edinburgh, where titled widows on limited jointures were common as blackberries in September. Her windows overlooked Kelvingrove Park and she was frequently heard to remark (especially during the visits from her older sister who dwelt in Heriot Row in Edinburgh) that 'for her, anyone could have your Charlotte Squares'.

She had quickly built up a select circle in Glasgow, drawn from old acquaintances and certain of her neighbours. Among these was one Mr Fox (the Old Tod to his cronies), a man who had appreciated as a youth the importance of steam propulsion and started to build ships designed for this method instead of trying to adapt steam propulsion to sailing hulls as many of his contemporaries had done. He had reaped the benefit of his foresight and founded a yard to build steamships in partnership with a wealthy India merchant, one McIan. Fox and McIan had become a name known in every port in the world. When McIan died and his son succeeded to his director's chair the Old Tod considered this young exquisite, who saw himself as the one aesthete in a philistine Glasgow and regarded the yard as a source of money which would pay for his extensive foreign travels and pay for the mass of assorted (in every sense) *objets d'art* which he brought back from them. The Old Tod then sought about for a more congenial partner who might keep the business solvent after his death, an event he did not regard as imminent but realised to be inevitable as he was well into his eighties. He had found this man in John Laidlaw, who combined a single-minded devotion to his work with an innate inventiveness which the Old Tod recognised as being an immeasurable asset to any business. The Old Tod, knowing Lady Angela's taste for 'folk with a *taste* to them', had taken him along to her house where he had been made welcome. At first the main attraction for him had been the excellent dinners, which were a revelation to a man who had suffered from Jimmie Gillies' cooking for so many years, and then he had begun to thaw and appreciate the amount of business conducted at informal meetings of this description. He had also begun to enjoy conversations which had nothing to do with ships and engines. There, a few weeks after Elspeth's death, he had met Hannah Lampeter.

It would be hard to say of these two which had been the pursuer and which the pursued. It was a mutual pursuit. Lady Angela watched the progress of the courtship with great amusement and with approval. It seemed to both the principals, an eminently sensible arrangement.

Hannah's attitude to Laidlaw was not wholly mercenary. A woman of energy and undoubted social talent she recognised in him a quality which her first husband had lacked; it was a quality she could not define, not being of a philosophic turn, but one which she was prepared to respect. If she had been asked to describe her attitude to him she might have said, 'He is a man of talent and energy in a position where he has come to need a wife with my ability. I can help him establish himself (and me) and he can relieve me of my endless striving and contriving.' In this she was quite right: he did need the kind of help she could give him and what was more important he had come to understand that he needed it. John Laidlaw was not a man to be contented with the exercise of his talents, he desired to have them recognised and acknowledged so that he could exercise them to the full. He needed someone to exert on his behalf (and that of Fox, McIan, Son and Laidlaw) those social graces which it had never come in his way to acquire and was now reluctant to learn for fear of looking foolish. Hannah fulfilled this specification admirably.

At all events the affair was quickly settled. Hannah wished for a London season for Araminatha and Phoebe as soon as it could be contrived and Laidlaw engrossed in the development of his new and revolutionary patent Valve Gear wanted to conclude this tiresome and distracting personal business as rapidly as possible. This was one reason why he had ignored . . . indeed had barely noticed . . . the failure of Janet to reply directly to his letters. It was necessary to get her off his hands because Hannah had delicately indicated her reluctance to have her on hers. Patterson's lad, his own daughter-in-law's brother, had seemed an obvious and easy prospect. To discover within a few months of his own wedding that Janet was unwilling to slip into her place in his scheme as smoothly as a properly milled cog in one of his engines was an irritating circumstance.

That morning from his office in the shipyard Laidlaw had sent a note to Hannah informing her of this check to their plans and asking for her advice (though not, of course, in so many words). Hannah, who had spent an exhilarating morning at the warehouse of Messrs Wylie and Lochhead, during which she had gladdened the heart of the salesman by ordering a great deal of expensive furniture for Laidlaw's house, discovered the note on her return to Lady Angela's.

The two women discussed this unforeseen hitch in the wedding arrangements over a light luncheon.

"There's nothing for it, my dear," said Lady Angela, "*you* will have to find her a husband."

Hannah was less than enthusiastic.

"A country girl never off the farm since she was born . . ." she said despairingly. "I number no farmers among my acquaintance and who else would have such a person. And if she doesn't go off I will have to take her about with my own two and how will that reflect upon them. She is sure to be some great lump of a girl with red hands and a Scotch brogue as thick as porridge. It's really too bad. It's enough to make one think again about the whole affair."

Her mother-in-law chose an apple and began to peel it.

"Best go and see the child before you do anything you may regret," she advised. "Your John is a remarkable man . . . it's possible his child is remarkable too."

"You forget," Hannah returned acidly, "I met the son . . .

and his perfectly unspeakable wife. Nothing remarkable about them I promise you except that they are the last people I would wish to have in my drawing room."

It was thus in no very good humour that Hannah stood waiting to be admitted on the doorstep of Laidlaw's house. It did not surprise her to have the door opened by the painter's boy: she was inured to the unlovely ways of Jimmie Gillies and her plans for the future did not include him. Nor did his include her, but that was another story. She smiled graciously upon the urchin who let her in. He seemed to have been dipped recently in pale green paint . . . the best spare bedroom as she recalled and then remembered with a surge of irritation that this room might no longer be a spare room.

"Is Miss Laidlaw at home?" she enquired.

"Is yon the awful bonnie lassie that came last night?" asked the urchin in turn and then jerked his thumb at the kitchen stairs. "She's doonby and there's an awful good smell coming up."

Hannah somewhat heartened by this description picked her way down the curving stone staircase and came upon an argument. Janet had a tray prepared laden with mugs of tea and had added to it a great pile of generously buttered hot scones. Jimmie, instructed to carry it to the painters, had mutinied and was glaring at Janet over the tray she was holding out to him.

"You're never going to give they creatures all they good scones," he protested. "They'll waste time from the work eating."

"They'll work the better for a full belly," said Janet, and Hannah winced slightly.

Janet thrust the tray at Jimmie and gave him a look which reminded him forcibly of her father.

"March!" said she.

Jimmie marched. He grabbed the tray with a violence which slopped the tea and did as he was bid with all the grace of a bad-tempered old he-goat.

"Well," exclaimed Hannah.

This was called forth less by Jimmie's behaviour than by the sight of Janet. Hannah's imaginary portrait of a coarse-grained, rough-handed awkward farm-girl vanished. Here was a beauty; here was a real beauty and, what was more, one of character. The brogue which Hannah had dreaded was there but in a form which could offend no one. For an instant Hannah imagined the faces of the Mamas if she were to sweep into Society's drawing rooms with a beauty like Janet in tow. Her mind moved swiftly, recasting her plans, as she came forward with her hands outstretched.

"So," she declared smiling, "you are to be my new daughter."

She took Janet by both hands and Janet, taken aback by this manoeuvre after her father's blunt warning, blushed and stammered something incoherent. Hannah kissed her on the cheek.

"I am sure we will be friends, my dear."

She looked about the kitchen and opened her eyes.

"Though after what you have accomplished in here today," she said admiringly, "you might well be thinking in terms of Cinderella."

She laughed and pulled Janet to sit down in one of the windsor chairs by the great iron range.

"Please put all thought of the wicked stepmother out of your mind," she begged with a twinkle in her eye. "I want to hear just what has happened to bring you hot foot to this *comfortless* house. My dear John . . ."

With a slight shock Janet realised that by this she intended her father.

". . . has asked me to procure a bed and bedding for you but my dear Mama-in-law says you are to come to us and I am to listen to no argument.'

This was not quite true but Hannah knew Lady Angela would welcome anyone so good to look at. Meanwhile Janet had recovered her aplomb and offered her visitor tea and one of the scones. Over this refreshment Hannah drew Janet out and won a heavily edited version of events at Glenfoot and a description of Donald which made her laugh again at Janet's expression of disgust.

"So like a man," she commented at last and patted Janet's hand. "Never mind my dear girl, John made the arrangements and he must unmake them. Meanwhile you can join my own two. They are so excited at the prospect of having a new older sister."

This was true. She rose and, having got Janet's promise to accompany her father to Lady Angela's house later that evening, she left. Janet closed the door behind her, reassured after an unpleasant morning and considerably relieved that she need not spend another night on a sofa at least a foot too short for comfort.

Hannah walked home thinking furiously. Her problem remained but in a different form. Janet was perfectly presentable or would be when she was properly turned out: she dwelled for a pleasurable moment on the prospect of buying her clothes. However, who would spare a glance for either of her two girls if they were accompanied by Janet. Obviously before the crucial London season started Janet must be married and out of the way, but with her looks there was no need to hunt about for some obscure bucolic suitor. Hannah was already considering which of several eligible candidates of her acquaintance would be most usefully connected when she mounted the steps of Lady Angela's house. She was of an economical turn.

Janet, repacking her valise, was conscious of a feeling of relief. Her stepmother seemed kind and, despite what her father had told her, perfectly ready to accept her as part of the family. She might have been less reassured had she heard the conversation between Hannah and her mother-in-law.

Lady Angela good-naturedly sent a maid to prepare a room for Janet.

"I gather from what you say that she is perfectly presentable," she remarked.

Hannah shrugged her shoulders.

"A trifle farouche, perhaps. She has a brogue but she has a pretty soft voice. She is a beauty, Mama."

Lady Angela's eyes opened.

"Oho!" she said and laughed.

"A real beauty. London would fall at her feet."

"So you've no problem after all?"

Hannah gave her a quizzical look.

"No one, no one at all, will give my poppets a second glance while she is there."

Lady Angela raised her lorgnettes.

"As pretty as that?"

Hannah nodded.

"So, Mama, we must dispose of her before Phoebe and Aramintha are presented next year. My dependence is on you. What wealthy, presentable, well-connected young man have you on your visiting list."

"Has she any money?"

Hannah shrugged again.

"I imagine my respected John would come down with something handsome if I ask it. I'll make it plain to him how the land lies when I see him."

"Does he dine with us tonight?"

"No. Nor does Janet. She told me she had the dinner on the fire . . . and I'll do her the justice to say that it smelled deliciously."

She cast a droll look at her mother-in-law.

The two women laughed and then fell to discussing the merits and advantages of different candidates for Janet's hand.

In the event it was a vain discussion, nor did Hannah have a chance to discuss a possible dowry for her new charge, because when Laidlaw appeared with Janet later in the evening he was preoccupied and nursed a cup of tea and a macaroon as if they were objects too precious to consume. Janet, conscious of being in some undefined way 'on trial', sat silently, as her habit was when she was unsure of herself, and spoke only to answer remarks addressed to her directly. She was an object of extreme curiosity to Phoebe and Aramintha who could not wait to get her to themselves, though they concealed this below their usual demure manners and responded to their grandmother's request for a little music with more alacrity than usual, being anxious to display their accomplishments to a new audience. To Hannah their ability to play and sing was a practical matter of increasing their value on the marriage market: she had little ear herself. Their prospective steppapa was barely aware of their existence, let alone their abilities, and the girls were content to let it remain so for they were in some awe of him. Lady Angela they disregarded as an audience, for well they knew she would be inordinately pleased with anything they did. Thus, it was for Janet alone they sang their ballad and she, liking music in an untutored fashion, made an admiring and appreciative audience. Nor did she provide any competition, for when Lady Angela politely asked her whether she played or sang she shook her head decisively.

"No, ma'am," she said, "I have never learned to play and I sing only the old country songs . . . and none too well at that."

At length Hannah suggested to her daughters that they should show Janet to her room and the three young people escaped the constraints of the drawing room. Janet was carried off to be questioned. This she endured with good humour, much as a cat endures the assault of kittens, and was distracted from her own worries and uncertainties by their artless confidences.

Phoebe, it appeared, was in love. A fat packet of letters was produced from an elaborate concealment.

"Mama would have a fit if she knew."

The writer was the missionary brother of an ex-governess of theirs and was presently in India attempting to convert the heathen. Janet admired his photograph, which was concealed behind one of Lady Angela in a silver locket worn, so she was assured, both day and night.

"There is just one awkward thing, Miss Laidlaw," said Phoebe earnestly, "he is poor, quite poor."

Janet had already taken Hannah's measure sufficiently to understand the implications of this.

"And his father was a parson. Mama does not expect us to marry poor people so that she has not had us taught *useful* things. I mean things which would be useful to poor people. I cannot cook, I have only once been in a kitchen. I fear I will make the most wretched wife for my dear Robert."

"You will be able to play the piano for the hymn-singing at prayer-meetings," comforted Aramintha.

"True . . . but would you not agree, Miss Laidlaw," pleaded Phoebe rather wistfully, "that it would be more *practical* if I knew how to cook."

Janet, warmed by her prospective sisters' evident liking for her and their rather pathetic naivety, laughed, and told them to call her Janet.

"I keep looking behind to see who this Miss Laidlaw is."

She also engaged to teach Phoebe to cook, if and when opportunity arose. Aramintha shook her pretty curly head when Janet enquired if she too wished to penetrate to the mysteries of the kitchen.

"Oh, no," she declared, "there is no need for that. I intend to marry well, if I can. It's different for Phoebe, for her affections are already engaged, but Mama has said there are sure to be some eligible offers for me when we go to London."

It appeared that this London season loomed very large upon their horizon. For Phoebe it had assumed the nature of a test of her fidelity and she had no fear of the outcome, only of her mother's determination.

"But I will be determined too," she declared, and Janet was ready to believe her, amused though she was at the high-flown language employed by her new relations which was, though she did not recognise it, that of novels obtained secretly from the lending libraries.

Later, in bed, she stared at the patterns cast upon the ceiling by the gaslights outside and wondered whether she might be included in their London plans and, if not, what she might do. She smiled sleepily.

"At all events," she thought, "I can cook and clean and nurse. I need never be short of employment . . . and I could always marry a missionary . . ."

Her last waking thought was to wonder how soon she would hear from Simon.

Down in the drawing room her father had told Hannah and Lady Angela the cause of his preoccupation.

"This Lord Staindrop is coming to Glasgow," he told them, "he is to visit the yard and the old . . . Mr Fox is away."

Hannah's reaction to this news reminded her mother-in-law of a gun-dog scenting a bird.

"He's recently opened some collieries in the north-west," Laidlaw continued, "and wishes a small fleet of coal-boats to trade with Ireland."

"And does he wish for Mr Fox's concern to build them?" asked Lady Angela politely, as Hannah appeared to be lost in deep thought.

"Aye," said Laidlaw heavily, "and it'll mean a good deal to us if he does. He's got other collieries and other businesses. But with Mr Fox away it means I must show him some extraordinary civility."

He cleared his throat and addressed his fiancée.

"I can't take him to the house, Hannah, for it's no near finished and in any event I'd not have Jimmie Gillies poison the poor creature: if I were to bespeak a dinner in some hotel in the town, Hannah, would you object to playing hostess for me?"

Lady Angela noticed with amusement that Laidlaw's suspicion of the gentry was in abeyance. Usually he entertained his business acquaintance to a beefsteak in an eating house near Finniestoun Dock.

"Were you not telling me, Hannah, that the gentleman at

Wylie and Lochhead told you that they had just refurbished Carrick's in George Square?" suggested Lady Angela, and was about to enlarge on this theme when she got a look from her daughter-in-law which was, as she declared later, as effective as a kick on the ankle.

"Of course I should not object," Hannah assured Laidlaw "and I am sure it is all most tastefully done . . . and I am sure I hope they have done something about the drains while they were about it, but all the same, hotel dinners are never so good or so intimate as those in a private residence. Such a pity the house is not yet ready . . ."

No one could accuse Lady Angela of being slow in the uptake, furthermore, she found in her daughter-in-law's schemes and machinations a deal of entertainment. It was plain to anyone who knew her that Hannah was, in the vulgar phrase, 'up to something' and Lady Angela hastened to comply with the unspoken request.

"It would be a far better thing," she amended, "if you were to bring him here. I'll provide a neat little dinner and I could invite the . . ."

"That would be quite delightful, Mama," interrupted Hannah, "just what anyone could wish for. But let it be just the family. These bachelors do so enjoy a glimpse of family life, do they not my dear?"

This last accompanied a roguish look at Laidlaw which went unheeded and indeed unnoticed, for Laidlaw, having achieved the main object of his visit immediately prepared to take his departure and return to the work which was waiting for him in his study. He promised to send at once when he had ascertained the date and time most agreeable to his guest. As the door closed behind him Lady Angela laughed.

"He is hardly a subtle wooer, your John."

Hannah nodded rather absently.

"True. But I think I prefer him so. One knows where one is." She yawned delicately behind her fan.

"I think I will retire."

"Indeed, I say you will not," said Lady Angela emphatically. "If I'm to play your game I'm anxious to know what it is."

Hannah sat down again.

"Staindrop," she said, "he's a widower, you know, and quite young; not yet forty I believe."

"Ah," said Lady Angela, "and wealthy, I don't doubt."

"Oh, yes," Hannah agreed, "but perfectly respectable, I give you my word. An estate in Derbyshire as well as the collieries and the business interests and there is property in London. It is an eighteenth-century creation I believe."

"What family?"

"The Pricketts."

"I knew a Gerard Prickett once," observed Lady Angela, "a self-important young man."

"The younger brother," Hannah explained, "chiefly remarkable for the size of his family. Nine to date with an annual addition."

"What one must admire in you, my dear, is your vast knowledge of these people. All the same, I think you are flying rather high. Which of the girls do you intend for him."

"Janet."

"Janet!"

Lady Angela stared.

"Janet," repeated Hannah, "Just imagine how useful. A large country house a few hours from Town and a superb Town house in Queensgate. With a ballroom too."

"I would advise you, my girl, not to count your chickens before the eggs are even laid," said Lady Angela drily. "Such a catch must be a wary bird indeed still to be single."

Hannah looked like a creamfed cat.

"I happen to know that he is anxious to marry again."

"Is he indeed?" said Lady Angela.

"He is. There is no heir to the title and very little love lost between him and his brother Gerard."

"Then why," asked Lady Angela, "is he still single?"

Hannah looked confidential.

"There is some doubt about his treatment of his first wife."

"Don't tell me the man's a Bluebeard!"

"No, no, . . . no such thing. He was married to Anna Bellamy-Crabtree and they did not suit at all. Constant quarrels. She ran away with some soldier or another . . . he was no one anyone knew, a native regiment I believe, and they were drowned in a shipwreck."

Lady Angela opened her eyes very widely.

"A salutary fate. The moralists would be delighted. There doesn't seem to be much doubt about that."

"Ah, but you see there was. Everything was hushed up because of the scandal and of course when it became known about the shipwreck everyone thought it was just a story he had had put about to cover things up."

"All the same, the Mamas might have their doubts but with such a catch as that . . ."

"Everyone had their doubts, and of course Gerard made it his business to spread the rumour that he ill-used her. But I happen to know . . ."

"My dear you always do . . . it is a constant source of entertainment to me . . ."

"I happen to know there was very little in it."

"How little?"

Hannah shrugged.

"They were an ill-assorted couple. She was wilful and spoiled. It was as much her fault as his, I imagine."

"Very likely," agreed her ladyship. "I knew her mother."

"I also know," Hannah went on, "that he has made a number of applications in various quarters and none of them has been successful. Unless he has been accepted since last April he must be fairly anxious to find a bride."

Hannah looked triumphantly at her mother-in-law.

"Janet is beautiful, fairly presentable and, what will signify much more to Staindrop, as healthy as she can stare. He wants an heir and he wants one soon. John can dower her, I suppose. What more could he ask?"

"What more indeed?" agreed Lady Angela. "However, I can see one possible halt to your scheme."

"What is that?"

"Janet herself. She's no meek little well-bred mouse to say 'yes Mama' and 'no Mama'. That's a girl of character."

"She is also no fool," returned Hannah. "What inexperienced girl with a modicum of commonsense would refuse even to consider such a prospect?"

# 5

THE MONTHS WHICH had passed since Janet arrived in Glasgow had been eventful and the campaign to marry Janet to Staindrop had been skilfully waged from the start. It had begun with the dinner party contrived by Hannah. Laidlaw had brought his guest to Lady Angela's house and he had been, even then, an object of considerable curiosity. Aramintha perched high and disposedly on the window seat of the small front parlour had peered down at the terrace. Laidlaw rarely employed cabs and he had not done so on this occasion, somewhat to his guest's discomfort on this particularly fine autumn evening; he and Staindrop had walked from the Yard and were thus in Aramintha's field of observation for some time.

"He's tall," she reported, "nearly as tall as your father, Janet . . . and his coat has a *vast* fur collar."

This was true: it also had a fur lining. Lord Staindrop, whose first visit to Scotland this was, shared the current English belief that Scotland was sub-arctic, barren, mountainous and inhabited by whisky-drinking industrial trolls or by red-legged savages in multi-coloured skirts. His baggage included a great deal of warm clothing. As a result, after a three-mile walk in the Indian summer evening he was a trifle heated.

"I think his hair is fair," said Aramintha, "but I can't see properly for his hat. But his whiskers are fair. He's got the most *lovely* whiskers. He'd be quite handsome really if his face weren't so red."

In this she was perfectly correct. When, some little time later, they came into the drawing room to make their curtsies to the guest this high colour had subsided and Philip, fifth Lord Staindrop, could be seen to be handsome enough in a rather florid way. His eyes were a very pale blue and a little protuberant, recalling for those who enjoyed gossip the unsubstantiated rumour about the second Lady Staindrop and the then Prince of Wales. He had a very fair skin which readily advertised both his state of mind and his physical well-being. His nickname at Harrow had been 'Peony' Prickett. Under the truly luxuriant whiskers and moustache there was hidden a full, rather sulky mouth: his hair was fair but not quite so luxuriant. The artifices of his valet concealed, or partially concealed, a certain thinning. He suffered the introductions in gentlemanly fashion, smirking, bowing and murmuring, "Charmed", "Happy", and other similar phrases. Hannah, who had a sense of theatre which in other times might have earned her fame as an impresario, had delayed Janet's arrival on the scene by a spurious errand to fetch a handkerchief. Thus, she came in when the company were already seated and Hannah noted with pride the result of a week of shopping and fitting: it was all she had hoped and more. Janet looked spectacularly beautiful; her dress was of a grey-blue silk and fitted her to perfection, displaying her firm and slender waist. Her hair had been arranged by Lady Angela's own maid, who, weary of making much of little, had welcomed the task of making the most of Janet's great cloud of thick dark hair. Hannah noted that she was not wearing the garnet set she had offered to lend for the occasion but only the old fashioned silver locket which had once belonged to Elspeth. When she came in and made her curtsey the men came to their feet with alacrity. Laidlaw came forward and presented her to Staindrop.

"My daughter, Janet," he said and there was an unmistakable note of pride in his voice.

Staindrop bowed, stared and murmured 'by Jove' under his breath. Janet was not conscious of his obvious admiration, so pleased was she to hear this pride in her father's voice. Laidlaw in his dry dutiful way had always been a good father, even at a distance. He had appreciated the quick intelligence in her and sent the books which fed it. He had never been anything but mindful of her but this was the first time Janet had felt that he was any way pleased with her or glad to have a daughter at all. Indeed she had been given very much the opposite impression, that she was an unlooked-for burden and a responsibility shouldered from a sense of duty only. His attempt to shed this load by marrying her to Donald had rankled. Now as she sat beside him she recalled he had met Donald only once or twice and on such occasions when he might have been spruced into some semblance of cleanliness: she could understand now how plausible Kirsty's story might have been and how likely it was to her father that she might want to make a match of it with a neighbour's son and a boy she had known all her days.

These thoughts were in her mind as the company chatted politely and waited for the bell to summon them to dinner and they gave to her expression something which had been lacking since she had seen Jock and Kirsty turn into the Glenfoot road end. Hannah looking across approvingly noticed that she had lost the 'guarded' look she had worn, as if she were prepared for the next blow that life had to offer. Lady Angela smiled benevolently and thought,

"I declare, the child looks quite happy for once."

On the way into the dining parlour Janet took her habitual glance at the hall table but there were no white rectangles on the dark wood: no letters by the evening post. Looking away from this she saw herself in the mirror above the table and knew a great pang of longing that Simon could have seen her like this instead of in her shabby work clothes. Perhaps, when his letter came it would be to say he would come to Glasgow. She mused on this during dinner, day-dreaming about his arrival. This suited Hannah very well for her one dread was that some turn in the conversation might call forth one of Janet's brusque and forthright remarks which could so easily repel one of refinement. In the meantime she was content to note that Staindrop's eyes turned constantly to Janet's end of the table.

After dinner there was music: Hannah insisted on this because by precluding conversation it helped to obscure the lack of common topics. Phoebe ploughed conscientiously through the sonata she had acquired for the occasion and then accompanied the nervous duet she sang with Aramintha. Hannah beaming on her 'poppets' did not miss the fact that Staindrop took his seat by Janet (carefully manoeuvred to a small sofa by Hannah) and whenever it was possible he addressed a few remarks to her. When Lady Angela enquired whether he sang he required little encouragement and in a somewhat reedy and uncertain tenor sang the 'Fair Country Maid'. Phoebe's accompaniment to this was equally uncertain but. as his Lordship took very little account of it for most of the song, this hardly signified. What did signify to Hannah was that Staindrop sang with his pale blue eyes fixed on Janet in a fashion she found a little disconcerting and Hannah found most promising. Afterwards he returned to his seat beside her and murmured something at which she blushed and jerked out,

"Obliged to you, my Lord."

A compliment, speculated Hannah and experienced something of the excitement of the deer-stalker as a fine stag begins to move into range.

John Laidlaw endured the music and the tea-drinking which followed with commendable good humour, but for him this was not altogether a social occasion and he had previously begged the use of the small breakfast parlour in which to talk business and there he took Staindrop when tea was drunk. Staindrop accompanied him with marked reluctance and took a prolonged leave of the ladies. Hannah with one swift speaking look at her mother-in-law drew attention to the fervour with which he kissed Janet's hand, an attention now a trifle out of date.

"I trust I may see you again before I leave Glasgow," he was saying, to which Janet smilingly agreed; he was after all her father's guest.

"I will ask your father to bring you to dine with me at my hotel," he told her, "it is the Grand Hotel at Charing Cross and they serve a very tolerable meal. And Mrs Lampeter, of course . . ."

This obvious afterthought caused no offence to Mrs Lampeter, who was experiencing something of the triumph of a playwright watching his creation come to life upon a stage and she accepted gracefully and effusively for them both. Laidlaw looked a trifle puzzled.

"I understood you were for London, the morn, my Lord," he observed.

Lord Staindrop looked a trifle conscious and brushed his moustaches upwards.

"Ah, yes, well, Laidlaw," he replied to this tactless remark, "I think perhaps that another day of discussions might be profitable, do you not? It might save me a further visit . . ."

Laidlaw in receipt of a discreet nudge from his betrothed and not unobservant of Staindrop's attentions to Janet agreed to this and made a suggestion of his own.

"As long as you are here you might care to see something of the country. I could arrange a steamer tour for you."

Staindrop closed with this offer with an eagerness very gratifying to Hannah.

"I should enjoy that exceedingly. Perhaps the ladies would accompany us . . ."

He turned to Janet.

"I know nothing of Scotland except that it produces the prettiest girls in the world. I would so much like to have a cicerone."

Before he retired with Laidlaw for a much-wished-for cigar and a glass of whisky (another Scottish product with which he was quite willing to become familiar) it was all arranged for the following day.

When they had gone Hannah turned triumphantly to Janet and kissed her on the cheek.

"*Well*, my dear!" she gloated, "You *did* make a hit!"

Janet endured this and other similar comments with a certain apprehension: it was plain what was expected of her. Having made an impression upon his lordship she must now make best use of the further opportunities offered. And to what end? Suddenly she felt beset, said her good nights brusquely and went to her bedroom. Here she was interrupted twice in the process of going to bed; once by Aramintha who bounced in as she was brushing her hair and struggling with the mass of combs and pins employed by Lady Angela's maid.

"Oooh!" exclaimed Aramintha and plumped herself down on the bed in an attitude which would not have pleased her mother, "it was just like something in a book!"

"What was?" asked Janet, disinterring a comb from a tangle.

"Tonight, of course!"

Aramintha clasped her hands.

"His heart left his bosom with one bound," she declaimed. "Oh, Janet . . . I *wish* I was you!"

"You'd be very welcome," said Janet rather wearily. "What haivers is this?"

Aramintha in the course of a week in Janet's company had inevitably become familiar with this word.

"It was nothing of the sort," she protested. "He never looked at anyone else after you'd come into the room. You could *see* what he felt. Oh, Janet, was ever anything so romantic?"

Janet knew a kind of exasperation.

"A few words and some common civility to his host's daughter?" she said, "You are a goose, Mintha."

Aramintha sat upright on the bed.

"It was much, much more than that, and you know it was. And he's going to stay on in Glasgow to see you again. You heard him. Your father didn't know about it. Oh, Janet . . . you will have us to stay with you when you're Lady Staindrop and have great parties and balls and invite all the eligible young men to meet us, won't you!"

"Out!" said Janet firmly and took her by the arm to the door.

Aramintha giggled and stood on tip-toe to give her a kiss on the cheek.

"You can be as Scotch as you like, darling Janet, but you know very well he was dreadfully smitten."

"Good night," said Janet and closed the door.

She was in bed and reading the *Fair Maid of Perth* when there was a discreet tap on her door and it opened to admit Hannah.

"You're still awake, my dear," she assured herself and closed the door gently. "Good. I was most anxious to have a word with you."

She smiled upon Janet.

"Such a pleasant man, don't you agree?"

"He's civil enough, ma'am," Janet allowed.

Hannah shook her head roguishly.

"More than civil, my dear. I would say . . . distinctly *épris*."

Luss School had not included French in their curriculum but the meaning of this word was clear. Hannah sat down on the end of the bed and her eyes sparkled with excitement.

"*What* a chance for you!" she exclaimed. "Oh, Janet, I could not be better pleased if it were one of my own two."

"But, ma'am . . ." Janet protested.

Hannah overrode her effortlessly.

"So handsome," she declared, "and very much the gentleman. To think of his singing a song to you! Such a delicate attention. So much more than I'd dreamed possible on a very first meeting. . ."

This incautious admission gave Janet plenty to think about

after Hannah had at last gone to bed. Before that she had succeeded in informing Janet of Staindrop's great wealth, of the extent of his Derbyshire estates and the glories of Staindrop House. Less honest than Aramintha, she had done no more than hint at the advantages of such a match to Janet's immediate family. There had followed some discreetly phrased instructions as to how Janet should behave on the following day, which had jarred more than a little.

"You must be a little more conversable, dear girl. I do realise that no man likes to have the conversation monopolised by his companion but there is a happy mean between chattering like a starling and sitting mumchance."

"Ma'am," protested Janet. "How can I? I should not think we have a single subject in common."

"Fiddlesticks!" Hannah said archly, "young people can always find at least one topic of interest."

Janet said that Lord Staindrop was not really very young and Hannah's expression stiffened a trifle.

"My dear child," she had said, rising from the bed, "it will not do to be turning up your nose at a good match because of a few years difference in age. Lord Staindrop is in his thirties and I do not consider this to be old. And he is *most* eligible. And you must marry, you know. I would not like to think you undutiful."

With that glint of steel gauntlet she had replaced the velvet glove, kissed Janet affectionately and retired to bed where she slept the sleep of the well-justified.

Janet had lain awake, her eyes open in more than one sense. Her prospective stepmother's kindness disguised a determination to be rid of her as speedily as might be: all the uncertainty and insecurity she had felt when her father had disclosed he was to be married returned. It was clear that she was not wanted in his household.

It was not that she found Staindrop in any way disagreeable. She admitted to herself that his attentions had been marked and flattering and that she had been flattered by them; but to be thinking of marriage at this point, marriage to a complete stranger, was discomfiting, even alarming. She wondered if she could mention Simon to her father to avert this kind of matchmaking and then rather hopelessly discarded the idea. He would be unlikely to regard those two brief letters as a sound basis for the kind of hopes she could not suppress. When she turned out the gas at last she found herself longing desperately for her mother's astringent good sense. She could have found a way out of this ridiculous dilemma. Almost she felt betrayed by Elspeth's death, as if her mother had left her to flounder from one crisis to another without a guide. When she did sleep the town was beginning to waken and she dreamed that Simon was drowning and while she rowed desperately to his aid the oars bent in her hands like barley-straws so that the boat would not move and she awoke sweating and sobbing.

In the morning there was still no letter for her and she went into the breakfast parlour in an unhappy frame of mind to endure Hannah's twittering speculations on the weather and what the day might bring forth. The gentlemen were to call for the party in a carriage at half past eight o'clock and to take them down to the Broomielaw where they were to board the *Carrick Castle* which sailed for Lochgoilhead at nine o'clock. Hannah oscillated between the window, where she scanned the terrace for a carriage and the sky for signs of rain, and the amply spread breakfast table where she consumed baps and honey (a Glasgow delicacy which had won her approval) and wondered aloud whether she should wear the new blue velvet walking dress she had put on which would spot if it came on to rain or her old grey flannel coat and skirt which would be dowdy but more weatherproof. Lady Angela solved this problem by offering the loan of a waterproof cape, called, rather improbably, the Zephyr Siphonia, which she had recently purchased from Thornton's of Jamaica Street and which she declared to be both waterproof and conveniently light so that Hannah might fold it into her handbag.

Hanah, her own troubles removed, turned her attention to Janet.

"That dress will serve very well," she approved. "Take your blue cloak with the velvet trim. And you should wear your new hat with the quill . . . most becoming."

"Have you an umbrella?" enquired Lady Angela buttering her third bap, "if not, I will lend you one of mine."

The carriage came at that point and in the bustle of departure Janet looked once more to see whether there was a letter but there was nothing to be found. Staindrop handed her into the carriage beside Hannah and then took his seat opposite. To his expressed hope for good weather for their expedition she responded with polite if distracted goodwill and Hannah smiled.

In Luss, Janet's departure had caused a train of events of which she was perfectly ignorant. Kirsty's letter, angrily demanding that he deal appropriately with the runaway and send her back to fulfil her obligations, John Laidlaw had torn up without showing to Janet and ignored. His letter to the laird removing the conditions of the sale of Glenfoot had been more productive. The factor had lost no time in coming up to the farm with the news that the laird had changed his mind. Mr Laidlaw could have the lease of Braeside renewed if he wished but they were to vacate Glenfoot immediately. At this bombshell Jock's jaw dropped and he stared dumbly and unbelievingly. Kirsty was far from dumb. She stormed at the factor who endured her abuse for a few minutes and then produced a paper.

"... he can't do this," bellowed Kirsty, "we were told we were to have this place! Here we are and here we'll stay. We'll have the law on you ..."

"There was," said the factor calmly, "nothing on paper ..."

"But the laird *said* ..." shrilled Kirsty.

"What he said then has nothing to do with your lease," said the factor. "You're in ahead of the term and the conditions laid down for the sale of Glenfoot have been withdrawn. Nothing was signed."

"What's a bit of paper?" said Kirsty scornfully, "we were told we were to have the place. I've got the letter."

"The letter was from your father-in-law," explained the factor. "It is not a legal document. Now, the laird doesn't wish to be hard on you and he asked me to offer you this "

He tapped the paper.

"... a nineteen-year lease of Braeside."

Kirsty thought of another aspect of the situation.

"What about our Donald?"

The factor shrugged.

"The conditions have been withdrawn," he repeated.

"You mean he's not to get it?"

"He can have it if you don't want it," said the factor calmly, "perhaps you have some other place in your eye?"

At this point Jock found his voice.

"But we shook hands," he declared plaintively.

The factor looked woodenly at them.

"There was nothing on paper."

After this visit there had been a return procession of farm-carts and stock to Braeside with Kirsty once more wearing her (rather battered) Sunday hat and cursing Janet every inch of the way. On the following day when the postie appeared he interrupted a stormy scene between Donald and his sister on the score of who was going to pay for the new pair of horses. Lachie's eyes gleamed at this choice item to retail during the rest of his round.

"Aye, mistress," he said, putting two letters on the kitchen table, "so you're back in the old place. I was inby Glenfoot and the new folk . . ."

Kirsty and Donald ceased their argument and gave him their full attention.

"What new folk?" they asked in unison.

"A lad from Stirling way," explained Lachie, "gentry. A friend of the laird's son. Full of wild schemes for the place like an egg with meat. Old mistress Elspeth will be birling in her grave I wouldn't wonder. Good day to you."

He left an angry and (for once) silent trio in the kitchen. One of the little boys, scared by this unaccustomed absence of noise, began to cry. Kirsty clouted him with fervour and then picked up the two letters. The first she thrust at Jock but at the second she stared with a kind of concentration of spite.

"If yon damned uppity bitch of a sister of yours expects me to traipse miles to post on letters from her fancy-man, she's wrong."

Jock held out his hand.

"I'll need to go down to the pier, the day," he told her, I'll take it."

"I'll see you in Hell first," Kirsty snapped, and flung the letter on the back of the fire.

"There!" she said triumphantly and wiped her hands on her grimy apron. "That'll learn her, the bitch."

The excursion 'down the water' was unexpectedly successful. It was a mellow golden day such as comes occasionally in October. The first part of the tour from the Broomielaw to Bowling was discovered by Mrs Lampeter to be 'interesting'. It was certainly not beautiful and both she and his lordship were taken aback by the stench which arose as the paddles began to churn up the inky water and they listened with their handkerchiefs pressed hard to their noses as Laidlaw pointed out various items of interest. They saw Messrs Tod and McGregor at the Kelvin's mouth with the skeleton of an Inman transatlantic liner on the stocks and a new steam-cruiser for the Royal Navy nearly completed at Napier's yard opposite. Hannah stood a-tip-toe to see the sheds and buildings which clustered round the hull of the big freighter which Fox, McIan, Son and Laidlaw were close to launching.

"It's not a big yard ours," said Laidlaw, "but there's room to expand. Fox has no wish to, though. It's a pity with shipping shares going through the roof at the moment."

After Bowling the smell diminished and the wind increased. The *Carrick Castle* began to roll slightly and Hannah begged for Laidlaw's arm to support her down to the cabin. Janet's offer to take her to the private Ladies' Saloon where she might lie down she declined with a meaning frown. Lord Staindrop had provided himself with a copy of *Tweed's Guide to the Clyde* and contrived to entertain Janet and himself by identifying various landmarks such as Dumbuck and Dunglas and the wide basins which marked the end of the busy Forth and Clyde Canal in which he took a decided interest. Staindrop was particularly pleased to be able to pick out the monument to Henry Bell on the Dunglas Rock although he was uncertain why this gentleman should be remembered. Janet was able to enlighten him and to describe in detail the first steamship to ply in European waters because her father had once made a working model of the *Comet* which had plied in Inchtavannach Bay till Jock had broken it. In return for this information he read to her the spirited account of the storming of Dumbarton Rock in 1571. In such an amicable fashion they passed the time until Laidlaw came to summon them to an early luncheon which was laid in the cabin.

When they had eaten, the two young people, as Hannah coyly described them, returned to a seat on deck far enough forward to avoid the noise of the paddles and they admired the wild scenery of Loch Long and the entrance to Loch Goil. Staindrop, delving once more into *Tweed's Guide*, found a poem by Tannahill, the Paisley poet, to the Lass of Arranteenie. He read aloud to her, soulfully but excruciatingly, so that Janet was forced to look at her lap and bite her lip and missed the ardent glance he cast at her as he read the lines,

> The langsome way, the darksome day,
> The mountain mist sae rainy,
> Are naught to me when gaun to thee
> Sweet lass o' Arranteenie.

The steamer chugged into the terminus at Lochgoilhead and the passengers were invited to disembark for a quarter of an hour. Hannah disclaimed any desire to do so and Laidlaw, who had had occasion to visit there before, said with feeling that he had no notion to be eaten alive with the midges. However, Staindrop undeterred by this gloomy prediction offered his arm to Janet and invited her watch the departure of those passengers who were booked through to St Catherine's in Loch Fyne.

"For it is the most singular conveyance I have seen in a long time," he said.

There were about a dozen well-laden people being herded into a capacious coach which made up in length what it lacked in breadth by an anxious agent armed with a vast silver watch and a waybill. Yoked to this vehicle were five shaggy Highland garrons who appeared like the somnolent and equally shaggy coachman to be much less eager to start than the agent. Lord Staindrop was much entertained by this conveyance and watched it rumble up the road towards Hell's Glen, declaring himself uncommon glad to be going no farther. At this point the gentle soaking west coast rain began to fall and he very gallantly took Janet's umbrella and held it over her until they reached the shelter of the cabin. Janet recalled days spent in the fields with no more protection from that same rain than a folded grain sack and thought how her mother would laugh to see her hoyden daughter treated as if she were made of sugar icing. She was still smiling at the imagined comments when they entered the cabin and Hannah looked at John Laidlaw with raised eyebrows as if to say, 'I told you so'. Which, indeed, she had just done.

Laidlaw, on the voyage home, during which the clouds wrapped themselves round the hills and gusts of rain blattered against the cabin windows, considered his daughter and his guest and an idea came to him. By the time the scurrying waiters served them with tea and a generous supply of buttered toast and jam and buttered scones and currant cake it had taken definite shape in his mind.

Fox in his hey-day had been a man of ideas but it had been McIan, the shrewd old merchant, who had had the money. Young McIan had more notion of spending than making. Fox would soon be dead. Suppose he could persuade Staindrop to become a partner; the man was wealthy enough for it to be a minor part of his activities so that he would not be continually interfering in the work of the yard. Laidlaw and Staindrop had a good ring to it for a name. The man had the right connections in London and knew enough about business to understand the present need to expand. He thought about it and looked at his daughter and his guest poring over *Tweed's Guide* and peering into the mist to see could they pick out Argyle's Bowling Green. When parts of it did loom through a gap in the rainclouds Staindrop remarked that it was no more like a bowling green than the Peak. Janet patiently explained the nature of Maccailein Mhor's grip on the country thereabout and the Highlander's liking for irony which had pitched on that sobriquet for the roughest, wildest and rockiest country. He appeared doubtful that such people as Highlanders could indulge in irony and doubted their ever having seen a bowling green. Janet changed the subject and pointed up to the head of Loch Long as they churned their way past the Dog Rock.

"It's only about two miles to Loch Lomond from Arrochar," she explained with a pang of homesickness at the thought of being so near her home. "Haakon the Viking king had his boats dragged over the pass there on tree trunks so that he could raid the loch."

It was a story which had fired her imagination as a child and she had often imagined the menacing square Viking sails on the loch and the fierce men looting and burning in the lands of Lennox. Staindrop listened with apparent interest but confided when she had finished the tale that history was a closed book to him.

"All those kings and dates and battles . . ." he said, "I never could master them, and of course we were never taught Scotch history. All the same, had I had a teacher as charming as yourself, who knows what might have happened?"

Janet, quite correctly, took this to be an indication of ennui and ceased to volunteer information, somewhat to Hannah's relief. Hannah skilfully turned the talk to a more acceptable topic,

Staindrop's own possessions, and the company was treated to a description of Staindrop House couched in the fashionable meiosis.

"You mustn't be imagining anything fine and grand like Chatsworth or Goodwood. Just a mere forty or fifty rooms, I give you my word."

Hannah skilfully kept him on the subject and they heard of the halls and the galleries and the drawing rooms. It was a little unfortunate that the parts of the house with which he was most familiar were the gunroom and the library where the presence of a desk gave him an excuse to sleep in the deep armchairs. His memory of the place was not equal to his pride in it. He conducted arguments with himself as to whether the Chinese drawing room opened off the gallery or out of the green saloon which even Hannah found a trifle tedious.

"And is your estate extensive?" she enquired after one such. "I am sure it must be very fine. Derbyshire is such a pretty county."

"A matter of some forty farms, I suppose," said his lordship.

"What kind?" asked Janet, her interest caught at last.

"I beg your pardon," said Staindrop.

"I meant are they hill farms or in the valleys?"

"Both, I imagine."

"Do you have a lot of arable?"

"I really couldn't say."

He looked a little shamefaced.

"You will be shocked to hear, Miss Laidlaw, that my agent attends to all that sort of thing. I scarcely know wheat from barley or one cow from another."

Before Janet could enlarge on this theme Hannah put another question.

"I have heard your gardens are uncommonly pretty," she said.

"Very true," he agreed. "My grandmother had them laid out by that fellow Brown. Miss Laidlaw will not be surprised to learn that we have a Scotch gardener."

"I expect he is a crotchety character," laughed Janet, "I never met a gardener that wasn't."

He agreed ruefully.

"I do hope, Miss Laidlaw, that I may look forward to the very great pleasure of showing you all these things some time in the very near future. It would make me very happy if you were to pay us a visit."

Janet, startled by this unexpected move did not reply at once and Hannah stepped smoothly into the gap.

"I am sure that is excessively civil of his lordship. Is it not Janet?"

"Yes," agreed Janet politely and considered her gloved hands. Suddenly the day's excursion had become menacing.

At dinner in the Grand Hotel that night Janet sat mumchance. The florid plush splendours of the hotel oppressed her and the food set before them was rich without being appetising. She had the sense of being nudged and edged in a direction she did not wish to go. A picture flashed into her mind of a ewe being separated from the flock by the dogs and she smiled at the homely memory. As she looked up she found Staindrop's rather protuberant eyes fixed on her and he smiled back as if he had been waiting for some such gesture from her. Hannah, who had disguised her irritation with Janet's silence under a flow of bright commonplaces, noted this exchange and gave a private sigh of relief. Laidlaw waited impatiently till the end of the meal when Janet and Hannah retired to the private sitting room and then broached his idea of a partnership over the port. He explained the circumstances:

"I cannot feel Mr Fox would object," he ended. "He kens fine that young McIan is so much lumber."

Staindrop listened in silence but by the time they rejoined the women to drink tea he had promised to consider the matter.

Consider it he did: in the train rattling south he weighed up the advantages of such a scheme. He required ships and would require in the future when his collieries expanded: coal was valuable only when it could be delivered to those who wanted to use it. A partnership of this nature would, at the least, ensure speedy delivery and a good price. And there was the girl; his thoughts lingered appreciatively over Janet. No family, of course, but perfectly ladylike and not a chatterbox. She was certainly a most attractive notion.

# 6

IT WAS THE circumstances of his return to Derbyshire which hardened an attractive notion into a resolve. His younger brother came, as in duty bound, to pay his respects to the head of the family and to announce, as he had done annually for ten years past, the arrival of yet another infant Prickett.

"A boy," he rejoiced smugly over a glass of madeira, "a fine healthy boy. Must be a great comfort to you, Philip, to know the succession is so perfectly secure. In the circumstances . . ."

He glanced about him at the pompous palladian plasterwork of the great saloon with a proprietorial air which nettled his brother almost beyond bearing.

The following day Lord Staindrop gave certain orders to a brass-founder and within a very few days a handsome tablet appeared in the unrelentingly Gothic chapel of Staindrop House. The late Lord Staindrop had undergone a conversion to a form of the Christian faith which found its expression mainly in stone. The decorous and unobtrusive apartment provided for private worship by the original architect of the seat dwindled to an oratory dominated by a painting of the 'Wedding at Cana' from the studio of an academician more renowned for acreage of canvas covered than for artistic eminence. It was also liberally provided with hassocks by the late Lady Staindrop whose own devotions took the form of polychromatic Berlin woolwork. Outside the gates of the park a new chapel had been built on which was lavished all the arts of the stone-carver, the glass-stainer, the wood-carver, the tapestry-weaver, the brass-founder and the silversmith in order to provide a setting fit for the devotions of a fourth baron. It was, perhaps, a pity that the first service he attended in it was his own funeral. As his heir, Philip, fifth Lord Staindrop, did not share his parents' religious fervours, the Gothic glories were enjoyed only by a few of the house-servants, such villagers as did not attend a red-brick Bethel at the other end of the parish and the incumbent who emerged from an obsession with archaeological matters once a week for an hour to conduct a service for them.

The Reverend Mr Jolly, summoned to attend at the installation of the tablet peered about him at the Gothic intricacies of the chapel as if he expected them to be quite different on a weekday and withdrew his mind reluctantly from a monograph he was composing for a learned journal on the Prediluvial Deposits of Derbyshire. The plaque on the wall before him read:

Sacred to the memory of
Anna Bellamy-Crabtree
late lamented wife
of
Philip Prickett
fifth Lord Staindrop
LOST AT SEA
1876
"Till the sea shall give up its dead . . ."

"Mmmm . . ." he commented, "quite, quite. Quite. Brass I see, and Gothic lettering. Perfectly in keeping. Excellent taste . . . in excellent taste. Just one small matter my Lord . . . I cannot recall . . ."

Lord Staindrop looked at him without enthusiasm.

"I cannot for the life of me recall . . . when your good lady died . . . did I conduct the service? It has quite slipped my memory."

"She was lost at sea," reproved his Lordship's bailiff.

"I see . . . of course. Foolish beyond permission. Tut! Of course . . . I will have great pleasure in dedicating this on Sunday."

"Tomorrow," rejoined his patron. "On Sunday I shall be in Scotland."

The following day Mr Jolly, after making a false start on the service of commination, made his nervous way through the dedication under the pale eye of Lord Staindrop, whose constant consultation of his watch indicated his anxiety not to miss the train to the north.

Once in Scotland he wasted no time. He went from the station to Laidlaw's office in the yard and asked permission to pay his addresses to Janet. Laidlaw, who had never quite believed Hannah's tale, concealed his astonishment and gruffly gave his consent. Staindrop, without more ado, began to discuss the articles of partnership he had brought from London, a discussion which took considerably longer than the first.

In the afternoon Staindrop called at Lady Angela's and was received with barely concealed rapture by Hannah. His enquiry for Janet was met with the information that she had gone for a walk in Kelvingrove Park. This had become a habit with her. After the novelty of town life had worn off Janet found the dawdling manner of it stifling and she missed very much the exercise and fresh air which she had enjoyed at Glenfoot. At first Phoebe and Aramintha had shared these walks but they found her pace too fast and her energy too great. Moreover, as the days slipped past and no word had come from Simon she had wanted to be by herself.

Staindrop, encouraged by Hannah to go in pursuit, found her on a bench sombrely contemplating an elevating effigy in bronze of a tigress and her cubs consuming a peacock. He halted beside her, bowed and then offered his arm to escort her back to the house. On the way, in a suitably secluded grove, he made her the offer of his hand. Janet, alarmed by this precipitance, pleaded that she had barely had time to make his acquaintance and asked for a little while in which to consider his obliging offer. He accepted this rebuff without overt pique and answered with a patronising air which indicated his belief that the eventual outcome was certain. He did not know that he had been spared a blunt refusal only because Janet was unwilling to cause dissension between him and her father.

Before he had left Woodside Terrace, Hannah had invited Staindrop to share a cup of tea and as he knew her for a friend he confided in her the outcome of his application. Hannah disguised her surprise and anger and dismissed Janet's reaction as mere maidenly modesty and assured him that she would certainly think better of it should he make another. Staindrop hummed and hawed at this assurance and departed to catch his train to London where, he said, he had neglected his business too long. Before he left he declared his intention to return in a fortnight or so. He left a hastily scribbled note to be delivered to Laidlaw saying that his first application to Janet had not met with much success;

> . . . I have to admit that I feel it desirable that a partnership such as we discussed should rest on a sound basis. I will, after all, have to play my part at a distance. It seems to me that in the circumstances it would be of great advantage to be your son-in-law. Should my hopes in that direction be dashed a second time [he wrote] I would have to reconsider the articles we initialled this afternoon.

Laidlaw read this and then consigned all women to a fate of which Jimmie Gillies, now beset daily either by his master's bride-to-be or his master's daughter, would most heartily approve.

Meanwhile Hannah had lost no time in saying exactly what she thought of her behaviour. The velvet glove came off completely.

"You cannot play fast and loose with such a chance as this," she had stormed. "Do you mean to try for a Prince of the Blood? You may be endowed with great good looks, nobody would deny this, but let me tell you you have neither birth nor breeding and too little money to gloss these deficiencies. How can you be so short-sighted? Not to mention so selfish and so ungrateful . . ."

Janet, overwhelmed by this attack and reluctant to mention Simon, inasmuch as after nearly two months of silence it would appear that the attachment she had fancied existed only for her, stammered a futile protest.

"But ma'am . . . after so short an acquaintance I cannot know if he is the man for me. We might not suit."

Hannah was scornful.

"You talk like a die-away heroine. Let me tell you that few husbands are ever the ideal. Every marriage is a compromise and it is the wife who must compromise. Don't talk such sickly stuff to me. And let me tell you this, miss, persons of our world do not marry only to oblige themselves. They marry to oblige their families. This would be a match of the utmost advantage to us all, the more especially to your poor father who has reached a positive crisis in his affairs . . ."

News had come that morning of the Old Tod's having had an apoplectic stroke.

". . . and you are to whistle it down the wind as if he was some tongue-tied rustic! "

She drew breath and chose her weapon.

"Having wasted this opportunity," she said bitterly, "you need not expect me to expend my energies contriving others. When we go to London in the spring you shall go to your brother. I have my own two to consider."

The door slammed behind her and Janet was left breathless and sore and conscious of nothing but a determination that whatever was to happen when Hannah went to London she would not return to Luss.

"I'll be a cook or a chambermaid sooner," she declared to herself.

She decided to appeal to her father, at least for some time to consider, but when she approached him in his study he merely fixed her with those brightly cold eyes and remarked,

"You're ill to please, lass, What irks you at this one?"

"Nothing," said Janet, "it's just that I . . ."

She struggled for the words which would explain how she felt but they would not come.

Laidlaw looked bleakly at her.

"I need a partner," he said. "The Old Tod is near done and young McIan takes an interest in nothing but his pictures and foreign whigmaleeries. He's talking of pulling out altogether. I need Staindrop. He has plenty of money, he's influential where I want influence . . ."

"Surely you can make a partner of him without my marrying the man?"

"Seemingly not."

He thrust the note from Staindrop at her, and watched her as she read it.

"Surely, lass, you could consider him. He'll be up in a fortnight to look at the plans for his collier boats and it's in my mind he means to try you again."

He rose and stared out of the grimy window at the overgrown back green.

"It's the sort of opportunity which doesn't come twice in a lifetime," he said.

Janet said nothing. She was thinking of the long years of separation and the comfortless life he had led and her mother's obvious remorse for this. She could sense the burning, driving ambition in this dour stranger who was her father. The opportunity he spoke of was his, not hers, and she sensed how he hungered for it. She knew he was asking her to do this for him; though he said nothing of it she was certain he must be thinking that the women of his family had done little enough for him though he had cared for them in his way. To anyone ignorant of her feelings for Simon, and this was everyone save herself, her refusal might indeed seem flighty and cross-grained.

Laidlaw turned about and saw her motionless by the door, her face rather pale and with the set wooden look which concealed her feelings.

"Don't look so gash, Jennie-lass, I'll not make you do anything you don't wish," he told her more gently. "But give the matter a bit of thought before he comes back again."

Janet nodded.

"Your good-mother's fit to be tied," he added. "She sets a deal of store by these matters. If you give him the go-by I doubt she'll not let you forget it in a hurry. Your life won't be worth living. She wants to send you back to Jock but I cannot have that. What's to be done with you I do not know."

Janet understood very well the warning he had just given her. Life in her father's new household would be no more pleasant than life with Kirsty. She left the study, returned the painters' cheerful greetings and set out for Kelvingrove Park.

On the way down to the fountain she almost decided she must write to Simon; then she counted up for the hundredth time the number of weeks since she had heard from him. It was too long. He must have forgotten her or thought better of keeping up her acquaintance. Perhaps his mother had persuaded him how foolish it would be to marry out of his own circle . . . if indeed, he had ever thought of marriage at all. She looked up at the Lady of the Lake in the centre of her little pond.

"I *can't* write," she said aloud and walked on.

She considered Staindrop. His manners were stilted and rather formal but there seemed no doubt of his admiration, though Janet, with a youthful cynicism, thought that his habit of presenting her with studied compliments as one might present a child with sugar-plums, a habit she found at once disconcerting and amusing would end if . . . if . . . she forced herself to look squarely at the prospect . . . if they were to be married. Janet was a country girl and she was not squeamish: Staindrop seemed gentlemanly and considerate enough. She was not revolted at the idea of his touching her as she had been by Donald. She admitted that given time she might come to like the man. However, there was more to marrying than being his wife. She thought with trepidation of the kind of life she would have to lead, for Hannah, who lacked imagination, had depicted it in detail, unable to understand that to be the wife of a wealthy, important and well-born man was not the ultimate dream of every girl as it had been hers when she was the same age as Janet. To Janet the social round, the obligations of a landowner's wife to tenantry and dependents, the administration of vast numbers of servants were more frightening than attractive. She doubted her ability to fill the role, a doubt shared by Hannah who had relished in prospect that of guide and tutor.

At the wrought-iron gates of the park she hesitated, looking through the bars: she remembered Staindrop's appearance at her side the previous day and willed passionately that Simon would appear as unexpectedly among the hurrying passers-by.

"He *must* come," she said aloud and drew a look of astonishment from a nursemaid with her charges undergoing daily exercise.

It was as if the bars of the gate were a symbol. If Simon did not come she could not wear the willow all her days, that was for the heroines of the lending library, and for that febrile world in which 'love' was the supreme arbiter in the choice of a mate Janet had little sympathy. Girls in her world married either because they had to, paying for a brief pleasure with a likely lad by years of grinding poverty and hard work, or else their marriages were family affairs more concerned with land and gear than with the prospects of personal happiness. To Janet marriage was an important and essential part of existence; happiness within that state a welcome bonus not a pre-condition. She had known it blossom in some unlikely places. The bars with their elegant rigidity spelled it out for her. If Simon did not come she must say 'yes' to Staindrop. There was always the chance, she told herself, that he might not risk a further rebuff.

She walked swiftly back to Lady Angela's, her decision taken: she could bear with Hannah's petulance and with banishment to Loch Lomond but without Simon she could not bear to add another disappointment to those which had already dimmed and distorted her father's life.

Simon did not come: at least, he did not come to Glasgow. By dint of a week's hard grind at his desk and by postponing some work he succeeded in clearing three days at the beginning of November in which he might discover why Janet had not answered his letters, the last of which had been a proposal of marriage. Kirsty had opened this one and read it before she sent it the same way as the others. Afterwards she set about her tasks with a kind of languor, conscious of a physical pleasure in having had her own back on the uppish bitch. This well-being had been abruptly dispersed by a letter in the same post to Jock from his father in which he commiserated with them over the loss of Glenfoot.

> I'd no notion that he would take it from you [he wrote] but if the new man is gentry that would explain why. They aye stick together, the gentry. By the same token our Janet looks to be going to join them. She has a follower, just now, a Lord Staindrop. He's a widow-man like myself though younger by a good bit and no family. You'll maybe see your sister Lady Staindrop yet . . .

To this news Kirsty reacted with a sour fury of jealousy which could find no expression but abuse of Jock, her children, the farm-servants and anyone intrepid enough to come within range of her tongue. The news spread rapidly through the village for Janet was popular and the agreement was that it was no more than her due and that Lord Staindrop, whoever he might be, was a fortunate man. Jock was teased about his high-born connections and once the first fury of Kirsty's jealousy was abated she too basked in this reflected glory. When Simon landed in Luss on a grim November day and engaged a room at the Inn, his enquiries about Glenfoot (made with a casualness which deceived no one in hearing, for Mary Ann had been busy) met with the disconcerting news that Glenfoot had changed hands and the old mistress must be birling under the neat grey stone in Luss Kirkyard over the changes that had been made there. Simon listened patiently to the tale of the new tenant's iniquities and asked nonchalantly what had become of the previous occupiers.

"Betsy and Dick's away to Inverbeg to a wee croft up Glen Douglas way," the innkeeper informed him. "And the folk upby say he's been working like the very devil at it."

"And Miss Laidlaw?"

The innkeeper had hoped to evade this question: he cleared his throat and looked a little uncomfortable.

"She's away to her father in Glasgow."

Simon was about to cancel his room and enquire the time of the next steamer to Balloch and the Glasgow train when the innkeeper's wife weighed into the conversation. Her husband was perfectly ready to permit Simon to find out the news himself but his wife was a forthright person and felt sorry for the pleasant young man. As she was to put it later to a somewhat despondent Mary Ann, 'Better a finger off than aye wagging.'

"Her brother Jock was saying that Janet's to make a grand match of it. A lord, no less. How's that for old Elspeth's lass? Mind, she's that bonnie and with the pretty ways of her I doubt she'll make a bonnie lady."

Simon, aware of her button-like eyes fixed on him, hid the shock this news had given him and decided to stay and discover whether the rumour was true. Before night he had had the same story several times. He heard it from Jock, who was down at the manse with a bag of grain for Mrs McMurdoe's hens, and he heard it from the purser who had engineered his first meeting with Janet. Below their pleasure in reporting this achievement of one of their number Simon could sense a sympathy which he found irksome and depressing. The next morning as he waited for the steamer which would take him to Balloch he wondered whether he should stop off in Glasgow and see her and have the story confirmed by her in person: as the *Prince Consort* approached he remembered the chilly stiff little notes which were all he had had from her and his own three unanswered letters. If they had been ordinary letters, to leave them unanswered would argue merely a lapse in manners, but these letters were . . . Simon admitted it grimly to himself . . . love letters. They demanded an answer, not to reply was a tacit indication that the feelings expressed in the letters were not shared. By the time he reached Glasgow his mind was made up. He caught the Perth train at Buchanan Street Station and arrived home a day earlier than his mother expected and in such low spirits that she at once sought around some way of raising them and hit upon the notion of a theatre party.

Meanwhile the fortnight had passed and Lord Staindrop was once more installed in the Grand Hotel. He spent the first day with John Laidlaw discussing the plans of his colliers and proposing certain modifications and accepted an invitation to dine, this time at number 14, Laidlaw's house, where he would be the first guest to honour the dining room in its pristine glories of carved and polished mahogany, maroon velvet, figured flock wallpaper and gilded plaster. Hannah had gone to the length of engaging servants, much to Jimmie Gillies' disgust, and had interviewed a number of them in the room which she had chosen to be her own sitting room on the first floor. They had awaited this ordeal in the hall and there Janet found a copy of the *Perthshire Advertiser* which had been abandoned by a candidate for the post of parlour-maid. She looked at it, half-hoping to find some mention of Simon and found one almost at once.

> ... among those present [wrote the reporter, describing a first night at the Perth Theatre] were Mrs Carnegie, Mr and Mrs Jamieson and their daughter Miss Kitty Jamieson who well deserved her soubriquet, 'Fair Maid of Perth', for she was looking very elegant in white satin trimmed with crystal embroidery on the bodice and blond lace. She was escorted by Mr Simon Lamington, who has so ably filled the place of the late lamented Mr Douglas. This rising young lawyer has been suggested as a possible Liberal candidate at the next election.

Janet let the paper drop and felt sick and shaken with disappointment and longing: only then did she understand how much she had been hoping against hope. And now there was no hope; the coy references which followed on the 'bonds of Hymen' and the expected 'union of two such long-established Perth families' rang grimly true in Janet's ears. She went upstairs into the room where she had removed the previous day, glad to escape, if only briefly, from Hannah's reproachful looks and bitter comments and Lady Angela's more forthright comments about girls who 'did not recognise when they were well off'. Even the sympathy of her two stepsisters was tinged with wonder and reproach.

"But Janet," Phoebe had said, "your affections are not already engaged, are they?"

Janet had agreed.

"He seems so handsome and so pleasant," Phoebe went on, "Why can you not like him? I think he is a charming man and if it were not for my dear Robert I would be in some danger, I promise you."

Aramintha's approach was more direct and she said all the things her mother had not said.

"Just think, Janet, of how you'll be able to help us. Think of that lovely house in London. We could stay with you there and there'd be no need to hire some poky little house. Mama says the place would be simply splendid for parties: it can set fifty covers in the dining saloon and there is a ball room with three crystal chandeliers. Oh, do think about it, Janet! I don't know how you can hesitate . . . I mean he's very handsome and not repulsive or fat or anything like rich men often are . . ."

Her father said nothing more but on Janet, mindful of the letters she had burned at Glenfoot, his silence pressed harder than did Hannah's reproaches.

That night after dinner, in the drawing room which still smelled slightly of paint in spite of all that Hannah and Janet had done to air it, Phoebe battled her way manfully through a sonata on the stiff new keys of the pianoforte delivered only that morning. It was a lively piece with trills and runs and glissades and arpeggios and it made an excellent cover for conversation. Lord Staindrop, joining the ladies with his host after no more than a token glass of port, took his seat by Janet. They exchanged a few commonplaces about the shocking weather and the fog with which the city was afflicted and Staindrop's journey. After a little while he leaned forward and looked into her face.

"It seems to me," he said, "you look paler than you were when I was last in company with you."

This observation had been prompted by Hannah, who had been at some pains to indicate that Janet might regret what she had done on his previous visit.

"I think perhaps town life does not agree with me," said Janet, forcing a smile, "I am not accustomed to it you know. I was bred in the country and I miss it."

"Even in winter?" he asked archly.

Janet nodded.

"Even in winter," she said.

For a few moments Staindrop considered the advantages of possessing a wife with whom town life did not agree: town life agreed very much with him. He decided to risk another rebuff. He was confirmed in the decision by a memory of Gerard escorting his brood round the portraits of bygone Pricketts in the manner of one preparing himself for a great destiny. At this point Phoebe and Aramintha launched themselves into a duet and under cover of this he spoke again.

"How do you think you might like the English countryside?" he enquired earnestly.

"I have never been to England," said Janet, "in fact I have never been from home at all until a few weeks ago. But I have heard that it is very beautiful."

"It is not so grand as your scenery," he admitted, "but it is held to be very fine near my home . . ."

He hesitated.

"Miss Laidlaw," he began, "the last time we met you asked me for time to consider the proposal I made you. Is it too soon to ask where this consideration has led?"

He took her hand, an action at once noticed by Hannah, who held her breath and prayed that her girls had at least another three verses of their song to sing.

"No," said Janet. "I have made up my mind."

There was a pause: Staindrop waited for her to continue but Janet found it harder than she had expected to burn her bridges.

"If your answer is to be 'yes'," he prompted her, "you will make me the happiest of men."

He peered anxiously at her downbent head to discover her response to this important if unoriginal remark. Janet lifted her head and saw her father's eyes fixed upon her.

"It is," she said clearly, "I am happy to accept your most flattering offer, my lord."

Outside the Landsdowne Road United Presbyterian Church in the Great Western Road there was a crowd of onlookers. Though this church served the fashionable areas to the west of the city it was not more than a few minutes away from the rookeries of the Cowcaddens and there was a scatter of ragged, barefooted children who slipped in and out of the groups of women, shawled housewives with their babies happed under the fringed tartans and white-capped servants with huge shopping baskets who were waiting for the church doors to open. A barouche appeared round the corner and drew up in front, the four white horses fidgeting and snorting steamy breaths into the frosty December air with white wedding favours on their bridles and on the driver's whip. Inside the church the organ thundered out the Wedding March from Lohengrin, the organist heroically attempting to use the three manuals, the two octaves and a third of pedals, the seven composition pedals and the thirty-six stops in a fashion which would do justice to the occasion. It was not every day that the Landsdowne Road United Presbyterian Church witnessed the wedding of a lord.

The doors opened and the bride appeared with the groom at her side. The crowd cheered good-humouredly and commented bawdily on the good looks of the happy couple; the barefoot urchins scampered expectantly round the carriage. Lord Staindrop, ignoring the throng with energy, handed his bride up into the conveyance and someone (he looked remarkably like Jimmie Gillies) flung a hatful of pennies and halfpennies on to the greasy cobbles just as he was about to follow her in. His ascent was thus somewhat lacking in dignity as the urchins closed in yelling, to grab as many as they could without regard to the members of the ceremony or the onlookers. The horses moved off, jerking at their bits and prancing, and turned down Park Road towards the bride's home. Behind the barouche there followed a string of carriages which halted briefly at the church to pick up the relatives and the guests. In the second of these rode Hannah Lampeter with a daughter on either side of her and a consciousness of achievement in her breast. In a very short time she and John Laidlaw would be taking the principal roles in a similar ceremony: it would be rather less elaborate, she decided, but sufficiently attended to give it dignity and avoid any suggestion of the 'hole and corner'. She stared out of the window at the assembled onlookers and smiled. There would be no largesse at her wedding. As the carriage moved off she leaned back against the squabs and began to compose a guest list, headed, of course, by Lord and Lady Staindrop.

In the first carriage Jock and Kirsty sat opposite John Laidlaw.

Jock was conscious only of a series of sartorial discomforts, tight shoes, tight, high collar, kid gloves and a high hat in which he felt uncommonly foolish. Kirsty felt discontented; a state to which she was accustomed. She concentrated upon her sister-in-law a mixture of jealousy and sour envy which even the possession of a new jet-embroidered silk gown which would astound the congregation at Luss Parish Church for many a Sunday to come and a fur-trimmed cloak could not assuage.

"Just fancy!" she ejaculated. "Her . . . a lady, no less. Our Janet a lady!"

Her father-in-law glanced up from the sombre contemplation of his grey gloves.

"I've kenned worse," he said drily.

"She's gotten herself a right stick for a man," sniffed Kirsty, who had not missed Lord Staindrop's ill-concealed dismay when he had met his new relations the previous day. "I still say she'd have done better to take our Donald."

"Janet will do fine," said Laidlaw and frowned down upon his gloves as though he was uncertain what they would do next. "And I've got myself the kind of partner I need."

Jock withdrew his mind from the speculations which had employed it, at to whether Mr MacMurdoe at Luss would consider the young and fashionable preacher at the Landsdowne Church to be sound in his doctrine; on the whole he thought not.

"I didn't take to the body myself," he said gloomily. "I hope he'll be good to her, the lass."

Kirsty sniffed again.

The wedding was duly reported in the *Glasgow Herald* at considerable length; the guests were listed, the presents were listed and the hymns were listed and the reporter waxed lyrical about the gowns of the female guests. The *Scotsman* duly mentioned it in a short paragraph on page seven. They, naturally, took little interest in the society of Glasgow but the wedding of a fifth baron was news wherever he might choose to be married. Simon found it and for some time after that alarmed his mother by his silence which she knew to be, in him, a symptom of acute unhappiness. He denied this with vigour and flung himself with energy and success into his work.

# 7

After a brief tour in Germany and Switzerland Janet and her new husband returned, first to Glasgow where they witnessed the wedding of John Laidlaw and Hannah Lampeter. This was a quiet ceremony, chiefly remarkable for the behaviour of Jimmie Gillies who became uncommonly drunk and resigned his cares into the hands of his master's new wife in a short pithy speech during the reception. It had to be short because his ex-master ejected him without ceremony. If, afterwards, he sought him out, found him a more congenial post in a sailor's drinking den and paid what was his due and a bit over, the guests were not to know and the incident was held to have enlivened what was otherwise a rather too dignified occasion. Janet saw the bridal pair on to the Belfast boat at the Broomielaw, for her father intended to combine his honeymoon with a tour of the Belfast shipyards, and then she and her new husband caught the train south. They arrived at Staindrop House, where Staindrop stayed for one night before taking the train to London, to his club, his business interests and certain bachelor pursuits.

The wedding tour had been brief but it had been long enough for Janet to discover that she had made a serious mistake. If love was not essential to a marriage, respect and liking were and she was unlikely to develop either for the man she had married. The gentlemanly manners so much admired by the Lampeters were, she soon discovered, for public use only: in private he was petulant, demanding and ill-tempered to a fault. The compliments, as Janet had predicted, ceased: what she had not considered was the contempt for herself implied in his using them to attract her. He made it very clear that her role was to breed him an heir and that he had married her for no other reason. While her upbringing had ensured that Janet was neither afraid nor amazed at the sexual demands he made on her, she was surprised and repelled by the crudity and occasionally even brutality with which he made them. She soon discovered her husband was a rather stupid man and with this went the obstinacy and conceit one might expect. He had two main interests, the increasing of his fortune and the exclusion of his brother from the succession to the title.

Janet, deposited thus unceremoniously at Staindrop, was too honest not to admit to herself that his absence was a relief rather than an affliction, accepted the condolences of the motherly housekeeper rather guiltily and mindful of Elspeth's dictum, 'aye do the work that comes to your hand', set about finding herself some occupation that would prevent her brooding on her mistake. In the house there was nothing to do: she could see that from the beginning. Mrs Summers cared for it with a devotion which Janet was unable to equal and was too sensible to challenge. She ordered the replacements of linen and china which Mrs Summers considered necessary, endorsed her instructions to painter and carpenter and accompanied her on ceremonial tours of inspection. In the gardens she found a fellow-countryman, dour and suspicious, who treated her tentative suggestions with ill-concealed contempt and a determination to ignore them. This amused rather than distressed her. MacRae knew his job and she was, in truth, not very interested in gardens.

It was about the estate she really wished to learn and the agent, Mr Denholm, found in her the enthusiasm and understanding for which he had looked in vain in the fourth and fifth Lords Staindrop. They became friends at once. He found her a quiet pony and taught her to ride: until that point Janet's equestrian experience had consisted of an occasional ride upon the rump of a Clydesdale. She escaped when she could from the callers who descended upon the house to inspect Staindrop's low-born bride and together they rode the length and breadth of Staindrop land, examining, inspecting, discussing . . . New schemes were instituted, trees planted, building was put in hand till the owner of these acres, becoming aware of these projects, came back to discover the reason for this unexpected drain on his resources. He found his wife in a critical mood. On being taken to task for misapplying his income she retorted that unless he spent a little less on his *menus plaisirs* and a good deal more in keeping his land in good heart that income would soon be substantially reduced.

"How can you expect high rents when the buildings are tumbling down and the ditches are choked?" she demanded. "And Elvan Hangar has been so neglected that half the timber in it is worthless . . . as for the state of the Home Farm, it's a disgrace."

Staindrop stared. During their brief acquaintance Janet had had little to say: she had found herself in a social atmosphere which was strange to her and among people, including her husband, with whom she had little in common. In such circumstances it was her habit to be silent and to listen, and Staindrop, uneasily conscious of his wife's bucolic origins, so unequivocally stated in her speech, had been glad of this and at no pains to draw her out either in public or in private. He had not realised that when Janet was sure of her ground she could show both initiative and determination. This rebuttal came as an unpleasant surprise. Nor was it the only one. At the losing end of an unexpected argument Staindrop reflected that the sooner she had other concerns to occupy her energies the better and enquired whether she was pregnant.

"You're crotchety enough," he observed resentfully.

"No," said his wife and rose from the breakfast table.

He demanded to know what she was going to do.

"I'm riding over to Carrbottom to see how they go on with the new cottages there."

"All this gadding about on horseback," he grumbled, "how can you expect . . ."

"You can expect nothing," returned Janet crisply, "as long as you are in Town and I am here . . ."

Staindrop went red.

"Such matters require your co-operation, my lord," she added.

"I suppose you mean you want to come and gad about the Town."

"Not at all," said Janet, "I mean that it is time you came and paid heed to your concerns here."

At the door of the breakfast saloon she turned.

"Your brother and his wife tell me they are coming to dine and sleep tonight," she informed him.

Staindrop consigned his brother to perdition over the cooling coffee and was tempted to do the same for a wife who was not proving to be the meek little broodmare for which he had bargained. She would have to come up to Town with him to keep her from meddling, he decided; uneasily, he wondered if she would come at his command.

There was yet another unpleasant surprise in store for him that day. His brother brought with him their father's youngest sister, Aunt Matilda Prickett, an unamiable eccentric with a dislike of men which was rooted in an unfortunate experience of her early youth. To this dislike there were no exceptions, but there were some men she disliked more than others. Her nephew Staindrop was one of these. Moreover, she was maliciously aware of the situation between Staindrop and his brother. Dinner was an uncomfortable meal: Aunt Matilda for all her spinster status had been brought up in the early years of the century and had no patience with a generation she stigmatised as mealy-mouthed. Over dinner she made some outspoken comments concerning Alicia's being pregnant again; animadverted on the stupidity of stud stallions, a reference calmly ignored by the target, Alicia's husband. Next she criticised the new-fangled way of serving the dinner, preferring the old fashion of having a number of courses from which one might make a choice of several dishes.

"Downright pinchpenny, I call it," she observed through a mouthful of lamb and green peas, and spattered the vicinity in the process. Janet looked amused at this and similar observations and at last drew down the harridan's attention on herself.

"Don't have much to say f'y'self," said Aunt Matilda with her eye on Evans the footman whose attempt to leave her with no more than a ladylike portion of an Italian Pudding she frustrated by grabbing at his coat-tails and hauling him back together with the coveted delicacy.

"No," said Janet, "I prefer to listen."

Aunt Matilda glared approval.

"That's the style," said she, "too much confounded gibble-gabble, these days."

She considered Janet, who looked back at her with a twinkle lurking in her eye.

"Good-looking gal, ain't you?" remarked Aunt Matilda, "healthy too . . . nothing die-away about yer . . ."

Janet agreed.

"Then why ain't yer takin' the wind out of Prickett's eye with an heir?" she demanded.

Janet choked on her portion of pudding and then laughed, to the unconcealed dismay of Alicia who had expected her to be overcome.

"Give us time, Aunt," begged Janet.

Aunt Matilda engulfed her pudding rapidly.

"Time!" she snorted indistinctly, "had six months, ain't you? Fine healthy stock . . . how long do you need?"

She scraped her plate noisily, licked the spoon and pointed it at Staindrop.

"Ask me," she accused, "it's your fault."

After dinner Aunt Matilda conformed to convention sufficiently to retire from the table with Janet and Alicia and leave the gentlemen to recruit their self-esteem with brandy and cigars. Alicia, with whom Aunt Matilda had been visiting for the past week, seized the respite offered, pleaded her delicate condition and retired before the tea tray was brought in.

"D'ye play?" demanded Aunt Matilda.

"No," Janet said, "I can sing a little, but only my own songs. I can't read music."

"Far too much caterwauling in the drawing room, these days," remarked her guest. "Sickly nonsense too, most of it."

She fixed Janet with a grey, grim stare.

"You look a sensible gal to me," she said at last. "Don't see you on the catch for a title. The money, was it?"

Janet flushed with anger and made herself remember that the speaker was a relative and a guest and old.

"No need to bite on the bridle," said Aunt Matilda, "speak your mind. Why did you marry my nevvy? He's like all men, crude, beef-witted and selfish, but he's worse than most. Got a nasty streak. If he was a horse I wouldn't breed from him. You don't like him gal . . . I can see that. Why marry him? The money?"

Janet, appeased by this plain speaking, shook her head.

"No . . . not that. Though my father . . ."

She bit off what she had been about to say.

"It was just that everyone . . . everyone I had about me seemed to think it was a good match . . ."

Aunt Matilda snorted.

"Everyone!"

"After a while it just didn't seem possible to say no."

To her surprise the old woman nodded her understanding.

"I'd not be your age again for a fortune," she observed. "Nowadays nobody could push me into what I know to be ill-considered."

The notion of Aunt Matilda being pushed into doing anything she did not want to do had not before occurred to Janet but she supposed it must have been a possibility: already she knew she was no longer the same green girl who had listened to well-meant advice from older people six months before. Her instincts had been right and their advice misplaced. Her train of thought was interrupted by Aunt Matilda thumping her on the knee with a heavy jet-studded fan.

"They'll be in before long," she said. "Always quarrel those two. They'd have been in before if I'd not been here. Before they come I want to say something. What do you know about Anna?"

"Staindrop's first wife?" asked Janet.

"The same . . . poor silly creature . . ."

"Not a great deal. Staindrop told me she was drowned. She was on a yacht and it was wrecked . . . something of that nature."

Aunt Matilda nodded.

"You haven't been about the Town at all and no one has gossiped to you?"

Janet looked a little uncomfortable.

"Mrs Summers . . . she is the housekeeper here . . . she did hint that they were not very comfortable together . . ."

The old woman gave vent to a high-pitched cackle.

"Comfortable!"

She thumped Janet's knee with her fan again.

"They fought like Kilkenny cats. And . . ."

She fixed Janet once more with that grim, grey eye.

"Eight years married," she asserted, "and no heir. Not even the whisper of one. She ran off, you know. Out of the frying pan and into the fire if you ask me. He was a young whippersnapper of a soldier. Borrowed his friend's yacht and carried her off. All very romantic I don't doubt. Pity he didn't learn to handle the boat. He ran it aground on the Isle of Wight and drowned both of them."

The sound of argument in the hall heralded the approach of the men. She thumped Janet for the third time.

"You get in a pickle, gal, don't run off with a soldier . . . come to me. I like you. I'll see he don't come making a nuisance of himself, I warrant ye."

Janet had no chance to do more than look her thanks for this unorthodox but obliging offer before the men came in bringing a whiff of cigar smoke with them, but she felt that she had found a friend.

At the end of June when Staindrop suggested that Janet might care to come to London his motives were nothing if not mixed. His first annoyance at her activities on the estate had died down when he realised that they were liable to prove profitable. Janet's lack of the kind of social gloss to which he was accustomed in his female companions he found irksome and embarrassing and he was not eager to parade his new wife before the amused and keenly critical eyes of London Society for fear of the caustic comments on his lamentable taste. He lacked the perception to see that other qualities which Janet possessed made that lack of polish unimportant.

However, he was still anxious to oblige John Laidlaw, whose influence in shipping circles might well frank his son-in-law on to some useful (and profitable) boards of directors: it would not oblige his father-in-law to hear that Staindrop was determined to keep his daughter out of Society altogether. In this he did John Laidlaw an injustice, as Janet's father was totally ignorant of Society and having got his daughter well and advantageously disposed he was prepared to put her out of his mind altogether and concentrate on more absorbing matters, such as the perfection of the Laidlaw Bearing. However, his wife was not prepared to let Janet drop out of sight: Hannah had two daughters to marry and Janet had had a key role to play in this project since the beginning.

". . . I do trust," she wrote at the end of a long letter, "that you intend to open the London house soon. The girls are so looking forward to a visit to you and a share in your London gaieties. They tell me you have promised them a ball . . . I did not look for this my dear, but I do not deny that it would be a blessing to have my little doves launched in such style . . ."

Janet's eyes opened widely at this gentle reminder: she could remember no such promise but knew well enough that Phoebe and Aramintha would probably recall what they were told to recall.

She was folding this letter and smiling rather ruefully at the prospect of having to find her feet in Town when her husband came down to breakfast. Among his letters was a coquettish reminder from his current 'flirt', one Lady Amelia Brambell, that he had not fulfilled a promise to attend her to the opera.

". . . and I must needs fall back on Jackie Ballard," she wrote in her sprawling hand, "but he is so *prosy* compared with my own Phillibilly . . ."

He grimaced slightly; such a pet-name was acceptable between the sheets, on paper it was embarrassing. He eyed the name of Jackie Ballard with distaste and foreboding. If he did not return soon Ballard would doubtless attain a similar idiotish accolade and he was not yet ready to relinquish the delectable Lady Amelia to any prosy buffoon like Ballard. But, but . . . he looked across the table to his wife presiding over the coffee-pot . . . Janet was still not in a satisfactorily promising way: he must take her to Town with him. He grimaced again at the prospect of the complications which must ensue to his pleasant urban round. He tried to visualise Janet moving among the elegant matrons and the gauzy debutantes. Though he was unimaginative to a fault, the picture of a seagull in a hen-run came into his mind and he dismissed it irritably.

"I mean to leave for Town tomorrow," he announced. "Do you care to join me in a week or so?"

Janet nodded.

"I'll send to open the Queensgate house," she said, with the air of one who had already made up her mind. "You can come there on . . . say, Monday."

Staindrop stared.

"And can you leave all your buildings and plantings so easily?" he asked sarcastically.

"Mr Denholm has it all in hand," she said, "and the Queensgate house has been shut up since your wife died. Mrs Summers says it must be in a real pickle."

"And is Mrs Summers modelling her speech on yours?" he enquired; Janet's Scotticisms irked him beyond measure. "I understood her to be a pattern card of gentility."

Janet flushed.

"I intend to invite my good-mither and my two good-sisters to bide with us a whilie," she returned deliberately, "and my faither . . . though I doubt he'll not come. And . . ."

She paused and smiled at him without liking.

". . . I thought it would be no more than civil to ask your Aunt Matilda to meet them."

He glared.

"That should certainly ensure that their visit is mercifully short."

Janet's London debut was smoothed and made comparatively easy by her new stepmother. Hannah exerted herself to do this mainly in her own interests. It would not serve if the Queensgate house were not an accepted part of the social scene, so the actors on that scene must be coaxed and hoaxed into accepting Janet as she was and not merely accepting her but making her welcome. Even Hannah knew better than to attempt to change Janet. For one thing she knew her limitations and for another she had developed a respect and even a liking for the girl who firmly refused to pretend to be anything other than she was, a Scots country girl. What was more, Hannah conceded that Janet had no need to pretend. She had a clear intelligence, a sense of humour and great commonsense. Her education at Luss school had given her a beautiful copperplate handwriting, her reading in history and geography, thanks to her father, had been considerably wider than most of the debutantes could boast and if she lacked knowledge of the complex interrelationships, official and unofficial, of her new circle of acquaintance this was an area in which Hannah was more than competent to coach her and Janet was interested enough in her fellow-creatures to learn willingly. For the rest, her beauty secured her the good opinion of the men and an indefinable quality of warmth and honesty secured her from all but the most confirmed of the backbiters among the women. After a somewhat breathless fortnight she found, rather to her surprise, that she was enjoying herself. Staindrop discovered that he had no need to blush for his bucolic bride and illogically resented her success in this, his own milieu.

Occasionally Janet remembered the figure of her mother asleep at the end of a hard day and protested at the frivolity and superficiality of the round of visiting, theatres, soirées, breakfasts and similar jamborees, but Hannah reassured her, tongue in cheek.

"It's not all so useless," she protested, "how else would we marry off our daughters. All this frivolity as you call it is a beautifully decorated shop-window to display our wares. Men don't care to go shopping so we make it as pleasant as possible with dances and dinners . . ."

". . . especially dinners," Janet put in with a vivid memory of her partner of the previous evening.

". . . and music and good wine and while they're enjoying these they consider our wares without ever being aware of it!"

Janet screwed up her nose at the pun and the maker twirled in front of the mirror, regarding herself in an elegant high-crowned hat decorated with blue ostrich plumes.

"And what about me?" she asked. "I have no daughters."

"Oh, we demonstrate to the customers what elegant creatures our chicks will hatch into."

Hannah invited comment on this contention with a tilted eyebrow, but Janet just smiled and took her parasol from her maid's hand. Hannah glanced out of the window.

"Your carriage is there. The Park will be crowded today. And no doubt Messrs Waring and Appleton will appear . . ."

These two gentlemen were her current quarry.

"I think you're wasting your time, Hannah," said Janet bluntly, "they'll not do."

"Why ever not?"

Hannah was taken aback.

"They're of good family," she argued as they rustled through the hall, "and they have money. And they are perfectly conversable."

Janet smiled her thanks at the footman who opened the door.

"They are a pair of tumphies, Hannah, and you know it fine."

"And what species is a tumphie?"

"And if Phoebe or Araminta lose their hearts to them they haven't the sense they were born with."

Araminta and Phoebe were already in the barouche and their

presence prevented Hannah from continuing the argument. Janet was not basing her contention solely on her impression of these two young men. Phoebe had persisted in her desire to learn the essentials of housekeeping and Janet, to the open scandalisation of the London cook, had been giving her lessons in the kitchen when the opportunity offered. The London cook and his satellites were bribed into silence. During these lessons Phoebe had confided that her intended was at present in India but wrote to her regularly through his sister who had been a governess to the Lampeters: he was due to come home in November when, so Phoebe declared, they would be married and return to India. Janet believed her. As for Aramintha, her eye had fallen on a young subaltern presently home on leave from the same country, and if Hannah concentrating her attentions on her pair of well-to-pass young ninnies, had not noticed this, Janet had. Aramintha, at least, would not need to bake scones. Young Lieutenant Marshall was the son of a wealthy India merchant.

The drive in the Park went much as such drives usually did. The coachman took his gleaming pair of high-steppers at a strict trot through the traffic and into the Park where there were twenty or thirty similar equipages, full of female Society enjoying the mild June afternoon in the company of male Society mounted on a variety of horses and riding as close to the carriages as they could press.

Before long, Messrs Waring and Appleton rode up sedately and took station on either side of the barouche whence they conducted a stilted conversation with Phoebe and Aramintha sitting demurely in the forward seats, protecting their complexions from the rigours of the June sunshine by means of elegantly ruffled parasols. It was as well for Hannah that she was too busy spinning wedding plans to hear much of this conversation which was of a triteness hard to equal even in a Society where triteness was equated with safety in any converse between young people of different sex. Janet, sustaining her share in observing the fineness of the weather and the pleasantness of the season, was surprised but not displeased to be distracted.

The distraction was mounted on a large grey gelding with a Roman nose and a barely controlled distaste for accompanying carriages. His rider was already known to Janet, to whom he had persuaded his hostess to present him at an evening party two days since. The hostess had hesitated, knowing his reputation, but being susceptible herself finally agreed. The distraction had introduced himself as an acquaintance of her husband, and Janet, to whom this was not a surpassing recommendation, had been fairly cool and distant. This had piqued Captain Jasper Pelham-Villiers, who was unaccustomed to such treatment.

Captain Jasper Pelham-Villiers took a fairly relaxed view of his military duties which left him plenty of time for his more serious ambition, which, so his fellow officers declared, was to make Don Giovanni's celebrated list appear rather abbreviated. As he was exceedingly good-looking, over six feet in height, wealthy, amusing, good-humoured and above all discreet, he had found plenty of women eager to help him achieve it. It was inevitable that Janet would catch his eye sooner rather than later as she was beautiful, young, married and apparently neglected by her husband. It was well known that Staindrop was still living at his club in spite of the presence of his wife at the Queensgate house. That this was due to the presence of his Aunt Matilda was not so generally known as she rarely appeared in a Society which she described as insipid.

Controlling his gelding expertly with one hand the Captain took Janet's hand and kissed it. It was a feat which so took her attention that she ignored the purpose of it.

"I've been hoping you would appear," he told her, "this daily parade is an intolerable bore without agreeable company."

This observation would not have obliged his current lady-love who was regarding him with disfavour from her carriage, now halted for the better convenience of the Captain under a tree at the side of the road. Janet was unaware of this presence though she was conversant with Pelham-Villiers's reputation, for Hannah had told her after that first encounter and was even then reminding her of the warning by nudging her discreetly in the ribs. Janet, however, saw little harm in a conversation with the most notorious rake in Town when it was conducted in an open carriage in which were three other people. She found the Captain's practised flirtation entertaining and considered his reputation was probably exaggerated: Hannah had a penchant for hyperbole.

Consequently she was less reserved than she had been at the evening party and he stayed by her side for some ten minutes. Society trotting by observed this and drew its own conclusions: it also observed the neglected lady order her coachman to drive on. Society prepared to watch the coming siege and keep an amused and penetrating eye on all the players in the drama.

# 8

ONCE BACK IN the house, Hannah lost no time in enlarging on the dangers of the situation. Janet laughed at her and Hannah was constrained to be blunt.

"I tell you, Janet, you can't afford even to *talk* to a man like that. Even now people will be saying that . . ."

At this point Aunt Matilda stumped into the drawing room.

"And what will people be saying, ma'am?" she demanded. "It's my experience that what most people say is always nonsensical and usually untrue to boot."

Hannah, who was used to treat Aunt Matilda much as an anarchist would treat an unexploded bomb, grasped at a possible ally.

"Jasper Pelham-Villiers has been making up to her in the Park," she told the old woman, "and she encouraged him."

Aunt Matilda sat down and grunted inelegantly.

"Did she? Then I expect they're saying you're his mistress, gel."

"What!"

Janet dropped her book. Aunt Matilda grunted again and then chuckled cavernously.

"None of yer modern milk-sops, Pelham-Villiers," she said not without relish. "And I'll tell you another thing . . . Staindrop won't like such talk, not he. Not before he's got himself an heir. He's like all men, a dog-in-the-manger."

She proved a true prophet. Staindrop, informed of the day's event by no fewer than three of his acquaintance, for once dined at home and took Janet to task for such an indiscretion. When she laughed at his agitation he flung off in a fury to speak to Hannah, ordering her to keep Janet out of Pelham-Villiers's way and accusing her in the same breath of playing the go-between. Hannah, angered by such implication, retorted, "Escort her yourself, once in a way, if you want to prevent such gossip. This is the first time you've been in the house in a week."

Staindrop enquired whether she expected him to live among a pack of penniless hangers-on and malicious old women and got what he deserved, for Hannah took a firm grasp on her temper and replied evenly that he would have plenty of leisure to do his duty by Janet.

"Lady Amelia will have to excuse you after next week, I dare say, when her husband returns. If you are there Pelham-Villiers won't come sniffing round. He's got some sense."

Staindrop, still in a tearing fury, stumped out of the little sitting room which Hannah had made her own and met with his Aunt on the landing. When she saw his state she grinned at him like a witch who saw her spells working and gave him some advice in terms which were plain enough to scandalise the butler in the hall below.

"Only got yourself to blame," she said and poked him painfully under the fourth waistcoat button with her fan. "Leave a pretty piece like your Janet alone for weeks as you've done while you trot like a pug-dog at the heels of some feather-brained trollop and all the town watches and you've got to expect that the men of the town will come making up to her. They've more sense than you seemingly. Tell you another thing . . ."

She considered him as if he were a somewhat grubby schoolboy.

"I wouldn't blame her if she decided to take advantage of his advances. Pelham-Villiers is twice the man you'll ever be . . . not that I'm throwing bouquets at him . . ."

"I'll pack her straight back to Derbyshire," he spluttered.

Aunt Matilda smiled nastily.

"Oh, but that really will set the fools laughing at you," said she, "married six months and daren't keep his wife in Town because he's used her so ill she'll be off with the first half-decent creature who looks her way!"

"Perhaps we could discuss me and what I am liable to do more quietly and in private!"

Janet stood in the doorway of her own room, her face white with anger.

"Goose!" said Aunt Matilda, "Not what you'll do . . . what they'll *say*."

She stumped back into her room and slammed the door so that Janet and her husband faced one another across the landing.

"You'll oblige me, ma'am, by returning immediately to Derbyshire and not exposing my name to any further scandal."

"Further scandal! Don't fear me . . . I'll not add to your efforts in that line! Do you think that kind folk haven't told me about the wee tawpie you have in keeping? What kind o' a man are ye tae content yersel' wi' ither mens' leavings?"

She curbed her anger.

"And if you think," she added, "that I'll leave here for just that kind of gossip to begin, you are wrong. If you wish to scotch it you move back in here and behave as a husband should and maybe the roving lads'll not get the notion that I'm waiting for them to come tapping on my window. But don't come yammering to me about scandal and you a speak for the whole Town."

Before Staindrop, now purple in the face, could say a word she went back into her room and locked the door, leaving him to spend a salutary hour in the library recruiting his *amour propre* with several glasses of brandy. At the end of it he had come, albeit reluctantly, to the conclusion that Aunt Matilda and Janet were right. For his wife to remove from Town at that point would give rise to precisely the kind of ridicule which he detested. The idea of a retreat to Derbyshire was not mentioned again. Instead, he set about detaching himself gradually from Lady Amelia (a costly business), removed himself from his club to the Queensgate house and escorted his wife to a number of functions at which he would not normally have deigned to be seen.

Society watched this development with amusement, perfectly conversant with the reason for it, and waited for Pelham-Villiers's next move. Society even had a good idea of who she might be. Staindrop danced with Janet at balls, rode sulky and mumchance by her carriage in the Park, sat by her side . . . or slept by it . . . at theatres and concerts, ate his dinner in her company and, according to the best below-stairs information, lay by her at night. Lady Amelia, in the meanwhile, transferred her favours to Jackie Ballard for whom she concocted a bed-name which even she hesitated to confide to paper.

However, Staindrop's new found uxoriousness did not have its much-wished-for outcome. By the beginning of August Janet was still not pregnant. She was, for all that, uncommonly tired of

London and of Staindrop, who made up for his enforced civility in public by his treatment of her in private. Janet found herself homesick for the coolness and the colour of her own country in autumn. She came to the conclusion that the only time of day when there was a breath of air to be had in Town was before breakfast. She had always risen early and she and her maid in bonnet and shawl and stout shoes fell into the habit of walking in the park before breakfast. Staindrop, who did not rise before eleven, did not know of this custom. Those of the household who did thought it unremarkable; all except one.

Pelham-Villiers, instead of shrugging his shoulders and looking about him for another name to add to his list, had found himself unable to put Janet out of his mind . . . or what passed for his mind, his brain not being the most exercised part of his anatomy. He found himself moping, hanging about theatres in the hope of catching a glimpse of her, riding in the Park for the fleeting pleasure of raising his hat to her in the face of Staindrop's scowl. One evening he found himself thinking, an unusual exercise for him at any time, how jolly it would be to come home to her without any nonsense about jealous husbands . . . to be mar . . . He caught himself up on the dread word, but the damage was done, the idea implanted. Pelham-Villiers was, as any of his friends male or female would bear witness, a man of action and he was not prepared merely to contemplate an idea however unusual it might be for him to have one. He decided to put this one into practice. He would elope with Janet, and if she could not become his wife she would be his *maîtresse en titre* and he would have no other but her. With the first steps towards this he was tolerably familiar, the difference between seduction and elopement lying mainly in the intention of permanence. After discreet enquiry he found an ally within the Queensgate house.

Lizzy the upstairs maid was romantic by inclination and she thought Pelham-Villiers was ever so handsome. She knew from Janet's maid a good deal of what went on behind the bedroom door and had taken a dislike to Staindrop. This was not entirely on account of the manner in which he treated his wife. Staindrop had encountered Lizzy on the stairs, considered her with unmistakable intention and had, as unmistakably, changed his mind. This was a slight hard to forgive and Lizzy was willing enough to help Janet to a different and more exciting partner especially when it meant a trickle of half-sovereigns into her pocket in return for certain information. Among the catalogue of trivia which she retailed in this way were two items of great interest. The early morning walks and the project of a shooting party at Sir Durward Ellis-Martin's box in Torridon.

Shortly after Pelham-Villiers had been told of these, the two early morning walkers in the Park encountered a rider shaking the fidgets out of that resty grey gelding; he was very glad to meet . . . and pass by with a greeting and a raised hat . . . an old acquaintance. Perhaps two mornings later he paused briefly to comment unfavourably on the grey's behaviour and wonder if it was caused by the cloudy skies and cold wind. On the third morning he dismounted and walked with them for a few minutes.

On the fourth morning the maid, for a consideration of five shillings, discovered that she had a sore throat and Lizzy volunteered to take her place. Pelham-Villiers's appearance was the signal for her to find a stone in her shoe and to lag behind. He made amusing conversation of a perfectly innocuous kind and Janet, who had always believed his reputation to be exaggerated, gradually relaxed her guard. On the fifth morning, about a fortnight after their first encounter, for he had been far too experienced to appear on every occasion, he heard with a sinking heart that Janet intended to leave for Derbyshire almost at once and was to spend most of September there before going to Scotland. She confided this to him because the idea of leaving Town and seeing Scotland again had lifted her spirits. Pelham-Villiers was much too clever to rush his fences and considered quite rightly that half past seven on a chilly morning was not a propitious time to urge a girl to throw her cap over the windmill. He wished her goodbye with no more than a warm handclasp and an ardent look and hurried away to extract from Lady Ellis-Martin an invitation to the shooting party due to assemble in Torridon on October the tenth. This was not difficult as Lady Ellis-Martin, like most of his hostesses, viewed his depredations with an indulgent eye and hoped her turn was coming.

His colonel when approached granted him the necessary leave, possibly reflecting that it made little difference whether the Captain neglected his duties in London or in wildest Scotland. Having secured his opportunity, Pelham-Villiers set about keeping himself in Janet's mind until it should occur. He arranged for a series of small anonymous gifts to be despatched to Derbyshire by the parcel post: too trivial to require close investigation by an alarmed husband, they were intriguing enough and sufficiently frequent to keep the 'anonymous' donor very much in the recipient's thoughts. Meanwhile, to avoid the startled comment of his admiring and envious acquaintance, and also to put in the time until October, he began to stalk another candidate for his list. But his heart was not really in it and she found him unaccountably obtuse in interpreting hints as to when she would be... unoccupied.

Hannah and her daughters returned to Derbyshire with Janet but Aunt Matilda decided to go to her nephew Prickett and console him for the loss of Alicia, who had died in a fever after the birth of her eleventh child and fifth daughter. Such consolation as Aunt Matilda had to offer might not apply the customary balms.

"I have made it my business," she wrote in her jagged spiky hand, "to tell him in no uncertain terms that he was solely responsible for her death. I said he was a selfish brute but he babbled on about the will of God. I said that God did not reside in his..."

At this point even country-bred Janet blushed.

"I thought his Alicia a poor thing," she went on, "but to abuse her as he did and then to call her death the will of God is too much for me to stomach."

Nor, as she made clear, did Prickett require much consolation.

"... you will not be surprised to hear that he has begun already to look about him for another wife. Twice he has mentioned a name to me in such a connection, saying that he cannot leave his little brood motherless. I was so bold as to say that I doubted if the lack of a mother was the lack uppermost in his mind. In any event I intend to remain here in the guise of consolatrice and chatelaine for some time and this should deter the eager candidates a trifle. Expect me when a decent interval after her funeral has elapsed... say ten days or a fortnight! After that I should arrive some few hours before the wedding announcements."

Janet communicated the contents of this letter to Hannah but did not let her read it, feeling that her stepmother had enough to bear without having her sensibilities outraged. Mr Waring had gradually melted from the scene. The departure from London had been marked by no particular attention, no hint of distress, no spelling for an invitation and for this cooling of his ardour (if what had never been more than tepid could be said to have cooled) she blamed Araminttha herself for failing to encourage his attentions. Mr Appleton, however, had written to her and included a kind message to Phoebe but made no mention of his having by a strange coincidence to have to come into Derbyshire to visit an aged relative. In such circumstances had Araminttha's other suitor found himself within an hour's ride of Staindrop. Lieutenant Marshall, who was an enterprising young man, had persuaded his father, retired from India to a hideous but magnificent mansion outside Manchester, to recruit his system, debilitated by recurrent fevers and equally recurrent chota pegs, by drinking the mineral waters at Matlock which lay conveniently near to Staindrop. From there he laid determined siege to Hannah.

In London Hannah had snubbed him (in the most tactful manner possible) because Mr Waring's unexceptionable family and very respectable fortune made him preferable. Hannah knew from experience the value of good connections. However, with Mr Waring reportedly paying his addresses to another and much more compliant debutante, Lieutenant Marshall's virtues became apparent and she came to consider him a very worthy young man and even to swallow the father's evident lack of gentility. Between them the Marshall's were in a fair way to persuading her to overlook the young man's grandfather, a handloom weaver now happily retired to potter about the mansion's gardens and to consider instead the size of the fortune which must come to the grandson.

Janet, who liked the young soldier and listened to his tales of India nearly as eagerly as Araminttha, played her part in the campaign by inviting them to stay at Staindrop. Her husband's grumbles at such ill-considered hospitality she ignored as the Marshalls ignored Staindrop's incivility. After a week the engagement was an accepted thing and Hannah had even come to regard it as a very fair match. She discovered, however, that young Lieutenant Marshall had inherited the ability to organise and the strong will which had built Abe Marshall's fortune: matters were taken, most civilly, right out of her hands and she found that she had given her consent to a wedding before the end of Lieutenant Marshall's furlough. Moreover, instead of being a fashionable London wedding or from the bride's own home in Glasgow it was to be in the Gothic chapel at Staindrop as soon as Janet and her husband returned from Torridon. Faced with a wedding in six weeks' time Hannah wrote to John Laidlaw for a draft on his bank and fled back to London to buy wedding clothes and provide raiment fit for the Indian climate.

One night when Janet was about to climb into bed there was a tap on the door. It was Phoebe, rather tearful, with a letter in her hand.

"Janet," she said, "Robert's written to say he can't be home before January."

There was a good deal behind this simple statement. Hannah's championship of the eligible Mr Appleton was subtle but it was exceedingly persistent. Phoebe had held out in London, braced by Janet's sympathy and the prospect of her Robert's arrival in November. Now, Robert's leave was postponed and Aramintha's engagement left her mother free to concentrate all her immense energies on Phoebe. And Janet would be in Torridon. While Phoebe was a sweet-natured girl neither of them had any illusions about the sort of pressure which would be applied and both knew that Phoebe found it hard to withstand such pressure. Janet frowned and clasped her hands round her knees.

"If I were you," she said at last, "I would let Appleton propose to you . . ."

She waved away Phoebe's protest.

"Refuse him . . . but not very convincingly. Let him think you might come round to it."

"But Mama will scold and scold . . ."

"Let her," said Janet. "As long as she thinks you might say 'yes' after a bit she won't bully too much. And she can't *make* you say 'yes'. While it's still hanging in the balance you accept your sister's offer to go with her to India."

Phoebe stared.

"But she hasn't asked me . . ."

"She will," said Janet firmly. "It's not unusual, you know. I'll have a word with young Abram. He'll understand."

"Mama will never agree."

"She will . . . if you refuse Appleton a second time."

"But he might not ask a second time."

"Then," said Janet, "she is bound to agree because she'll think you're going to be left on her hands and everybody knows that girls who go out to India find husbands almost as soon as they land."

Phoebe went away, doubtful and apprehensive but a little comforted and Janet lay awake listening to Staindrop stumbling about in his dressing room. She was astonished by the wave of dislike and distaste she felt for this man who was her husband. She reflected she could solve other peoples' problems but her own was grimly insoluble. Always honest with herself she had admitted long ago that she detested this man she had married and found the prospect of a lifetime tied to him almost insupportable. What was worse, after nearly a year of marriage there was still no sign of an heir. She considered the idea of life with Aunt Matilda and smiled faintly. It would be nothing if not entertaining but Aunt Matilda was seventy-two; in the nature of things refuge with her would be short-lived. The alternative was to run to her father, but she knew very well that neither he nor Hannah would countenance her leaving Staindrop. She looked at a little filigree basket filled with sugar almonds which stood on her bedside table, the latest of the bibelots to arrive from her 'anonymous' benefactor. There was a ready refuge indeed, but one likely to be even more fleeting than with Aunt Matilda. She considered how she might find a refuge for herself: the trouble was that she could not find employment as a governess . . . her accomplishments were few and of the wrong description. Few Mamas wished to have their daughters instructed in the making of scones. She had no money at her disposal and so could not buy a farm . . . she found her mind going round and round the possibilities and impossibilities like a mouse in a barrel.

The dressing room door opened and Staindrop came in. He brought a gust of stale cigar smoke and a smell of brandy: he was also in a vile mood in which he would wreak his resentments upon her. Janet looked at him her face expressionless but inside she seethed with rebellion. Somehow, she vowed silently, some day I will get away from this man.

However, the following day they travelled north together in apparent amity. Staindrop beguiled the journey with cigars, which rendered the compartment blue with smoke, while Janet read. Once they were across the border he began to comment contemptuously on the Scottish countryside, Scottish weather and Scottish habits. Janet, absorbed in Mr Disraeli's *Sybil* and trying more or less successfully to identify some of her London acquaintances in that *roman à clef*, scarcely heard him. She was by now inured to this form of baiting. Her refusal to be drawn exasperated Staindrop and his remarks became more and more outrageous. Not far outside Glasgow the train made an unscheduled stop. Staindrop rose, let down the window with a bang and glowered out into the dusk.

"Typical," he grumbled. "Damned, bare-arsed savages . . . can't speak clearly or organise correctly. They aren't fit to have railways. We should wait until they're civilised before we build them in this barbaric country."

Janet looked up from her book in alarm as a furious voice retorted from the platform outside.

"And who're you crying a bare-arsed savage! I'll give you savage!"

A face distorted with fury appeared at the window and a grimy hand grasped at Staindrop's lapel. He pulled away and stared at this apparition in horror. The intruder glared round the compartment, saw Janet and with his free hand took off his old-fashioned blue bonnet to reveal a white line where it had protected his forehead from the grime of the nearby steelworks.

"Begging your pardon, lass," said the intruder with a friendly grin which vanished when he returned his attention to Staindrop, "Just let me tell you something, my mannie . . ."

The train gave a preliminary jerk and clank and the hand clasping the bonnet grabbed for the frame of the window.

"Don't you dare to come in here!" shouted Staindrop. "I will summon the guard!"

"Yon shilpit wee English felly? Man, I could eat him to my tea."

The train began to move.

"You'll fall!" cried Janet, "it's moving!"

"Let me tell you," said the apparition, unmoved by this warning, "if it wasn't for Jamie Watt, one of your bare-arsed savages, you wouldn't have a bloody railway, you stinking, scone-faced sasunach . . ."

He disappeared as suddenly as he had appeared just before the train gathered speed.

"I tell't the bastard!" they heard him announce triumphantly to his fellow steelworkers on the platform.

Janet returned her gaze tactfully to her book while her husband composed aloud the letter he would write to the management. As he knew neither the name of the place where the episode had occurred nor the name of the apparition Janet felt no concern. She was jerked out of her suppressed amusement by a blow on the face. Staindrop stood over her his own face distorted with temper.

"You enjoyed that, you bitch," he shouted. "Don't deny it!"

Janet felt the anger blaze up inside her.

"I won't," she snapped. "It's aye a pleasure to hear a boor repaid in his own coin."

"The reply was another blow which nearly knocked her off the seat. Her husband snatched up the fallen book and flung it into the darkness outside the open window where it fluttered and vanished. Janet bit back an exclamation of pain, glared at the angry man and then as calmly as she could rose to straighten her hat in the mirror. That done she sat down again and stared out of the window. Staindrop swore, slumped sulkily back into his seat and lit another cigar.

John Laidlaw was not at the station to meet them: nor was he at Woodside Terrace. The parlour-maid O'Malley, who had replaced Jimmie Gillies, admitted them and gave them a note.

> Sorry I couldn't be with you. We have a pickle of bother down-by at the yard. Have your dinners and wait on me. I'll be home before ten. JL

He came in just before they had finished a meal eaten in silence. He was too preoccupied to notice the atmosphere. Without ado he summoned food and began to explain his troubles to Staindrop.

"If I don't take care we could be swallowed up," he explained. "We have the room to expand and this naval contract needs that. If Stenson get the contract they will need it. The Old Tod says we haven't the money to tender . . . I say we must look for it. At this stage we can't afford not to tender. If we don't we go under . . ."

Janet, her head throbbing, excused herself on the grounds of weariness. Her father glanced at her perfunctorily as they rose and then his blue gaze sharpened.

"Aye, lass, ye look real far through. Are you well enough?"

Staindrop looked at her and flushed scarlet.

"I'm fine and well, thank you, father," she said quietly, "I'll see you in the morning."

She went out and her father looked after her for a second, frowning, before he returned to the matter of the new frigates to be built for the Royal Navy. Staindrop listened carefully: he was a man who took profit seriously and he had invested a good deal in the yard. It was not long before he agreed to find another party to back a tender from Fox, McIan, Son and Laidlaw. He knew a neighbour in Derbyshire who had recently opened a colliery who might be interested. Laidlaw, who was not a man to let the grass grow under his feet, produced paper and pen and Staindrop sat down in the study and wrote a letter of invitation to his neighbour to come to the yard and see for himself. They sealed the agreement with a glass or so of whisky and Staindrop went upstairs while Laidlaw found a stamp and went out briefly to put the letter in the pillar box at the end of the terrace. When he came in again he went upstairs and passed the door of the spare bedroom. From inside came the sound of voices: it was apparent that his son-in-law was thoroughly displeased about something for he was shouting. The heavy doors and thick walls of the house prevented him from hearing what was said, but he hesitated and frowned. After a few moments he shook his head and went into his own room.

Staindrop had come up to the room and discovered that Janet had disappointed, yet again, his hopes of an heir. His reaction to this news was predictable. He stormed at her accusingly:

"You don't want a child!" he shouted. "You're preventing it . . . you yokels have your methods . . ."

Janet denied this angrily and he silenced her with another blow and after that she said nothing but lay and listened to his abuse.

In the morning, Staindrop, as he often was after such scenes, was sulkily polite. It was a mood which lasted no longer than his sitting down to breakfast. A letter had arrived for him from a London acquaintance which included among a mass of trivia the information that Captain Pelham-Villiers was to make one of the houseparty at Torridon. It was a faintly malicious letter, the outcome of an amusing hour at Staindrop's London club where his friends had speculated on the possible outcome of such an encounter with great invention. The news provoked another scene; the presence of O'Malley restrained him a little but once she was out of the room he let fly more abuse at Janet, accusing her of playing him false with every man to whom she had ever addressed a civil word. O'Malley, her ear to the keyhole, treasured every word to repeat to the cook. At length Staindrop strode out of the house to hail a cab and go down to join his father-in-law at the yard as they had arranged. Janet went to the drawing room where she read a book without attention and came to a decision.

The men returned shortly after six and Staindrop went to his room to change for dinner while Laidlaw went to his study, as he always did, to open the letters which had arrived for him by the evening post. When he opened the door Janet was there, sitting on the sofa where she had spent her first night in the house and staring into the fire.

"Hey, lass," he said, surprised, "what are you doing in this old den of mine. I'd have thought you too much the fine lady now to sit among all the dust and the reek of tobacco."

"I'm smoked like a kipper by Staindrop's cigars," she said. "Your pipe is nothing to them."

Laidlaw chuckled at this and she sat and watched him fill his pipe and light it with ritual care before she spoke. A picture came into her mind of him sitting in the Glenfoot kitchen on one of his rare visits and packing his pipe with the same precision. He turned a keen eye on her once it was set going.

"Well, lass?" he asked.

"Father," she began, ". . . could I come home, do you think?"

"Of course lass . . . where are you now, may I ask? You'll aye find a welcome here."

She shook her head.

"I don't mean for a visit. I mean to stay. For good."

Her father stared at her and laid the pipe on the chimney-piece. "You want to leave Staindrop?"

Janet nodded. Laidlaw turned away and drummed his fingers on the mantel-shelf.

"It's a bit hasty, isn't it, Janet?" he said at last. "Young people aye have their ups and downs, I understand. What's it all about."

"We just don't agree."

Her father made an impatient noise.

"That's no reason and fine you know it."

Janet swallowed. It was proving harder than she had anticipated to tell him about the man she had married.

"I know you'd words last night," he told her. "The whole household must have heard him. What was that about?"

"He wants a son," she said. "There's no sign yet."

"If that's all that's in it . . . your mother was four years married before Jock was born. You tell him that."

"I did," said Janet.

"Well then?"

"It makes no difference to . . ."

She hesitated.

"Makes no difference to what?"

She put her hand up to her jaw where a bruise was beginning to appear and swallowed again.

"He . . . he . . ."

Her voice faltered.

"In the name of the Kingdom!" he said roughly, "what is the matter with you? There must be something if you're wanting to leave him."

Janet considered her hands as if the answer might lie there.

"I've no liking for him," she said at last. "I don't think I ever could have."

When it came to the point she could not bare her humiliation to the stranger who was also her father; she could as easily have taken her clothes off before him. There was also the grim fear that he might laugh . . .

"That's no reason, lass," he said impatiently. "How long is it? A year? Give him a chance before you come running home."

"You'll not have me back then?"

"Janet, lass, you don't lack for sense. Use it. Don't provoke the man. Fine I know your sharp tongue; you had that from your mother."

There was a trace of bitterness in his voice and Janet remembered the letters she and Simon had found in the attic. Evidently he was thinking that she was like her mother in more than her sharp tongue. She tried desperately to find the words which would explain the dilemma but they would not come.

"Och, you can come if you must," he told her grudgingly. "I'll not shut my doors to you. But Hannah'll be sorely put about and I doubt she'll not go out of her way to make you welcome. And I'll tell you to your head, lass, you couldn't have chosen a worse moment. I need his backing on the board over the head of this Navy contract and what's more he's finding me a backer . . . I tell you it's damned awkward."

He lit his pipe again.

"Look, he's not such a bad lad," he suggested. "I know he hasn't got much up here . . ."

He tapped his forehead.

". . . but you're well provided for. Everything a girl could want, Hannah tells me. And the bairns'll come in time . . ."

Janet stood up hastily; there was a note of pleading in her father's voice which she could not bear. It struck a false note for her. Her father was strong, stern, a distant titan who should never need to beg.

"I was haivering, I suppose," she said. "Never heed. We'll come about, I dare say."

She left the room.

John Laidlaw looked at the door through which she had gone and frowned. On an impulse he crossed the room and opened it to call after her. He saw the whisk of her gown as she ran upstairs and heard a door close. He debated whether to follow her but decided against it. Back in his study he stared at the pile of specifications on his desk and cursed.

He had no further conversation with his daughter until he bade her goodbye the next morning. Staindrop was giving directions to the cabbie who was being obstinate about understanding his passenger's English speech and Laidlaw handed Janet into the cab. She sat forward on the worn leather seat to say goodbye and he glimpsed the blue mark on her jaw. He stared in dismay.

"Janet," he said gruffly, "if there's something you didn't tell . . ."

"No father," she said quietly. "Nothing. Never heed what I said. I was tired after the journey, that's all."

Staindrop climbed in and prevented Laidlaw from pursuing the matter, but he stared unhappily after the vehicle as it rumbled down the terrace.

"Damned women," he muttered but there was little conviction in his tone.

Once inside his study again he remembered something he had meant to tell her. Characteristically he sat down, there and then, and wrote an account of his meeting with an up-and-coming young lawyer from Perth who had come to draw up a contract for the building of a steamer to ply on the River Tay.

"He said he was acquainted with you when he visited Luss a year last summer and asked to be remembered to you. I told him what I could remember of your grand London doings . . ."

He paused, his pen poised above the paper, as he recalled the earnest face of the young man.

"A pleasant young man, I thought, and all his wits about him. You'd need to get up early to get the better of him . . ."

The last paragraph gave him some trouble.

> I'm not easy in my mind about you. If Staindrop mishandles you or anything of that nature I beg you will not consider the affair of the contract. Blood is thicker than water they say and I have no wish to see you unhappy.
>
> I am affectionately,
>
> Your father.

He folded this missive and was about to address the envelope when he recalled that he had forgotten to find out their address. He cursed again and laid it aside till he should hear from Hannah. For the next fortnight he found himself inundated with work: negotiations over the frigates, tussles over the backing, plans for the expansion of the yard, contracts, drafts and amendments of drafts. Hannah, equally immersed in wedding plans, did not write for some time. At the end of three weeks he had a brief uninformative note from Janet herself, dealing almost wholly with scenery and weather. He ignored the content but copied the address on to the now grimy envelope which he disinterred from a drift of plans and specifications. The next day Luke, the groom cum boot-boy took it to the post and it arrived in Torridon some four days later on the heels of the worst November snowstorm for sixty years.

# 9

THE ELLIS-MARTINS described their Torridon retreat as 'our little shooting-box in the North'. Lady Ellis-Martin had inherited the estate from her grandfather, a thousand acres of rocky shore and pathless heather moor, and a ruined tower above a bay. Her husband, who had amassed a fortune based on the supply of cheap boots to the armies of other nations, built a new castle beside the ruin with a wealth of towers and turrets, battlements and shot-windows which the builder of the original fortalice would have been puzzled to defend. He also stocked the heather moor with grouse and gamekeepers, very obligingly providing the crofters he was forced to dispossess in the process with their fares to Canada in an elderly sailing craft chartered for the purpose. The new castle could accommodate more than twenty guests, whose needs were met by a host of servants drawn from the little town of Oban thirty miles away. To reach this fastness it was necessary to take the train to Oban and there, in good weather, the Ellis-Martins' steam launch would be waiting at the pier to take visitors and their luggage round the point and up the tiny Loch of the Rowans to the castle bay. In bad weather a light car drawn by a plodding garron would jolt the visitor over thirty miles of moorland track. For those hardy enough there was a steep path over the hill to the head of the loch, five miles of sheep-track and from there either a long row down the loch or a tramp along the rocky shore.

Janet and her husband arrived at the castle by sea on a golden evening. The tide was making and there was no wind so that the *Princess Deirdre* slipped almost silently up the loch, a feather of smoke from her funnel, her gay red and white awning reflected in the silken water and a wake spreading behind her like a peacock's tail. She nudged gently along the little stone jetty where two gillies were waiting to take the baggage up to the castle in a handbarrow. Beyond the boathouse, where half a dozen rowing-boats lay waiting for those who preferred fishing to shooting, a governess-cart drawn by a garron, another kilted gillie at its head, was ready to take the passengers. Janet cramped from half a day in the train and the boat looked at the broad grassy track and said she would prefer to walk the half mile or so to the imposing stone terrace on which the parasols and self-conscious tweeds of earlier arrivals could be seen. Staindrop signified that he would walk with her by a long-suffering shrug and handed their two fellow-travellers up into the cart.

These were a widow, one Mrs Baberton, and her daughter who were invited to a number of such parties on account of their skill at whist. In view of the unreliability of the weather it was advisable to have some form of indoor amusement: moreover, Miss Baberton played the pianoforte in a competent almost professional way and was quite happy to play accompaniments for singers or waltzes for impromptu dances without exacting payment in the form of long and tedious sonatas, as other amateur pianists were prone to do. They were also well known to be first with all the news. Lucy Baberton had not been so engrossed in her novel as to ignore the signs of ill-temper in Lord Staindrop during the journey. Her mother, sharing the contents of a lunchbasket had glimpsed a bruise on Janet's jaw which she had hoped to conceal with a high ruffle on the collar of her blouse and a lock of hair drawn forward. This circumstance was enough to alert them and as they bumped slowly up the curve of the drive in the governess-cart they watched their fellow-travellers walking along the grassy path and saw with intense interest that they were obviously exchanging 'words'.

These 'words' concerned Jasper Pelham-Villiers.

When they were joined by the Babertons Janet had exerted herself to appear as usual but Staindrop had continued to sit mumchance and stare out of the window. As they were walking up the path his bottled-up bad temper found expression.

"If I see you as much as look his way," he threatened, "you'll pay for it, I promise you."

Janet said nothing but strode on up the path. Staindrop, more accustomed to pavements, found himself falling behind and was forced to trot a couple of paces in order to come level.

"I suppose you think I haven't noticed all those trinkets and sweets arriving for you . . ." he panted, "I suppose you think I am a fool . . . blind and deaf to boot, eh?"

Janet stopped so suddenly that he almost bumped into her.

"I've good reason to," she said bluntly, "it would take a born gomeril to concoct such a tirrivee out of next to nothing. Captain Pelham-Villiers is the merest acquaintance and will remain so. If you want me to make a speak of us both I'll do what you say and ignore him completely. And if you hit me again I'll go back to Glasgow at once and leave you to explain why."

She did not wait for an answer to this but walked briskly over the last twenty yards to the terrace steps at the top of which the earlier arrivals waited to greet them. Staindrop stumbled behind her his face red with anger and the guests glanced meaningly at one another.

By dinner time all the guests had arrived and a score of interested pairs of eyes watched the first encounter between Staindrop and Pelham-Villiers. Janet, despite her dread of some humiliating scene, was reminded irresistibly of two collies at Luss Games walking stiff-legged round one another hackling while the crowd watched with interest and a degree of apprehension. The encounter passed off uneventfully as such encounters most usually do: Staindrop had recovered his temper, or as much of it as would let his commonsense prevail. He had decided to conceal his suspicion and dislike. The two men shook hands with apparent cordiality and Pelham-Villiers greeted Janet with no more than a bow and a warm smile which she returned rather distantly. The slackening in tension was almost perceptible . . . indeed it might have been called disappointment. The Babertons had been busy since their arrival and expectations had been whetted.

The hall in which the guests were gathered was the heart of the castle. It was lit by a cupola of an incongruously Muscovite description and lavishly panelled in dark oak. On every panel hung either a weapon or a trophy; pistols, pikes, spears, halberds, targes, swords, stags' heads, stuffed fish, horns, and antlers in alarming profusion. It was almost heated by two vast fireplaces which burned mounds of peat and all round the walls stood suits of armour regarding the assembly grimly through a variety of slits and apertures. A carved screen lined with leather diverted the draught from the huge, iron-studded, oaken front doors and opposite these a magnificent oak double staircase climbed to the gallery. Here the oak panelling gave way to stone, ameliorated by tapestry hangings which depicted in primary colours a number of improbable medieval episodes, animated by the draughts which billowed and rippled them. From this gallery opened the main suites of rooms and the corridors which led to the various towers. The Staindrops were lodged in the West Tower. From the window they had an incomparable view of the loch.

After dinner Janet excused herself before the men appeared in the drawing room on the grounds of a headache. In her room she took the pins out of her hair and let the heavy plait uncoil to her waist. She had left Maisie behind in Derbyshire. She was busy replaiting it when there was a tap on her door. She turned her head, frowning, and after a short hesitation called, "Come in!"

The girl who entered was about her own age and height: she wore the uniform of the female servant, cap and streamers, black dress and plain linen apron but her friendly smile had nothing to do with the mim, shuttered expressions of London servants.

"I'm Seonaidh, mistress," said she, "herself says I am to wait on you, if you're needing anyone."

"Seonaidh?"

"Aye . . . Seonaidh MacAllister. It is my father is gamekeeper here."

Janet smiled at her.

"I am Janet too."

The girl beamed back at her namesake reflected in the mirror and began to undo the row of buttons down the back of Janet's dress.

"There now," she said comfortably, "like in name, like in nature . . . so they say. Would you fancy a nice cup of tea in your bed, mistress?"

Gradually the houseparty settled into a kind of routine. The men breakfasted late and then set out to fish or to shoot. The women either donned 'sporting' outfits of tweed and heavy boots and tramped the moors with their menfolk or went for ladylike strolls about the policies under sensible umbrellas. Those who did not wish for outdoor exercise played cards, read desultorily and animadverted on their host's choice of books. They hugged the fires, embroidered, gossiped and wrote interminable letters to their less fortunate friends saying how much they were enjoying their visit. These Alastair the captain took daily to Oban in the steam launch.

Janet, encouraged by Seonaidh's father, started to learn to fish and Miss Baberton who could, characteristically, already cast a fair line usually came with her, somewhat to Janet's relief: she did not wish for a solitary encounter with Pelham-Villiers. This gentleman, watching for opportunities to open his campaign, found himself frustrated at all points: during the day Staindrop dogged his footsteps assiduously, while at night Janet seemed always one of a group. On the day when he pleaded a wrenched ankle and let the guns go out without him, Janet decided to go with her hostess to Oban in the launch. October was nearly over and the party due to break up in ten days' time before the chance came for him to press his suit.

It began on a day such as occasionally comes late in October, warm, still and sunny with a high pale sky. The men went out early to shoot on the far ground and arrived to find the gillies and loaders already there and in high spirits. Ellis-Martin enquired the reason for all the laughter.

"It is Angus, here," they told him, "seven girls he has, seven! And the oldest near old enough to be married. And last night his wife had a fine boy."

Ellis-Martin presented the proud father with a sovereign for his new son and called for whisky from the lunchbaskets to wet the infant's head. When the ceremony was over the butts were allocated and Staindrop found himself with Angus for his loader right out on the flank.

"We will not be seeing many birds here," observed Angus, unpacking cartridge boxes, "they will go over east to west into the wind."

Staindrop took up his position, his gun resting on top of the low turf wall.

"So Angus," he said, "you have a son and heir?"

"A son, aye, m'lord, but devil the thing have I for him to heir," grinned Angus, "not with nine mouths to feed."

"But you'll be glad to have a boy, I dare say?"

"Aye m'lord. I've aye wanted a laddie and I'd just about given up hope of him. My Morag's not as young as she was, you'll understand."

In the ordinary way Angus would not have spoken as he did. Staindrop was not popular among the loaders because he was a poor shot who tended to take his frustrations out on those who attended him and was, as they saw it, close-fisted with his sovereigns and, what was worse, with the whisky flask. But Angus had had a long anxious night and his breakfast had been early and scanty; the drams and his deep pleasure in having a son combined to make him confide his secret in a man he scarcely knew and did not like.

"We asked the wise man at Ardtornish," he explained, "and he said to lie together outside in the dark of the moon and we would be sure to make a son. And so we did . . . so we did. A fine healthy boy he is."

Staindrop frowned into the distance.

Angus nodded.

" 'Under the sky and the ground beneath you'," he quoted, "and a rare job I had to persuade herself to it . . . it was just not decent-like, says she, and it took a good dram in her . . ."

He chuckled reminiscently.

Staindrop bagged no birds that morning and at lunchtime he told his host that he had letters to write and would walk back to the house. When he reached it he made for the library and hunted out an almanac. What he found there made him nod: he made a face at the deer's head above the book-case and slammed the book shut.

"Dammit," he muttered, "it's worth a try."

The fine weather lasted another day but on the second morning after the birth of Angus's son a smirr of cloud appeared over the sky and the loch was ruffled by little gusts of wind. Janet on her way along the shore passed the boathouse and found MacAllister hauling the heavy cobles well up upon the shore.

"I doubt we're for a blow," he explained, "and it's to be a devil."

He surveyed the sky and the sea knowledgeably.

"Winter's coming early this year."

He pointed at the line of deer on the other side of the loch picking their way among the rocks and the heather clumps.

"They should be up in the high corries still. They can smell a storm coming."

Janet agreed. She had seen the same happen at Loch Lomond.

"How long before it comes?" she asked.

"A day and a night," he prophesied, "and it'll be bad taking that long to arrive. Quick come, quick go they say."

He shook his head gloomily and Janet remembered Betsy and Dick discussing the look of the ben at evening in the same fashion and knew a great pang of homesickness.

That afternoon the temperature fell rapidly and the sportsmen came home early, stamping their feet and crowding about the fire to warm their hands while the servants hovered about with offers of whisky and cherry brandy. Staindrop accepted a stiff whisky and drank it, looking anxiously out at the approaching darkness. He refilled his glass and tossed down another three fingers with a gasp and a grimace before he went in search of Janet. She was in the library writing a reassuring letter to Phoebe.

"Put on your cloak," he told her, "I want to talk to you. We're going for a walk."

Janet looked up in astonishment. Staindrop was not given to fortuitous exercise and fresh air.

"Now?" she asked, "It's almost dark."

"Needn't go far. Never get a moment's privacy in this place. People in and out all the time."

His words were underlined by Pelham-Villiers's appearance in the library door. He too had been in search of Janet but checked at the sight of her husband. Staindrop scowled and gave Janet an unceremonious push towards the door.

"Fetch your cloak. I'll meet you in the hall."

Janet hesitated briefly but decided that an argument in the circumstances could be tactless. By this time she was in no doubt of Pelham-Villiers's feelings towards her and nor was any member of the houseparty. In fact, though none of the leading characters was aware of it, there was a flourishing book on whether Janet would succumb to Pelham-Villiers and another, just begun, on how long Pelham-Villiers would persist in his pursuit if she held out. Already he had remained constant for longer than anyone could recall.

"Tell you what it is, Mama," Miss Baberton had remarked

the previous evening, "he's got a leveller at last. He's in earnest this time."

Her mother deplored her mannish choice of phrase and pooh-poohed her reading of the situation, claiming to have known Jasper since he was in his cradle and even then his nursemaids dursn't venture too close. Miss Baberton had chuckled at the comment but maintained her opinion which was not far from the truth. Pelham-Villiers had found Janet becoming an obsession with him: her coolness and elusiveness he blamed on Staindrop's presence, not on indifference to himself. Even at the worst, he argued, with unusual humility, she must prefer himself to that chilly pompous ass of a husband. His own feelings towards Staindrop startled him by their violence: he was accustomed to ignore husbands except as obstacles to be overcome or dupes to be hoodwinked. To find himself consumed with desire to do a husband some painful injury merely because he exerted some trivial marital privilege such as taking Janet by the elbow or, as now, giving her a push, was a new and unwelcome experience. He felt the blood throb under his high collar as Staindrop went past him into the hall. The urge to land his fist in the middle of that peevish countenance was overpowering. He watched Staindrop pace up and down the hall for a moment and then turned away trying to control his dislike. He gripped the chimney-piece and glared at the stag's head which presided over the fire, calling it by a foul name which, poor beast, it had done nothing to deserve. He heard a snatch of conversation in the hall.

"Hurry up for any favour!"

"Staindrop, it's cold and almost dark . . . whatever it is, surely it can wait."

Staindrop made an impatient noise and Pelham-Villiers heard Janet exclaim as he seized her arm.

"I tell you it can't wait. It's got to be tonight. Come along, do!"

A swirl of cold air and a cavernous thud as the front door closed indicated that they had gone out. Jasper threw his cigar into the fire and swore again. Then, on an impulse he would have been puzzled to explain, he turned on his heel, grabbed an ulster from the cluster hanging in the cloakroom and went out after them.

The light was almost gone and he could see no sign of them

anywhere. He decided, wrongly, that they would keep to the drive and set out along it feeling more than a little foolish. In fact Staindrop had turned to the left and hurried Janet over the rough grass under the windows until they came to the ancient low arch which led into the ruins of the old fortress. This was now roofless, four thick walls pierced occasionally by narrow windows and rising to a height of nearly fifty feet. Up one side protruded the stumps of a staircase and in the beamholes of the first storey straggled the ragged ends of birds' nests. The Ellis-Martins had placed a bench inside but it was rarely used for the interior was dark and dank. The grass was kept scythed but it was not a pleasant place.

Staindrop pushed Janet through the arch and kept his hand on her arm. They could hardly see one another.

"Lie down," he said.

"Are you out of your mind?"

She jerked her arm away but he caught hold of her cloak.

"I said, lie down," he said between his teeth and began to force her down on to the grass. Janet bewildered, resentful and more than a little frightened tried to resist him which was unfortunate because Staindrop needed the stimulus of resistance to help him try to carry out an intention he knew to be irrational. In a curious way the struggle justified his behaviour and the need to use force released the violence which festered inside him. The episode became brutal.

They struggled in the dark and Staindrop cursed ceaselessly at her, calling her by the foulest names he could think up as she tried to break away from him. He gripped her wrist and she bent her head and bit hard. He snatched his hand away and hit her on the face with his fist, after which she staggered back dazed and sick, her head singing, and fell over a fallen roof-slab in the grass.

"You'll do it," he grunted, "you'll do it if I have to break your damned neck!"

If Janet had understood in the slightest what he was about she might have been less terrified; she knew very well how his lack of an heir had become a festering sore over which he brooded and which had turned his normal fraternal dislike of his brother into a sour murderous hatred. However, the scandalous story of Angus's method of achieving a son and heir had not yet passed beyond the castle smoking room and Staindrop could not bring himself to explain to her what he wanted and why. He was not an articulate man and he was well aware of Janet's contempt for him and familiar with her sharp tongue. Not only that, but he had come to believe, rather than admit that he might be barren himself, that Janet did not want a child and was taking steps to prevent one and thus she would not agree to what he wanted. In his rather confused mind the only way to achieve what he wanted was to take it by force. What he had not bargained for was Janet's ability to resist. For all her slenderness she was no die-away miss. He found himself compelled to use more force than he wished.

When she fell he could not discover for a moment where she was till in the dimness he saw a movement as she tried to stand up. He moved over to prevent this and fell over the same roof-slab which had been her downfall. Janet, by now quite convinced that he had gone out of his mind and meant to kill her, gathered up her skirt which had been torn away from the waistband in her struggle and ran through the arch. Her face felt stiff and swollen already and there was the taste of blood in her mouth.

Behind her Staindrop scrambled to his feet and stumbled in pursuit though he could barely make out the shadow ahead running over the rough grass towards the loch. Janet heard his panting and quickened her pace with some notion of trying to hide from him in the boathouse. In her haste her light slipper came off and was lost and she caught her bare foot on a tussock and fell headlong. Her elbow struck a rock and she gave a whimper of pain, for it hurt her very much, and then was sick.

Jasper, pacing aimlessly back up the drive, heard her running through the grass and then the fall. Cursing under his breath he ran towards the sound and nearly fell over her crouched in the grass.

Staindrop, who had stumbled twice, picked himself up for the second time and heard Pelham-Villiers's shocked exclamation as he came upon Janet. He stood uncertainly, wondering what to do. At such a moment Janet would be unlikely to regard his advent with any great pleasure and Pelham-Villiers would almost certainly jump to uncomfortably accurate conclusions . . . he was familiar with Angus's story.

Muttering with frustration and embarrassment he retreated to the keep, meaning to remain out of sight till Pelham-Villiers was elsewhere. He had no desire to come into dinner with a black eye.

# 10

Gently Pelham-Villiers tried to lift her to her feet and felt her shivering. When she felt his hands on her Janet gasped and tried to push him away. Pelham-Villiers was not a particularly clever man but he had a sort of instinctive kindness and a degree of imagination. He did not need to be told what had happened . . . or why: Angus's recipe for getting an heir had become a matter for bawdy comment over the port and the situation between Staindrop and his prolific brother was common knowledge. He gentled her as he might have gentled a nervous horse, murmuring nursery endearments and reassurances and constantly stroking her hair. When she had stopped shaking he produced a large linen handkerchief and let her wipe her face.

"Better?" he enquired.

Janet nodded.

"Let me take you in now. It's cold."

"Not the hall," said Janet and her teeth chattered, "I'm not fit to be seen. I . . . I had a fall . . ."

Her voice broke slightly and Pelham-Villiers, sensing the humiliation behind that speech, knew a savage desire to knock Staindrop's teeth down his throat. None of that coloured his next speech, which was a matter-of-fact offer to take her round to the gunroom door.

"There'll be no one in there just now," he said, "all in the hall swiggin' sherry . . ."

"I lost my shoe," discovered Janet.

"Never mind your damned shoe," he said and picked her up.

After a few steps through the thick grass he was hoping that this chivalrous gesture would not prove too much for him. Janet was tall and it was an uphill quarter of a mile to the gunroom door. However, he set her on her feet in the gunroom only slightly out of breath. He livened the fire and lit a branch of candles. When he turned round he was shocked at the way she looked. Her bodice was ripped apart, the buttons gone and her sleeve hanging off. There was a cut under her mouth and where the torn sleeve revealed her arm he could see a series of savage red marks which would become bruises. Her hair, usually so neat and smooth, was hanging down her back in tangles.

"Perhaps you would ask Seonaidh to come to me," she suggested.

"As you like, but I think you need this first."

Ellis-Martin had left his flask on the cupboard. He filled the cap and made her drink. She obeyed and shuddered at the bite of the spirit, but found the familiar taste and smell comforting because it reminded her of Betsy for whom whisky was the prime and only medicine for minor ills. He saw some colour come back into her cheeks and smiled.

"Now I can feel more comfortable about you," he observed, "a minute ago you looked ready to knock on Peter's Gate. I'll fetch your maid."

He went to the door, hesitated and turned.

"Where did you fall?" he enquired.

"In the Old Tower," said Janet. "It was dark and the ground is very uneven . . ."

Pelham-Villiers nodded and left the room. He did not return. He felt the moment to be unpropitious and in any event knew a very lively desire to gratify another impulse. A word to the housekeeper and he went to his own room to change. Seonaidh arrived in a few minutes, clucking with concern, and helped her up a narrow back-stair to the West Tower where she provided a hot bath, ointment for the bruises and scratches, a bowl of broth and a sleeping draught begged from Lady Ellis-Martin. She then built up the fire expertly with peats and left Janet with a cheerful good night and a wish that she might feel no worse for her fall in the morning. Outside in the passage she waited for a moment and heard the bedclothes flung back, the sound of bare feet on the wooden floor and the key turned stealthily in the lock.

Seonaidh nodded to herself and made a comment in the Gaelic which cast some doubt on the ancestry of men in general and of one man in particular. 'A fall indeed,' she thought, 'some fall . . .'

Pelham-Villiers, meanwhile, had investigated the hall and the other rooms where the party was used to congregate before dinner. Staindrop was not to be seen. He went outside again. By now it was almost pitch dark and there was a wind rising. At the archway leading to the Old Tower he paused and listened. He could hear someone pacing to and fro inside and see the glow of a cigar. Just then the noise of the gong which was sounded to summon the company to dinner came faintly from the house and he heard the figure inside sigh and begin to walk towards the archway. Pelham-Villiers flattened himself against the wall to the left of the arch. The only light left was in the west where the last dregs of daylight were draining from the sky. The man inside the tower emerged and was silhouetted against this tiny glimmer.

"Staindrop?" whispered Pelham-Villiers. It would be too embarrassing if the figure turned out to be another member of the party indulging in a preprandial breath of air.

"Who's that?" responded the unmistakably peevish voice and the figure turned towards the enquiry. Pelham-Villiers, with a sense of gratification more common to other occasions, landed him a heavy blow in the stomach. For a second he considered his victim groaning and retching on all fours and then he hurried away to join the company.

The skill of the cook was wasted on the diners that night, so intent were they on the rumours which were flying around. Lady Staindrop sent a message by her maid to say that she had had a fall while walking and while not badly injured she was shaken and wished to keep her bed. Lord Staindrop did appear eventually while they were discussing the roasted grouse, but he was a poor colour, clearly unwell, said little and ate less. Pelham-Villiers, on the other hand, ate a hearty meal, conversed cheerfully and ignored Staindrop with energy and point. By the next morning the wildest stories were circulating; some circumstance being lent to these by Miss Baberton, who left her mother's room late after a session of delicious speculation and had seen Lord Staindrop rattling angrily at his wife's door and demanding admittance in a furious whisper.

After dinner Pelham-Villiers had seen his host alone and declared his intention of departing the following day.

"For if I don't, Durward, I will assuredly murder Staindrop."

Ellis-Martin looked up from his brandy and demanded the reason for this homicidal probability.

"Not your usual way with husbands," he chuckled.

Pelham-Villiers looked down his nose.

"Can't tell you . . . not the thing. But this I will say, Durward. The man's a blackguard . . . peer or no peer."

"Strong language, Jasper," commented his host, "thought you were the only blackguard in this party, 'pon m'soul I did."

He guffawed and filled the glasses again.

"Blackguard I may be," said Jasper, "but there are some things I would not . . . could not do to any woman. Not to the worst trollop of them all . . . let alone my own wife."

With which none too cryptic comment he went to bed, where he lay stroking his bruised knuckles with a reminiscent smile and dreaming of an uxorious future in the comfortable conviction that Janet's mishap would persuade her to give him what he so much wanted.

He was not the only one to lie awake. Janet's sleeping draught lay untouched as she planned what she would do next morning to the last detail. When she had done that she lay staring into the dark, waiting for morning, her mind going round and round endlessly. The shock of Staindrop's behaviour had worn off and she began to see his action in perspective. What she saw she did not like. Ignorant of the reason for his action and conscious that she had always, in a current elliptical phrase, done her duty, his brutal beating assumed a frightening aspect. She had not found any quality in Staindrop which she could respect nor any that she could like but she had never before suspected that he might be out of his mind. She shifted restlessly at the grim notion and the twinges this movement produced reminded her of the violence which he had used. She would, she *must* leave him. The difficulty was where she could go: her father would not receive her, he had as good as told her so, and Hannah with her eye upon Society would do nothing to persuade him. Aunt Matilda had promised aid but she was in Derbyshire and Janet had barely money enough to carry her back to Glasgow. Briefly she thought of Jock, but the ill-tempered malicious face of Kirsty intervened: there was also the presence of Donald just over the hill. She decided to go to Betsy and Dick; they would shelter her until she could find some work. She would find a post as a housekeeper. Better to work for strangers than stay with . . . her mind boggled at the word which arose in it. The decision taken she put her mind to the immediate difficulties of reaching the station at Oban without being seen and persuaded to return. She soon arrived at a solution to this problem; while she was working out the details she heard her door handle being turned. The door rattled against the jamb, once and again.

"Janet! Janet!"

Her husband's voice was hushed but urgent. Janet did not answer.

"Open up damn you!"

The door rattled again.

"I want to talk to you. I've *got* to talk to you! Open this damned door!"

Janet sat up and swallowed the sleeping draught. Before the scrabbling at the door was finished she was drifting off to sleep.

She did not hear another visitor to her door an hour or so later when the household had at last gone to sleep. When the visitor got no response to his discreet taps he took a letter from his pocket and slipped it under the door. When she woke up with a jerk after a nightmare just as dawn was breaking the white square on the shining oak floor was the first thing she saw. She lit a candle and read it. It was from Pelham-Villiers and was, had she known it, unique. The Captain was at all times unwilling to set pen to paper: written evidence was so damning.

> My dearest Janet, [he wrote] you must let me offer you a refuge from that brute. It makes me writhe to think of you in his clutches. You must know by now how much I revere and adore you. I ask nothing better than to be your stay, support and comfort . . .

If these words had a familiar ring to Janet it was scarcely surprising, they were from a play she had witnessed not two months before.

> . . . I beg you [he continued] flee with me before he does you more mischief.

The next paragraph threw the Captain upon his own resources and had a distinctly military flavour.

I will proceed south tomorrow by the first available train and await you in London. Please rendezvous with me in Harpenden's Hotel in Eden Square. Send to tell me the approximate date and time of your arrival and I will be there. By then I will have plans to leave the country and transport arranged. Bring no baggage. I will attend to everything.

Please believe me to be your most devoted,

Jasper Pelham-Villiers.

Janet smiled over this ardent missive and shook her head. She refolded it and laid it on the dressing chest as she set about preparing for the day ahead. It was still there later that same day when Staindrop came into enquire peevishly of the empty room when she meant to leave her bed. He found it of absorbing interest.

The steam launch left for Oban every morning soon after eight. Alastair collected the letter-bag from the Castle together with his list of commissions for the day. If any of the guests wished to go to Oban his departure was deferred to suit their convenience. On the morning after Janet's 'fall' there were no guests wishing to use the launch, so Alastair hurried down to the jetty just before eight with one eye on the threatening sky.

"There's snow in it, right enough," he muttered to the engineer, "a bitter winter it will be with snow in November month."

The engineer was a Glasgow man who regarded bad weather as a discomfort and not a disaster. He grunted a casual response and spread a shovelful of coals meticulously over the palpitating hearth. He had no potatoes still in the ground or sheep on the hill. Alastair looked at him with irritation, wishing he had not taken on this summer job; no English money would make up for the loss of his sheep. He looked again at the sky and the grey sea and then beckoned irritably at the figure hurrying down from the Castle. She wore the black stuff dress of the household staff and wrapped around her the tartan bar worn by the women of the district, muffling her face and covering her hair. Alastair waved her impatiently into the cabin.

"Is there any others to come?" he asked.

"No the day," said the girl, "just mysel'."

A lowlander from her accent, he decided, as he cast off the mooring line and stepped aboard at the stern, giving an expert shove of his booted foot which sent the little launch swinging out into the loch, stern first.

"We'll not be taking our ease this day at all," he called down to the engineer, "you'll need to be whacking her up a bittie, Tam."

Something of the idiom had stuck after a summer spent in the company of the Glasgow engineer. Tam obligingly 'whacked her up' and the *Deirdre* set off down the loch like a duck in a hurry, a curl of white foam at her bows. The girl in the cabin did not come out to exclaim at the bright brasses as they usually did but stayed below, her head bowed and her face hidden by the plaid. Alastair opened his mouth to pass the time of day with her but noticed the bundle in the bottom of the basket. It was tied in a grey woollen shawl and through the knitting could be seen the various colours of the clothes inside. A shabby carpet bag leaned against the basket. Evidently she had been turned away from the Castle and from her attitude was in no mind to discuss her wrongs. The little craft surged on, pitching as the waves at the mouth of the loch got shorter and steeper.

At Oban the girl stepped hurriedly ashore. Alastair stepped after with the mooring line.

"Are you to be coming back with us?" he asked as he bent over the bollard.

The girl shook her head and Alastair patted her on the shoulder.

"Don't you be fretting, now," said he, "there's better places and them not ninety miles from nowhere at all. Good luck go with you, mo chridhe!"

The girl muttered thanks and hurried away to the little new station with its bright paint. She would have time and to spare for the train, Alastair reflected, for it was not due to leave until after noon. He turned away to the pile of supplies waiting for him on the quay and began to carry them on board, promptly forgetting all about his passenger. There was a constant coming and going of girls at the big house during the summer as the English housekeeper wrestled with the prejudices and inadequacies of local domestic assistance.

Back at the Castle Seonaidh gloated over her new possessions.

There was to be a ceilidh at the house of her uncle this night. She would go in the beautiful wine-coloured silk dress and open her aunt's eyes as wide as they could stretch. She folded it carefully and placed it on her shawl. It would never do to wear it for the long walk over the hill; however, she abandoned the idea of 'making an entrance' in a braw gown from London only reluctantly. Her eye fell on the ruin of the dress which Janet had been wearing the previous night. It was a thought muddy but that was dry and would brush off readily enough. The torn gathers of the skirt would be easily cobbled back into the waistband. As for the ruined bodice, that was no problem for her own Sunday gown was about the same grey colour but plain-like without the buttons and braid. The bonny big cloak would hide its shortcomings. She threaded a needle and began to sew. It was her monthly day off and she had permission from the old Cailleach to stay away till morning and now her lady was gone she had a half a mind to stay away altogether. When the skirt was done she put it on and the cloak over it, took up the bundle which contained the silk gown and the box of trinkets she had had in thanks from Janet for the use of her black stuff gown and tartan plaid. She slipped out of the side door for fear the Cailleach might see her and find a task.

She should have known the signs of approaching weather as well as Alastair for she had been born only ten miles away: she should have realised that to use the hill road when snow was threatening was dangerous. She did realise this but pinned her hopes on its being too early in the year for heavy snow; at the worst, she thought, she would get a right drooking and the grand cloak would keep out the most of that. The wind was blowing out of the north, a thin arctic breath. Seonaidh huddled into the thick velvet-lined wool and pulled up the hood with its cosy trimming of fur and hurried up the path to the hill road. Two people saw her. It was a pity when they were the last people to see her alive that they should take her for somebody else.

In the station at Oban Janet waited on a bench; the wind was rising minute by minute and whistled through the cast-iron pillars. She drew the coarse tartan plaid about her and shivered. There was a fire in the waiting room, for twice she had seen the porter go inside with a scuttle of coal, but it was essential that no one should see her closely enough to know her again. The hands of the clock moved slowly through the morning. Janet, who had eaten nothing since luncheon the previous day, noted with a pang the time when the rest of the party would be sitting down to a late breakfast. Her mind dwelt longingly on the dishes of buttered toast, the piles of hot rolls, crystal dishes of heather honey and white butter: she could almost smell the porridge and cream, the chafing dishes of bacon and eggs, grilled kidneys, herrings and haddocks. She remembered the vast pink ham which stood on the sideboard for those who preferred a cold breakfast and her stomach churned and protested at such memories. In the bitter cold the bruises she had collected the previous evening stiffened and ached.

At half past eleven the train backed into the platform and clanked and huffed itself to a standstill. Janet picked up her bundles and climbed into a third class compartment, glad and grateful to be out of the wind. Gradually the compartment filled up. A shepherd with his cringing dog and a smell of whisky so strong that it was almost visible sat down opposite Janet and fell asleep, noisily and immediately. Then came two old women, grey-haired and toothless, talking incessantly in the Gaelic. Just as the whistle blew and the train lurched the last passenger climbed in, a fishwife with a heavy creel of fish fresh from the boats ready to hawk round the inland clachans. However, she was not the last passenger to board the train. There was a clatter of hooves and a shout "Hold the train!". The fishwife paused as she refilled her clay cuttie pipe and stared at the scene outside.

"A bonnie chentleman, chust!" she observed approvingly. Janet kept her head low and the plaid well over her face. She knew the bonnie gentleman's voice.

The train trundled rhythmically along the lochside and then turned for the long climb inland. Heavy clouds covered the sky and soon flakes of snow began to scud past the windows.

"Sneachd!" exclaimed the two old women and shook their shawled heads forebodingly, "geamhradh moch, Dhia!"

Before long the snow thickened so that it was not possible to see more than ten yards into the swirl. The train stopped and the fishwife got out, grumbling that she would never win home before night, and leaving a souvenir of her presence in the combined stink of herring and thick black pigtail twist. After she had slammed the door the shepherd's dog whined and nudged at his master's knee. He got a savage kick for his pains and yelped piteously. The porter peered in at the door evidently looking for someone, saw the shepherd and cursed!"

"Duncan . . . Duncan Rhuaid . . . are you wanting to go on to Stirling again!"

The herd staggered to his feet and got out, his dog slinking about his heels. The door was slammed again, the window closed and the train chuff-chuffed into the snow. At the next stop the two old women scrambled down and toddled away into the whiteness, their woollen shawls pulled tightly about their ears and still mumbling away in the Gaelic. Janet, peering out, saw that the ground was white; the snow was beginning to lie. The compartment, empty of people and innocent of heating, grew colder and colder and the train went more and more slowly. By this time Janet was so hungry she felt faint and ill and the cold bit at her savagely.

When the train stopped again she peered out, trying to see where they were. She could see nothing except a white whirling wilderness. There was a long wait and then someone came past under the door shouting something. Janet let down the window and leaned out to hear better but she was too late. Someone was leaning from the window to her right.

"What did he say?" she asked.

"He wass saying that the halt at Fraoch is chust the matter of a mile away and we should all be walking there to find food and shelter for the night."

"Isn't the train going on?"

"The engine will not go, they are saying . . . we must wait for one coming from Stirling and it not likely to be here till morning."

Her informant opened his door and jumped down on to the track. He was a small farmer or a crofter she judged. She looked along towards the other end of the train and then ducked back hastily into her compartment: Jasper Pelham-Villiers was leaning out of a first class carriage and shouting questions at the guard. Even in the snow she could see and hear him plainly enough.

Janet tried to think: presumably the passengers would have to spend some time at the Halt before a train came to pick them up. They would almost certainly have to spend the night there. Pelham-Villiers would be certain to find her out in such close quarters as a mere Halt suggested and afterwards . . . well, it would be hard to avoid assistance which she did not want and which would lead to . . . tired and hungry and beset as she was it would be strange if she did not succumb to whatever he had to offer. She looked out of the other door, flinching at the blast of snow which hissed in at her. She reasoned that if there was a Halt there must be some form of habitation near by. There was plenty of daylight left. Surely in that time she could find shelter. If the worst came to the worst she could always find the railway line again and find her way to the Halt. She pushed the door wide open against the cold blast, collected her bundles, sat down on the floor of the carriage and launched herself down on to the permanent way. She landed softly on a drift of snow which had already built up against the wheels.

Afterwards, when she thought about this action, she was to decide that she must have been a little light-headed with hunger and fatigue even to consider so fool-hardy a thing. It was not as if she was some town-bred sasunach. However, at the time it seemed a reasonable alternative to becoming Pelham-Villiers's latest mistress. Janet was not given to rationalising her feelings but at that point she was, as she might have put it, scunnered at men: her brother had betrayed her, her father had sold her for control of a business, her husband . . . her mind shied away from what he had done. To put herself into the hands of another of the detested species seemed the ultimate foolishness. She scrambled down the embankment and began to walk across the moor into the wind.

The cold cut and clawed at her, the snow swirled and scurried endlessly, covering the heather tussocks with a treacherously smooth blanket over which she stumbled and floundered. After a while she realised she was not going into the wind any longer, that it was blowing on her left cheek: memories returned to her. She could hear Dick's voice as clearly as if he were standing under the lamp at Braeside and telling the story of the laddie who had run from the army at the Dumbarton Rock.

"Wandered in circles," Dick had said, "you could see them plain as print in the snow when it was thawing. Wandered round and round like a cow on a tether and never kenned it."

She pulled up for a moment and stood peering into the storm:

if she was going to find safety she must think and not panic and walk in circles till she lay down and was covered with snow and slept away to death. If she walked with her back to the wind, she reasoned, she would find the railway again. She turned herself until the wind pressed the plaid against her shoulders and was about to go back when she heard the bleating of sheep. She listened intently thinking it might be her imagination. In Dick's tale of the soldier laddie, it had been a herd with his dogs who had found the body in the spring of the year. Then she heard them again, nearer this time, and then, silently as a ghost a black and white dog lollopped into her view, checked at the sight of her and barked. Two whistled notes came out of the whiteness and the dog vanished in response. Janet realised her good fortune slowly because she was numb with cold and weariness.

"Herd! Herd!" she called out rather feebly, "Can you tell me where to find a house?"

Her voice seemed to be whirled away on the wind and she tried again. The dog materialised at her feet again, barking purposefully and the bleating sounded nearer. A figure loomed out of the whirling whiteness: tall, broad and made to look broader by the plaid wrapped about his body and shoulders. He wore an old-fashioned broad bonnet pulled well down over his face and there was a crook in his hand. He put it out in her direction almost as if to ward her off and Janet remembered the tale of the white fairy, the ban sidhe who foretold death. Her plaid and skirt were white with snow and her aspect ghostly enough, she didn't doubt, and she had life enough in her to chuckle at the idea of being taken for a ghost. It was that chuckle which persuaded the herd that she was real and human. He had his own reasons for expecting the ban sidhe.

He addressed her in the Gaelic, coming closer and peering at her. The dog vanished at a gesture and the bleating presences pressed more closely round them.

"I haven't the two tongues," said Janet apologetically, "I'm from Loch Lomondside."

The herd spoke again.

"I wass asking what you are doing here by your nainsel'. It is ten mile to Tyndrum and wicked weather in it."

"The train is broken down and stopped," Janet explained. "I

went to find shelter for the night. I didn't know how far we were from houses."

The herd put out his hand in a thick knitted mitt and took her basket.

"Best you are coming to my house," he said, "my wife iss sick but you can care for yourself I dare say. It is a mile or two yet but Borb will take us . . . and the sheep, poor beasts."

They moved off at the slow pace of the flock and he put himself on the weather side of her, screening her from the worst of the blizzard. Borb appeared and reappeared chivvying the sheep along in front of them. They seemed to be following a track or road because the snow lay thinly under their feet, blown away by the wind, and there were no harrassing clumps of heather.

"What road is this?" she asked as they plodded along.

"The old road of the cattle," he said, "in the days of the black cattle the men of the Isles wass driving their beasts to the tryst at Crieff by this road. My house iss may be a half mile beyond."

That last half mile seemed endless to Janet: they were at the house before she could see it, a long narrow thatched building crouched under a burden of snow. The herd thrust open a low door and put her basket inside.

"My wife iss sick," he repeated, "go you in and dry yourself. I must see to the sheeps."

He nodded and turned the corner of the little building.

Inside it was dark. A faint glow indicated a dying fire. Janet moved towards it gratefully and found peats in a basket and a handful of dry heather kindling. In a minute or so the heather blazed up and she built a wall of peats about it. In the light it cast she saw a lamp on a hook above the table and a jar of paper spills on the chimney-piece. She reached for the heavy, polished brass object and lifted it down. A shake indicated it was full of oil; the chimney was clean. The heavy oil smell reminded her of the kitchen at Glenfoot. The light it gave revealed a small, rather bare, stone-floored room: a small table stood in front of the one small window and on it a huge brass-clasped, leatherbound Bible. Under the lamp was a round pedestal table and two home-made chairs. The only other furniture was a dark oak dresser as old as the house with a litter of baskets and wooden berrycombs on the rack below and blue-patterned plates standing on the shelves above the two wooden armchairs with patchwork cushions on either side of a plaited rag rug which lay in front of the fire.

Janet was warming her hands and crouching over the growing fire when she heard a rustle of movement behind her. She spun around and saw that there was a box-bed set in the wall opposite the fire and a woman peering at her from the shadowed interior.

# 11

"Co?"

The voice was hoarse and feeble.

"My name's Janet, mistress. I was caught in the snow and your man brought me."

Janet moved to the bed and looked at the occupant. She was comparatively young, not much older than Janet herself, but her eyes were huge and sunken and her face seemed all bone.

"The man of the house," she said in English, "he was telling you I was sick?"

"Yes," Janet agreed.

The woman in the bed lay back on the pillow.

"My stomach," she said, "it is a sickness in my stomach. Can you be getting yourself a bite to eat?"

Janet considered the comfortless untidy bed.

"Let me make you more comfortable," she said. "Are you warm enough?"

"The man of the house will see to me."

Janet did not insist. The kettle on the swee was nearly empty so she filled it with the dipper from the bucket and swung it over the fire. The meal girnel stood at the end of the dresser and she measured out enough for brose into two of the blue delft bowls and set another handful to soak for gruel. When that was done she took off her wet plaid and replaced it with a dry shawl from her bundle. Her wet boots she removed and set to dry beside the dresser and padded about in stocking soles. The gruel was drained into the only saucepan and she thickened it gently at the edge of the fire and then poured it into a bowl. There were horn spoons in the dresser drawer.

"Can you fancy a bowl of gruel, mistress?" asked Janet.

The woman in the bed sat up slowly and peered at the steaming bowl.

"Gruel?" she said.

"Aye. Smooth as cream I promise you."

The sick woman took the bowl and the spoon, propped herself against the wall and began to eat.

Janet set out the blue bowls on the table and was wondering how long she could wait for the herd to come when in he came with a swirl of snow about him and Borb at his heels. He had a pail in his hand, half full of milk. Janet, remembering how Betsy greeted Dick, poured hot water from the kettle into a wooden tub and put it on the dresser with a linen towel she had found on a string above the fireplace. He gave an approving grunt, hung his soaking plaid to drip behind the door, added cold water to the tub and, fetching soap from the fireside press, washed his face and hands. When he had dried himself the brose was ready, steaming on the table with a jugful of the warm fresh milk beside it and a lump of butter. The rest of the milk was now in a broad earthenware pan setting before the fire.

Janet ate ravenously of the brose and the new milk and felt that she had never tasted anything so delicious. The sick woman held out her empty bowl and her husband took it from her with an approving look. The meal was eaten in silence except for a muttered blessing asked before the spoons were lifted. When it was over and the dishes washed, the herd reached for a pipe from the mantelshelf, filled it and sat down. Janet set the tub on the table for his wife to wash and had her out of the frowsty bed with a shawl round her. There was fresh bed-linen in a bothy kist at the bottom of the press so she made up the bed with clean sheets and refilled the earthenware het-piggie she had found among the blankets. The sick woman returned waveringly and Janet helped her in and made her comfortable.

When she had emptied the tub and the chamberpot outside the herd puffed out a cloud of smoke and spoke at last.

"Can you be sleeping among the hay in the loft?" he asked, "it's warm up there above the beasts and we have just one bed. There's bedding in the kist, a pillow and mebbe two-three blankets."

Janet agreed willingly to this arrangement, her whole body crying out to lie down and rest and never mind where.

* * *

In the morning she climbed down the rickety ladder, stiff and sore, to find the breakfast ready on the table and the herd sitting beside his wife on a creepie stool. Janet apologised for oversleeping and the herd shook his head.

"Tired you must be," he said, "and no wonder."

He indicated the porridge steaming on the table and Janet sat down muttering her thanks. The pair watched her eat in silence.

"Mistress," said the herd when she had finished, "I am Lachlan MacAllan and this is my wife Ealasaidh."

"And I . . ."

Janet paused.

"Janet, they cry me," she said and hastily borrowed Betsy's maiden name, "Janet McLaren."

"Aye," said Lachlan, "you'd be meeting somebody at Stirling, likely?"

Janet shook her head.

"I was for Stirling," she agreed, "but there's no one looking out for me. No one to fret."

There was another short silence.

"You would be looking for a situation, likely?"

Janet nodded.

"Would you be considering staying here with us a whilie?" Lachlan went on. "We're in sore need with Ealasaidh sick and there's a penny or two put by will make it worth your while."

"Chust till I am well," said Ealasaidh. "Fine I know it is dreich here for a young one with nobody passing. A few weeks, chust."

Janet looked at Lachlan. His face was without expression but in its very stoniness was the information Janet expected. Ealasaidh was never to get well. For a man like that to ask a chance-met stranger to stay indicated the greatness of his need.

"I am from the north," he explained, "and have no folk hereabout and . . ."

"They are thinking down there that it is a witch I am," Ealasaidh interrupted and chuckled.

"Woman of the house, be silent," he told her harshly.

"If she is to stay, then she must know."

They looked at Janet for a moment.

"And are you so?" Janet enquired smiling.

Ealasaidh smiled back.

"And if I am, are you feart?"

Janet shook her head.

"Then you are for staying?"

"I am."

Lachlan's face did not change but he brought his fist down on the palm of his hand with a great smack. Ealasaidh leaned back into the bed recess with an expression of relief.

"Well," said Janet and she began to gather up the porridge bowls, "time you were off to your work, Lachlan, and high time I was at mine."

As she went about the cottage that day discovering what was to be done she considered her decision. Accidentally she had come upon the perfect hiding place: no one would be likely to search for her in this remote spot. If people near by were curious about her, she could be a cousin of Lachlan's from the South. The hue and cry for her could not echo as far as this moorland and even if it did Lachlan and his wife needed her help badly enough to keep her secret if she asked them. Ealasaidh was at the fire as she came to this conclusion, her hands held out to the blaze and comfortable enough with an upturned creel for a footstool and a nest of pillows and blankets. Janet was combing the long dark hair.

"So you are a runaway?" said Ealasaidh suddenly.

Janet jumped and dropped the comb.

"You are so a witch!" she exclaimed.

Ealasaidh chuckled.

"I may be," she said, "but there is plenty to see for those who have eyes."

She reached for Janet's left hand.

"You are married."

She tapped the broad gold ring and then spread out the white fingers with their carefully shaped nails.

"And it is a long time since you worked with your hands . . . so, you are married to a rich man."

She pushed up Janet's sleeve and pointed to the now blue bruises along the inside of her arm then patted her swollen face.

"And someone has mishandled you sore."

Janet pulled her arm away.

"And McLaren is not your name," Ealasaidh went on. "And

how is it, will you be telling me, that anyone as bonnie as yourself should be wanting to hide away in such a place as this."

Janet began to plait the hair.

"You may not be a witch," she observed drily, "but I can understand how folks might think you were."

Ealasaidh laughed again, but said no more until Janet set about the baking.

"You may have married a silver spoon," said she, "but you had none in your mouth when you were born."

Jane smiled and shook her head over the baking board. Later she removed her wedding ring.

Few newspapers came to that remote place but Lachlan told Janet that Mr Duguid the minister received six copies of the *Scotsman* by the carrier once a week on a Wednesday. Having learned this she made it her business to walk down to the village on Thursday morning to visit the dark and smelly Jennie-a'-things which was kept in one of the low stone cottages which lined the wide road. There she bought certain items, including four ounces of Lachlan's fierce tobacco, and enquired for a newspaper. She was advised to 'spier at the Minister's sister' and thereupon bore a determined attempt to discover why she should want such an unchancy thing as a newspaper with smiling and uninformative politeness. She did, however, take the opportunity to explain that she was Lachie's cousin come to nurse Lachie's wife and was rewarded by a keen curious glance.

"So you are up there with that one," said the old woman, "she has the Sight, so they say."

"And so have we all, if we look carefully enough," said Janet and handed her the coins. "Good day to you."

Miss Duguid was a middle-aged grey-haired woman with a slightly harassed air. She was in the kitchen supervising a baking of scones when Janet tapped on the back door of the manse and she listened to Janet's request with only half her attention as she kept a platoon of maurauding hens at bay.

"I'm throng," she said, and Janet warmed to the accents of her own lowlands, "but go your ways into the Minister's study and you'll find them on the table. Little enough time either of us has to read them. I put half of them past unopened. Down the lobby there . . . first door on your right."

She aimed a shrewd kick at the boldest of the hens, shut the door and returned to her scones.

The study smelt of tobacco and mouldering books and was achingly cold, but on the table lay six newspapers. Janet began to look through them and came on the item she was expecting almost at once.

DISAPPEARANCE OF PEER'S WIFE

> We regret to report that Lady Staindrop, wife of Lord Staindrop who recently acquired a large interest in Fox, McIan, Son and Laidlaw, Shipbuilders, has disappeared from the Torridon shooting-box of Lord and Lady Ellis-Martin.
>
> Shepherds and gillies and the male guests at Drumore Castle have been out on the moors in the most inclement weather searching for Lady Staindrop, who was last seen taking the path which leads to the moors . . .

This puzzled Janet a trifle.

> . . . so far they have found no trace of her and in consequence of the recent unseasonable and severe weather the gravest fears are being entertained for her safety. The police at Oban are anxious to question Seonaidh McAllister who left her employment at the castle on the same day and Sergeant Deuchars has travelled to London with Lord Staindrop in order to question a military gentleman who left the houseparty to rejoin his regiment on the day the disappearance was discovered.

The remainder of the item consisted of a list of the guests at the houseparty and a catalogue of the various bags made during the previous fortnight on the Drumore moor. Evidently the *Scotsman's* 'man in the West' combined the role of police correspondent with that of Society columnist. Janet looked quickly through subsequent issues but could find no more. She replaced the papers as she had found them, thanked Miss Duguid, who bade her welcome to read the paper anytime she might wish, and left to return to the cottage.

As she walked the six miles to her refuge she considered what she had read. It seemed likely that if she did not reappear her death would be presumed . . . once Staindrop was satisfied that she had not eloped with Pelham-Villiers. She paused, looking across the bleak landscape to consider the consequences of such a presumption. With a surge of bitterness she came to the conclusion that while Jock and Betsy and Dick might grieve for her and Aramintha and Phoebe would miss her for a space (till both were safely married) there was no one else to be greatly affected. Hannah's use for her was now less and her affection was superficial at best. She could not forget that her father had closed his eyes deliberately to the way that Staindrop had mistreated her under his own roof. To Janet it seemed plain that his partnership was more to him than she would ever be. If she were dead he might feel some grief but it would be tempered with relief that no threat now existed to the partnership. As for the rest of her acquaintance they would forget that she had ever existed within the month. At the thought of her husband she shuddered: her face was still painful enough to remind her that he had tried to kill her (as she believed). It seemed a fair enough conclusion that once he was certain she was not cuckolding him he would rejoice. It was as well he respected the conventions enough to wait some time before seeking yet another heir breeder. By now she knew that few of the Mamas would welcome his attentions. If, as seemed likely, any version of the events at Drumore became known in Society he would be regarded warily indeed. It was scarcely a recommendation to have two wives run from him. She might be easy about his remarriage for a time. To 'die' would give her breathing space, time to decide what to do. It would mean that no one would be looking for her; she could rest in peace indeed, inasmuch as she could sleep at night. She walked on, having decided that she would not inform anyone of her survival.

Perhaps Janet was a little harsh: it is not always wise to judge how people feel about you by the way they treat you. It was certain she underestimated the anxiety and distress which her disappearance was bound to cause, possibly because she underestimated the affection which people had for her. She forgot about Jasper and Aunt Matilda, who both loved her in their fashion. She had been hurt and trapped and frightened and her instinct was to lie low and play dead, like a fawn in a brake. It was a slightly more adult version of the childish plaint, 'when I'm dead they'll be sorry'. Nor did she consider at this point, how difficult it might be to 'come back to life'. About Simon she had tried to train herself not to think at all but halfway back to the cottage she had a sudden picture of him discussing the item in the *Scotsman* across the breakfast table with his handsome bride. She wondered bitterly if he would realise that the Lady Staindrop in that paragraph was Janet, that unsophisticated rustic with whom he had enjoyed a brief holiday encounter.

However, in one matter at least she was completely at fault: her husband was undergoing a singularly uncomfortable interlude. Like every other guest at Drumore Staindrop had immediately linked Janet's disappearance with Pelham-Villier's departure. The letter which he had found gave him real grounds for such a presumption and he took little interest in the search which was organised. His fellow guests considered it face-saver only and the 'book' was closed and monies paid (a circumstance which was to cause some acrimony later). Staindrop, rattling southwards in the London train, felt angry and humiliated, not alarmed. He was confident that Janet would be discovered under Pelham-Villiers's protection either in London or in some continental resort. Staring out at the bleak November landscape he savoured the letter he had written to John Laidlaw before he left the castle in which he had vented his feelings in a mélange of incoherent abuse and wild threats. He had promised to spare Janet nothing; had blamed her behaviour on her low origins and ill-breeding; had declared his intention of realising his interest in Fox, McIan, Son and Laidlaw without delay in order to sever once and for all any connection with such an ill-omened family. The contemplation of John Laidlaw's chagrin when he read this epistle comforted Staindrop a trifle as his train huffed sullenly into Euston Station. Another consolation was the prospect of confronting the guilty couple at some point in the very near future.

His man of law was less sanguine about such a confrontation. He, like many of his fellow-lawyers, had come to regard Pelham-Villiers as a kind of recurrent decimal in Society's matrimonial causes, but so far none of them had been able actually to cite the gallant captain in any of these causes. In fact Mr Bagley was accustomed to describe him, when in discreet legal company, as a 'deuced slippery customer'. Staindrop's brusque demand that he track down the guilty pair at once he greeted with pursed lips and raised eyebrows. Even the letter did not cheer him.

"It is our experience, my Lord," he observed, "that this is more easily said than done and while this letter may constitute an invitation to . . . er . . . misconduct, we have no proof that Lady Staindrop did in fact accept it."

Staindrop spluttered indignantly.

"These are hardly grounds, my Lord, to base such a . . ."

"Grounds! Grounds!" bellowed Staindrop, "The letter, what more grounds d'ye need?"

Mr Bagley stood *his* ground.

"I am bound to observe, m'Lord," he observed, his hands joined at the finger-tips and his eyes considering his client's disordered cravat, "that Lady Staindrop did not seem to me the kind to . . . as you might say . . . throw her cap over the windmill."

"Much you know about it," growled Staindrop. "Get your people on to it without delay."

Mr Bagley shrugged and acquiesced.

However, his report a week later was highly unsatisfactory. His informants reported, so he told Staindrop with a certain amount of concealed pleasure, that Captain Pelham-Villiers was living a bachelor existence.

Staindrop snorted his disbelief. Mr Bagley coughed gently and added a particularly galling piece of information.

"You might not be aware, m'lord, but I have been told, and very reliably, that Captain Pelham-Villiers has himself been making extensive enquiries into the present whereabouts of Lady Staindrop. His intimates say he is most exercised in his mind about her safety."

Staindrop glared at him.

"It would appear that he did expect her to meet him in Town," Mr Bagley continued, "and when she did not do this he was worried and distressed and gave orders to his man of business . . . who is by way of being a friend of mine . . . to prosecute a discreet search in the North."

He glanced at his client, who looked stunned.

"A search which has had no result."

Staindrop grunted incredulously and returned to the Queensgate house where his mood was not improved by a brief, dry note from his father-in-law who demanded concrete proofs of his daughter's defection, displayed a disquieting knowledge of Staindrop's deficiencies as a husband, and ended by telling him that whereas he had no power to prevent Staindrop's selling his holding in Fox, McIan, Son and Laidlaw the shares were at present at rock-bottom and likely to remain so. The rumour Laidlaw had so carefully set about to produce this result, he did not repeat. Staindrop cursed, crumpled the single sheet and hurled it at his valet who came in with the brandy decanter.

As the days passed and Janet did not reappear, Society began reluctantly to question the correctness of its conclusions. Pelham-Villiers was giving a spirited impression of a heart-broken man and it was whispered that he had lived in unbroken celibacy for close on a month. A number of versions of the events which had taken place on the eve of Janet's disappearance began to circulate and Staindrop, feeling a distinct drop in the temperature of his social surroundings, decided it was time to see how matters were in Derbyshire. He was far from pleased to find that they were in an excellent way.

He arrived to find the house humming with preparation for Aramintha's wedding, with guests arriving by every train and Aunt Matilda presiding over the festivities with a grim spine-chilling good humour. Not only that, but as Laidlaw refused to leave Glasgow, Staindrop found himself required to give the bride away. Hannah had had something of a disagreement with her husband over the matter.

"It will present a very odd appearance if you are not present," she informed him chillily.

"It will seem odder if I do come," he retorted. "I'm damned if I'll stay under that man's roof after all I've heard."

"Rumours and exaggerations," said Hannah reprovingly, "the merest backstairs gossip. To stay away merely gives credence to such reports and can do nothing but harm."

John Laidlaw removed the pipe from his mouth.

"I'll not go, woman. Save your breath. Those letters he wrote about Janet were not rumour. Nor was his trying to persuade Loughton to pull out."

The backer Staindrop had found had resisted his neighbour's persuasion to remove his money from the yard.

"A perfectly natural indignation in the circumstances . . . he thought himself very much injured when he wrote them."

"And I considered myself much injured when I received them," he returned. "Forby, with the way he's behaving over the business I've too much in hand to leave it."

This was true. He was in the process of buying Staindrop out by means of a complicated network of nominees while the share prices of the yard were still low. The news of two new contracts, one for a new Atlantic passage-boat, he was keeping secret until this necessary task was completed. For this reason he was conducting all the negotiations himself and this involved much work. However, he refused to admit to Hannah or even to himself that he still hoped that Janet might appear on his doorstep as she had done when she first came to Glasgow. Her set face when she left in the cab for Torridon haunted him more than he cared to acknowledge.

However, Hannah entertained none of her husband's qualms.

"I made sure, my dear Philip," said Hannah at the first opportunity, "that you would not wish to give further matter for the slanders going about by cancelling dear Aramintha's wedding. We both know what people would say if we were seen to be at outs. And what better way could there be to keep the gossips at bay than for you to stand sponsor for Aramintha?"

She tapped him playfully with her fan.

"We older people have to keep an eye to these things, you know," she confided, "life has to go on. I feel for sure that dear Janet has simply decided to take a little rest from Society. She was not bred to this life and you and I were, you know. She would not want us to spoil dear Aramintha's great day on her account."

Staindrop acquiesced, sulkily and ungraciously.

Nor had Janet cause to worry about Phoebe. It was Aunt Matilda who solved her problem. Among the wedding guests was young Mr Appleyard, and Hannah was blatant about providing opportunities for him to 'speak his heart', as she put it. The night before the wedding Staindrop had taken refuge in his study and was making inroads on the brandy and most of the other guests were either playing cards or knocking the balls about in the billiard room. Mr Appleyard, Hannah, Aunt Matilda and Phoebe were gathered in the music room. At the start there had been one or two of the younger guests but they had been dispatched by Hannah on one pretext or another and Aramintha had been sent to bed to get her beauty sleep. Phoebe had been persuaded to play an affecting piece for the pianoforte which purported to describe the Siege of Vienna. Under cover of the thundering, if hesitant, arpeggios in the bass (gunfire) Hannah suggested to Aunt Matilda that tomorrow would be a long and tiring day.

"Not for me," responded the old woman, "I don't intend to raise a finger. Leave that to you and that Summers woman."

Gunfire gave way to a cavalry charge and Hannah had to raise her voice over the galumphing chords.

"You must be tired," she bellowed.

"Stuff!" retorted Aunt Matilda.

"Would you care for tea in your room?"

"If I did, I'd ask for it."

Hannah leaned forward.

"Might as well leave them to themselves," she urged, just as the galloping hooves gave way to twittering birds in the Vienna woods at dawn (trills in the treble) and both young people looked at her in surprise and embarrassment. Phoebe made a crashing discord and blushed an unbecoming scarlet. Young Appleyard looked down his elegant acquiline nose.

"Waste of time," said Aunt Matilda, "you don't see what's under your nose. Girl doesn't want to marry him. Got someone else in her eye I wouldn't wonder."

Hannah swallowed her wrath and discomfiture.

"Dear Aunt," she cooed, "always so droll."

Aunt Matilda gave her a look of contempt.

"Droll!" she snorted. "What d'ye take me for? A pet parrot?"

Truth to tell she did indeed have the look of a bird but it was more vulturine than psittacine.

"Girl!" she demanded.

In six months she had not succeeded in learning which was Phoebe and which Aramintha and she addressed them both impartially in this fashion.

"Girl! If this young fellow-me-lad popped would you say yes?"

Phoebe went a little pale and then looked defiantly at her mother. She knew if this chance was lost there would never be another.

"No, Aunt Matilda."

The old woman chuckled.

"Sensible girl," she approved, and then turned on the unfortunate Appleyard and poked him painfully with her jet-studded fan. "Dunno if you'd intended to pop, young fellow, but if y'do my advice to yer is don't."

With which masterly resolution of the situation she retired to her room and rang for her customary night-cap, which was not a fiddle-faddling cup of tea but a glass of brandy with hot water and lemon.

"So droll always . . ." Hannah began lightly with a steely determination to mend the situation. She turned her batteries upon young Appleyard, but he hastily bade them both a polite good night and retired to his room where he considered Aunt Matilda's advice and found it good. To be rejected is never pleasant and young Mr Appleyard had sufficient *amour propre* not to invite it. He stayed for the wedding but avoided both Phoebe and her mother and left as soon as he might.

Downstairs Phoebe wept absentmindedly as her mother animadverted on her the hard lot of widowed mothers, her folly in whistling such a catch down the wind, and her ingratitude. Warming to her subject Hannah painted a grim picture of Phoebe's immediate future and cited Aunt Matilda as a fearful example of what she might become if she persisted in this lunacy. What was Phoebe going to do, Hannah enquired dramatically, when she had brought her mother's grey hairs in sorrow to the grave. Did she wish to end her days starving in an attic? And did she expect another London season with Janet playing fast and loose in this inconsiderate fashion and her dear John fixed in Glasgow (a touch of acid informed her voice at this point) like a limpet to a rock. She would have to content herself with some provincial if, indeed, she could manage to land one. Phoebe, her mind in India, suffered these predictions in tearful silence which so exasperated her mother that she was forced to dismiss her unsatisfactory daughter to bed as if she were still six years old.

At the reception Aunt Matilda slashed yet another Gordian knot. After it had been in full cry for an hour she peered round the crowded room at the guests.

"Young fellow-me-lad gone?" she enquired in piercing tones of Phoebe who was sheltering under her lee as a yacht might take refuge under the guns of a battleship.

"Yes, Aunt."

Aunt Matilda nodded.

"Did he pop?"

"No, Aunt."

Aunt Matilda gave her a painful blow with her fan in token of appreciation.

"Mama kickin' up a dust, is she?"

"Mama is a little displeased with me," admitted Phoebe.

"I'll lay she is."

The old lady peered at her.

"Tell the truth, girl. Who is he? And don't prevaricate."

She emphasised this with another blow from the fan.

"He's a missionary, Aunt. In India."

Aunt Matilda gave a snort of contempt which rattled the display of Prickett silver on the sideboard.

"Missionary!" said she, "a missionary. I've no opinion of them."

Phoebe went slightly pink.

"It is *my* opinion that signifies, surely?"

The old woman considered her, her eyes narrowed.

"Oho! Mama has left us some spirit, has she?"

A third blow from the fan followed, harder than before, and Phoebe winced slightly.

"India, eh?" said Aunt Matilda reflectively and turned her head like a vulture searching for a likely corpse until she saw the bridegroom, trim and handsome in his regimentals.

"A soldier . . . now, that I can understand," she muttered, "but a niminy-piminy, namby-pamby, psalm-singing . . ."

Her hand shot out and grabbed Phoebe's skirt.

"Stay here, girl," she commanded and at length caught young Marshall's eye. He said later that he had actually felt hers drill into his back. She beckoned to him with her fan in a manner which left no room for misunderstanding her wishes, or thwarting them for the matter of that. Young Abram, who had conceived a liking for the formidable old lady, came over at once.

"Yes, ma'am?" he enquired.

"That girl, y'wife," said Aunt Matilda, "not much more than a babe."

"Yes, ma'am," he agreed, smiling, "I feel I'm robbing the cradle."

"You'll be goin' back to your regiment, I suppose?"

Abram nodded.

"Immediately, ma'am. They're at Dehra Dun."

"You'll be busy, I don't doubt. You're a duty officer . . . none of yer pups on the staff?"

"Very busy, ma'am . . . we've a hundred recruits to put through their paces."

"Whatsername . . . Araminta . . . what'll she do while you're busy?"

Abram frowned.

"I presume she'll do what the other wives do."

Aunt Matilda snorted again and a number of heads turned at the uncouth noise.

"Guzzle, gossip, get fat and get into mischief, eh?"

She emphasised this suggestion by a home thrust from the fan just above the third shining brass button of his red coat. Abram withstood this assault in the best tradition of the British Army only gasping very slightly.

"I'm afraid you're right . . . in some cases," he admitted.

"What she'll need is a companion."

Abram's expression became alert.

"Ah," he said softly, "yes. I agree. I had hoped to ask Phoebe to join us later. For a cold weather, perhaps."

"Stuff," said Aunt Matilda, "when d'ye sail?"

"In a week."

"Take the girl with you."

Abram's expression was a mixture of consternation, dismay and a consciousness that it was neither kind not polite to let such emotions show before Phoebe.

"Aunt, I can't . . ." protested Phoebe at this ruthless ordering of her future. "You can't ask them to take me with them on their wedding trip!"

"Do them good not to live in one another's pockets for the whole journey. Sickly stuff! You'll prevent them getting tired of their own company."

It would be wrong to say that Aunt Matilda carried her point there and then but nevertheless when the bridal pair clattered down the drive in old Abe's elegant new barouche drawn by a team of matched chestnuts which drew gasps of envy from most of the male guests present, Phoebe stood pledged to join them in five days at Tilbury docks and a letter requesting a cabin for her had already gone to the post. With it had gone another to her Robert expressing her delight incoherently and illegibly and telling him that before very long she would be landing at Bombay.

# 12

THE WINTER HAD begun early and it lasted long. Twice the meal ran short and Lachlan struggled down through the drifts to fetch more. Janet's hands reddened and swelled with the cold and her nails cracked and broke. The cottage lost its comfortless look as she contrived curtains and cushions. Lachlan, kept within doors by the wicked weather, made a day-bed for Ealasaidh and Janet padded it with sheep-fells so that the invalid could spend more time out of the dark box-bed. She also relieved Lachlan of the outdoor work about the house and took the old cow in charge. There was a scatter of hens too and she learned their laying places so that Ealasaidh could have the egg-nogs which, as the months passed, came to be all that she could stomach. A time came soon after Ne'erday when the move from box-bed to day-bed became too much of an ordeal and she stayed on the day-bed both day and night. Twice when there was a brief thaw the doctor from Dalmally drove up in his battered trap and examined her, chatting cheerfully, not to say libellously, about the people in the district. The second time he came Janet followed him out to the trap and he gave her a big blue bottle.

"It'll be a hard passage, lass," he told her, and there was no cheerfulness in his face then. "This is laudanum. I've written the instructions on the label but . . ."

He hesitated.

". . . don't stint her when she needs it. If you need more send Lachie. I'll look inby again soon."

He drove away and before the hard weather closed in again the Minister tramped up to the cottage, looking like an older version of Lachie himself in plaid and bonnet, thick knitted stockings and moor boots. He came into the kitchen while Janet was preparing the dinner and introduced himself brusquely.

"James Duguid, Minister of this parish. You'll be Lachlan's cousin Janet, I doubt."

Janet dispelled the doubt and began to unwrap the Reverend Mr Duguid, who appeared, when divested of plaid, ulster and a series of knitted comforters, to be a spare man in his fifties with a rather grim, grey eye. Janet plied him with tea and scones from the girdle and listened to his conversation with Ealasaidh approvingly. He made a short prayer for her recovery and then settled down to give her the gossip of the district. Ealasaidh was too weak to respond much but she evidently enjoyed the Minister's astringent view of his parishioners. He came to the end of a scurrilous anecdote about one crofter, notoriously close-fisted, who had postponed his marriage thirty years until he could find him a weel-tochered may and had recently wed a wealthy widow who was now leading him a life of it, made an acid comment on the love of money and reached for the big brass-clasped Bible.

"Lachie'll not object if I read a bittie out of his regular daily stint?" he said with a twinkle.

Lachlan read aloud three chapters before bed every night and three extra on Sunday. He had begun on Leviticus 7 the night Janet arrived and was now making his way through the second book of Samuel and nothing, neither the genealogy of Kings nor the heathenish customs of the early fathers would deflect him. Mr Duguid turned to the Psalms and read the twenty-third psalm in comfortable matter-of-fact manner which took its high promise for granted. After that he rose, asked a blessing and began to recocoon himself.

Janet set him on his way and saw his cheerfulness drop from him as his outer coverings had done.

"Puir lass," he said, and Janet saw a tear under the unsentimental grey eye, "even wi' paradise in prospect it is a cruel and unforgiving way to leave this world."

He stumped on a pace or two.

"There is a basket o' comforts . . . jellies and such . . . which my sister put up for her. I left them ahint the door. Send me the basket when opportunity offers. And gin she asks for me, send. I'll come some way."

The 'comforts' were of little use. Ealasaidh could take nothing but liquids and she grew weaker by the hour. Janet shifted her bed into the kitchen to be near at night, for the lambing had begun in the worst that a Highland spring could do and Lachlan was seldom at home. A half-dozen orphan lambs were added to Janet's cares, but Ealasaidh liked to watch them feed, smiling at their greed for the bottle.

Soon the pain which had attacked at intervals over the winter came to stay. Janet sent Lachlan to Dalmally for more laudanum and lambed a handful of scraggy ewes herself in the frank behind the cottage where she was in earshot of Ealasaidh's whistle. The snow vanished at last and there was heat in the sun, but Ealasaidh was obviously sinking. Lachlan went about his work but he kept near the cottage and he had less than ever to say.

One night Ealasaidh seemed a little better. The pain was less and she welcomed a spoonful of broth. She looked at Janet reaching for the blue glass bottle.

"Leave it a time," she whispered, "it is not living to be dreaming all the while."

Janet laid it past again and sat down on the chair, her hands in her lap.

"Shall I read to you?"

Among later baskets of 'comforts' brought by Mr Duguid had been books; not just works of devotion such as you might expect of a manse study, but novels. They had enjoyed Mrs Gaskell, Currer Bell and Mr Dickens during the winter nights; even Lachlan had listened, despite his suspicion of fiction, because Ealasaidh had forgotten her weakness in listening. This time she shook her head very slightly.

"What will you do?" she asked.

Janet did not pretend to misunderstand.

"I will go to the town," said she, "and find a situation."

"Would you not be staying with Lachlan?"

It was Janet's turn to shake her head.

"No," she said.

The winter had proved to her that it was not possible to go back. Once she might have married a farmer and lived all her days on a farm and been content. Now she could no longer face such a life. It was not the comfort she missed, or the luxury or the frivolities of Society, it was simply that she missed the sense of enlargement, of being in touch with the world. She could no longer lead the kind of life which Lachlan could offer her and be happy. Janet was not the kind of person to wonder whether this inability argued a deterioration or a development in her character but she could recognise facts. Almost as an afterthought she added, "I am married."

Ealasaidh smiled faintly and seemed about to say more when the pain caught her. However, she had said enough to jerk Janet into taking stock of her situation. The parallel with her mother's death struck her forcibly and reminded her of her mother's advice. For the first time she realised how accurately Elspeth had foreseen what would happen to her. This time, she promised herself, she would be ready.

The end could not be delayed; by the time it came no one could want to delay it, least of all Ealasaidh. Janet did her last service and played her unobtrusive part in the ceremonies which followed. People who had never come to see Ealasaidh in life came to see her dead and laid in her coffin, to eat and drink on the other side of the wall and follow the pony cart with the plain pine box upon it until they reached the low grey church.

When it was all over Janet walked back to the house with Lachlan, the six miles covered in silence. Once in the house Janet repacked her few possessions. Lachlan watched, still wordless. After a short while he reached into the box-bed and produced from a recess inside, a japanned box. From that he removed an old leather purse and counted out ten sovereigns which he held out to Janet, still without a word. Janet looked at the gold and shook her head.

"It's myself that kens fine," said Lachlan at last, "there is no gold in the whole wide world could pay you for what you have done."

He put the coins in a little heap on the table and from his jacket pocket brought out a little gold chain with a curiously shaped device hanging from it; a triangle made out of what looked like golden nails.

"Herself said you were to have this. You would not be feart at it, she said, and it would be a minding."

Janet stared at the trinket.

"She was an Egyptian, then? I wondered."

"Aye, a gypsy," said Lachlan. "I met her at the horsefair at Strathpeffer and there was never no one else for either of us. My folk was wild-angry and hers no better so we came South. But the folk here . . . they never took to her, nor she to them."

"What will you do now?" asked Janet, her eyes on the day-bed pushed against the wall.

Lachlan looked at it as well.

"It's chust the two months to my term and I will be going North again. My father's at the fishing and needs a hand."

He pushed the little heap of coins at Janet.

"We saved to put a bairn to the school and then to the college maybe, but there was never no bairn. You have it Janet, I've little wish for that money. For a lass alone a little siller can be a protection and herself would have liked fine for you to have it."

He gave her, besides, several treasured items of Ealasaidh's wardrobe; a set of lace collar and cuffs of fragile point lace which might have graced the Chevalier's ball in Edinburgh, a linen petticoat heavy with crocheted flounces, a shawl of Indian silk so fine it would slide through a wedding ring, patterned in colours which glowed like jewels in that dimly lit little room. To these he added a heavy grey silk dress and a pair of barbaric gold earrings and a woven straw double basket to hold them all. As she buckled the straps around this he stared down at her.

"It is not easy for me," he said, "not easy at all to say what is in my heart . . . but I am glad it is yourself will have these little things of hers. She loved you. And . . ."

He swallowed and turned away.

"My ways were not always her ways. My Faith lies in the Book and in my Redeemer. I have no wish to traffic with . . . other powers."

He hesitated.

"But she laid it upon me. She dreamed for you. I was to tell you . . ."

He frowned into the dying peats.

"There are three dead, she said, and two must be recalled before the fankle's undone . . . but when there's life there's hope. The chain will fall off."

Janet stared at him in bewilderment.

"What did she mean?"

"She said you would know that better than I. I have done as I promised. It is all over."

His voice sounded as bleak as the north wind.

He went with her as far as the drove road and she was conscious of his standing motionless and watching her out of sight as if her departure was the real end of the day's ritual for him. After she turned the shoulder of the hill she thought of him returning to that quiet house with the empty room and wondered whether Ealasaidh lingered there for him and if he put her from his mind because of his stern rejection of those 'other powers'. She grieved bitterly for him.

Before she caught the train to Lochearnhead there was time to call on Mr Duguid as he had requested. Once again she knocked on the back door and the clerical hens strutted and clucked about her ankles. Miss Duguid answered her knock, this time less distrait and rather more welcoming. She admitted Janet through a narrow aperture designed to limit the hens' sphere of activity and latched the door on an intrusive beak.

"Whiles I think I'd do better to buy my eggs from Mistress Moir. These creatures, they'd roost on the Minister's own chair if I'd let them."

This time the Minister's study was almost warm and he was writing at his desk. Miss Duguid ushered Janet in.

"Miss McLaren, James."

The Minister rose and shook her hand for the second tme that day. He pointed to a chair.

"Sit down, lass, sit down . . . you look worn to a thread. Libby, perhaps a cup of tea?"

Miss Duguid disappeared and could be heard giving orders in the kitchen. Her brother rootled among his papers.

"You mentioned you might look for a situation in town," he said.

"Yes."

"If you would consider going to Perth I might be able to be of service to you. I was in a charge there for many years and have a wide acquaintance."

Perth. For Simon's sake she was prepared to think it a pleasant town. Besides, it was not far, barely an hour in the train. She wondered if she might see Simon in the street once in a while. It was a small place, not like Glasgow or London.

"That would be very kind of you. Thank you."

Mr Duguid peered at her anxiously.

"Lassie, you look fair no weel . . ."

"It's been a long day," she admitted.

"And a hard winter," he added. "You'll bide here with us till the morning train."

Janet found herself petted and cossetted and put to bed in a chilly room which smelt of new-ironed linen and lavender. In the morning she came down to find that both host and hostess were already out. Mr Duguid had set forward on an eight-mile walk to visit a sick woman at the other end of the parish and his sister Libby was bullying a newly-delivered mother in a tiny air-less room behind the smiddy. On the breakfast table was a sealed envelope with an address on it. And underneath was a message on a scrap of paper.

> This good lady was a member of my congregation in Perth. She has a large circle of acquaintance and may know of a suitable situation for you. God bless you and go with you. J.D.

Beside these was a bundle of newspapers with advertisements underlined. Jinty the manse servant brought her tea and porridge and was disposed to linger, avid to hear about 'her upbye'. Partly to be rid of her, for she had no wish to talk about Ealasaidh, Janet opened one of the newspapers. Almost at once she saw a headline.

> TRAGIC DISCOVERY AT DRUMORE
>
> A body believed to be that of Lady Staindrop was yesterday discovered on Drumore Moor. It was accidentally come upon by a gamekeeper halfway down a steep slope below the path which leads over the hill to Oban. Evidently Lady Staindrop had wandered off the path during the untimely snow storm which occurred on the day of her disappearance, fallen and broken her limb and been unable to reach the path again. The corpse was in a poor state of preservation but has been identified by her next of kin from various articles found on and near the body. The funeral will be after the enquiry.

Janet looked blankly at the brief paragraph and could hear Lachlan's voice as he quoted his dead wife. 'There are three dead she said.' Here was one who would not be recalled. Sickened, Janet read the list of clothes and trinkets found by the corpse and recognised the things she had given to Seonaidh . . . and one or two that she had not. There could be no doubt whose corpse it was. Jinty returned with a boiled egg, spoil from those maurauding hens, and exclaimed at the guest's appearance.

"Mercy be here, mistress, you look like a ghost!"

Janet smiled faintly and looked again at the paragraph. It was an eerie feeling to be supposed dead.

"I don't wonder, I'm sure," she said.

Perth Station was a bustling place, a junction for every main line in Scotland. The platforms were thronged with hurrying passengers laden with travelling rugs and luncheon baskets. Porters clattered by with trolleys piled with luggage, trunks, hampers, gun-cases and rod-cases; lean men in homespun knickerbockers led gun-dogs about and abused them when they cringed from the noises, men leaned out of carriage windows and bellowed questions which were lost in a cacophony of clanking wheels and hissing steam. Janet, accustomed to silence and loneliness, found it confusing and alarming but was reassured by the ticket collector who lacked a leg, lost at Balaclava with the Black Watch. She enquired timidly how to reach Rose Terrace and he considered her and her bundle and her straw basket for a moment; then he jerked his head for her to stand aside while he dealt briskly with the remaining arrivals from the eastbound. When they had all departed, walking towards the town or hailing the cabs which waited in the station square, he nodded to Janet to follow him, and with his crutch under his arm he swung easily along to where they were unloading a parcels van.

"Gaun near Rose Terrace, Chic?" he asked of the youngster holding the head of a morose piebald horse.

"Aye," said Chic, "I've boxes o' books for the school."

"Can ye tak' this lassie?"

Chic considered his prospective passenger with enthusiasm.

"Aye!" he said roundly and spread a newspaper retrieved from a nearby bench on a corner of his dray.

"Sit you there, lassie," advised the old soldier and lifted her luggage on the vehicle before he helped her up. "Chic'll hae ye there inside hauf an 'oor . . . aye, an' he'll gie ye a' the clash forby."

He sketched a salute and swung off on his crutch before she could thank him properly.

The piebald, after some degree of blasphemous encouragement, hauled his burden through the arch and into the square. Chic swung himself on to the other corner of the dray and flourished a battered cartwhip in a meaningful way and the piebald heaved himself into a lumbering trot towards the West Port.

Perth town was nearly as busy as Perth Station. In South Street a herd of fat cattle, headed for the mart, were disputing passage with a variety of vehicles and the crossing at the West Port was jammed with lowing cattle and cursing carters. Chic picked his way dextrously among the mêlée and by dint of putting his near wheels on the pavement emerged into South Methven Street. They clopped past the handsome new buildings there and turned right and Janet got her first view of the North Inch, a wide expanse of green grass which bordered the Tay. It was dotted with white where linen had been spread to bleach and groups of women stood about with washing baskets on their hips and gossiped in the thin spring sunshine. In the centre was a group of children playing a game with bat and ball and all round the outside there ran a narrow strip of smooth close-clipped turf which Janet recognised as a race-course. She remarked on this and Chic nodded.

"A braw day, Race Day. The toun's fair packed wi' gentry an' that an' a' verry free wi' their siller . . . an' the horses is braw."

He clouted the piebald's rump with the butt of his whip to remind him of the business in hand and turned left.

Rose Terrace was a row of elegant stone houses which faced the river across the Inch. In the centre under a pediment in the Greek style a crowd of schoolboys was emerging, noisy and book-laden.

"Yon's the Academy skailin' for its denner," said Chic and looked tolerantly at the crowd which swarmed on both sides of the cart and hurled basic insults at Chic and his horse and his cart; at his passenger they stared and whistled. Chic grinned at them and made a sweeping gesture with his whip of which they took no notice whatsoever.

"You'd never think," he confided when the howling crew had gone hurtling towards the town, "that they laddies was frae a' the best families in the toun. Aye and there's some great folk in the country don't send their laddies to they English schools. It's a grand school, the Academy."

He doffed his bonnet to a tall figure in a tall hat who strode towards them, his hands clasped behind his back.

"Yon's the Rector himsel' . . ." Chic breathed reverently, "ma brither wis at the school, he's a clever lad and comin't oot tae be a minister an' he says yon lad can use the belt like a guid un."

The revered figure waved at them.

"Have you my new books, Gow?"

"Aye, sir."

"The janitor will take them in."

The Rector looked curiously at Janet, raised his hat and walked on. Chic indicated to the piebald which had taken advantage of the exchange to come to a halt that it was time to move on.

"Whit number dae ye want?"

"Seven."

"Mistress Frazer?"

"Aye," said Janet.

He drew up outside Number Seven and Janet looked curiously at the house. Outwardly it differed very little from others in the row: three floors and an attic lit by gracefully proportioned windows. A narrow 'area' under the steps which led to the front door gave light to a basement kitchen. She thanked Chic, who helped her off the dray and handed down the bundle and the straw basket before he headed back to the Academy and the waiting janitor.

Mistress Frazer was not helpful. She read Mr Duguid's note and sniffed.

"It is a number of years since I last heard from Mr Duguid," she said.

She examined Janet in the same captious manner and seemed no more impressed by her than she had been by the note.

"And have you any experience of good service?" she enquired, but it was plain from the outset that she considered it a forlorn hope. Janet, conscious that her experience was not quite what was intended by her inquisitor, made a poor hesitant job of her reply. Mistress Frazer sniffed again, this time in a final manner.

"I doubt I cannot think of anyone of my acquaintance who might have a situation to offer you."

The stress on the last word was faint but enough to sting.

"There might be some work at the George," she suggested grudgingly.

Janet came up the steps of the area into the terrace. It had been made very plain that servants or would-be servants did not make use of the front door. She paused, uncertain where to go next: should she try to find lodging and look for work in Perth or should she go to Glasgow. In some ways its would be easier to lie low in a big city. She knew a feeling of hopelessness and was tempted for a second to give up the whole charade and go back to Woodside; perhaps, after all, they would not try to send her back to Staindrop. Perhaps he would refuse to have her back. She thought of the commotion there would be, the reproaches and the sarcasm; of the newspapers and the sensation in London circles, and she flinched. Better to try to find work where she was and keep in hiding, for a time at least: as she walked across the wide North Inch she felt suddenly very alone.

At the George she found that a vacancy for a chambermaid had been filled less than an hour before and another was unlikely to occur. Her request for a night's lodging was received coldly and granted only when she produced a gold sovereign from her purse. The chambermaid who was sent for to show her to the tiny room under the attics where she was to sleep made no effort to carry her basket but whisked quickly up the staircase until they were out of earshot of the landlady.

"Here," said her guide, turning on the second landing, "is that right enough that I heard you asking for a situation?"

Janet nodded.

"It's myself just came here this very morning. Bridie's my name."

Janet put down the basket.

"Are you really wanting a situation?" asked Bridie. "Sure, if I was out of a job I'd not be wasting the ready staying in this place. They can't count in pennies here, you know, shillings and pounds is all they've heard of."

Janet agreed that she really wanted to find a post and Bridie cocked her head a little on one side.

"You could be after trying the place I just left," she suggested. "It might suit you. You look quiet-like . . . not like me."

She giggled.

"Where is this place?" Janet asked.

"It's with a Mrs Carnegie. Finicky she is, with one son and she thinks the sun shines out of his arse. Mind, she's a real slave driver; she's aye *at* you. You'd need the strength of a horse and the patience of the blessed saints themselves to work there long, so you would. Sure, wasn't I the fourth one to leave her in a sixmonth. Half the girls in the town have been there."

Janet noted down the address and set out to discover whether Mrs Carnegie would employ her. For the second time that day she found herself in Rose Terrace, this time outside Number Twenty-one. Profiting by her experience of the morning she knocked at the area door, was admitted grudgingly by a grim-faced lady's maid who, after a prolonged consultation behind closed doors, ushered her into a sunny little back parlour.

Janet found herself looking at a very small elderly lady who stood in the doorway, neat and composed, her mittened hands folded at her waist and a pair of mild blue eyes gazing over rather than through a pair of pince-nez which, unlike most of the breed, straddled her nose at the correct angle. She was dressed in the style of twenty years before in a hooped skirt and fringed dolman of black watered-silk. On her head was a formidable cap, laden with lappets and frills, immaculately gophered. From a waist still remarkably trim hung a chatelaine of worked silver on which were needlecase, thimble, scissors, pencil, ivory tablets and a bunch of keys which rivalled that of a jail turnkey.

"Good day?" said she enquiringly.

"Mistress Carnegie?"

The elderly lady nodded.

"I understand you require a parlour-maid. I would be pleased if you would consider me for the post."

The mild blue eyes considered Janet for a full thirty seconds and then Mrs Carnegie nodded again as if she approved of what she saw. She smiled.

"It would be a refreshment to have such a bonny face about me," she said unexpectedly, "Come away and sit down."

There followed an interrogation over a cup of chocolate (Mrs Carnegie detested tea) during which Janet had to keep all her wits about her: her carefully prepared tale of service in Drumore Castle and the call to nurse her cousin's wife was carefully examined before she fell heir to the post just vacated by Bridie.

# 13

BRIDIE'S ESTIMATE OF the qualities required by the holder of the post was a little exaggerated. Mrs Carnegie's standards of performance of household tasks were rigid and meticulous but her approval could be won and Janet won it. Number Twenty-one was not a difficult house to run: the cooking, which was surprisingly elaborate, was done by a Frenchman and everything else, except the care of Mrs Carnegie herself, by Janet. Guilbert, the cook, was considerably older than his mistress. He had accompanied a refugee from the Revolution of 1848 to a haven in Scotland and when that gentleman died had spent some time as a scullion in the kitchens of Rossie Priory where he had revealed a talent for cookery. From there he had moved to the household of one Mr de Launay McPherson, a landed gentleman whose mother had been a French refugee from the first French Revolution and whose youngest daughter Christine, or Kirstie as she was more usually called, had inherited his services on the death of her father and retained them ever since. His English was fluent but as it was heavily accented in a mixture of broad Scots and Languedoc it was hard to understand. However, this did not appear to have handicapped him in any way: though he had never married he was visited frequently by three sturdy middle-aged men whom he treated with paternal affection and who accorded him filial respect. Their respective mothers also visited Number Twenty-one on occasion, a circumstance which Mrs Carnegie ignored with dignity.

Janet soon discovered that an ability to work comfortably with Guilbert was the real criterion for Mrs Carnegie's approval of a domestic: this she found easy for it was impossible not to like the hot-tempered, dark-eyed little man. His seventy-odd years had whitened his hair and deprived him of teeth so that he lived on broth and bread, but he still cooked with enthusiasm for such as as could eat and in Janet, educated by her months among the flesh-pots of London, he found an appreciative pupil.

Mrs Carnegie, while exacting in the whiteness of the linen and the gleam on the china, glass and silver, ate so little that Janet carrying an almost untouched chicken down to the kitchen again, wondered aloud if M'sieu Guilbert was not sometimes discouraged. He shrugged enormously and said, "Ver' muckle. But soon Mr Shimi will be hame, Janette an' he eat . . . when he content he eat like six horses."

"Madame's son?" asked Janet. "Does he live here?"

"Indeed aye."

"Where is he just now?"

Guilbert frowned and shrugged again.

"Feeshing, mebbe. He like weel to feesh."

"Will he be home soon?"

But Guilbert could not tell her this; instead he went off into a long list of M'sieu Shimi's favourite dishes which conjured up for Janet a comic picture of a rotund young man with a knife and fork in his hands and a napkin tucked into his collar, French-style.

The next day in the middle of the morning Mrs Carnegie's silver bell tinkled in the breakfast parlour. Janet, cleaning knives on a block of bath-stone, put off the old kid gloves she used and the green baize apron, set her cap straight and ran upstairs. Mrs Carnegie was writing on cards in the elegant Italian hand she had learned as a girl.

"Ah, Janet, lass," she greeted her, "you've been with me now . . . what is't, three weeks?"

"A month about," said Janet.

"Aye," said the old lady," well now you're well acquent with my ways I've to have some friends in. About a dozen for their dinner on Friday."

"Yes, ma'am."

"Just a bite o' dinner and a game at the cards," said Mrs Carnegie, "and mebbe a tune on the pianoforte. Best clear off the shawl and the cheeny or Mistress Jamieson will put a flea in my lug. 'It's an instrument o' music,' says she, 'no a chimney-piece.' Her daughter's a bonnie singer, aye . . . bonnie."

She pushed a pile of cards towards Janet.

"Ye'll take these about the town for me, Janet. No need to waste siller on the postie."

Janet shuffled the handful of white pasteboard slips.

"There's just the ten here, Ma'am."

"That's right, lass, ten guests, my laddie and myself. Twelve."

"Aye, Ma'am."

She turned away:

"I'll tell Guilbert myself," said Mrs Carnegie, "or like enough he'll take the tid."

Janet smiled.

"He'll be pleased, I think."

"Aye, likely," said the old lady drily, "I'm an ill wifie to cook for. Away with ye."

The little household revolved in a bustle of activity. Guilbert himself, followed by an urchin with a vast market basket, shopped for fish, meat and vegetables. Janet discovered that the rooms she cleaned every day required to be cleaned again from floor to ceiling. Clean curtains had to be hung and every bibelot washed in hot soapy water. By Friday the house gleamed and shone and smelt of soap and polish and delectable food.

Included in all these preparations had been a pair of rooms on the back of the house over the stables. Mrs Carnegie kept no carriage, preferring to walk on her errands and calls in the town, "I've no lost the use of my legs, lass" and to hire a gig or a landau from the livery stable in South Street for errands which took her farther afield. The coachman's rooms over the empty stable had been converted into a neat bachelor establishment. She opened them up saying, "My Shimi can be private here and needna do the pretty gentleman to all my old tabbies. An' he can have his friends inby for a glass o' the eau de vie without their needing to take heed of me."

Janet looked about her at the shelves of leather-bound books, the comfortable easy-chairs and the capacious writing table under the window. It was a pleasant retreat.

"You think I spoil yon laddie, hey?"

Mrs Carnegie fingered the stoneware tobacco jar and sighed.

"Well, mebbe I do, mebbe I do. I'd no other bairn but him and I was thirty past when he was born. And he's been good to me."

Janet set about the bookshelf with her duster.

"He's been away fishing, so Guilbert tells me."

"Aye. He went off with his rods and bitties in a great tiravee the day before you came. No warning. Just packed his bags and tell't his clerk to deal with the business in hand."

Mrs Carnegie frowned at the jar in her hand.

"But I've a notion it wasn't just fish he'd on his mind. I doubt his clients'll no be best pleased. But he's young yet . . ."

A picture of the son of the house was beginning to build up for Janet: greedy, spoilt and indulged. She hoped that what had proved a pleasant haven would not be disrupted by his reappearance.

Friday came and there was still no sign of him. Janet found herself playing sorcerer's apprentice in the big kitchen until at five o'clock a tap at the area door heralded the arrival of one of the small boys often to be found in Guilbert's kitchen, chewing incredulously on unheard-of delicacies. Guilbert enwrapped him in a linen dish-towel and supervised a thorough cleansing of neck and ears and hands. Janet he dismissed to tidy herself and to assume the black stuff gown and lawn cap, collar, cuffs and apron. She brushed her hair and when it shone plaited it into a chignon in the nape of her neck. As she came downstairs Mrs Carnegie emerged from her room, robed in pale grey silk and a cap which was a frivolous froth of Venetian point. She approved Janet's appearance and asked about the state of affairs below-stairs. Reassured, she instructed her elderly maid to look after the ladies, a superfluity which that grim female took somewhat amiss as indeed she took most things.

In the drawing room the hostess fidgeted from chair to chair, straightening the ornaments and then returning them to their original position and occasionally as if drawn by a magnet going to the window and peering discreetly through the screens of Darvel lace.

Timidly Janet enquired if she should keep the twelfth cover: so far there had been no sign of her employer's son. Mrs Carnegie nodded emphatically and drew out a letter from her reticule.

"Friday, he says," she reassured herself, "and Friday it will be . . . ah, here they come! Quick, Janet!"

For the next half hour Janet admitted the guests, escorting the ladies to the somewhat daunting ministrations of Miss Johnson in the best spare bedroom and indicating to their escorts the apartment at the rear of the hall where they might leave hats and cloaks. She took particular note of the Jamiesons. It was unlike Mrs Carnegie to let anyone influence her arrangements unless it might be this spoiled and careless son of hers; but it had been in response to a comment of Mrs Jamieson's that Janet had cleared the pianoforte of its burden, two superb embroidered Chinese silk shawls, three groups in Bow china, a photographic portrait of the late Mr Carnegie in a silver frame draped with a black velvet ribbon, some assorted curios such as an ostrich egg, a Japanese painted fan and a hideous brass idol from India with a multiplicity of hands and a bland uncaring expression. All these treasures had to be found other homes, no easy task in number twenty-one because Mrs Carnegie regarded an empty surface as a challenge and an opportunity and possessed, moreover, a vast complex of family connections serving in various capacities in every part of the Empire, all of whom sent home innumerable tokens in response to her conscientious supply of thoroughly entertaining letters.

Mrs Jamieson was a portly pleasant woman with a bluff, no-nonsense manner who bullied her large absent-minded husband in a kindly fashion and quite blatantly adored her daughter. Kitty Jamieson was tall, elegant and pretty in a style to be found in the engravings in the *Ladies' Magazine*. Her eyes were of that pale blue charitably described as forgetmenot and set wide apart above a fashionably acquiline nose and a rosebud mouth. Her hair was light brown and intricately dressed in a series of bands and puffs. Her time in number twenty-one had been long enough for Janet to collect what the ticket-collector had called the 'clash o' the toon' and she knew that Miss Jamieson was currently considered the Fair Maid of Perth . . . and she was not ill-dowered. Moreover, she recalled a certain item in the *Perthshire Advertiser* and wondered what had become of the projected engagement between her and Simon. The downtrodden Mr Jamieson was engaged in the manufacture of linen . . . though this was not stressed by either his wife or his daughter . . . and in a good way of business. Mrs Carnegie, whose view was that the best was only just good enough for her son, had evidently fixed upon this paragon to be his bride.

That this plan was neither unknown nor unwelcome to her choice was obvious enough. When Janet ushered mother and daughter into the parlour downstairs where the party was assembling Miss Jamieson kissed her hostess and demanded, "Dearest Aunt Kirstie, where is that wicked and neglectful Shimi of yours? I declare you have enticed me here under false promises."

Mrs Carnegie patted her on the cheek with a delicately painted silk fan (from Cousin Murdoch's boy in Shanghai).

"He'll be here. He'd no miss an evening in your company, my lass."

However, the company had proceeded in pairs to the dining parlour and conversation had dwindled in profound respect for Guilbert's soup before he arrived. Janet was on the point of descending to the kitchen to assemble the second course ready for Guilbert's acolyte to carry up for her when she heard a cab drive up to the door. She called downstairs that there might be a short delay in serving the second course and hurried to open the door. The cabbie came in and put down a valise under the great bronze gong (Robert, the eldest nephew was currently with the army in Burma). His fare was still on the pavement retrieving his rods. A voluminous Inverness cape disguised his shape but Janet's picture of a rotund little man vanished like smoke. She picked up the valise and took it to the door which led to the stableyard ready to remove later. When she came back the tall figure had dumped his rod-cases on the carved wooden chest, paid off the cabbie and was engaged in removing the Inverness cape. He turned about and confronted Janet just as the door of the dining parlour opened and his mother came out.

"Evening, Bridie, am I . . ." he began smilingly, but when the light from the candles on the table fell on Janet's face he stopped and his face went quite white. He stood staring speechlessly at her and his mother who had advanced on him shaking her head reproachfully, halted in alarm at his appearance.

"Shimi . . . you're ill. Janet, fetch me a glass of eau de vie!"

She pushed him down into the carved wooden chair and Janet went hurriedly to the tantalus in the dining parlour where the guests were looking puzzled and a little alarmed. She could have done with a sip of the brandy herself. The greedy, spoiled, plump mother's darling she had pictured, the beloved 'Jimmie' was Simon Lamington. And he had recognised her.

Janet's room in number twenty-one was high up under the

roof and her window looked out over the Inch to the Tay and the wooded slopes of Kinnoul Hill on the farther bank. After the last dish was dried and put away and all traces of the evening's visitors had been eradicated as if they had been disease-ridden beggars instead of welcome guests, Mrs Carnegie dismissed her household to bed. Janet climbed the narrow red-druggeted staircase to the attic floor, weary, confused and anxious. The feeling of having escaped, of having gained a haven had been abruptly dissipated and she wondered what to do. Bleakly she considered yet another flight and, not for the first time, wondered what was to become of her. She undressed and made ready for bed but sat up staring across the Inch which was faintly lit by a sliver of moon, remembering what had happened that evening.

On her reappearance with the brandy Simon had recovered somewhat. He stared at her as she brought the glass.

"This is Janet," his mother had explained, seeing him stare. "Bridie has left us and Janet taken her place. Take this."

She pushed the glass into his hand.

"Man, Shimi, but you look gash," she went on, "ye might have seen a ghost. What have ye been at, west the country, there?"

He drank a little of the brandy and handed the glass to Janet.

"Perhaps I did," he said, looking her straight in the face. "I was at a funeral while I was away. In the West."

His mother, who had the passionate interest in death and the ceremonies of death of a Scotswoman of her age and generation pressed for information.

"Nobody of your acquaintance, Mama," he told her. "I met her while I was in the West last year. I hardly knew her. In fact..."

He looked at Janet again.

"I hardly had time to get to know her at all."

"A client, I suppose," said his mother comfortably, "and did she leave much that you'd to go traipsing off, West the country there, to her burial?"

"A few rowan berries, Mama," he said, "that was all."

"Now you're haivering," said Mrs Carnegie.

He gave them a fleeting smile.

"Now Mama, can I come into dinner without changing. I've been travelling all day and I'm starved."

The rest of the evening went very much as Mrs Carnegie had

planned. The guests retired to the drawing room after dinner and the elders went at once to the card-tables ready laid out at one end. The young people, Kitty Jamieson, Simon and another couple, recently married, gathered about the pianoforte. Janet, coming in and out with candles and glasses and eventually the tea tray, had had plenty of opportunity to hear Miss Jamieson sing and agreed with her employer that she was a bonnie singer. Nor could there be any doubt about her penchant for Simon. Every song was sung to him alone and all her attention was for him. The rest of the company might as well not have existed. About Simon's state of mind it was not possible to be so certain. He looked preoccupied. When she brought his tea cup he muttered very quietly,

"I must talk to you."

She nodded but Kitty Jamieson was too close to venture on an answer. He asked for sugar and Janet brought the tray of cream and sugar across in time to hear Miss Jamieson say, "What's this, Shimi, I thought you didn't care for sweets?"

"A slander," he returned, "at least in present company. I thought we were to hear 'When the Swallow Comes' . . . or are you too weary?"

She looked pleased and returned to the pianoforte to hunt through her music. Under cover of the introductory chords Simon helped himself to the smallest piece of sugar he could find.

"You needn't be afraid," he began, in an undertone, "I won't . . ."

He was interrupted by a demand for sugar at the whist-tables where an animated (not to say acidulated) post-mortem on the last rubber was in progress and Janet had had to move away but she had felt sufficiently reassured not to pack up that very night as she had almost determined to do.

Only one incident contrived to cheer her during the course of that interminable evening. She heard Mrs Jamieson say to her hostess that she thought she was very unwise.

"She is by far too pretty," she said. "I think you should be rid of her as soon as maybe."

Mrs Carnegie had responded by a sturdy defence.

"Haivers," she had said, "handsome is as handsome does and Janet's as neat-handed and sensible a lass as I've had in the house."

Mrs Jamieson's next remark had not been audible but the sense of it was plain.

"Haivers," said her hostess again, "as long as Kitty's about he'll not have any sheeps' eyes to make at any other lass, however pretty she may be."

It seemed to Janet that Mrs Jamieson was not reassured and she felt unaccountably cheered by this.

Simon had volunteered to escort the Jamiesons home and so there had been no chance to speak with him again. Janet sighed and climbed into bed.

Nor did the following week provide an opportunity for the talk he wanted. It now became obvious that Number Twenty-one was run for Simon alone. Janet, busied all day under Mrs Carnegie's keen eyes, realised that for the past month the household had been almost inactive: from the day of Simon's arrival Bridie's parting complaint had some justice. Janet caught up in a series of tea-parties, card-parties, musical evenings and other aspects of the Perth social round, all of which needed nearly as much preparation as the dinner-party, found herself occupied to the full. Nor was Simon himself idle. He had to pick up the threads of his law practice and it was soon obvious that pressure was being put on him to stand for Parliament in the Liberal interest. Janet observed the comings and goings of solemn high-collared gentlemen whose consumption of assorted wines and liquors was as great as it was inconspicuous. When he was at home his mother supervised his well-being, presiding over substantial breakfasts in the early morning and summoning luncheon or tea and hot scones as soon as his footfall was heard at midday or in the evening. At night there were guests or engagements elsewhere when he escorted his mother (and presumably Miss Jamieson). Moreover, Janet did not go out of her way to seek a meeting. She felt shy and unready to explain the circumstances which had brought her there.

Janet had her time off after luncheon while Mrs Carnegie was laid down on her bed and Guilbert retired to his room beside the kitchen with half a bottle of wine, never more and never less. She formed the habit at this time of putting on her plaid and walking along the river bank, watching the salmon fishers and the small boys tumbling and splashing in the shallows mother-naked to the reiterated outrage of respectable females, expressed in letters to the *Advertiser*. There was a clump of willows just beyond the race-track and there, in fine weather, she could sit unseen and read volumes borrowed from the shelves of number twenty-one. Mrs Carnegie, whose idol had been and remained Sir Walter Scott, had conceived a mild approval of Mr Dickens . . . in despite of the vulgarity of his themes; there were other novelists too. Thackeray, Mrs Trollope and her prolific son. To these Mrs Carnegie on discovering Janet's liking for reading had made her welcome.

About ten days after Simon's arrival she was sitting in this retreat with Copperfield open on her lap and wondering, rather bleakly, if, like David, she could seek sanctuary with an eccentric aunt, or whether Aunt Matilda would return her to Staindrop for the pure delight of embarrassing her nephew. She heard someone call her name and looking through the screen of leaves she saw Simon. He saw her at once and gave a coin to the urchin who helped Guilbert in the kitchen and who had evidently got to know where she went in the afternoons. Ian pulled at his disreputable cap and ran away, his bare feet flashing their blackened soles above the rough grass.

Janet closed her book and waited till Simon came and sat beside her.

"Well," he said, "you're an elusive creature, Lady Staindrop."

# 14

JANET SAID NOTHING but her heart thumped and the balls of her thumbs pricked . . . for what reason she hardly knew. Simon plucked a blade of grass and began to harass a busy party of ants about their own business among the roots of the willow.

"I think," he said, "you owe me an explanation. I was at your funeral, after all. And a very moving ceremony it was."

Janet said nothing to this and he went on.

"The Minister mourned this poor creature cut off in the flower of her youth, very eloquent he was. Your father and brother were there in their blacks . . . and your brother suspiciously red about the nose and green about the gills. You'd a mourner in him, I reckon. Your sister-in-law and your stepmama were perambulating heaps of crape and concealing veils . . ."

He looked directly at her.

"Concealing very little, as I should judge. Lord Staindrop was impatient, even embarrassed, I thought. Perhaps it was the story which was all over Oban . . . or it might have been the military gentleman who arrived late and wept noisily and continuously all through the ceremony."

He raised one eyebrow at her, inviting comment, but Janet shook her head.

"He seemed to have a notion that Staindrop was responsible for your untimely demise. I heard him mutter the word 'murderer' more than once. And your father seemed stiffish with his noble son-in-law. Your stepmama, however, made up for this. Staindrop was sulky as a bear."

Janet's mouth twitched as she pictured the scene. Simon smiled.

"But for one trifling circumstance I think I too would have found some amusement in the affair."

Janet looked at him and found his smile had vanished.

"I believed that you were dead," he said simply.

Janet blushed to the roots of her hair.

"How in the world do you come to be here?" he asked. "Here, of all places."

"It's a long story," said Janet.

"I've all afternoon," he invited.

"I hardly know where to start," Janet told him.

"If it's any help I know something of your life with Staindrop. The military gentleman was staying in the same hotel and he waxed confidential. Even allowing for his partiality you seem to have had a good deal to bear."

Janet plunged into her story, skating over the episode in the old keep as best she might, and explaining how she had been sent to Number Twenty-one by Bridie.

"I suppose," said Simon at last, "it's not so surprising as it might seem. My mother keeps a lively kitchen of it and there aren't many ready to tolerate Guilbert. We have had a positive procession of Doras and Bridies over the years. Didn't you realise this was my home?"

It was his turn to blush.

"Or perhaps you had forgotten."

Janet denied this emphatically. She reminded him that his mother had married again so that her surname was different from his own and explained how she had mistaken 'Shimi' for Jimmie.

"It's the Gaelic version of Simon," he explained. "I had a nurse from Frazer country and she called me that and my family do to this day. I wish . . ."

He hesitated and evidently changed what he had been going to say.

"And now," he said, "what do you plan to do?"

"I'm happy where I am for the time being."

"Fiddle," he said impatiently, "this is no life for you. I've been thinking all week. Tell me, have you ever thought of emigrating?"

Janet shook her head.

"I've no money . . . nowhere to go and no one to go to."

Simon laughed.

"As to that . . . my mother has relations in every corner of the British Empire. As for money . . . it could be arranged."

"But what should I do?"

Once more he seemed to change his mind about what he was going to say.

"You could farm," he suggested, "or you could set up a boarding house, or a shop."

"I suppose I might," said Janet.

She felt unenthusiastic: the prospect of taking such a step alone was daunting, even unwelcome. She felt somehow chilled and unhappy. For the first time she fully realised her predicament. She was alone but not single, dead but still alive . . . and with the need to stay alive. Almost she wished it was she and not her namesake who lay in that grave in Oban. Simon rose and put out his hand.

"Take a little time to think," he advised her. "There's no need to decide at once. But you can trust me. I won't do anything you don't want, I promise. But I hope you'll let me help."

He released her hand and they began to stroll along the bank.

"You didn't say . . . how did you come to be at my funeral?"

"I read the report of your death in the paper and I went across to the West to find out what had happened."

He looked bleak as if he was recalling how he had felt.

"I was at the procurator-fiscal's hearing in Oban," he told her. "It all sounded very conclusive. Why did Seonaidh's people never enquire after her, I wonder."

"I think she may have told them she was going to try for a situation in England. They wouldn't expect to hear from her. She couldn't do more than write her own name and she was a heedless limmer at that," explained Janet. "But what a thing to happen . . . poor lass."

They walked in silence for a few moments.

"When will you come back to life?" Simon asked at last.

Janet didn't reply directly.

"I won't go back to Staindrop . . . I won't."

Simon looked worried.

"You might have to tell people you were still alive," he said. "What if Staindrop decided to marry again?"

Janet nodded.

"I know," she said. "I know. All I wanted was a breathing space . . . I didn't mean to vanish for ever."

Simon stopped walking.

"And what about the weeping soldier?" he asked.

Janet laughed and Simon thought inconsequently that it was her laugh he would remember if he was never to see her again.

"Och," she said, "he was a great tumphie!"

It was Simon's turn to laugh at this description.

"He was at some pains to signify that they were burying his heart in that grave. He said as much later in the day to anyone who would listen," he told her.

"It was just because I didn't fall down at his feet the very instant he looked my road," she explained. "All the others did, you see. There had to be something singular about me."

Simon chuckled again.

"I'll commend his perspicacity, at least."

Over the next week or so Janet obediently considered emigration and the prospect of a solitary life in a foreign country. She did not find it attractive and was honest enough with herself to admit that Simon was the reason for this. She knew she should make plans to leave Number Twenty-one but put off doing this, reluctant to face the fact she should not stay. Simon and she exchanged hardly a word in that time but it needed no words to tell her that he felt much as she did. She wondered at his silence while she had been in Glasgow but there was no chance to ask him. She went through the busy days living from minute to minute and trying not to think about the future. One Tuesday afternoon the silver bell tinkled once more and Janet hurried to the small breakfast parlour. Mrs Carnegie was engaged in sealing a letter. New-fangled envelopes she did not trust.

"Master Shimi is for Edinburgh and Parliament House for the next fortnight," she announced. "And I am worn down by all my jollifications. I'm for Strathpeffer to drink the waters . . . foul as they are. Miss Johnson's to go with me and I'll see she drinks them too. Maybe they'll sweeten her temper."

She turned in her chair to look at Janet.

"I've hired a wee house for a month and a couple of lasses with it. This letter is for the lawyer to confirm it."

She tapped the letter.

"Guilbert will go with me. You can't get food fit to eat in yon place. I want you, lass, to bide here by yourself. I need somebody to see after the place, keep it fired and aired. I'll not abide a foosty house. You'll not be lonely?"

"No, ma'am."

"You'll be at the books, I warrant you," prophesied her employer. "And none the worse for that. When Master Shimi comes back he'll just take a room at the George Inn till I return."

In two days time Simon left for the Edinburgh train with no more farewell than a look exchanged over his small valise. In three days his mother, Miss Johnson, Guilbert and an inordinate amount of meticulously packed boxes left to catch the Inverness train in a hired fourwheeler. Before they left Mrs Carnegie inspected the horse, a lugubrious, rack-ribbed elderly grey. She considered his angles for a moment and then dug her parasol into the driver's own well-covered ribs.

"We'd do better with yourself between the shafts," she said, "yon poor beast's as old as I am myself."

She turned to Janet, who was standing on the steps, her cap-streamers fluttering in the wind.

"You'll write to me, Janet lass," she told her. "Just once or twice to give me the news and tell me all's well."

She fumbled in her reticule and produced a couple of sovereigns.

"These are for you, lass," she said gruffly. "You can take the penny stamp out of them and maybe have a shilling or two to spend. You're a good worker, Janet, and light on your feet. I cannot abide to be waited on by cart horses."

Miss Johnson, waiting to help her employer into the cab, sniffed at this thrust.

Startled, Janet looked at the coins in her palm while Mrs Carnegie hoisted herself nimbly into the overloaded cab and tapped on the roof to give the driver the office to go. The last she saw of them was Guilbert's gnarled hand waving at her from the window.

Alone in Number Twenty-one for three peaceful weeks Janet spent the mornings doing her duty by the house and her afternoons wandering about the city. The evenings she spent reading. Occasionally, she told herself she should be making plans to leave, to go abroad, but always she fell asleep before she could do this. One Monday evening about three weeks after they had gone she took her letter to the post. On her way back she met a ragged man handing out playbills, and mindful of the two sovereigns still in her purse she took one and learned that,

THE PHOENIX PLAYERS
PRESENT A SHORT SEASON OF
SHAKESPEARE
in the new theatre in
PERTH
Mr Benenden and his Company
will present
AS YOU LIKE IT
HAMLET
and the Scotch tragedy
MACBETH
at the following times and with seats at
the following prices.

She noted that the play for that night, the last of this season, would be *As You Like It*, which was a favourite of hers.

The theatre stood a little back from the High Street but announced its presence with a board overhanging the pavement. Janet found a number of people anxious to book seats for the evening's performance but managed to secure a seat on the balcony, rather to one side. With a rising feeling of excitement she went back to Number Twenty-one and laid out on the bed the heavy grey silk gown which had once belonged to Ealasaidh, the gold ornament and the embroidered shawl. She washed, brushed her hair and plaited it into a crown. The dress fitted well enough and was sufficiently long to hide her thick, sensible shoes. The mirror in the hall showed a handsome girl, somewhat unfashionably gowned. The clock in the drawing room struck seven. It was time too go. Janet drew her shawl about her shoulders and began to have qualms. No matter how she might look, it was not at all the thing for girls or young women to go to the theatre unescorted. If she did she would be conspicuous and this was undesirable . . . for any number of reasons. She hesitated, conscious of the folly but reluctant to give up her treat. The memory of the stiff price she had paid for the ticket decided her, she pulled the shawl up over her head so that her face was half hidden, pulled on her gloves and opened the front door. On the doorstep, key in hand, stood Simon.

He considered the figure in the doorway appreciatively.

"I don't wish to appear captious," he said at last, "but this is no way to avoid attention."

Janet retreated into the hall again and pulled off the shawl.

"Fine I ken," she said impatiently, "I was wanting to go to the play, but you're right. It'd be daft."

Simon followed her in and closed the door.

"Half Perth would be wondering who you were and the other half busily trying to find out."

Janet sighed agreement. Simon looked at her for a moment and grinned.

"Wouldn't it be rare sport," he said, "to give them something to talk about."

Janet looked at him enquiringly.

"What you need," he said, "is a hat with a veil . . . and an escort."

In the event Janet saw *As You Like It* from a box. Mrs Carnegie's wardrobe, ransacked by her son, had provided a hat and a thick veil and Simon himself was her escort. They were a little late and came into the box just as the lights were dimming. As the curtain quivered and rose she asked, "I meant to ask . . . what did you come to the house for, tonight?"

Simon looked down at her unsmiling.

"Do you want me to say I came for a book which I could have borrowed from my friend . . . or to tell you the truth."

Janet felt the blood beat in her ears and she gripped her hands together under the shawl. Simon turned his head to look at the scene on stage.

"I came to see you," he added almost inaudibly, "because I couldn't stay away any longer."

Janet saw and heard very little of that first act but when the curtain went down it seemed that she had not missed a great deal. Simon was scornful.

"Celia must be nearly as old as my mother," he commented, "and what is more her memory is going. She was prompted twenty times if she was prompted once. She and Rosalind are more like grandmother and granddaughter than sisters."

When the house lights went up for the first interval Janet edged her chair to the back of the box and pulled the veil down over her face. Simon, however, leaned on the edge of the box and waved to his acquaintance in the stalls. This included the Jamiesons who were present, *en famille*, in the fifth row. Janet shrank back even farther into the shadow, wishing she had not yielded to temptation but stayed at Number Twenty-one and finished *Can You Forgive Her*. She could see Miss Kitty leaning forward trying to see into the box and combining this activity with gay insouciant smiles to Simon whenever he looked her way.

The lights dimmed at last and the music began.

"Mr Jamieson will come knocking on our door during the next interval," he prophesied.

"What will we do?"

"Leave it to me."

He laughed and took her hand.

"Whatever can we have been thinking of to come here."

Despite this, and the elderly Celia and an exiled Duke whose sojourn in the forest had evidently given him a severe cold, not to mention a Touchstone who could not hold a tune, the play laid hold upon them both and at the next interval the expected tap on the door still startled them. Simon squeezed Janet's hand, opened the door and went out, closing it behind him. For five minutes or so Janet was conscious of a barrage of stares, not only from the Jamiesons but from all the 'guid folk' of Perth there present and curious to discover who this stranger within their gates might be. She inched her chair as far behind the pillar as she could and bent her head to study the programme. Amongst such interesting items as Mr Rattray's recent purchase of prime Havana cigars and Mr Anderson's promise to build a kilt to any measurement within the week she discovered that Mr Benenden's world-renowned players were due to appear for a short season at the new Theatre Royal in Glasgow. Simon returned at last and closed the door firmly on Mr Jamieson's curiosity. He was looking mischievous.

"You are a widow," he informed her, "not recently bereaved but still not wishful for company. Your husband was a university friend, you understand, to whom I owe a debt of hospitality. You are staying privately and it was as well I had no notion of where that might be for he'd have had it out of me."

He began to laugh.

"Lie like a lawyer, they say. I must say I wish the play had been worth all this cloak and dagger work."

The lights dimmed again as the ushers turned down the gas and the somewhat puny orchestra struck up the incidental music, not a little hampered by the absence of at least three important members. As the curtain went up it revealed the woodland set which for some younger members of the audience bore a striking resemblance to that used in the pantomime Babes in the Wood earlier in the year.

Touchstone was giving a painful rendering of 'It was a lover and his lass . . .' when Simon leaned over to Janet and murmured, "It might be as well if we slipped away before the curtain."

Janet agreed.

Cutlog Vennel was ill-lit and ill-paved and Janet stumbled as they were hurrying along to be well away before the rest of the audience emerged. Simon grabbed her arm and Janet once again felt her thumbs prick and the blood beat in her ears. Once on the better-lit pavement of Horse Cross she tried to pull her arm away but Simon held it more tightly and she had the sensation of being caught up on a great wave or in a high wind. He said nothing but she caught a glimpse of his face under the gas lamps and it seemed to her to have lost the teasing humorous look it had worn earlier. He walked fast, almost as if he had forgotten she was with him.

The open space of the North Inch stretched in front of them. Behind the clouds scurrying before a west wind there was a moon and the clumps of bushes and trees were visible. Simon struck out across the grass towards the house, but halfway across he stopped short and pulled Janet roughly round to face him.

"Do you know I've been in Perth since two days after my mother left?"

He took her by the shoulders and shook her slightly.

"Do you know why?"

"No," said Janet and swallowed hard in an attempt to control her breathing, "not unless the fish were rising."

He shook her again.

"Damn the fish!" he said, "I came because I couldn't stay away. I've trailed you round the streets . . . I've waited outside the house at night. I can't eat . . . I can't sleep . . . damn it, Janet, I can't even *think* . . ."

He pulled her roughly against him and hugged her till she could scarcely breathe. She struggled to free her arms and he loosed his hold only to tighten it again when she put them round his neck. After a while he began to kiss her in kind of desperate hungry fashion which roused her so that her legs trembled underneath her. He stopped as suddenly as he had begun and held her close and she could hear the rapid thump of his heart.

"Jennie, in God's name, what are we to *do*?"

She could not answer.

"You know," he went on, "I went home after I saw you and I told my mother I meant to get married. I was coming back as soon as my work would let me . . . and when I did you'd gone and the village was full of the grand match you were to make. Why, Jennie, why? I made sure you felt something of what I did. Why marry that . . . that creature . . . of all people?"

Haltingly Janet tried to explain something of the pressures which had ended in the Landsdowne Road ceremony.

"If you'd come to Glasgow, "she said, "if you'd written . . ."

"But I did write," he broke in, "I wrote three times and never an answer."

They had begun to walk slowly towards Rose Terrace, but at this revelation they both stopped.

"I never had your letter," said Janet. "If I had you'd have had answer I promise you. I thought . . . I thought you'd gone home and thought better of . . . of . . ."

She stopped.

"I suppose Lachie's mother must have forgotten to tell him I wanted my letters sent to Glasgow. Lachie's no genius; he'd just take them up to Glenfoot and to Braeside in the ordinary way. And I suppose Kirsty destroyed them."

"But why would she do that?"

Janet began walking again.

"A dozen reasons and no reason at all. She wanted me to marry her brother Donald. You met him, remember?"

"How could I forget?"

"And if not him, then she'd work hand-in-glove with my father I don't doubt. My brother-in-law, Lord Staindrop," she mimicked, "I can hear her at it."

"And the no reason at all?"

"Jock and I were good friends," she said, "when they were wed I was . . . well, fine you know I've a bitter tongue and I never thought she was the person for him."

They reached the steps of Number Twenty-one and stood outside.

"And what is to be done?" asked Simon unhappily.

Janet did not answer at once. She knew very well what had to be done and the prospect made her want to cry out with misery and resentment.

"I'll make you a cup of tea," said she matter-of-factly, and went up the steps to unlock the door. In the hall she kindled a taper at the candle left burning on the stand and lit the gas. Simon closed the door and stood watching, his face rather white. He didn't move until she went towards the kitchen steps.

"I don't want any damned tea," he said and took her by the arm. "Come in here. We've got to talk."

Mrs Carnegie had accepted gas as a utilitarian convenience with which to light kitchen, hall and staircase but in her parlours she preferred candlelight. Simon lit the branch of candles on the chimney-piece and turned to face Janet, who stood quietly in front of the empty grate.

"Are you staying here tonight?" she enquired.

"Am I?" he asked and took her hands.

She pulled them away.

"It would distress your mother . . . and if Miss Kitty came to hear of it . . ."

"Confound Kitty . . . and my mother. Look Janet, we can't marry, not unless you come to life and even then we can't be sure that . . . that Staindrop would let you go. And it would take months, years even."

"I know."

He came closer.

"Remember I said you should emigrate? I was thinking, we could go to Australia . . . we could be man and wife there. Who would know? And from what I've heard of the place who would care if they did?"

Briefly Janet considered such a prospect and let it go with such a sense of regret that she could hardly speak.

"Your mother . . ."

"I'll see she is cared for. She won't suffer."

Janet shook her head.

"And there's yourself," she went on. "I've heard what folk

say of you. You go to Australia and you'll destroy all you've built here and in Edinburgh."

"That's not important. I don't want success without you. It won't be worth having."

Janet could not answer this: she just swallowed and shook her head again. Simon pulled her to him and his grip on her arms hurt.

"Jennie! Jennie, I know you feel something for me. Please come with me, *please*!"

"I can't," she blurted out, "I can't! I want to more than anything I ever wanted . . . but it would be wrong."

"Wrong!"

He let go of her and flung over to the window.

"This isn't wrong. It was wrong to marry a man like Staindrop if you like . . . that was wrong, a sin, a crime . . ."

From behind he looked much younger. Janet wanted to follow him over but she dared not.

"It was wrong," she admitted, "I know that now. But it hurt no one but me . . . and him in a way."

"And me!" came from the figure at the window.

"That I didn't know or there's no one on earth who could have made me do it."

He turned about at that.

"Then why?"

"Because if I do what you ask there are so many people to be hurt and disappointed. Your mother would never get over losing you, it would kill her . . ."

"She could come out to us."

Janet smiled faintly at this notion.

"You're nothing of a gardener, Master Shimi. There are some plants you can't transplant. She fairly lives for you and by you . . . if you run off with her own servant she will die of the shock and the disgrace of it."

His fists clenched.

"I can't bear it that she should think of you as that . . ."

"I'd rather she thought of me as a servant than as the whore who made her old age miserable."

They stared at one another.

"You don't mince your words, Jennie," he said at last. "But then you never did, did you?"

"No," she said and they both smiled at the memory of his encounter with Donald.

"And," she went on more gently, "I'll not harm you."

"How in the world could you harm me?"

"All too easily . . ."

Her voice broke.

". . . all too easily . . ."

She ran out of the room and upstairs as fast as she could and locked the door of her room behind her. She flung herself across the narrow bed and lay face down, too distressed even to cry. She heard Simon follow her and waited, her heart thumping like an engine.

"Jennie! Jennie!" he called.

She said nothing.

"Jennie, please!" he entreated, "open the door."

Janet put her hand to her mouth in the effort to remain silent.

It was long after midnight before he left at last. She stood by the door and listened to him go slowly down the stairs and the tears ran down her face. The front door slammed heavily and from her window she watched him stride across the Inch, a shadow in the starlight. When she could see him no longer she turned from the window and stood for a moment wiping the tears from her cheeks and gathering her resolution for what had to be done.

# 15

SOME TWO HOURS later Janet sat down to write a note to Mrs Carnegie.

Dear Madam, [she wrote]
I am sorry but I must leave you without notice which I do not care to do but there is no help for it. I hope I leave everything as you would wish to find it. The keys of the house I have sent to Mr Lamington at the George Inn. I hope you will have no trouble finding someone to take my place. My thanks for your kindness and my regards to M. Guilbert.

Janet.

This she set upon the hall table and put the smiling brass buddha upon it (a souvenir of cousin Lachlan's short stay in Siam). The streets were all but deserted at that hour but Janet pulled her tartan plaid well over her head as she hurried along to the station.

In the booking office the clerk was nodding beside a generous fire.

"When will there be a train to Glasgow?" she asked.

She had decided to seek shelter with Betsy while she gathered her wits and decided what to do. Her money would not last long.

The clerk blinked and yawned and glanced at the clock.

"Glasgow train in five minutes," he told her and selected her ticket. "Return?"

"Single," said Janet and her throat ached as she said it.

The clerk gave her the pasteboard slip and the change from the second sovereign.

"Platform Two," he announced.

Janet was about to go along the passage which led to the platform when she saw a familiar figure waiting at the foot of the iron bridge over which she would have to cross in order to reach Platform Two. Simon had evidently worked out for himself what she was likely to do. She hesitated and shrank back into the shadow of a pillar. She longed to go to him and knew if she did she would never leave him again. She clenched her hand and pressed her knuckles painfully against the grimy sandstone. There was a rumbling of iron trolley wheels and a large party of people came through the arch from the station square, accompanied by what seemed to be an inordinate amount of luggage; there were trolley-loads of trunks and hampers. The party talked ringingly among themselves and demanded in equally carrying voices a quantity of second class tickets to Glasgow. There were four women with the party. Janet made up her mind what she must do.

She slipped out from her shelter behind the pillar and touched the arm of the woman nearest to her.

"If you please," she requested, "may I travel with your party? My friend has been taken ill and cannot come and I don't care to travel alone at night."

The answer to this was drowned in the screech of brakes and the whistle and thump of the engine as the train drew in, but it was evidently in the affirmative for she took Janet by the arm and bustled her along the passage in a flurry of porters and trolleys and travelling rugs and dress baskets. Simon was thrust aside by the hurrying party and given no opportunity to look at their faces as they passed under the pale gas-light. The last she saw of him was from the compartment window, still waiting forlornly at the bridge.

The train jerked and Janet was cast on to the lap of a fellow-traveller. Only one of the lamps in the compartment was still lit but she could see the four other women besides herself. The oldest was the one on whom she had fallen, a large and imposing woman in a hat decorated with plumes. In the other corner sat a younger woman who had taken off her hat and was patting her coils of magnificent shining black hair; even in that dim light she attracted attention. Her eyes were beautiful and if her features were too pronounced for fashionable prettiness her face was of the kind that people remember. The remaining two sat together opposite her, huddled into shawls. The compartment was filled with a powerful smell of eucalyptus.

Janet apologised and took her seat opposite the older woman.

"No matter, no matter," said she with a gesture which was just a little too studied for the occasion. The train gathered speed and plunged into the tunnel. The younger woman got up to close the window against the smoke and smuts. It was stiff and she had to struggle with it before it finally slammed shut.

"The worst thing about our honourable profession," she said, and her ringing voice took Janet back some six hours, "is the midnight travelling. One feels like a ghost . . . no, less positive than that. I declare I do not know whether I am this one . . ."

She laid her hand on her bosom.

". . . or that one."

She pointed at the window where she and her companions were mirrored against the dark.

"Save it for the customers, dear girl," said the older woman. "We're too weary to appreciate your flights."

Even in that dim light Janet could be certain of her company. The dark young woman had been Rosalind and the older of the two other women, Celia. She had fallen among the players.

'Rosalind' pulled down the blind with an impatient jerk and hid their reflections.

"What I want to know, my dears, before you all fall into stertorous slumbers, is what are we to do about tomorrow?"

The older woman sighed and removed her imposing hat, bestowing it on the seat beside her.

"No doubt Mr Benenden is considering the matter," she pronounced and withdrew a shawl from the carpet bag at her feet and wrapped it around her head and shoulders.

"No doubt," returned 'Rosalind', "Mr Benenden is presently considering the contents of his second bottle."

"Hush!" said the older woman and made a gesture of her gloved hand towards Janet.

"It is hardly a matter to be kept dark when one considers his condition on stage tonight. That was an announcement as public as might well be."

'Celia' raised her head and spoke for the first time.

"He had the most distressing head cold," she said catarrhally.

'Rosalind' leaned across and patted her knee.

"So did you, my love, but you didn't find it necessary to pickle yourself in brandy before you appeared."

'Celia' retreated into her cloud of eucalyptus fumes and 'Rosalind' addressed the carriage at large.

"Tomorrow we are supposed to open in Glasgow with *Maddalena.* It's mawkish rubbish but the house is sold out and we *have* no Maddalena. And our respected manager instead of trying to replace poor Amanda is drinking himself into his customary stupor."

"How is poor Amanda?" enquired the older woman.

"How should she be," said 'Rosalind' impatiently, "poor Amanda has a broken leg . . . and if Benenden knew his business which he does not he would sue the proprietors for leaving a staircase like that unlit."

The other woman beside 'Celia' raised her head and Janet remembered that she had played 'Audrey'. She had a broad plain face but when she spoke her voice was beautiful.

"I went up to see her in the Infirmary before the first performance. She was in pain but she hasn't much fever and the nurse said she would be more comfortable in the morning."

"Matters could be worse," said the older woman.

"But it'll be two months before she can come back to us," 'Audrey' added.

"And we need a Maddalena for tomorrow night . . . for heaven's sake . . . tonight!" said 'Rosalind'.

"We'll find somebody in Glasgow," the older woman told her wearily.

"Maggie, my own, we will arrive in Glasgow in an hour in the chill grey dawn and we will then go to our respective and sordid lodgings . . . I have been in Glasgow before, friends . . . where no doubt Benenden will sink into swinish unconsciousness. By the time we arrive at the theatre he will still have found no one. And poor Dora will have to take the part . . ."

"No," said 'Celia' with decision. "I will *not* play the part of a girl, not again. I'm twenty years too old."

"And even if he has found someone she will not know her words and we will stumble through with the prompter saying half her lines and the rest of us filling in the rest."

"You're too severe," said Dora—'Celia' and sniffed lugubriously, "Ten sides. Any actress could learn it in an hour or two."

'Rosalind' seemed to exude exasperation.

"*If* he finds someone and *if* she is an actress."

Dora raised her head.

"And there's the appearance . . ."

"That's what I'm trying to tell you!" exclaimed Rosalind, "It can't be just any little trollop . . ."

"Oh, Jess," implored Maggie, "do calm down and let us get some sleep. With the best will in the world we can't do anything about finding someone in the train. You can stir the guv'nor into action when we get to Glasgow."

"Oh, very well," agreed Jess — 'Rosalind' rather sulkily and she too pulled a warm woollen shawl out of her bag. "Do you want me to turn down the lamp?"

Maggie nodded.

"I'll do it," volunteered Janet, for the lamp was in a bracket above her head. She got up and stretched to the little brass screw on the side. The tartan plaid about her head fell back and showed her face.

Janet rarely considered how she looked. Her mother's pride in her had never found a direct expression and she had discouraged 'vanity'. Certainly at that point her appearance was the last thing on her mind. But Jess, idly glancing at the stranger in their midst, caught her breath in astonishment and wonder. In the soft lamplight Janet looked almost unbelievably beautiful: her profile and complexion were always flawless, but in the ordinary way their effect was lessened by her expression. Janet was always composed and cheerful. At that point her pallor and the faintly haggard look caused by her present distress gave her an unaccustomed ethereal quality. Jess gave a little yelp.

"In the name of all the Nine Muses at once!" she exclaimed, "it *is* Maddalena. Or have I fallen asleep and dreamed one?"

Janet dropped her hand from the lamp and stared in bewilderment. Jess rose and pressed her down into her seat again, peering intently into her face.

"Who are you?" she persisted, "what are you?"

It was Janet's turn to wonder whether she was awake or asleep.

"Janet," she stammered.

"And what are you?"

She gave a breathless, almost hysterical laugh.

"A ghost," she said.

Jess stepped back, disconcerted and stumbled over Maggie's feet.

Maggie chuckled.

"Served with your own sauce, Thalia," she said, "for any sake leave the child alone and go to sleep."

"But Maggie, rouse yourself, *look* at her!" demanded Jess, making a quick recovery. "She's Maddalena to the life!"

Maggie obeyed and her eyes widened.

"She is . . . she is indeed," she agreed. "But you're distressing the poor girl."

Jess ignored her and appealed to the other two.

"Dora! Alice! Look at her!"

Janet the object of four intent gazes felt that she had to get the situation under control.

"My name is Janet," she repeated, "and I am going to Glasgow to . . . to . . ."

She faltered and to her alarm, tears came to her eyes at the consideration of her desolate condition.

". . . to find a situation," she continued more firmly.

"I do not . . . nay, I will not believe that you are a servant," said Jess with a kind of arrogant certainty.

"Then you must," said Janet clearly, "because that is what I am."

"Her voice is good," commented Maggie, who had sat up and was considering Janet with interest.

"Clear and strong," agreed Dora, "there is a brogue but it is slight.

". . . to find a situation . . ." repeated Jess, her eyes fixed on Janet's face. "Have you not got one to go to?"

Janet shook her head.

"You can learn by heart?" pursued Jess.

"Yes," said Janet with a memory of Bible chapters repeated at her mother's knee.

Jess clapped her hands together once in a sharp startling sound and began to rootle in her bag.

"Jess, have some sense . . ." protested Maggie. "You can't just abduct a chance-met stranger."

"This is not chance," Jess announced dramatically, "this is Fate."

"Besides, this is Scotland. Some people here believe the theatre is the Scarlet Woman, the original den of iniquity . . . do you?" she asked Janet.

"No," said Janet, "no, not at all. In fact I was in the theatre tonight. I saw you."

"A pity," said Maggie, "we were not at our best tonight. Far from it, in fact. Our Celia broke her leg about an hour before the performance and poor Dora had to take the part . . ."

"It must be fifteen years since I played the part," sighed Dora, "I couldn't remember a line."

"And we have a fearful epidemic cold going about . . ."

"Here . . ." interrupted Jess and pulled a battered bundle of pages out of her bag and thrust them into Janet's hands. "Your part is Maddalena: you are a tragic beautiful girl, deserted by your lover and wishing to enter a nunnery but pursued by two hateful suitors who quarrel over you. The father of one of them . . ."

"Jess!" said Maggie, "Listen, you can't . . ."

"Why not?" asked Jess and looked down at Janet clutching the grimy script. "You've no place to go, have you Janet?"

Janet shook her head.

"You can stay with us and that means you'll have a roof over your head at least. You might even get paid if the house is full enough. And if we have a proper Maddalena it might *be* full."

"But Jess, I don't suppose she's ever been on a stage in her life! Have you?"

"Never," said Janet.

Jess snorted.

"What has that to say to anything. Neither had you when you played your first role, neither had I."

She turned back to Janet.

"We're offering you a place with us . . . perhaps a career, who knows. If you have it in you and with a face like yours who knows indeed! Surely you'd rather try something like this than slave for some thankless family all your days?"

Like every actress she gave full value to the words she used and the phrase 'all your days' echoed in Janet's mind like a tolling bell.

"And you'll help us out of the fearful dilemma," Jess coaxed, her intensity dropping from her like a cloak. "Please, Janet, even if you hate it, it'll give us time to find someone else. Otherwise . . .

well, the company could collapse. It doesn't do to let your audiences down in the big towns. And what would happen to us all I hardly dare think."

Janet laughed unexpectedly. Suddenly she felt reckless, she had nothing to lose.

"I won't be any use," she warned them, "but I'll try."

The atmosphere in the stuffy compartment suddenly became gay and warm.

The journey to Glasgow took about an hour and a half. By the time the train clanked into the station Janet knew the bones of her part and was word-perfect in the first two scenes. She had always been a fair mimic and had a good ear for tone and inflection so that her travelling companions from regarding her as an barely acceptable stop-gap had come to realise that she might be more than that. They coached her enthusiastically and she learned fast. When the train came to a halt Jess rose and clapped her hands again with an air of triumph.

"If you can move, my girl, you will do, indeed you will."

That night, very late, Janet lay beside Dora high under the roof of a Bath Street lodging house. She should have fallen asleep immediately for it was more than forty hours since she had been to bed, but instead she lay awake and wondered if Simon was lying awake too. A passion of longing and unhappiness arose in her so that she had to turn her face into the musty pillow in case she should cry out and waken poor cold-stricken Dora who lay snoring beside her. In a desperate effort to think of something else she went over in her mind the unbelievable day which had just passed.

Jess had taken her straight from the station to Renfield Street where she had bullied the nightwatchman into letting them into the theatre. By midday Janet was word-perfect in all her scenes and familiar with her main moves: she was then fed with porter and hot pies fetched from the inn on the corner and before these were finished the rest of the company began to assemble, greeting her with astonishment and relief. Janet was swept at once into a full rehearsal. Inevitably she lost her lines from time to time in these new circumstances, but the company rallied to her assistance with a will and by the time Mr Benenden arrived at half past three in the afternoon, trailing an aroma of stale brandy and a bewildered, tow-headed little trollop, she was tackling her scenes with a degree of confidence. Benenden, erupting into the orchestra stalls, was hushed by those members of the cast not engaged in the affecting scene where Maddalena discovers too late that her lover was not dead but in the army and she was pledged to marry the richest of her suitors to save her father from the gallows.

Benenden watched this new and unexpected acquisition in stupefied silence for a few minutes and then slapped the trollop on her ample bottom and recommended her to return to her previous employment in the Princess Theatre . . . which took a broad view of entertainment. The company then rehearsed till an hour before the curtain went up for the evening performance, with Benenden shouting and coaxing and cursing to pull the performance together.

Though Janet's part was central to the play it was not large. Benenden as the profligate father and Jess as the jealous sister of Maddalena's lover having the lion's share of the action. Any time she was off-stage she was seized by a tiny wizened woman dressed in rusty black with a permanent *chevaux-de-fris* of pins in her puckered mouth who thrust her into a trio of grimy peasant costumes, somewhat too large for her, and then crawled round her pinning and tacking frantically and muttering prophesies of disaster through the pins.

At last Benenden had confessed himself almost satisfied and dismissed them to find something to eat before the curtain went up. Jess thrust Janet down on to the vast plum-coloured plush day-bed in their dressing room and sternly bade her rest. She sent out for a plate of hot sausages and fried potatoes, which they shared, Janet discovering a surprising appetite for this plebeian fare. They were interrupted at the meal by Benenden's nephew, the lover conscripted into the army, who looked round the door in his improbable regimentals to announce,

"Looks like a good house . . . and a queue for the gallery!"

Whereupon Janet lost her appetite. Somehow she had never considered the idea of doing her part before hundreds of people. However, there was no time to consider this aspect for long because Jess handed her over to Dora, who dressed her in the first of the peasant dresses as if she had been a child and then made up her face. Janet, who had never worn cosmetics of any kind, found this distracting and fascinating. One after the other the cast wished her good fortune and before she had time to panic she was on stage and among the furniture and the faces which had become so familiar during the long day. In a kind of ethereal trance of exhaustion (which suited the unbelievably angelic Maddalena very well) she played the part as she had been taught. The audience, their eyes on her lovely face, forgave her occasional inaudibility and the (surprisingly few) prompts and applauded wet-eyed and vociferously when at last the curtain fell on her flower-strewn corpse. When the curtain fell for the last time the company with that emotional unanimity of enthusiasm and affection which can so readily seize any theatrical group embraced her and congratulated her and thanked her tearfully before Jess swept her off to eat a late and nasty cold supper in the depressing dining parlour of the Bath Street lodgings. The taste of the bitter stewed tea reminded Janet suddenly of Mrs Carnegie, who so disliked the brew, and then of Simon to whom she had given scarcely a thought for the past twelve hours and more. She felt as if she had betrayed him, knowing that he must have been trying to discover where she had gone all that long day, and she who rarely cried at all, let alone in public, burst into tears there before them all and was swept off to bed in the attic room by Dora in a cloud of compassion and eucalyptus fumes.

# 16

To her astonishment Janet found herself able to earn her living as an actress. She became a member of the company and retained the part of Maddalena even after Amanda returned. She was given small parts in most of the productions and was the understudy for Amanda. The consensus was that if Janet was not an inspired actress she could do well enough ... and of course there was always her appearance. There was also her readiness to help in other ways, to mend costumes, to dress wigs or bundle playbills and programmes. On the latter she figured as Gianetta Spettrale, in memory of her first encounter with the company. Another reason for Benenden's retaining her services was the theatrical tendency to be superstitious. Janet had come to seem a mascot: since she had arrived the run of ill-luck which had reached its climax in Perth had ended and the company had prospered. The two-month season at the Theatre Royal was followed by a Christmas season in Edinburgh, then a most profitable (and exhausting) tour which took them to Inverness and Aberdeen.

Janet, immersed in a life quite unlike anything she had ever known before, worked all her waking hours and tried not to think of either past or future. She discovered the theatre to be a world of its own with little contact with the real one outside its own concerns and this gave her a sense of security. Who would ever dream that Gianetta Spettrale was in legal fact Lady Staindrop ... or for the matter of that, Janet Laidlaw, farmer's daughter. To spend her time pretending to be other people, in particular, people whose griefs and dilemmas were resolved (whether by death or marriage) before the fall of the final curtain helped her to forget her own, seemingly insoluble, problem. She worked at learning this strange new craft as hard as she had worked at farming Glenfoot or learning to be the chatelaine of a great house and a member of

Society. It was bred in her to 'do well whatever came to her hand'. By the end of December Benenden was accustomed to describe her as a 'useful little artiste' and the rest of the company were beginning to wonder how long she would be content with the small unimportant roles she was given.

Occasionally she worried a little about returning to Glasgow, so close to her father. Even in Inverness and Aberdeen she went out very little and when she had to, wore a bonnet with a thick veil. In the theatre she might feel completely secure; as far as she knew none of her own family had ever visited a theatre and Hannah affected to despise provincial offerings and did her play-going in London.

The Phoenix Players at the end of their tour were offered a six week engagement in Glasgow. It was conditional upon Benenden expanding the repertoire with two more plays. He decided to put a new French play into rehearsal, *The Lady of the Camellias*, and to give the leading role to Janet.

At first Janet refused and told him she must leave the company if they were to play in Glasgow again. It was some measure of what she had achieved that he spent a whole morning persuading her to take the part. She explained something of her predicament, saying she had relatives in Glasgow and a circle of acquaintance and was anxious to avoid them. Intrigued by the hint of mystery, Benenden set himself to overcome this difficulty. She should wear a fair wig for Marguerite . . . nothing was more disguising than a change of hair. He would bill her as the daughter of an Italian political refugee; that would put people off the scent . . . and provide some useful publicity. She could be excused from the smaller parts which did not involve a heavy make up and when she repeated her triumph as Maddalena she could wear the same fair wig. He would see to it that she went to and from the theatre in a closed cab. Janet, unwilling to leave the shelter provided by the company, agreed to all this much against her better judgment. Later, in the light of what happened she wondered whether in her heart of hearts she had really wanted to be recognised and to emerge from the limbo into which she had thrust herself. At all events she accepted the part and before long had little time to worry about possible recognition.

Marguerite was a heavy part and Janet was left with no time for regret; she had barely time to eat or to sleep. She certainly had no time to read the newspapers. If she had, she might have read an item which would have reminded her forcibly of her situation. It appeared in *The Times*, not an easy newspaper to come by in Glasgow, on the morning of the first performance of the *Lady of the Camellias*.

> A marriage has been arranged and will shortly take place between Martha Sharpe, oldest daughter of Sir John and Lady Sharpe of Eaton Square, London and Leigh Park, Sussex and Philip Prickett, fifth Lord Staindrop, of Staindrop House, Derbyshire.

Aunt Matilda read the news in the breakfast parlour at Staindrop. She had installed herself there since Aramintha's wedding, thus effectively denying the proprietor the use of his own seat as he blasphemously refused to come within twenty miles of her sharp tongue. A further reason for his absence was his brother's having embarked upon a second edition of his family with a second wife and being all to ready to spy out their future among the halls and heirlooms of Staindrop: moreover, the Sharpes were fixed in London and it was there that Staindrop had to remain until the knot was tied. Thus, there was no one to hear Aunt Matilda's bellow of combined derision and indignation when she read the announcement except an impassive footman who heard her muttered, pointedly Rabelaisian speculations concerning his employer's ability to sire children with a stony face and then repeated them with gleeful embellishments in the servants' hall, which remembered Janet kindly and was indignant.

*The Scotsman* printed this engagement in a neat paragraph on the second page, which mentioned Staindrop's connection with shipbuilding and then recalled the tragic fates of the previous Ladies Staindrop. The writer wished him a happier outcome to this third attempt to find connubial bliss. It was Mrs Carnegie's habit to read items aloud to her son while he drank his tea and ate his scones. She chose this one as an example of English depravity . . . Mrs Carnegie had a wholesome suspicion of the morals and customs of her southern neighbours . . . and one which might give her an opportunity to discuss his own matrimonial prospects which he seemed to be allowing to go by default. Kitty Jamieson, piqued by his neglect, was showing disquieting signs of responding favourably to another, more attentive suitor. When told this he had shown no emotion but relief and frivolously commissioned his mother to choose a good wedding gift. Moreover, he had not been himself for the past few months, his cheerfulness had vanished and his zest for work: he seemed to plod through the weeks, to take no interest in anything. Mrs Carnegie was taken aback, not to say alarmed, by his reaction to a piece of news which she considered to be of no intrinsic interest at all and which concerned persons they did not know, nor indeed want to know. He stared at her and his face was as white as a sheet. He left his tea undrunk and his scone half eaten while he packed a bag and went to catch the evening train to Glasgow. To her exasperated enquiries about where he was going to eat dinner and what she and Guilbert were to do with the meal presently preparing for him he gave only vague and distracted answers and went striding off to the station as if he needed to walk all the way to Glasgow. He forgot he was due to speak at a meeting in the assembly rooms that evening, which annoyed the hard-working Liberal agent very much.

John Laidlaw noticed the paragraph because it appeared just above the Shipping Intelligence. He frowned at it for a few seconds before he pointed it out to Hannah.

"Only to be expected in the circumstances," said she, and sighed for opportunities gone.

She considered the paragraph and then brightened.

"I believe we are related. Remotely, I allow, and through a cousin of a second marriage, but there is a connection. I must write what is proper."

She bustled into the little room she had made her boudoir to compose a suitable epistle. John Laidlaw lit his pipe and smiled rather sourly.

Kirsty and Jock, visiting in Woodside Terrace in order to celebrate their tenth wedding anniversary in a suitable fashion, heard the news from Laidlaw, and Kirsty bridled in her customary aggrieved style.

"Four month," she sniffed. "No much respect there. Hardly cold in her grave."

"Considering," said her father-in-law brutally, "that she'd been dead a sixmonth before she was put into it . . ."

"Father . . ." protested Jock, who had helped to identify that body.

Kirsty bridled again at such coarseness but her mind was not really on it. She and Jock were to visit the theatre that night for the first time in their lives and this loomed far larger on her horizon than the marriage of a man she hardly knew and did not like.

On the day that the announcement appeared in *The Times* Staindrop attended a dress-party at his fiancée's house, there to accept the congratulations of his acquaintance. If there was a degree of reserve among those who had heard a version of the Drumore episode (and there were considerably more of these before the evening was over) he was determined not to notice and his bride-to-be, a woman in her late twenties, plain and rather stupid, was too pleased with having landed such a catch, albeit a somewhat battlescarred one, at her advanced age to see the commiserating looks or notice the *sotto voce* exchanges of the guests.

Halfway through the evening the butler announced a latecomer.

"Captain the Honourable Jasper Pelham-Villiers!"

Staindrop's future parents-in-law stared at this announcement, for to the best of their knowledge the gallant captain had not been invited. He came in on the heels of this announcement and surveyed the guests with a stern and contemptuous expression. Under his arm was a copy of *The Times* and round his sleeve a broad black crepe band. He strode to where his host and hostess stood by the fire, the engaged couple one on either side of them. Staindrop scowled hideously at this intruder and turned his shoulder on him to speak to another guest, who was too fascinated by events to pay any heed.

"Lady Sharpe, Sir John . . ."

Captain Pelham-Villiers bowed solemnly.

"May I beg your forgiveness for this intrusion," he went on, "I am aware I was not invited to this . . . this happy gathering . . ."

His handsome face twisted into a formidable sneer. He surveyed the crowd of Sharpe and Prickett relations gathered to honour the occasion and sneered again. He addressed himself to Staindrop.

"And, my lord, I find it easy to understand how my presence might cast a blight upon the proceedings for you."

He considered with distaste the huffy countenance of Staindrop and then flourished the newspaper at him.

"... but when I read this unspeakable ... this iniquitous announcement ..."

A babble of indignant protest emanated from the group before the fire but Captain Pelham-Villiers accustomed (from time to time) to make himself heard on the wide expanse of Horse Guards' Parade overcame it without effort and those who had not so far noticed the imminent contretemps turned their heads to stare.

"... iniquitous I say," declaimed the gallant captain, "I would never have believed that loving parents would have sacrificed a tender innocent young girl for the sake of empty social position."

Sir John and Lady Sharpe stared at him, as they might have at a savage Ashantee who had invaded their drawing room, in incredulity and alarm. Their daughter Martha simpered and hid her pudgy face behind her fan when she heard herself described in such terms and by such a person. Her upbringing had not been so sheltered that she had not heard of Captain Pelham-Villiers and his proclivities. The captain lowered his voice dramatically: in such moments as he could spare from his more serious pursuits he was an enthusiastic playgoer and had made a study of the greatest tragedians. Not even the eminent Mr Henry Irving could have bettered the effect of his next pronouncement.

"Are you aware, sir ... I repeat, are you aware that you have affianced this innocent lamb to a man who is, in my eyes and in the eyes of God, no better than a murderer?"

The company drew in their breath and stood speechless. Lord Staindrop's face reddened alarmingly and his eyes bulged. Captain Pelham-Villiers drew himself up and pointed at the prospective bride, who shrank back against the what-not and precipitated a large number of very ugly ornaments to a well-deserved end.

"Will you see your daughter married to this cold-hearted Bluebeard?" he demanded, "to a man, nay, to a fiend in human form who has already disposed of two wives? I appeal to your sacred duty as parents to consider what you are doing!"

He dropped his arm and turned upon Staindrop.

"As for you, sir ... you are shameless and evil and I will defend this contention with my blood ... with my blood, sir. You may name your weapon and I will meet you when and where and how you may please!"

He glared about him at the assembly, most of whom were uncertain whether to exclaim or to applaud.

"I have the honour, ladies and gentlemen, to bid you all a very good night."

He bowed again and withdrew, leaving Lady Sharpe in tears at the havoc wrought among her cherished bric-à-brac, her daughter more than halfway to hysterics, Sir John in a considerable danger of apoplexy and the rest of the guests impatient to leave and describe to those unfortunate enough not to have been present at this exhilarating end to a very dull evening. Staindrop, without a word to his affianced bride or to her parents, left the house and returned to his lodgings where he gave his valet a very bad quarter of an hour.

The following day eager eyes scanned *The Times* in expectation of another announcement, 'that the marriage arranged would not now take place . . .' but they were disappointed. For Sir John and his lady, Staindrop House and the growing Staindrop fortune cast a flattering light upon their owner's previous marital misfortunes and they decided it would be un-christian . . . to say the least . . . to condemn poor Lord Staindrop on the flimsy evidence of the bad opinion of a most notorious rake. In this decision Miss Martha fully concurred, for she saw clearly if she missed her chance here all her younger sisters would be married before her (a fate too grim to contemplate) and she could be left at home for the rest of her days to help Mama and dust the china ornaments. Marriage, even to a possible Bluebeard, must be better than such a fate. Besides, she was quite sure that her dearest Philip's two previous wives had been perfectly horrid women and their demise due to the merest accident, whatever horrid people might say. Certainly the last Lady Staindrop had been a horrid common Scotch girl with a perfectly frightful brogue, for all her friends had told her so.

Her dearest Philip, sulking in his rooms in Albany, received her note on hot-pressed scented letter-paper and learned that she would stand by him no matter what. He made an unprintable comment and hurled the effusion into the fire where it joined the ashes of two other letters: one was a formal note of congratulation from his brother, who reported gleefully on his dear Jemima's continued good health in her present delicate situation; the other was from his Aunt Matilda, who advised him in terms the reverse of delicate that he was making a fool of himself (if that were possible when Nature had done a fair job already), that he should cut his losses, admit his shortcomings (here she was specific) and live single instead of making himself a laughing-stock with a niminy-piminy, pudding-faced piece half his age.

At about the same time as Miss Sharpe's letter was delivered at Albany a station fly drew up at Staindrop House. A veiled woman got out bearing a copy of *The Times* in her hand. On hearing from the butler that his lordship was in Town and only Miss Matilda Prickett in residence she asked to see her. In a very short time there was a maelstrom of activity within the house, with servants toiling up and down the stairs with bags and valises and dressing cases and a barrage of orders emanating from the storm-centre, who sat black-clad and grim on the chest in the great hall underlining her demands with thrusts of an ebony walking cane. Such a precipitate departure gave rise to unbridled speculation in the servants' hall. An embittered bootboy who had been found in possession of an uncleaned pair of Aunt Matilda's shoes was heard to express the hope that she and her cane would never be heard from again.

Earlier that same evening Kirsty and Jock had set out for the theatre. This form of celebration had been suggested by Kirsty and had not been well received at first by Jock, who dreaded what the Reverend Mr McMurdoe at Luss would say if ever he came to hear of such a throughither proceeding. For Mr McMurdoe the difference between the entrance to the pit of Hell and the entrance to the pit of a theatre was nonexistent and he would consider Kirsty and Jock as lost souls. Such a consideration could prove embarassing; to be groaned over sepulchrally in church was not to everybody's taste. However, Kirsty had been insistent.

The various theatrical offerings in the city had been passed under consideration: one theatre was in a low part of town and Kirsty was not prepared to pick her way to it through the scraps and orange peels of the vegetable market. Another nearer the west end of the town was presenting a lurid and blood boltered melodrama which concerned a murder in Glasgow itself. While Kirsty would not have objected to such an offering she could foresee certain difficulties in describing her exploits to the less favoured inhabitants of Luss parish. A third featured the Mongolian Monster who could carry three grown men around in his teeth and Sally LaSalle the Saucy Soubrette: the audience for this, Kirsty considered, would be by no means as refined as she could wish. Another theatre was closed owing to a disastrous fire. Consequently, the Theatre Royal was the only possible choice and despite Jock's gloomy disapprobation seats had been booked there for the *Lady of the Camellias*. Kirsty had no notion of the plot but thought that flowers of that nature must be refined. She had ordered for the occasion a gown of puce satin trimmed with ecru lace and jet beads and a confection of feathers and flowers and beads with which to deck her sandy hair, all of which made her resemble an elaborate sugary pudding. Jock, uncomfortable in his collar, his tight shoes and his conscience sat gloomily beside her in the cab which rattled them along Sauchiehall Street with its new shops and brilliant gas lamps to Renfield Street. Kirsty, revelling in her new finery and the dissipation ahead, chatted away about the shops and the people and the play they were about to see while Jock bit the knob of his cane and made no answer.

The wide doors of the theatre were decorated with gaudy posters which described in elaborate phrases the excellence of the play and talents of the company who were presenting it; they waxed especially eloquent about that 'rising star in the theatrical firmament, Gianetta Spettrale'. Jock, sweatily clutching the tickets for which he had paid what seemed like a king's ransom, stared at the names of those for whom he was about to compromise his chances of eternity. They appeared to him foreign for the most part, English and French, and this was sure proof of depravity. He sighed deeply and followed the usher up the wide shallow steps of the grand staircase with its red carpet, white paint and gilding to the plush-covered seats in the middle of the Grand Circle on which Kirsty had insisted.

They were early and for some time sat in solitary splendour as the rows gradually filled up. Jock morosely considered the programme, for which he had been asked to pay the outrageous sum of three pence, while Kirsty subjected each dress which entered to a searching (and usually disadvantageous) comparison with her own apparel. When at last the gas lights were turned down by the uniformed ushers and the curtain looped itself upwards to reveal the glittering Parisian scene, she settled her skirts and prepared to enjoy the unfamiliar sensation of debauchery with an obscure sense that she had at long last got the better of Janet.

The gorgeously dressed guests at Marguerite's house (Benenden had spared no expense on this production) danced and gossiped gracefully among the gilded furniture (by kind permission of Messrs Wylie and Lochhead). Eventually Marguerite herself came through the double doors with her admirer in pursuit and leaned breathless against the sofa down left. Kirsty and Jock sat bolt upright as if they had been jerked by a single string. In the half light they stared at one another and then back at the stage.

"It's awfy like her," murmured Kirsty uncomfortably, "could be her very double."

Jock was trembling. This vision of a dead sister in such a place as he believed the theatre to be, was a portent. He rose to his feet and, without heed for the feet of those in the row, tramped and stumbled his way to the door. Kirsty, thus abandoned, stood up to call him back, was told hissingly to sit down and did so, then thought apprehensively of what Jock might be about in the lobby and rose to leave to a commotion of complaint which could be heard even on the stage. 'Marguerite' in the midst of her flirtation with 'Alfred' heard it and supposed someone to have fainted.

Kirsty found her husband in the lobby with two ushers, who had pushed him down on one of the couches which stood by the wall and were loosening his collar, alarmed by the colour of his face. Under the weatherbeaten tan he had gone as pale as curd. Kirsty, alarmed, sent one of the ushers for a dram, her recently acquired 'refinement of speech' dropping from her like a scarf in her anxiety. Jock clutched at her hand like a drowning man and muttered,

"It's a judgment . . . a judgment . . . that's what it is."

He shuddered and Kirsty sat down beside him to calm his fears.

"Yon's no a ghost," she assured him, "just a lassie as like her as she can spit . . ."

Jock shook his head and his teeth chattered against the rim of the glass.

"It's Janet," he said, "her face . . . her voice . . ."

He gulped the whisky.

"Haivers," declared Kirsty, "we both saw her put in the ground did we no?"

"Aye," said Jock, "and I saw her afore she was coffined."

He shuddered again.

"But yon play actress was Janet. I tell you, Kirsty, it's a judgment on us . . ."

His voice began to get louder and Kirsty, seeing the ushers glance uneasily at one another, tried to talk sense into him.

"Man, take a hold of yerself. A'body's a double so they say, and yon actress-creature must be our Janet's. Come on back in and you'll see it's just a likeness."

Jock shied like a horse at the idea.

"Na, na! I'll never peril my immortal soul again in sic a place," he told her and added more quietly, "I tell ye, Kirsty-lass, it's been a sore lesson to me."

He beckoned one of the hovering ushers and told him to call a cab. His pallor had gone but he had an air of decision about him which reminded Kirsty of her father-in-law and made her realise that there would be no more visits to the theatre. He would not stay in the unhallowed place even to wait for the cab in shelter but went out on to the pavement in the bitter February night. They paced up and down to keep warm and Kirsty noticed a gas-lit sign which read STAGE DOOR down the alley at the side of the theatre, and she had an idea. If Jock could see the actress wifie close to he might realise that it was just a haiver on his part: likely enough the hussy would be nothing like Janet.

"Ask the cabby to wait on me," she told her husband and walked up the narrow pend, her satin skirts held carefully high above the grimy setts.

The stage-door keeper was a man of habit. He checked in everyone in the cast and the stagecrew and then waited until he heard the bell which told him that the curtain had gone up on the first act. He then strolled round to a favourite hostelry and drank a whisky and hot water, one only, and returned after this refreshing interlude to guard the door during the first interval. Thus, when Kirsty pushed open the door and peered into the gas-lit passage there was no one to bar her way and ask her business. She saw a staircase at one end of the passage and could hear voices coming from that direction so she went towards them. A gaggle of party-guests came down the stairs and passed her in a gust of greasepaint, cheap scent, sweat and hot, none-too-clean cloth. She went up the stone stairs as far as a half-landing where a faulty gas-jet bubbled and spluttered. Above her on the upper landing she could see the elaborate white satin skirts which 'Marguerite' had worn on her entrance, swagged and draped over a cage-crinoline and caught up by knots of artificial rosebuds and brilliants. Kirsty paused and looked, hidden in the shadows.

'Marguerite' was evidently waiting to make an entrance for she was listening intently to the murmur of voices onstage: her head was bent so that the pale ringlets hid her face. Kirsty was about to speak when 'Alfred' came running up the stone stairs two at a time and joined the white satin clad figure. Kirsty strained to hear what they were saying.

". . . miss your cue," said Marguerite.

Kirsty's heart thumped. It was the same clear decisive voice that she remembered and now, offstage, the Scots accent was unmistakable.

"Never, my love," said the elegant 'Alfred' cheerfully. "Born in a prop-basket, as they say. Never missed an entrance in my life Had some close calls, though . . . when I've been . . . well . . . distracted. Like I am now."

He seemed to make some advance towards Marguerite, for the white satin skirt swayed and moved farther away.

"I believe you."

Kirsty forced herself to remember the open grave in the Oban kirkyard and the heavy oak coffin which was lowered into it.

"Aren't you going to ask why I am distracted?"

"I hope I've more sense. We're on."

The two figures pulled at a flimsy lath and canvas door and a stream of limelight fell across the upper landing for a minute, and showed their faces. Kirsty gasped.

"It *is* Janet!" she said, "It can't be anyone else!"

# 17

THE CAB DREW up outside Laidlaw's house and disgorged Kirsty and Jock. Kirsty left her husband to pay and scuttled up the steps, her headdress askew and her satin skirts held high to reveal that she had baulked at the purchase of silk stockings and wore hand-knitted grey wool ones under all her finery. She was just at the top of the flight when the front door opened and John Laidlaw thrust forth the neat young groom who had taken the place of Jimmie Gillies.

"Send it at once, Luke," he was saying. "Take a cab . . . take that one! Quick now!"

Luke, clutching a piece of paper, pushed past Kirsty and leapt for the cab just as the cabbie began to turn his horse.

"It must arrive tonight!" Laidlaw called after him and then turned a sardonic eye on his daughter-in-law.

"Aye, aye, Kirsty, you look fair put about," he remarked and held the door for her. "And you're early back, forby. Did our Jock get cold feet at entering the place of sin?"

"You'll not be so joco' when you hear what I've to tell you . . ."

"Do you tell me that? Well, we've news for you too."

He pushed her ahead of him into his study. A tall young man rose as they came in and she looked at him with a feeling of apprehension.

"You've met Mr Lamington, have you, Kirsty?"

Kirsty swallowed and shook her head.

"No to speak to," she said.

Laidlaw raised his eyebrows.

"A slight acquaintance for you to do sic an ill turn," he observed. "If you wish to meet my daughter-in-law, Kirsty, Mr Lamington . . . this is her. If you don't, in the circumstances I'll not blame you. Just try and let on she's no here. Mind, she's hard to ignore whiles."

Simon bowed very stiffly.

"And what am I supposed to have done?" blustered Kirsty.

"Fine you ken what you did. Did you read his letters afore you destroyed them, woman?"

Kirsty went scarlet and Laidlaw considered her with contempt.

"Aye, you can see she did. I doubt you'll not be over-pleased woman at the news Mr Lamington brings us. Our Janet's no dead. We buried another girl up there in Oban. Mind, he doesn't know where she is and hasn't seen her or heard from her since August month but he's sure she's alive . . . aye."

He sat down and began to fill his pipe. It was Simon's turn to flush and he counter-attacked briskly.

"She can't have seen this notice in the paper or you'd have heard from her yourself."

"You'd best have proof of what you say," Laidlaw told him. "or yon Staindrop'll have your hide, lawyer or no."

"If it's proof you're after . . ." began Kirsty who had begun to recover from the encounter but she was interrupted before she could get any further by Jock who came into the room still wearing his tall hat and a preternaturally solemn expression. He gaped at the sight of Simon, but his father spoke first.

"Aye, Jock lad, you look as if you'd met up with old Nick himself. Take your hat off man, for any favour, or you'll have my Hannah on her high horse. She's a fair stickler in sic matters."

Jock, distracted, took off the hat and looked about vaguely for a place to set it down. Impatiently, his father took it from him and spun it into a corner of the room. Kirsty pounced on it and brushed the nap with her elbow.

"I'll thank you to mind that we haven't all got money to throw away," she protested.

"Indeed?" said Laidlaw with a meaning look at the puce satin skirts.

"It'll be a lesson to me all my days," announced Jock.

"Man, I don't give a docken if you wear two hats!" said his father, but Jock took no notice of this.

"To see my own sister in yon haunt of sin . . ." he went on, "flaunting herself abroad . . ."

Suddenly he had all his father's attention.

"To see your own what?" he demanded.

"That's what I was trying to tell you," shrilled Kirsty, "I've all the proof you need. Your daughter's no dead, she's a play actress. I saw her the night with my own eyes, aye and I heard her."

"Is that right enough?" Laidlaw demanded of Jock.

Jock nodded lugubriously.

"Get your hat, Mr Lamington," said Laidlaw. "We'll away and get at the rights of this matter."

At that time of the night cabs were scarce and the two men walked the length of Woodside Road to Charing Cross before they met with one so that by the time they reached the theatre the play was over and the audience pouring into the street. Laidlaw told the cabbie to wait and left him to fend off the home-going playgoers and strode purposefully into the foyer. Simon followed more slowly, looking about him, and his eye was caught by a name on one of the playbills.

"Look!" he called to Laidlaw, who was looking about for an usher, "come here and look at this."

Laidlaw came and read out the name to which Simon was pointing.

"Gianetta Spettrale," he read. "Well, what of it?"

"I would translate it as Janet Ghost," said Simon and laughed.

Laidlaw considered the poster further.

"It can't be her," he decided. "It's the name of the actress playing the heroine of the piece. She'd not be able to do that, not straight off surely?"

Simon smiled.

"All the same," he said, "I think if we ask for Miss Spettrale we will find she is Janet."

"Where would we ask?"

"At the stage door."

However, when they arrived at the end of the alley they found a number of others on a similar errand and could not reach the door where the stage-door keeper stood guard like Cerberus. Laidlaw waited and watched the various members of the company emerge and pair off with individuals in the waiting throng.

"Might be at a dance," he grumbled. "Ever danced Strip-the-Willow, Mr Lamington?"

At length the crowd about the door had thinned enough to let them reach the door and Simon approached Cerberus with a suitable sop. Laidlaw urged this, for, as he said, from the sound of him Simon was more familiar with stage doors than a good-living man ought to be and could pronounce yon unchancy foreign name. To Simon's enquiry the door keeper returned a wary look.

"You're wasting your time," he told him. "She never sees no one. And there's plenty ask."

"If you could just say . . ." Simon began when Janet appeared. She looked harassed and was being followed by the 'Alfred' of the piece, young Benenden, who was evidently anxious to take her to supper.

"No," Janet was saying, "no, I told you earlier. I don't care to eat so late. I just want to go home."

Benenden looked downcast.

"But I've got it all arranged," he protested, "a few nice people and some chicken and stuff. You *ought* to celebrate once in a while . . . especially when the piece has been such a hit . . ."

"No," said Janet again. "I'm sorry, Dickie, but I've told you time and again I won't go out. It's no use asking."

She pulled her cloak round her throat and turned to hurry away before he could argue further. She came face to face with Simon, who had turned at the sound of her voice and was standing under the flickering gas lamp. Her face went white and she gasped with shock. Then Laidlaw stepped into the little circle of light, looked at her and shook his head. Simon suddenly realised that his companion was no longer a young man.

"Aye, lass," said Laidlaw, "so it's true."

He put out his hand and patted her clumsily on the arm as if to reassure himself that she was really there. Janet caught at his hand and held it for a few moments while she collected her wits.

"You gave me such a shock . . ." she stammered, "however did you . . ."

At this point young Benenden stepped forward.

"You appear to be distressing this young lady," he said in his grandest manner, "kindly unhand her."

Laidlaw hardly spared him a glance.

"Away with you, laddie," he said. "This is no business of yours."

Benenden swelled indignantly.

"Anything which distresses Miss Spettrale must be my concern," he declared.

"You might have told us, lass," said Laidlaw. "To let us think you dead . . ."

His face worked slightly and Janet suddenly understood for the first time what she had done. A great surge of remorse overcame her and she burst into tears. Laidlaw for the first time since she was a tiny child took her in his arms. Simon stood quietly by with a lump in his throat, waiting till she should remember he was there. Benenden, however, was not content to wait.

"Sir!" he exclaimed angrily, quite unable to understand what what was happening, "who are you, sir? What is this? I cannot permit you to molest this lady."

Neither Janet nor her father took any notice of him and he turned to Simon uneasily.

"This man is old enough to be her father," he complained, "I cannot just stand by and . . ."

"He *is* her father," said Simon.

"Oh, indeed?" replied Benenden and it was clear that he did not believe a word of it (he was not an actor for nothing). "I am to understand that this is a family reunion?"

"Yes," said Simon.

"And I suppose you are her brother?"

"No," said Simon.

"What is your role in this touching affair then?"

"I hardly know," he admitted. "You might call me her legal adviser."

"A likely story," said Benenden with a sneer he had used to great effect in Act IV.

This exchange had given Janet and her father time to recover and for Laidlaw to recollect his surroundings.

"We can't talk here," he declared. "You'll come home with us?"

Janet nodded and then tried to dry her eyes on the edge of her cloak. Simon provided her with a handkerchief.

"We never meet but we have to dry one another," he remarked with a smile.

Janet smiled back and tears came to her eyes again. Simon put his hands lightly on her arms.

"You will have to learn not to smile at me like that," he said rather unsteadily, "it has a drastic effect."

"I don't understand and I know I shouldn't tell you but I'm

so happy to see you again," she said impulsively. "I've been so empty with missing you. How did you find me out?"

"You haven't seen the notice in the paper?" he asked and her smile faded.

"No. We've just opened in this piece and it has been . . . well, very hard work and there was no time to read them."

"Staindrop's to marry again," said Simon.

Janet stared at him for a moment and then seemed to take her decision.

"Well, I always knew it would have to happen some day," she said. "And perhaps it was time . . ."

She looked at her father, who was standing by her, and put her hand through his arm.

"Let's go home and discuss what's to be done."

Benenden felt he had been ignored long enough.

"And where are you taking her?"

He moved in front of them and challenged Laidlaw.

"None of your concern," said Laidlaw and waved him away like a pestering fly.

"I intend to make it my concern!"

"Oh do stop your nonsense, Dickie, and go home. You can tell your uncle I may be late for rehearsal tomorrow."

"What!"

Laidlaw stopped in his tracks.

"You're not going back to yon place?"

Janet looked at him rather helplessly and Simon stepped smoothly into the breach.

"The cab's waiting," he reminded Laidlaw. "We can discuss this inside."

As they climbed into the cab, with Simon facing Janet and feeling slightly light-headed with the shock and delight of seeing her again, Benenden ran after them and hailed another cab.

"Follow them!" he said grandly and then was conscious of a faint worry lest he should have to follow them far. Pay day was two days off.

At about the same time Staindrop was sitting in his rooms making further inroads into the brandy and wondering whether he could put in an appearance at his club without being twitted about Pelham-Villiers' dramatic appearance at the Sharpe's evening party when his valet came in with a telegram. In view of his more recent correspondence, he eyed the yellow form with understandable suspicion. Its brief contents made him stare in consternation and then curse. Almost without a pause he began to bellow orders at his valet to pack a night bag for him immediately and then call a hansom to take him to catch the night express for Glasgow.

After he had left in a black bad temper, the valet, nursing a singing ear and a long-standing grudge, picked up the slip of yellow paper discarded in the sitting room. He read it and, as he was intimately acquainted with his master's affairs, its contents made him guffaw in a most unseemly style and help himself to a measure of brandy which had also been left untended in the haste of his master's departure. As he sat at ease by his employer's fire and considered that gentleman's dilemma he evolved a pleasant scheme to embarrass him still further. He gulped the last of the brandy, tucked the telegram into an inner pocket and set out to find another set of bachelor apartments a few streets away.

An hour later, with a very generous cheque safely tucked into the same inner pocket, he was strolling along one side of Queen Square thinking contentedly of the neat and commodious lodging house in Bayswater which he could now afford to buy and the pleasure he would take in relinquishing a situation where the opportunities for peculation only barely made up for his employer's chronic ill-temper and heavy hand. As he planned the furnishings and appointments of the Bayswater house he was passed by a hansom cab racing hell-for-leather in the direction of Euston Station with a familiar figure leaning out over the apron and shouting encouragement to the Jehu. The valet was so struck with the situation he had precipitated that he leaned against the railings of the nearest house and laughed until he attracted the attention of a policeman on the beat, who approached suspiciously and demanded if he might be drunk.

At Woodside Terrace the gas lights still burned. Hannah, returned from her card party, had been regaled with the whole story by Kirsty and with some difficulty had elicited corroboration from Jock who was still in what appeared to be a state of shock and sat disconsolately muttering to himself about hell-fire and Mr McMurdoe. Hannah demanded to know whether Staindrop had been informed and when she was reassured on this point set herself to wait until her husband should return. Her feelings were mixed: she was not an unnatural woman and to believe Janet dead and in such distressing circumstances had caused her grief, considerable grief. She had been the more grieved by Laidlaw's obvious remorse that he should not have acknowledged Janet's plight in his anxiety to retain Staindrop as a partner. Moreover, in the months she had passed in her company Hannah had come to have an affection and a good deal of respect for her stepdaughter and had known a qualm or two at the part she had played herself in bringing her to such a pass. To discover she was still alive gave her pleasure at first but this was gradually swamped by resentment, first at the unnecessary distress she had caused and then at the commotion her reappearance was bound to create.

She suddenly interrupted a tirade from Kirsty about how she had always known that Janet would come to a bad end by exclaiming, "Whatever can we say to Lord Staindrop?"

Kirsty stared.

"Never mind him . . . what's Jock and me to say in Luss? Him an elder in the Kirk and that much respected with a sister in yon place flaunting herself like a Jezebel!"

Jock groaned.

"She has painted her face and tired her head . . ." he declaimed, "in the portion of Jezreel shall dogs eat the flesh of Jezebel."

Hannah blenched slightly at this.

"I think, Kirsty, that the shock has been rather too much for John . . . perhaps he should lie down on his bed?"

However, before he could be persuaded to do this the cab drew up at the door and Kirsty, at the window, reported on its occupants.

"Father," she said, "and yon fancy-man of Janet's . . . and there's a wifie just getting down . . . in the Name . . ."

She turned to face the room and let the heavy curtains fall together.

"To think she has the brass face to bring her sin to this house! It's Janet herself!"

Janet's entrance to the drawing room was greeted by a spiteful tirade from Kirsty which dealt confusedly with sin and pride and hell-fire and what the neighbours would say and how Jock would never be able to hold up his head again. Laidlaw interrupted her.

"If you're that much concerned with sin, woman, away up to your room and think on the sin of covetousness and jealousy. You've played your part in this fankle . . . aye, and no small part!"

He turned his angry gaze on Jock, who was staring at his sister as if he expected Jehu to ride his chariots over her at any moment.

"And take yon gcmeril with you," he added roughly. "Lord knows you're well-matched, for spite and bigotry have aye slept in one bed and brought forth grief."

Kirsty, much affronted at such plain speaking, burst into noisy tears and flounced out of the room. Jock followed her without a word.

"They'd rather have you dead, it seems," said Laidlaw bitterly and then saw Janet's face.

"Sit down, lass, and never heed," he said gently and put her in a chair.

Simon drew up another and sat just behind her where she could be sure of his presence.

"Ring for yon O'Malley," said Laidlaw to his wife and it was a measure of his state of mind that he had forgotten the courtesy with which he was used to treat her. "I doubt we could all do with something."

Hannah, tight-lipped, rang for the parlour-maid and ordered a tray with food and drink. When she had done this the first awkwardness had passed. Laidlaw took a deep swallow of his whisky.

"We'll have no talk of whys and wherefores," he announced and fixed Hannah with a bright blue stare. "Let it suffice I know why she did what she did and to my mind there was reason enough. There'll be no reproaches. We've enough to do seeing how matters can be mended."

"But to leave us in ignorance," protested Hannah, "to cause us such grief and distress . . . some explanation is due."

"I am sorry," said Janet quietly, "I am truly sorry. But I had little reason to suppose at the time that anyone cared very much what happened to me."

Hannah began an indignant protest but was silenced by Laidlaw.

"I have thought since," he said heavily, "that you might well think this. We must have seemed unco anxious to get you off our hands one way or the other. And I should have learned more about the man Staindrop than just the depth of his pocket."

"But whoever would have dreamed that he would ill-treat her," Hannah defended herself. "He was always so very much the gentleman when we were in company with him . . . and so attentive."

"A gentleman whose first wife had run away from him," returned Laidlaw. "You never told me that and you must have known of it. Did you tell Janet?"

Hannah fell silent, a bright patch of colour on each cheek.

"And you never told me he misused you," he said to Janet. "I had it from your maid after you were . . . afterwards."

"I tried once," said Janet.

"Aye," he agreed sombrely. "And I'd not listen. It was during the negotiations for the Naval contract. I needed Staindrop then. It would have dished me to lose him. I told myself it was just female haivers. I should have known better . . . you're not given to haivers, lass. It's kept me awake this many a night . . ."

"I'm sorry . . ." said Janet almost inaudibly, her hands clasped tightly in her lap. Simon stirred in his chair.

"I can understand why you might keep close at first," said Hannah accusingly, "but afterwards, when you thought about it . . . did you not *think* of the distress . . ."

Janet explained about Ealasaidh and how it became impossible to leave her.

"And after she was dead," she went on, "I read about my own burial. It was a shock . . . I can't tell you . . . It began to seem more and more difficult to admit that I was still alive and later . . ."

She glanced over shoulder at Simon.

"I had another reason to stay close."

She did not explain further. Hannah looked at Simon's expressionless face and drew her own conclusions.

"As for you, young man," she said coldly, "I gather you've known these six months that Janet was alive and you said never a word to those most concerned. I do not think that this was a very honourable action."

Simon looked at her seriously.

"It would depend, ma'am, on your definition of honour. Miss

Laidlaw confided in me to a certain extent. She seemed afraid that you and your husband might insist on her returning to Staindrop and this . . . this was not agreeable to her. In such circumstances, it would scarcely have been honourable to betray her confidence until something like this engagement made it necessary. And also made it less likely that he would demand her return."

Hannah's raised eyebrows and pursed lips made it clear that she did not accept this explanation but she said nothing more on that head. There was something more important.

"What if he does demand it?"

There was a brief silence.

"We can discuss this in the morning," said Laidlaw. "We're all tired."

"I think we should clear the air," said Hannah. "We can be sure of one thing, there is going to be a considerable scandal. I think the best thing would be for Janet to return to her husband."

There was another silence.

"For her sake," she added, ". . . and ours."

Janet looked at her and for a moment appeared very like her father.

"No," she said.

Hannah appealed to Simon.

"Surely, Mr Lamington, as a lawyer, you must admit that a wife's place is with her husband."

Janet rose from her chair.

"This is a pointless argument," she told them. "Even if he wants me to go back, which is very unlikely, I won't go. I'm not afraid of him any more but I could not live with him again, not now I've escaped."

"And what will you do?" asked Hannah. "Become a servant again? That will reflect well upon your family, I must say."

"I mean what I say," said Janet. "Make no plans for this season which include Queensgate or Staindrop House for I will not be there."

Hannah flushed angrily.

"I'm tired, father," Janet went on. "Is there a bed for me here or could someone call me a cab to go back to Bath Street."

"I'll have a bed made up for you," said Hannah huffily and tugged at the bell, "and one for Mr Lamington, I suppose."

When this was done Janet rose to say her good nights.

"We'll talk again in the morning," promised her father.

"I'll be of the same mind still," she warned him, smiling, and for the first time since her childhood kissed him on the forehead.

"But I'll promise you this," she added, "I'll not disgrace myself, or you . . . or anybody else."

She looked over her father's head at Simon and there was no smile on her face. He understood what she was saying.

"Did you know Mr Lamington is to stand for Parliament, father?"

"It's not yet certain," he returned, not taking his eyes off her face. "I am still considering the prospects of emigration."

They looked at one another for a moment.

"I think you should put it from your mind," said Janet in a low voice. "Good night."

The sleeping carriage attendant on the Glasgow train was pleased to find that all but three of the sleeping berths were taken for the late night train. He made an assessment of his charges and reckoned that none of them were good for more than the customary shilling. However, before the train was well out of the station he was cheered by the appearance of the guard.

"Two women wanting two berths," he said. "Old griffin and a widow with a nipper. Got any?"

"Might 'ave."

"Reckon she might spring you arf a crown . . . might be more. She's a one right enough, the old 'un."

"Send 'em along," said the attendant.

He was engaged in settling this party when another latecomer appeared and demanded to know whether there was a berth available. The attendant demurred: he preferred to keep a berth in hand in which he might snatch an hour or two of sleep in the dead hours. The latecomer was evidently in an evil mood for he became abusive. Nor did he (which was more to the point) produce any reasonable incentive to forgo this strictly unlawful privilege. The attendant endured his abuse with an unexpressive countenance but resolved not to give way on any point. As he was to say later to the guard over a cup of tea, "If 'e'd been civil and slipped me a florin I'd have given 'im a coupla blankets and a piller."

As it was the latecomer stalked back to his first-class smoker where he huddled into his fur-lined coat and glowered into the night through a haze of tobacco smoke which drove the only other occupant out to find a less asphyxiating seat. As he left the compartment coughing, he nearly collided with a tall military-looking gentleman who accepted his apologies with great good humour and continued on his way to the sleeping carriage where by dint of two persuasive sovereigns and a good deal of banter he obtained the last vacant berth.

Consequently, Captain Pelham-Villiers spent a comfortable night in contemplation of a lover's meeting at the end of the journey. Why the object of his affections had failed to let him know she was still alive did give him slight pause but he fell asleep eventually in the comfortable certainty that there must be some acceptable explanation, even of this. Staindrop, on the other hand, huddled sleeplessly in his compartment, morosely wondering if ever there was another man so beset with matrimonial complications. His head began to nod in a combined fug of cigar smoke and self-pity and somewhere near Carlisle a signalman saw, in the centre section of the Scotch express, a madman dancing about his compartment and beating at himself with his hands. Staindrop had fallen asleep during his third cigar and it had dropped from his flaccid mouth and burned a large hole in a prominent place on the front of his shepherd's plaid trousers; the area of woollen underwear which lay below was also damaged and his attention had been drawn to the occurrence when the cigar stump had begun to burn the skin which lay below that. The compartment was filled with throat-catching stink of burning wool and later with the echo of bad language when Staindrop discovered that his fool of a valet had not packed another pair of trousers in his nightbag.

O'Malley, the parlour-maid, rising at six to light the fires in Woodside Terrace, toiled up the stairs with buckets of coal and down them with buckets of ashes and muttered imprecations on the extra work caused by unexpected visitors. The previous night, by dint of eavesdropping, she had pieced together a garbled version of Janet's story and she went into her room with a certain superstitious awe, meaning to look carefully upon the face of one who, according to her information, had been dead for a year.

However, she found Janet both alive and awake and in a wrapper of a very elaborate description lent her by Hannah.

"... And there she was writing a letter and all in the bitter cold," O'Malley reported to the cook, "pretty as a picture she is and a smile as sweet as honey."

The cook was still half asleep and far from pleased with her lot.

"Six for breakfast instead of four and never a word to me. She's a play actress so that young mistress Laidlaw was saying. A disgrace that's what it is and in a gentleman's house. Look outside and see can you see the milkman, Biddy. There's just a drop left for our tea and it's on the turn."

There was no milkman in sight but O'Malley emerging from the kitchen door into the area found Dickie Benenden huddled on the steps, more than half frozen but convinced that such a vigil must convince Janet of his undying, self-sacrificial devotion ... if only she could be informed of it.

"Miss Spettrale?" he demanded through chattering teeth, when O'Malley had got over the turn he had given her and which she declared had taken two years from her allotted span. "Miss Spettrale, is she all right?"

"Miss Janet, you mean?" said O'Malley. "She's as right as ninepence. Up and about and writing a letter."

"Tell her I'm here," he chittered, "and assure her I am hers to command if I can be of assistance."

O'Malley was gratifyingly impressed by such heroic sentiments but thought privately that he would be of more immediate use if he were not set solid with the cold.

"Sure and I will," she said obligingly, "but won't you come in for a heat at the fire?"

Benenden shook his head.

"I'll not enter till she bids me," he said nobly. "But tell her I am here if she needs me."

O'Malley went in and then remembered something. She put her head round the door.

"And who shall I say is here?" she demanded.

"Tell her ... Richard, Richard Benenden," he said and opened his eyes for a second to see whether she recognised the name. But O'Malley was not a playgoer. She preferred the halls.

The cook was less impressed by his devotion and went out with the rolling pin to invite him to leave at once. Benenden did not deign to answer.

"Richard?" said Janet when she heard the news, looking up from the letter she was writing to Staindrop, "oh, it's Dickie, the great gomeril. Oh, tell him to go home. I don't need his help or anyone else's."

O'Malley reported a few minutes later that he would not go until he heard from her own lips that she was unscathed. Janet gave an exclamation of exasperation.

"I'll get dressed and come down and rid you of him."

In a very few minutes she came down to the kitchen to the scandalisation of the cook and went into the area where she dismissed her swain in a few crisp sentences.

"Away home and get your breakfast for you'll get none here."

Cook measuring out the meal for the porridge heard this with relief.

"A fine Alfred you'll make tonight, croaking away with the cold like a frog in a puddle."

Benenden attempted a protestation of devotion but was stopped ruthlessly.

"This is all haivers and you know it. You've fallen in love with every leading lady you ever had, so they tell me. Now home with you."

He went off, rather downcast, while she watched to make sure that he left. A clatter of hooves drew her attention and a cab came up the terrace at a canter. The door swung open before it came to a halt and a tall figure leaped nimbly down and handed the driver a coin, waving the offer of change loftily away. The new arrival turned about to survey the house and at once saw Janet staring in disbelief from the area. Before she could retreat hc came down the area steps three at a time and seized her in a rib-cracking embrace.

"Alive!" he exclaimed, "Alive and more beautiful than ever. I could not believe it!"

Janet struggled free.

"Please stop it," she protested. "Where on earth did you arrive from?"

Pelham-Villiers released her reluctantly, conscious of two faces behind the barred kitchen window. Cook and O'Malley had never spent a more entertaining morning.

"From London by the night train," he told her. "I came the very instant I heard you were found. I asked the cabbie if he knew where your father lived and he did and here I am."

Janet regarded him with a kind of resigned despair.

"This promises to be a memorable day," she said. "You'd better come in. I can't leave you on the doorstep after a night journey, much as I would like to."

She led him into the kitchen where he endeared himself to his audience by bidding them a cheerful good morning. Janet was less cheerful.

"Please show Captain Pelham-Villiers to the breakfast parlour," she requested. "And I don't doubt he'd like some breakfast."

Cook sighed but not deeply. As she said herself, she did like a proper gentleman.

The uninvited guest was immured in that apartment and Janet escaped upstairs to finish dressing. O'Malley had just taken the captain a preliminary cup of tea out of the cook's own pot, "For sure, isn't he a fine man and isn't it a cold morning and him all the road from London!" when all three of them were startled by the peremptory jangling of the front door bell. Cook dropped the bellows with which she was quickening the fire with a view to preparing a dish of bacon and eggs and rushed to the area window where by dint of inserting her head between the bars and peering upwards she could see a pair of legs. This pair was stamping about impatiently and was clad in trousers very much too short and too wide.

Lord Staindrop had had to find a replacement for his ruined garment. He had not deemed it suitable to conduct such an interview as he anticipated with an erring wife either tightly buttoned into a fur-lined overcoat or displaying a hole as large as his fist in a strategic area. He had intended to make the purchase at his leisure when the shops opened for business, but the sight of a familiar and much-hated figure hailing a cab had jabbed him into more precipitate action. He had taken the next one and ordered the driver to take him at once to the nearest tailor's where he had hammered on the door until the owner came down, unshaven and indignant, from his breakfast and was constrained to supply him with a pair of trousers.

It was a little unfortunate that the tailor's clientele seemed to be drawn from a circle which made up in girth what they lacked in height. In desperation Staindrop had seized upon the pair which most nearly fitted him, though they were far from satisfactory. He paid exorbitantly for them because the tailor protested vehemently that he was bound to deliver them that very day and to a very good customer. Staindrop put them on and refused to remove them and left the tailor clutching three sovereigns.

O'Malley heard the bell as she came out of the breakfast parlour in giggling disorder. Jasper's reunion with the love of his life had not impaired his lively appreciation of other females. She also heard an impatient hammering on the panels of the door. Straightening her cap in the hall looking-glass she opened the door, a lengthy process for there were bolts, bars and chains enough upon it to protect the Bank of Scotland, and was nearly pushed over by Staindrop's entrance.

"Where is my wife?" he demanded. "Tell her I will see her at once!"

O'Malley, simply gaped. This was a morning she would remember for some time.

Staindrop made an exasperated sound and removed his overcoat. Looking about he saw a light in the breakfast parlour. Thrusting open the door he went in to find Pelham-Villiers at ease by a bright fire sipping tea as if he had been a guest of long standing. To Staindrop, conscious of an unshaven chin, his spruceness was an affront.

"You! I knew it!" said his lordship with concentrated loathing. "I said all along that you were at the bottom of it. I should have expected to find you here."

"I say," enquired the captain, fascinated, "did you know you had got on some other fellow's trousers?"

"Never mind my damned trousers!"

O'Malley had recollected herself sufficiently to close the front door, much to the fury of the cabdriver who was about to make an entrance in search of his fare. At Staindrop's bellow of anger she decided that someone must be told of this invasion so she lifted up her print skirts and fairly scuttled up the staircase. She knew Janet was up and dressed and able to come quickly and she was none too sure what the mistress would have to say to this early morning visitation, so she ran up the second flight to Janet's room.

"It's your man, mistress and him and the other gentleman at it, hammer and tongs!"

Janet followed her downstairs with a sinking heart to face what she knew would be a difficult interview and one she had hoped to avoid by writing a letter. She found that matters had reached a crisis.

Staindrop and Pelham-Villiers were shouting at one another in the parlour, the front door bell was pealing away as if the latest caller were swinging on the end of the bell-pull. Cook and O'Malley had roused young Luke to answer it because they were unwilling to run the gauntlet of the hall, and after the morning's events the blessed saints alone knew who might be at the door this time.

"You're a philandering villain," bawled Staindrop, "you ought to be cashiered!"

"You're impugning the honour of your own wife!" Jasper returned in ringing tones. "You are the villain, sir!"

"Honour!" spluttered Staindrop, "Honour! What honour has she left to her, the trollop!"

"I say you shan't miscall her!" roared Jasper. "I'll defend her good name with my life . . . sword or pistol or fists . . . name your weapon, sir, name it! I will prove you wrong!"

"I'll call her what I please," declared Staindrop. "Any woman who would run off to live under your protection is a whore and a trollop even to consider such a loose living scoundrel!"

For answer to this he got Jasper's fist in his face. It was not a considered blow, merely a swipe born of exasperation, but it sent him staggering back through the parlour door into the hall where he cannoned into Luke trying to cross unobserved to the front door. They both came down in a heap just as the door swung back against the wall with a crash. O'Malley, in her haste to inform Janet, had forgotten to lock it. The cabman came stamping into the hall, describing his passenger in terms which could only have been understood by a fellow-Glaswegian, to discover the defaulter on his back on the hall carpet with a large mustachioed figure standing over him in a pugilistic attitude. A slim youngster sketchily dressed in breeches, shirt and his stocking-soles was attempting to extract himself from this perilous situation. The cabbie's flow of abuse dried up and he gaped. Behind him through the open door strode Benenden, who had returned at the sight of two gentlemen arriving at the house in evident haste, to discover what these early arrivals portended and to assure Janet of his support through any emergency, which he did over all the commotion in tones calculated to reach the gallery of the largest theatre in Glasgow. At the head of the kitchen stairs stood O'Malley who was in hysterics and cook, clutching a frying pan in which the eggs still spat and frizzled, reiterating that this was not what she had been used to in a gentleman's establishment and were all these people staying to their breakfasts.

Janet, bemused, regarded the scene from halfway down the first flight. She sank back on to the step behind. There was a movement behind her and she turned to see Simon, who had turned out to see what all the commotion was about. Behind him on the half-landing were grouped the rest of the household in various stages of disarray, huddled behind Laidlaw who was clad in trousers and nightshirt and clutching the brass poker from the drawing room.

The situation might be said to be getting out of hand.

# 18

After an hour or so the company had been called to order. Hannah had taken Staindrop away to offer him a much-needed shave and a pair of her husband's trousers, which, if they were a trifle too long, made him appear less like a clown in a circus than his hasty purchase. She also gave him a substantial breakfast in her own sitting room and listened sympathetically to the tale of his woes. The cabdriver had gone, together with a large tip, and a story which would earn him free drinks for a month. Janet had convinced Benenden that neither her life nor her virtue was endangered and despatched him to the theatre to say that though she must miss the morning rehearsal (she was playing Bianca to Jess's magnificently aggressive Katharina in the *Taming of the Shrew*) she would be in the theatre for the evening performance. Simon, with a resigned and amused glance at Janet, had undertaken to entertain Jasper, who was superbly impervious to any hint that his presence was superfluous and even to Laidlaw's blunt request that he should leave. Over an equally substantial breakfast he had confided to Simon his innermost feelings and even asked whether Simon, as a man of the world, considered that Lady Staindrop might contemplate accepting his protection.

"It would be a bond more sacred to me than any marriage tie," he assured Simon through a mouthful of bap.

Simon, who had become familiar with the gallant captain's reputation, reflected that there were a number of husbands who would vouch for this. Thus, when the company foregathered in the dining saloon 'to settle the matter' Jasper was also present, though nobody really knew why. By that time, too, the atmosphere was comparatively calm. The company seated themselves around the dining table and immediately took on the aspect of a board meeting with Laidlaw in the chair . . . which was, perhaps, not unintentional.

Laidlaw began the discussion himself by declaring that they had met to discuss the situation which had arisen following Janet's reappearance. No one, he said, could but rejoice that she was safe and sound and was acclaimed for this sentiment by a hearty 'Hear! Hear!' from Jasper who, baulked of the seat next to Janet by Simon's superior tactics, had taken one opposite and was exasperating Staindrop by gazing ardently at her. However, Laidlaw continued, there could be no doubt that there was a certain awkwardness attached to this happy reunion . . . certain difficulties were bound to arise . . .

At this point Simon interrupted.

"The situation is perfectly clear," he said in his best courtroom manner. "All that will be necessary is for his lordship to intimate to his fiancée that their marriage cannot now take place.

"But things cannot just be left as they are," protested Hannah. "For all our sakes the situation must be regularised. It is really most unsatisfactory."

This was greeted with a loud 'Hear! hear!' from Staindrop slumped sulkily beside her.

"Lord Staindrop has also said to me that he would be quite willing for Janet to return to him as his wife and would not contradict any . . . er . . . explanation we might put about to cover her prolonged absence."

There was a rumble of protest from Jasper which culminated in the word 'Never!' Hannah ignored him.

"I think," she said, "it would be best for all concerned if she were to do this."

She paused and looked about the table to see how this suggestion was received: Jasper looked incredulous, Laidlaw doubtful and Simon expressed no emotion at all.

"We would need," Laidlaw said heavily, "to have some assurances about her treatment . . . it would seem not to have been very satisfactory in the past . . ."

"Hah!" snorted Jasper significantly and glared along the table at Staindrop.

"I am sure," Hannah said, "these little misunderstandings can be smoothed over."

Jasper gave vent to another 'Hah!'

"Such minor contretemps do arise from time to time in early married life," Hannah continued, "and I feel that . . ."

Jasper rose to his full height and twirled his moustache.

"I do not call what occurred at Drumore a minor contretemps," he declared and pointed a minatory finger at Hannah, who looked down her nose.

"You were not present, ma'am, on this occasion. Your step-daughter was forced against her will to go for a walk on a cold dark evening with her husband . . . with what purpose I can only conjecture . . . and I discovered her some ten minutes later, her gown torn and stained, her arms bruised and scratched and her face . . ."

He swelled with emotion.

". . . her pretty face swollen, bruised and cut."

He paused and pointed at Staindrop.

"Someone . . . I have no proof of whom . . . someone had given her a severe beating."

He looked contemptuously around the table.

"You may call this a minor contretemps if you choose," he said, "you may even accept Janet's explanation that she had a severe fall . . . Hah!"

He glared at Staindrop.

"She was shaking with terror when I found her . . . trembling like a leaf. Something had frightened her and I am convinced that 'thing' . . ."

He packed the syllable with a wealth of distaste and pointed again at Staindrop.

". . . was none other than her husband."

There was a prolonged pause and the company looked at one another.

"You will agree, sir, that your daughter is not easily frightened?" Jasper enquired of Laidlaw whose face was grim.

"Aye," said Laidlaw.

"And are you prepared to hand your daughter back to a man who would do that to her?"

"No," said Laidlaw. "No."

Simon spoke suddenly, the words forced out of him by a sudden surge of anger. This was the first time he had had any but Janet's much-modified version of the events which had driven her to run away.

"Oh, that's excellent hearing!" he said bitterly. "But is no one going to ask Janet herself what she wishes in this?"

Everyone looked at her and she coloured under their gaze.

"I'll not go back," she said quietly. "It's not because of what happened. I thought Philip a monster at the time, but . . ."

Jasper snorted.

"And you were right!"

Staindrop half rose from his seat and Janet quickly intervened in an attempt to lighten the atmosphere.

"One thing I have learned in the theatre and that is that men do strange things when they are jealous . . . and I suppose Staindrop had reason to think . . ."

Jasper snorted again and leaned forward.

"*That* isn't why he attacked you. He knew there was nothing in it whatever he may have said. I'll tell you why he attacked you . . ."

He blurted out the story of Angus's recipe for getting a son. It was received in bemused silence by Janet and the men, though Hannah gave an exclamation of distaste and hid her face. Janet looked at her husband.

"If he'd explained what he wanted and why, I'd have laughed at him and he knew it. So he didn't try and I thought he'd run mad and was trying to kill me because of him."

She nodded at Jasper.

"I could wish, my dear, that he had had reason."

Janet took no notice of this gallantry.

"I never dreamed that was what he intended . . ."

Hannah recovered her composure.

"If you now understand why this unfortunate affair occurred will you not now consider returning?" she suggested. "It would be by far the most satisfactory ending to the business."

Janet shook her head.

"No, I won't go back. Not because of what occurred but because he dislikes me as much as I dislike him, because he has a foul tongue and I have a bitter one and because this disagreement would be bound to end in violence again. It would be my fault as much as his."

There was a short silence.

"Very well," said Laidlaw, "we'd best leave it at that."

"Oh, no, we will not!" said Staindrop and sat forward.

"Everyone's had his say and now you can listen to mine. I married because I wanted an heir. Do you suppose I'd have taken a trollop out of a Scotch farm-yard for any other reason?"

Simon and Jasper both came to their feet at this but Laidlaw waved them to their seats again.

"Hear him out," he said grimly, "you'll have your say later."

"It's true anyway," added Janet. "Nor is it the first time he has told me so."

"I still have no heir," said Staindrop. "Now it seems I can't have a wife. Well, I tell you I won't have my brother's ill-conditioned brat in my shoes. I'm a young man still and I'll have an heir one way or the other. If you won't come back and do what is no more than your duty . . ."

He glowered at Janet.

". . . I'll rid myself of you and marry someone who will."

There was a fraught silence.

"I can do it," he assured them. "If Janet is obstinate I will divorce her in the courts for criminal conversation with both of these . . ."

He pointed at Simon and Jasper.

"You will have to resign your commission," he said, "your regiment has turned a blind eye to your philandering to date . . ."

This was not quite accurate; Jasper's fellow-officers regarded his amatory exploits much as they regarded the mess trophies, as proof of communal prowess.

". . . but they'll not stand for an open and public scandal. As for you, you provincial pup . . ."

He turned on Simon.

"There'll not be much left of a career in politics after that," he sneered. "They're great hypocrites, the Scotch."

This was followed by another silence. Staindrop leaned back in his chair and drummed his fingers on the table. Janet had gone as white as a sheet. Hannah regarded her rings and Laidlaw clenched his hands as if to prevent them flying out at his son-in-law. Jasper rose to his feet and his theatrical airs dropped away from him like a coat.

"You are such a cur, Staindrop," he said quietly. "I'll tell you this to your head. Rather than see Janet tied to you I'd be proud to stand beside her in the courts and damn the consequences. And

I'd do it even if I was never to see her again. You do your worst."

He snapped his fingers.

"I agree in every particular," said Simon and came to his feet as well. "With your permission, Mr Laidlaw, Captain Pelham-Villiers and myself would consider it a privilege to see his lordship off the premises."

Jasper's face assumed an expression which reminded Janet forcibly of her old sheep-dog at the prospect of a walk on the hill and she had to subdue her amusement even at such a moment.

"Just a minute," she said, before her father could speak, "I can't believe you are serious, Philip. Surely you don't mean to do such a dastardly thing rather than see your brother at Staindrop?"

"I am perfectly serious," he said mulishly.

"You're prepared to destroy two perfectly innocent people to gratify a personal spite at your brother?"

"You're forgetting yourself in all this innocence," he sneered. "You'll not be welcome anywhere but your own farm-yard once I'm done with you."

"I knew you for a stupid man," she said quietly, "and a sulky obstinate one, forbye. You're overquick with your hands when you're crossed and unfaithful as a tom-cat but I never realised before that you were wicked. I'll come back," she told him and her voice trembled slightly. "I'll come back because I must. But I'll come back in my own good time and when I do . . ." her voice strengthened, ". . . I'll lead you such a dance of it you'll wish you'd never been born."

No one in the dining saloon had heard the front door bell ring again. O'Malley, eating a belated and well deserved breakfast, had jumped in her chair.

"Merciful heaven," said she, "not another of them! I declare I don't know whether I'm coming or going, this day."

"Eight for breakfast," said the cook. "The dear knows how many will be for lunch at this rate."

This time the callers were female. A pale woman in her late thirties, heavily draped in widow's weeds, stood on the doorstep with a girl of maybe five or six holding her hand. The child was so wrapped against the Caledonian chill in shawls and comforters that it was a task to discover the sallow little face within them. Behind them stood a small, thin, elderly woman dressed in purple silk with a formidable bonnet and an umbrella nearly as tall as herself.

"Is Mr Laidlaw at home?" enquired the old lady.

"He's engaged just at the moment," said O'Malley, her ear cocked nervously at the double doors of the dining saloon, "but maybe you'd care to wait?"

"We would," declared the old lady and marched in holding her umbrella much as a soldier might hold a sword when approaching a suspected ambush. The widow sidled after her and the little girl wrested her hand from her mother's and began to remove the upper layer of shawls.

"What name shall I say?" asked O'Malley, giving aid where it was needed as one comforter was tied in a knot just where the child could not reach it.

She missed the glance which passed between the two adults.

"Prickett," said Aunt Matilda. "Miss Matilda Prickett and her niece and great niece."

"Please to come this way," said O'Malley and set off up the staircase to the drawing room where she intended to leave them with Jock and Kirsty. This pair had been firmly excluded from the dining saloon by Laidlaw, who declared that he could not be doing with Kirsty's screeching all morning and if Jock had no more to contribute to the matter in hand but inapposite quotations from the second book of Kings he could spout them to Kirsty who, it seemed to him, would be the better of some Christian teaching. After which not even Kirsty insisted on attending and they were waiting abovestairs in the drawing room with Jock staring gloomily at the wall wondering what Braeside was at in his absence and Kirsty speculating avidly and aloud on the outcome.

O'Malley, who had taken Aunt Matilda's measure even during that brief encounter, wondered gleefully what she would make of the young Mrs Laidlaw, whom she detested. She looked behind to see if they were following and to her horror she was in time to see Aunt Matilda listening with evident interest at the dining saloon door. As she watched she heard her say, "Wait where you are till I call", then open both doors and march in.

O'Malley did not wait to see what happened next but fled wailing downstairs, holding on to her cap and streamers and calling on Saint Bridget to protect her. In the kitchen she took refuge with the cook, who was fulminating about the fact that still no one had bothered to tell her how many would be in for luncheon. The news of the arrival of another three potential guests left her momentarily speechless.

Aunt Matilda's unheralded appearance reduced the company in the dining room to a similar condition. She surveyed them as if they were unsatisfactory merchandise in a warehouse.

"Aha!" she observed and poked Staindrop painfully in the chest with the ferrule of her umbrella. "Thought I'd find you here."

Staindrop scowled.

"And Janet, I heard from Staindrop's man that you'd turned up again," she observed. "Thought I told you to come to me if you got in a pickle. Should have written me, girl. Don't care to lose m'friends at my age. Upsettin'. Puts me off my feed."

"I'm truly sorry, ma'am," said Janet. "I was thoughtless. I would not wish to cause you pain."

"Don't doubt you'd your reasons," said the old lady and poked Staindrop in the midriff again so that he squirmed where he sat. "And here's one of them. Been makin' yourself unpleasant as usual?"

Simon, standing behind Janet, bent down and whispered.

"Who *is* she?"

"His aunt."

"Lord," said Simon reverently, "but she is a real tartar. I hope you will introduce me later."

"Been tryin' to get the girl to come back I suppose. Still tryin' to take the wind out of your brother's eye. Just like your father. Never would face the facts, m'brother. Went religious."

She glared about her.

"Ain't anyone goin' to offer me a chair?" she enquired.

Jasper ushered her into his with an air and she repaid him with a steely grey glance.

"Still sniffin around?" she observed. "I commend your taste but not your sense. Ought to know when you're beat. She won't have you. You haven't the brains for her. Plenty of everythin' else I gather," she added with a salacious chuckle, "but not brains."

She pointed her umbrella at the door.

"Off with you. Family business and we don't need you. Tell him Janet. He won't take it from me."

Obediently Janet looked up at her crestfallen admirer.

"I appreciate your kindness and your concern, captain," she told him. "And I'd like you very well in the ordinary way, but I can't return the feeling you say you have for me . . ."

He looked downcast and took her hand.

"Truly?"

"Truly."

"Never?"

"No," said Janet. "But thank you, dear Jasper."

He kissed her hand and moved to the door.

"It would give me such pleasure to deal with you as you deserve, Staindrop," he said regretfully, "but I can't help but feel I leave you in the most capable hands."

He kissed his hand to Aunt Matilda.

"Your most obedient servant to command, ma'am," he declared. "If you were thirty years younger what a pair we would make."

"Impudent scoundrel," said Aunt Matilda and shook her umbrella. "I'd have you broken to bridle, don't doubt me."

"I don't," he grinned. He bowed to Hannah and left the room.

O'Malley, summoned to fetch his hat and coat, saw him leave with regret.

"That's one gone," she told cook.

"There's still nine," said cook morosely.

"Now," said Aunt Matilda. "Let's conclude this business. Who's he?"

The umbrella pointed at Simon.

"Simon Lamington, ma'am, a lawyer. Very much at your service."

"My service, indeed," she snorted incredulously, "when anyone can see with half an eye that you and Janet are besotted on one another. If I'd believe that I'd believe anything. But it might be useful to have a man of the law. You can stay."

She turned to Staindrop with much the same air with which she was used to approach a well-spread table.

"Now . . . where was I?"

Wickedly, Simon prompted her.

"His lordship's father would not face facts, ma'am."

"Ah," said Aunt Matilda. "Yes. Gettin' old. Can't keep to the point. Point's this. You probably can't get brats, Staindrop. Seven years with one wife, a year with another and never a sign. Best face it."

She considered her nephew with distaste.

"Just as well, if you ask me. However . . ."

At such a thrust Staindrop finally lost his temper and jumped out of his chair scarlet with fury.

"You keep your long nose out of my affairs, you evil-minded, foul-mouthed old hag!"

He advanced upon her shaking his fist and Janet cried out. Simon and Laidlaw moved swiftly to intervene but they reckoned without the umbrella on which her nephew all but impaled himself.

"Had a nasty temper from a whelp," she observed. "Now sit down you great oaf and listen to what I've got to tell you. If you want a wife you've got one . . . for all the good that's likely to do you."

"I'm aware of it," he said sullenly. "I've seen to it she knows it too."

He looked across at Janet.

"Janet's not your wife," declared Aunt Matilda, "and what is more, she never has been."

She grinned gleefully at the stunning effect of this statement and without moving from her seat called out piercingly, "You can come in now!"

The double doors opened and the widow who had arrived with her came in. She put back her veil and looked at Staindrop.

"I take it you remember me, Philip?"

"Anna!" he gasped. "But I thought you were in Ind . . ."

Too late he realised the infelicitous nature of such an admission and went an unappetizing yellow-grey colour. A short silence fell.

"I trust you can witness to that remark, Mr Lamington," said Laidlaw at length.

"I can," said Simon, "and I fervently hope I may."

Anna, questioned gently by Simon, explained that she and Alan Eldon, the soldier with whom she had run off, had been taken off the wrecked yacht by a French fishing smack which had landed the party at St Morlaix in France. The only other person aboard had been Eldon's ex-batman, a Jerseyman, who had returned from the French port to his native island. Alan had changed his name to Bourtree and they decided to take passage to India where he had found employment as manager of a small tea plantation in the hill country. There small Anna had been born and there, some six months ago, Alan had died of a fever. Anna decided to come home and had settled in a village not far from Bakewell.

"Why did you not come forward when Staindrop announced he was to marry two years ago?" demanded Hannah.

"I did not hear of it. We had no communication with home. We rarely saw newspapers and because Alan had friends among the soldiers we seldom left the plantation for fear we should meet with them. I had written to Philip to warn him that I was alive, but he did not reply."

Staindrop shifted uncomfortably.

"The first I knew of this marriage of his was when I saw Lady . . ."

Anna hesitated and looked across at Janet who chuckled.

"It seems that I'm neither fish, flesh nor good red herring," she said. "Best call me Janet."

"I saw the notice of Janet's death. It didn't seem sensible or kind to say anything at that point: there had been enough distress from what I could understand. It was when I saw this new notice that I felt I could stay in retirement no longer."

She produced the cutting from *The Times* which announced Staindrop's engagement to Miss Sharpe.

"As soon as I saw this I went to Staindrop Hall but found he was in Town . . ."

"*I* was there, however," interrupted Aunt Matilda with evident satisfaction, "and I was in no doubt what we should do. So we went to Town."

"There we found Staindrop had gone North," said Anna.

"And why," added Aunt Matilda.

"So we took the cab on to the train . . . and here we are."

"We'd have been here sooner," Aunt Matilda informed them, "but we breakfasted at the Grand. I'd no wish to encounter Staindrop on an empty stomach."

By midmorning the party had diminished. Staindrop had taken himself off to engage rooms in an hotel for his new-found wife and himself. Shaken by the unexpected appearance of Anna he had agreed to Laidlaw's proposals, which were designed to minimise as far as possible the discomfort and scandal. There was no way in which these could be avoided altogether but everyone present agreed that a spectacular trial for bigamy could be of benefit to nobody.

"Wouldn't object to seeing him in prison," said Aunt Matilda regretfully, "but it would be uncomfortable for the family."

Hannah agreed fervently.

"And what is to happen to . . . to Lady Staindrop?" asked Janet who had stayed silent during the discussion, letting the feeling of release seep through her like a calm tide and conscious of Simon by her side. The little girl, a solemn rather sallow mite, had made for her with the confidence of a child never rebuffed.

"Pretty lady," she had approved and climbed on Janet's knee to regale her with tales of India and the supreme virtues of her *ayah* who told stories about animals.

Anna, who had also been silent, flushed slightly.

"I am known where I live as Mrs Bourtree," she said, "and I could go back there and stay. But . . ."

She hesitated.

"I would like to have more for Joy than the confined life I lead. She will be pretty some day."

"She'll go back to you, nevvy," interrupted Aunt Matilda, "told me so in the train. Best thing all round if you ask me. If she can stand it."

"Oh, good of her," said Staindrop resentfully. "And if I won't have her?"

"You're in no position to bargain," said Laidlaw. "She is your wife."

"After what she's done?" said Staindrop indignantly, "and that child!"

"Silence, nevvy. There's plenty of sauce for the gander here. Want me to name all the trollops you've had in keeping since you were first married? No brats though."

"That is quite a different matter," returned Staindrop, his face scarlet.

"I cannot for the life of me understand why it should be so," said his aunt.

Janet laughed at this blow for feminism, worthy of John Stuart Mill himself, and Simon remembered a hot August afternoon on Inchtavannoch. He had only once heard her laugh since that day.

Staindrop sullenly agreed to accept Anna and the child and Aunt Matilda gave them some astringent advice while Janet glanced anxiously at the clock. She was due for rehearsal at noon.

"Brazen it out," she told them. "There'll be other scandals soon enough. And if he raises his hand to you, Anna, just say 'I thought you were in India.' That'll bring him to heel."

## POSTLUDE

SOME MONTHS AFTER Janet's return to her family she was sitting in a cane chair in front of a small white house from which a stretch of smooth grass sloped down to the edge of the loch. From where she sat she could see the woods of the southern shore of the loch and against the dark green a plume of white steam as the *Prince Consort* prepared for her morning journey to Ardlui. Two swans sailed across the little bay where the house was built and a family of half-grown ducks dived and swam in a convoy. The postman had just called and paused in a leisurely fashion to share a pot of tea and discuss local affairs.

"Your brother's never been over to see you?"

This was a comment, not a question, and Janet made no reply. Lachie shook his head.

"Nothing like a good Christian to hold a grudge," he said sadly. "There's whiles I wonder if Mr McMurdoe and me mean the same person when we talk about God. Never you heed, Janet lass, he'll come round. He's a good, big, soft lump your Jock."

His expression changed to one of malicious amusement.

"And if she never comes round it'll be too soon. I reckon. She's near her time and carrying all before her like a Glasgow Baillie."

He went on to give her some news of the district.

"Mary Ann's never been out of the bit since she got yon new boat. The house is aye full. She's got a lord with her just now. A wee shilpit creature he is too but a cheery soul with a word for everybody. Never seen a fish in a fortnight but it doesn't put him up nor down. And your Betsy was down about the other day and in for a crack with my Jean and said that Dick was after the next croft down the glen to run more sheep. He'll get it, likely... he's done well."

Janet agreed and Lachie swallowed the rest of his tea.

"I'll need to be going," he said and shouldered his bag. "I'll leave you read yon bundle in peace. You've surely added pounds to my load this last month, you and your man. My Dougal's at me for the foreign stamps."

Janet promised to save them and Lachie trudged down the path to the rickety jetty where he had tied his boat.

There were four letters addressed to her in the pile. She picked up one of them with a certain sinking of the heart. It was postmarked Perth and the writing was the elegant hand of Mrs Carnegie. She opened it rather reluctantly but was greeted by an unexceptional opening:

> My dear Janet, [she wrote] Please forgive a foolish prejudiced old wife who deserves to be neglected for the rest of her days. I am ashamed of my behaviour.
>
> Simon came to see me and never even mentioned my not attending your wedding or the wicked letter I wrote you. It was such a pleasure to see him as he used to be, full of jokes and teasing me and in such good spirits. When he left I determined to write to you and try to mend matters between us. I was at my desk a good half hour before I could think how to begin. You have made him so happy, my dear girl, that even if you were what I once thought you I would have to forget it and want as much as I do now to welcome you as my daughter. Please, before you go to London, give me an opportunity to make amends. My house is yours until you find somewhere of your own. Shimi of course knowing my liking for interfering in other people's affairs has commissioned me to look for a place for you and I enclose a list of addresses.
>
> He told me all your story and I must say I consider that you were very shabbily treated. But no doubt you will wish to forget your misfortunes and I will say no more on that head. He made me laugh till I cried by his description of 'Aunt Matilda' and her playing the *dea ex machina* and I had to beg him to leave off...

Janet smiled at the memory of this Homeric episode and went

on reading the letter which gave her news of Perth and a kind message from Guilbert and ended;

"... and believe me yours very contritely, Christine Carnegie."

Janet resolved to answer that letter before the day was over. The one flaw in her happiness had been Mrs Carnegie's opposition to her son's marrying someone who had not only been her servant but whose reputation had been distinctly curious. This letter lifted a great weight from her shoulders for she had no wish to come between Simon and his mother.

She picked up the next letter without enthusiasm. It was from London and the writing was Hannah's. It was long and full of chat about people Janet had known and might know again but Janet skimmed over it until she came on two pieces of news which caught her attention.

... I met that Miss Sharpe who was engaged to Staindrop. She showed me her ring and told me she was to marry Mr Stephen Jones who is a relation by marriage of my cousin Jeremy. He is a pleasant young man and intends to take orders as his uncle has a living for him in Berkshire.

Janet was pleased at this news. She had always felt that Miss Sharpe had had rough treatment in the matter of that engagement.

I met Captain Pelham-Villiers at the Consetts the other night and he asked kindly for you. He has a current *belle amie*, I am told, so he is not pining away. I find that the memory of what occurred is fading and being buried under the current scandals. By the time you and Simon come to Town I doubt if you will experience much embarrassment. I am so glad that Staindrop's part in the affair was hushed up and your father did not press the matter to a court case. That would have been too embarrassing for us all, whatever the outcome. It is better to try to remain on good terms and I must report that I had a bow in the park from Staindrop, who was driving with his wife. While Anna is not received everywhere ... one could not expect that ... her friends have been kind. They had the little girl with them ...

Like Mrs Carnegie's the letter ended with a list of possible houses for her, this time in London.

> ... I think the last on the list would be most suitable, for it is within walking distance of the House but far enough from the river for your not to be troubled by the effluvia. It has been quite unspeakable this summer ...

There was a fat letter from India and Janet recognised Aramintha's eager scrawl. The contents consisted mostly of a paean of praise for the infant Abram.

> ... grandpapa is to come out for a cold weather and will escort Baby and me Home for a few months so I will see you and you will have the great privilege of meeting Baby. I am sure you will adore him. My Lord and Master sends his salaams.

Aramintha ended with a long message from Phoebe, who had been posted with her Robert to a station in the hills. Janet folded up the flimsy sheets and turned to the last letter, which she handled much as if it had contained an explosive. This was not unlikely for it was from Aunt Matilda who wrote but seldom and only when, as she put it, she had something worth writing. Her letters were thus never without interest. This one was no exception.

> ... I visited Staindrop House last Monday [she wrote] as I feel it my duty to see that all is well with Anna. Imagine my astonishment to be greeted by a smiling Staindrop! He invited me to partake of a glass of brandy to 'toast his news' as he put it. I needed it for other purposes. The news was that Anna is in whelp! I was never more taken aback. Staindrop is quite beside himself with this achievement and took great pleasure in twitting me on my previous opinion of his prowess. He keeps her in cotton and she is as smug as a cat on a cushion. I held my tongue, which as you know is always a great trial to me, and did *not* recommend that he pass the male servants under consideration but I will certainly be concerned to examine the

child's physiognomy once it is born. I left early. He gloated over me in a fashion I can only describe as revolting . . .

Janet dropped this missive into her lap and laughed. Simon, approaching from the water's edge, heard the sound and wished not for the first time that he was a poet and not a lawyer so that he could find the words to describe Janet's laugh. She heard his approach and her face lit up with pleasure until she took in his appearance. He was coatless and shoeless and soaked to the skin, carrying his boots in one hand and a vast salmon in the other.

"Simon!" she exclaimed, "Not again!"

"I'm afraid so," he said rather sheepishly.

"Whatever am I to say to your consituents when we go back," she demanded, "if you are lost in the depths of Loch Lomond? They could never abide another by-election so soon."

"The thing is," he said, laying down the salmon with care on the grass, "I am rather too large for small boats and I do tend to get to my feet in moments of excitement. It's the lawyer in me. Over I went and wee Alec couldn't get me in again so he towed me ashore and then went back to rescue my rod. But I brought you our supper. Isn't he a beauty?"

"Take him to the kitchen and give him to Alison and I'll find you a towel and some dry clothes . . . if you've any dry clothes left to your name."

"Now then . . . don't scold," he begged.

"When we go to Town I won't dare let you go near water," she declared. "You've only to see it to fall in it. I am not going to tow you out of the Serpentine twice a week. I shall tell Hannah we want a house as far as possible from the river."

"My mother should have warned you," he admitted.

Janet remembered and smiled happily at him.

"Oh, Shimi, she's written to me . . . *such* a kind letter. I feel quite afraid because I don't think I could be any happier than I am."

"I hope you have some dry clothes for yourself," said her husband, "I've warned you before about smiling at me when I'm wet. You get wet too."

And in spite of all her laughing protests she did.